DEATH

BEHIND EVERY DOOR

Also by *New York Times* bestselling author Heather Graham

THE REAPER FOLLOWS
SHADOW OF DEATH
CRIMSON SUMMER
DANGER IN NUMBERS

The Blackbird Trilogy

CURSED AT DAWN
SECRETS IN THE DARK
WHISPERS AT DUSK

New York Confidential

THE FINAL DECEPTION
A LETHAL LEGACY
A DANGEROUS GAME
A PERFECT OBSESSION
FLAWLESS

Krewe of Hunters

THE UNKNOWN
THE FORBIDDEN
THE UNFORGIVEN
DREAMING DEATH
DEADLY TOUCH
SEEING DARKNESS
THE STALKING
THE SEEKERS
THE SUMMONING
ECHOES OF EVIL
PALE AS DEATH

FADE TO BLACK
WICKED DEEDS
DARK RITES
DYING BREATH
DARKEST JOURNEY
DEADLY FATE
HAUNTED DESTINY
THE HIDDEN
THE FORGOTTEN
THE SILENCED
THE BETRAYED
THE HEXED
THE CURSED
THE NIGHT IS FOREVER
THE NIGHT IS ALIVE
THE NIGHT IS WATCHING
THE UNINVITED
THE UNSPOKEN
THE UNHOLY
THE UNSEEN
THE EVIL INSIDE
SACRED EVIL
HEART OF EVIL
PHANTOM EVIL

Cafferty & Quinn

THE DEAD PLAY ON
WAKING THE DEAD
LET THE DEAD SLEEP

* * * * *

Look for Heather Graham's next novel
MARKET FOR MURDER
available soon from MIRA.

For additional books by Heather Graham,
visit theoriginalheathergraham.com.

HEATHER GRAHAM

DEATH
BEHIND EVERY DOOR

ISBN-13: 978-0-7783-6808-3

Death Behind Every Door

Mira
22 Adelaide St. West, 41st Floor
Toronto, Ontario M5H 4E3, Canada
BookClubbish.com

Printed in U.S.A.

In loving memory of E.D. "Dan" Graham, my father,
the Great Scot, or Mr. Clean to the neighborhood kids, one of the strongest
and kindest men I have ever been privileged to know. I thank him for the
stories of the "homeland" with which he regaled me when I was young
stories of heroes, great battles and human nature—because, of course,
history is most often written by the victors!

And for Clan Graham, of course!

CAST OF CHARACTERS

The Krewe of Hunters—
a specialized FBI unit that uses its members' "unique abilities"
to bring justice to strange or unorthodox cases

Adam Harrison—
philanthropist founder of the Krewe of Hunters

Jackson Crow—
supervisory field agent, Adam's chosen leader for the team

Angela Hawkins Crow—
original Krewe member, exceptional in the field and on research

The Euro Special Assistance Team, or "Blackbird"—
a newly formed group created to extend the Krewe's reach
into Europe to assist with crimes abroad

Luke Kendrick—
six-four, green eyes, dark hair, a Blackbird agent
with a military and police background

Carly MacDonald—
amber eyes, dark hair, a Blackbird agent known for
her effortless ability to work undercover

Mason Carter—
six-five, blue eyes, dark hair, recently promoted to field director for
Blackbird, working with Special Agent Della Hamilton in France

Mark Billingham—
detective chief inspector, on-site for Luke's first
crime scene investigation

David Morton—
about thirty-five, friendly brown eyes, thick brown hair,
front desk clerk and owner of Graystone Castle bed-and-breakfast

Malcolm Finnegan—
a tall man, solid and dependable, inspector and senior officer

Brendan Campbell—
clean-shaven head, determined and intelligent leader
with the National Crime Agency

Clayton Moore—
owner of the Gordon House property

Ben Pratt—
owner of the Gordon House property

Jim and Terry Allen—
owners of the Vicky Inn

Hamish Inverness—
a helpful spirit, died at the Battle of Culloden in 1746

Kenneth of Clan Menzies—
another benevolent ghost, died at the Battle of Falkirk in 1298

Daniel Murray—
a young man working undercover with the National Crime Agency

PROLOGUE

Remington House
South London

The dirt was the first giveaway. Nothing might have been obvious to the casual observer walking by the ruins of Remington House, but when he'd been called out to join Detective Chief Inspector Mark Billingham, Luke Kendrick already suspected that the killer he'd been tracking had taken up residence in the United Kingdom.

And the dirt was the first giveaway.

It was filled with bone fragments.

Luke knelt, gingerly sifting through the pebbled dirt. At first, he found nothing but tiny fragments that he collected in an evidence bag. Then he found a larger piece and studied it carefully. A forensic crew needed to be called in, but he had something to go on. He'd found a finger bone, a phalanx, that suggested someone with long hands, perhaps a musician…

And perhaps that meant nothing. Maybe it was just his imagination, him personifying something he hadn't begun to define other than that…

It was human.

And he couldn't help but picture the situation that had brought him here, the old manor back in the States where police had discovered so many incomplete skeletons, so much blood and acid, so many furnaces...

All evidence that pointed to the man known as America's first serial killer, H. H. Holmes, the alias of the infamous Herman Mudgett, and his "Murder Castle," where dozens had come to attend the Chicago World's Fair in 1893.

He realized Mark Billingham was looking at him.

The Englishman was a solid officer—a man so concerned with the reports of screams having come from the area along with a rash of missing persons that he wasn't the least offended by the fact an FBI agent from the US might be a person who could help him. Nearing sixty, Billingham still stood as tall and straight as a ramrod and he'd managed to keep an incredible head of thick, silver-white hair.

Luke rose and offered the evidence bag to Billingham. "Human remains, beyond a doubt. While I don't have a medical degree, I've been around long enough—"

"Indeed," Billingham said dryly. "I, too, am able to recognize a human finger."

Luke grimaced and nodded. "Right. Of course. We need to rip the place apart. I'm going to suggest you get Forensics out here as quickly as possible, though I believe whoever was perpetrating the crimes here has moved on."

"I'll put in the call but, while we wait, I'd like to explore the rest of the place," Billingham said.

"Of course."

They had only come as far as the entry. Once, Remington House had been the crowning jewel in a massive noble estate. But after being bombed in World War II, it had passed from owner to owner, all hoping to restore its grandeur, all discovering the fantastic sum needed to do so. It had recently been taken over by a historical society, one still in the process of acquiring the necessary paperwork and funds to restore the manor structure itself. Once, however, the grand entry had led to a massive ballroom and stairs to an open balcony overhead, which led into bedrooms and guest rooms, while the dining hall and servants' quarters had led to the left.

"I'll head up and you'll take this floor?" Billingham asked.

"Sure. No, wait. I believe there was a basement. I'm heading down," Luke told him.

"That was where..." Billingham began. He shook his head. "I read the reports. The man who carried out the horror in the US was—"

"Killed," Luke said flatly. "Yes, he was shot when he tried to use one of our forensic people as a shield, threatening to slit her throat."

Luke knew that for a fact. He'd been working undercover and had been with the team who had discovered the small inn aiding the H. H. Holmes Society. And while he hadn't been the one to shoot the man, he had been the one to give the order to take the shot. They all knew that it was regrettable. They didn't take human lives unless they had to. Nathan Briar, the killer they'd trailed and cornered, had died without giving them information they desperately needed.

But since his blade had rested against the throat of Debbie Lyons and tiny rivulets of blood were already seeping down her neck, there had been no choice. But the two-hundred-year-old manor where Nathan Briar had been practicing his depravities had been purchased by a shell corporation in the Cayman Islands and that just kept leading the best techs in the world down a rabbit hole. But in that old edifice, they'd found acid vats, a giant furnace, all kinds of chemicals and of course...

Bits and pieces of human remains.

And then one more thing. A scrap of paper that hadn't quite made it into the fire with a happy face and a short message.

"The H. H. Holmes Society."

"Basement, of course," Billingham said. "I'll go with you, if I may."

"Of course," Luke assured him. "The entrance to the basement is usually around a kitchen or a food staging area in older places, so we'll head there first."

They did.

They followed old stone steps down below the earth, the wooden handrails long ago rotted and fallen apart.

But in the dark dampness below the main structure, Luke immediately saw what he had feared. A massive furnace recently used. Wooden tables, stained with blood. And as Billingham switched on his heavy-duty flashlight, they immediately saw that, placed in a far corner of the room, someone had been left to greet them.

A skeleton.

Set on a stand, with its wired hand and finger bones lifted to the forehead in a salute.

Luke shook his head, inhaling a deep breath. He looked at Billingham and said quietly, "Detective Chief Inspector, I'm truly sorry to say I believe the H. H. Holmes Society has now traveled to your jurisdiction."

"Did you kill the wrong man?" Billingham asked, frowning.

"No, sir. You're missing the point. The H. H. Holmes *Society*. We have been desperately searching through the dark web. Someone out there is creating a…league of killers, all hoping to imitate and outdo the man known as America's first serial killer. Some even suspect he might have come to London before he created his Murder Castle in the US. And he might have begun his killing career as Jack the Ripper. But for the present—"

"There's a *society* of such killers?" Billingham said with horror. "But how—"

"As of now, we're working on little but theory," Luke explained. "And a scrap of supposedly burned paper our forensic team was able to salvage. Also...body parts. But there are differences now—forensic detection is light-years better, we have fingerprinting, DNA—"

"Enough to catch *a* killer," Billingham said. "But an unknown number of killers?"

Luke stared at him solemnly. "Along with our scientific methods being better these days, so is underground communication online. Out in the open, botanists find other botanists, new moms find other new moms, and killers also find like-minded friends."

"Then we can shut them down—find the head of the snake and hack it to pieces!" Billingham said passionately. "Between our international tech departments—"

"I believe we have some of the best people in the world," Luke assured him. He hesitated.

Murder was as old as humanity. Murder could occur over love, jealousy, greed and a dozen other factors. Those murders could usually be solved.

But this situation...

Herman Mudgett, aka H. H. Holmes, had not been a man who looked like a crazed killer; rather, he'd been highly educated, receiving his doctorate from the University of Michigan, one of the most prestigious schools of his day. He'd been a ladies' man, charming, intelligent, so much so that he had been very successful at convincing and seducing people, many to their deaths. He went through much of his life appearing to be an upstanding and well-admired businessman.

He liked money; many of his murders had to do with insurance fraud, and in the end, he was arrested first for his financial crimes. Insurance fraud was one of his favorite schemes to get money—of course, this often meant murdering someone to get his hands on that money. And it was after his arrest that the true purpose of his Murder Castle had been discovered. He'd confessed after he'd been convicted of many of his murders, but even in his confession he attempted to deceive, confessing to murdering some who had still been living at the time.

He had written in his last missive to the world that he had felt no more about destroying the bodies of those he'd killed with acid or fire than he might have felt burning any inanimate object.

He'd talked about being Satan or the son of Satan. Maybe, as a true psychopath, he wasn't that far off.

Luke realized that Billingham was looking at him, waiting for him to speak. Before he could respond, the detective chief inspector took the initiative.

"In other words, I'm not just looking for a serial killer—I'm looking for several? At least until we find whoever has that dark-web site going?"

Luke nodded grimly. As he did so, his phone rang. He excused himself to Billingham to answer the call.

It was Mason Carter, recently promoted to field director for their Special Circumstances Unit, European Division.

For a time, he and Della Hamilton had been the only special agents in the European Division. And then...

This.

Mason and Della were in France, following a request from Interpol. But Luke knew something was wrong the minute he heard Mason's voice.

"You need to get just north of Edinburgh. As quickly as possible. Special Agent Carly MacDonald is checking into Graystone Castle, and we've been contacted by Interpol—several people heading to the Highland Games being held in the area have disappeared. Of course, everyone knows what happened in the United States—"

"Right. That's why I'm where I am now," Luke reminded him.

"I know, but I think we're looking at an active site. People who had mentioned to others they might check out Graystone

Castle are among those who can't be reached. I know you're already working at a site, but... I think this is going to take precedence. We gave her the go-ahead—she knows what we're up against, but everyone needs backup. Can you get up there quickly? She went in as a tourist."

"She's not among the missing already, is she?" Luke asked. "I haven't worked with her—"

"No, no, but from her report, nothing we've come across so far resembles the Murder Castle so completely. It is a centuries-old building and it's been refurbished in an interesting way. I believe she's going to need backup as quickly as possible."

Luke looked at Billingham.

"I'm on this. We've got bodies, but the killer is gone. Trust me—we're good," the man told him.

Luke nodded. He knew Billingham and his people were among the best.

"Luke?" Mason said over the phone line.

"I'm here."

"Well, get there, quickly, please. Graystone Castle is now a bed-and-breakfast. But from what we're hearing..."

"What?" Luke asked.

"It's just like 'Hotel California,'" Mason said dryly. "From what we've learned so far, people check in—and they don't check out."

CHAPTER ONE

Graystone Castle had been operating as a bed-and-breakfast for several years before the games came to the small town just north of Edinburgh. And as every hotel room, B and B, guesthouse and short-term rental in the area filled up with visitors, so did Graystone Castle.

Carly MacDonald checked in alone, smiling as she chatted with the man working behind the desk, Aaron Miller—according to the nameplate on the desk—a fellow of about thirty-five or so, medium in height and stature, with friendly brown eyes and a mop of thick brown hair.

He accepted her driver's license and credit card politely, but she wanted to get him talking.

"This is fantastic!" she told him, as if she were unable to hide her enthusiasm. "Incredible and wonderful. I'm staying in a real castle! Oh, and of course, you...you work here? You own the place?"

She already knew he owned it. And if evil deeds were afoot as they suspected at headquarters, he was most likely the perpetrator. And with what had happened back in the States...

It was important that she keep up her charade, that of a starry-eyed American who was thrilled to be staying in a castle.

"I got lucky!" he told her. "The place was truly going down-hill, and I managed to get a great loan. I mean, how many Americans get to buy a bona fide castle? Okay, so it's no Buckingham Palace. But here's a map for you."

"Wait! You *are* the owner?" Carly asked, accepting the map of the place he handed her.

"I, um… Yeah. Sorry. Aaron Miller. And, yeah, it's cool! And you can do lots of exploring and imagine the good old days—or not so good, sometimes. Bad things happened here, too. Of course, the place was built in the 1400s originally, and you know, the Scots and English were at one another's throats forever! Disloyalty, well, you know. Hangings, beheadings…but I guess it was cool if you were royalty—on the right side of whoever had the most power! So. Here's the courtyard in the middle sur-rounded by four walls. Three floors, the third being the mu-seum part of the place—you'd be surprised how much medieval stuff you can still get at auctions and yard sales here. The sec-ond floor is guest rooms, first floor we have the kitchen—new and modern—the dining hall, the ballroom, the entry—where we are now—and the sports room with the great doors to the courtyard. So! I take it you're here for the Highland Games?"

"Oh, yes. My grandparents were from Edinburgh!" Carly told him. "They're gone now and I grew up in Daytona Beach, Florida. But… I guess I'm here in their memory! Thanks so much. I'd love to talk more about the history of the place. It's so fantastic! I'm so jealous—I'd love to own a castle!"

He was looking at her oddly and she grinned. Genetics could be strange. Her father's parents really had been born in Edin-burgh and she knew the area well—part of the reason she'd been chosen to go undercover here. But her mother's mom's parents had been born in what they called Persia and was now modern-day Iran. She had inherited dark hair and amber eyes from that branch of her family, and she probably didn't resemble at all what someone might think of as a Scottish American.

"I, umm—" he began.

"Right. I don't look Scottish. Perfect American!" she told him, grinning. "A mix of many backgrounds. Hey, I had one great-great on my dad's side who fought in the American Revolution. Anyway, whatever mix I am, there's a part of me just still not believing I get to stay in a real castle—and wishing I could buy one!"

He laughed. "Does your family know you're staying in a real castle?" he asked her.

His accent was strange. Scottish? Someone wanting to be Scottish or pretending to be Scottish? Maybe he was thinking that a Scottish accent was a better way to welcome tourists to a Scottish castle.

"Are you kidding? I didn't tell anyone. Couldn't afford to bring them on a trip like this—and it's just one that, well, I've wanted forever."

"So, no one knows you're staying here. I'll keep the secret!" He smiled. "And I got ya! I grew up in Chicago. I wanted a castle, too! Well, of course, honestly, I could never have afforded it if I hadn't turned it into a bed-and-breakfast. Oh, yes, complete breakfast every morning. I hope you'll love your stay."

"Oh, I know that I will!" Carly assured him. "I know I will!"

"Happy to have you," he told her. There was an odd note in his voice as he said the words, and something about the way he looked at her.

She smiled, accepted her key, hugged the map and headed up the steps to the second floor, ignoring the newly installed elevator—for the time.

Of course, considering what they were up against, the elevator itself might be a murder room. Still, if a killer was being clever at all, his mechanisms wouldn't be so public and so obvious.

He'd grown up in Chicago. He'd always wanted a castle.

And there had been something about the way he'd said he was happy to have her...

And happy, of course, that no one else knew she was here.

In her room, she first threw herself on the bed, pretending to love the ambience of the room. She stood after a minute, walking to the drapes, opening them, looking out at the courtyard. There were handsome lawn chairs grouped together within areas of beautiful foliage, a croquet setup, a tennis court and a nicely modern hot tub.

It was really the perfect vacation place.

But there was a camera in the room somewhere—that was the way the members of the Holmes Society worked. And she was being watched right then. That was something that could get the man arrested.

But there was much more at stake.

Human lives.

Still, she didn't want to be watched. She had to find the camera and a way to innocently cover it. Hopefully, it wasn't in the ceiling.

It wasn't. It was conveniently close to the closet, hidden behind a hook. Perfect.

She hung her jacket on the hook, blinding the camera. This man might well be an acolyte of Holmes, but he was nowhere near as clever. Now...

If the room itself was rigged, he was going to have to *assume* he'd knocked her out or killed her with noxious gases.

And now, with the camera knocked out, she could assure her gas mask was within easy reach, still hidden among her things should he enter her room unannounced, but easily available when she needed it.

Cameras in the room might be enough to bring out local authorities. But how long would it take and just how deeply might they investigate? And if someone here was in danger...

Could they be found quickly enough?

It was time to roam the castle. She'd start with the third floor just like a good tourist. Out of her room, she took the next flight of stairs to the third floor, where the man had, indeed, displayed his many historic treasures. Against the raw stone of the castle walls, the items truly appeared to be museum quality. He'd done an amazing job. Tables displayed medieval combs, perfume bottles, tankards and more. Coats of arms, from many families, filled the wall, along with...

Shields. Knives, swords, crossbows...

She could only wonder if any of them had been used recently.

There were a few other people in the museum. A mom with two boys stood nearby, and she smiled as they acknowledged each other. A pair of older teens, a young woman and a young man, obviously on a date. And a man studying one of the old paintings on the wall intently, uninterested in the others.

So, has anything in this room been used recently?

And were the old dungeons in use again, with a rich cache of torture and killing machines, old and new? After all, H. H. Holmes had made use of something resembling a medieval rack.

This was a castle. And a killer was playing a cunning game.

She had to play it better. Play to naivete. Find her way to the basement...

Or, as it had once been and might now be, the dungeon.

A dungeon, equipped as the basement of the Holmes's Murder Castle had been equipped in Chicago in the 1800s.

She had to find it.

Before it could be put to further use.

The driving time from south of London to Edinburgh could be as much as seven-plus hours—depending on traffic, just like anywhere in the world. Knowing that another agent was already in play didn't make Luke happy. They all knew they were up against something so evil that describing it as *heinous* would be an understatement.

But he put a call through to Carly. She answered it cheerfully, greeting him as if he were a long-lost friend. He knew, of course, she was worried her calls might be heard, accessed or even recorded. Which would be fine. They both had new burner phones.

He and Carly had never met but he greeted her with the same enthusiasm. She went on and on, assuring him she was fine, telling him about a marvelous museum full of shields and weapons and even medieval household goods.

"Lots of hours of daylight left! Oh, feel free to call again. I'll probably head to bed at about ten, which is hours and hours and hours away. There are games tomorrow, and I want to be there bright and early, so…"

Ten. Ten o'clock at night was the witching hour. She'd been letting him know she'd studied the situation and nothing happened during the daylight and early evening hours. Probably because the owner/manager/desk clerk had to keep his eye on those who were associated with locals or even playing in the Highland Games until he was clear to work on his Holmes Society business without failing as a host.

Luke had received the report regarding what they knew about the disappearances in the area. And what they knew about the man calling himself Aaron Miller.

The curious thing about the man was that his fingerprints gave them nothing. His face came up in no version of facial recognition. He was apparently American—despite his strange accent and speech—and he had purchased the place as an American through a bank in the Cayman Islands.

Who he really was, no one knew, but according to the law, he'd done nothing wrong. He had no record.

He had no past at all.

It had been Adam Harrison, founder of the Krewe of Hunters, who had heard of a friend disappearing while they headed to enjoy a stay at a bona fide castle. Adam had engaged Special

Agent Angela Hawkins Crow to research the disappearance. She
was second in field command to her husband, Jackson Crow,
and a simple genius when it came to finding out information
through a computer.

She hadn't found his friend.

She'd found other disappearances. And since Luke had been
the agent to discover the horror in the United States...

Luke was here now, driving as fast as he dared without bringing down the local authorities to reach the castle north of Edinburgh.

The concept behind the horror going on was still mind-bog-
gling—even to him, and he'd seen a lot of the bad that humanity
could perform during his years with the FBI. And yet, in this
age of social media itself being a major influencer on the beliefs
of millions—perhaps billions—of people in the world, the dark
web finding followers shouldn't be so shocking.

But that the means and methods of a historical serial killer
could be embraced by a group—a society—still seemed to be
something beyond horrid. While there had to be a main player—
a founder for such a group—they were left to scurry around
finding the membership and whatever castles or schemes the
killers might have concocted to emulate Holmes.

At first, Luke had believed the so-called society would be
based and working in the United States. After all, H. H. Holmes
was known as *America's* first serial killer. But then again, there
were those—including the man's great-great-grandson—who
believed that Holmes had traveled to London and been known
as Jack the Ripper there.

None of his guesswork or theories mattered right now. Mason
Carter and Della Hamilton were working at a suspected site in
France while he had been sent to London and Carly had been
sent to Edinburgh. Since their "special" unit of the FBI was still
under formation, most of their technical help had to come from

headquarters in the States; when boots on the ground were necessary, it meant that they had to move quickly.

Halfway through his journey north in the United Kingdom, he wondered if he should have asked about getting a chopper for a lift to Edinburgh. He could have gotten a car from some agency in the area. Headquarters had let the local authorities know that foul play was suspected; they had been already aware, but local queries had given them nothing.

They were standing by and ready to assist.

But he'd decided that coming in as another American tourist was the best plan. He called Carly's number and was grateful to hear her answer. She once again told him about the beauty of the place and how she wanted to head to the Orkneys afterward to study stone monoliths there that might have been precursors to Stonehenge. But he didn't mention he was going to come in himself just in case their host was savvy enough to be monitoring calls and texts.

He didn't have that much farther to go, just a few hours more, and she should be fine.

But he had to keep a strict hold on his use of logic and theory here.

Because he had been the one to go into the "castle" in the States. He'd been the one to find Special Agent Brenda Roberts on the table in the dungeon, and he'd been too late to stop the horror and torture she'd suffered. He tried many times to remember that he'd stopped the killer before he'd finished with Special Agent Julio Rosello, and that Rosello was now recuperating at a hospital in New York and expected to make a full recovery.

He just knew he'd never live with himself if he arrived too late again.

There had been two of them there. But Angela hadn't discovered the dark-web society of imitating killers until after the case—well, until after the case that had only been the beginning.

They hadn't known then the disappearance they were investigating might have been the result of knockout gases and other forms of rendering a victim incapable of fighting back. They hadn't known about the many cameras and listening devices and chutes to dispose of those too quickly done away with. They hadn't been expecting a modern version of an H. H. Holmes Murder Castle, one that made subtle and cunning attacks so much easier and…

So much more enjoyable, according to Gary Houghton, the killer whose death Luke had been forced to order to save an agent's life.

Watch them, watch them inhale the gas, watch their horror as they realize something has gone very wrong. They can't reach help as the room is spinning. And then! Watch them when they see they're bound to a table and next to it there are all kinds of knives and razors and then…

He gritted his teeth and gave himself a serious mental shake. He needed to be a true professional. He needed to remember both procedure and instinct. He needed…

He'd gone to the site this morning and they'd found the remains of the dead. That killer was still out there—somewhere. Billingham was on it.

But Carly MacDonald couldn't really understand what she was up against yet. He needed to get there; he needed to concentrate.

And stop whatever was about to happen to her, no matter how aware and savvy she might be.

Carly found the stairs to the basement.

They were hidden behind a large board that had been covered with information regarding the Highland Games.

She pretended to be studying the names of contestants in the caber toss as others passed her, two women in their early twenties, giggling about "what men wear under their kilts," and a married couple with a boy, talking about another son who was taking part in the games.

When they had passed her by, she slipped behind the large board. And as she suspected, she found the stairs.

Ancient, chipped stone. They led down to pure darkness.

Well, at one time, the basement or dungeon here had been a place for prisoners. She could imagine that during Scotland's history much of it had been very bloody indeed. The space below had seen a great deal of pain, suffering and death.

She hesitated just a second, wondering that with all the death that had gone on...

The castle was advertised as haunted, of course. But so far, she hadn't encountered any of the departed. Maybe they were there, just watching. Maybe they were enjoying the show.

She doubted that. Since her first encounter with a dead World War II soldier at Arlington, Carly had not met a single soul who was evil. That made her wonder, of course, if there really was a hell, a place of eternal fire, or perhaps just eternal darkness.

She did know that sometimes good souls stayed behind and befriended one another, and they seemed to have a mission that had to be completed before they moved on. Some stayed for their own families. Some stayed to help find their killers. Others stayed without really knowing why, other than to guard a place perhaps, or be there when they were needed, whatever place in time that might be.

"I could use a friendly haunt!" she said softly.

Wrong move.

No haunts appeared.

But a minute later her host was there, calling out.

"Hey! Hey, get back up here, please! This area is off-limits to guests. Way too dangerous. Please!"

Furious with herself, she forced a smile and started back up the steps. She had a coworker heading her way. When he arrived, one of them could occupy their host while the other headed down to the basement/dungeon.

She now knew the entry.

That would make it easy.

"Oh, hey, I'm so sorry!" she said, going up the stairs and looking at Aaron Miller as if she were truly upset with her lack of proper guest behavior. "I guess… I love the place! I am so, so fascinated. I realized there were steps behind the board—"

"Yes. Behind the board. Dark, dark steps! Hey, we have liability here, too, you know," he said, truly annoyed with her. "I'm afraid I'm going to have to ask you to—"

"No, no, please, please! Don't ask me to leave. I promise. I'll stick to the well-lit areas where I know we're allowed to be!" she swore.

He smiled at that. "No, I wouldn't want you to have to leave. In fact, it would be great if you were to stay forever!"

He wasn't lying, she knew. He'd love to have her forever— buried somewhere in the castle walls!

"You're too sweet!" she told him. "And I promise, I'll be a better guest! Oh, what do you suggest for a dinner place? I'm going to head out and get something to eat, and then I'm going to go to sleep to get ready for my early day tomorrow!"

"Oh, I like Micky's—it's casual, but truly local. They serve haggis!"

She smiled. "I hear that there's fantastic fish in this area."

"Nothing like Scottish salmon!"

"See you later!" she said. She started up the steps to the second floor and then asked, "How do you do it? You own the place, you run the place—"

"I have a great cleaning crew, and I have little notes to put on the registration desk that say 'Back in five minutes!' so that I can escape now and then and check on everyone's welfare."

"You do an amazing job!" she told him.

He smiled. "You haven't seen the half of it yet!" he said lightly. In a teasing manner.

She smiled as if she were even more impressed. She'd never

see the other half of what he did—not if she was half the agent she had worked hard to be.

She hurried back up the stairs, deciding she really would go and get something to eat. He probably hadn't lied about the local restaurant being great.

But before she left, she returned to her room and moved things about, making sure she knew where everything was—exactly—so that she'd know if anyone had come in while she was gone.

Because Aaron certainly had access to his guests' quarters.

Once out, she found her rental car parked in the sweeping drive that fronted the castle. With the restaurant's address in her GPS, she drove toward food.

Food was definitely necessary, though she hadn't thought about it until she'd been caught in the stairwell.

The restaurant was charming. The building that housed it was nowhere near as old as the castle, but it had a charming Victorian facade. She was greeted by a friendly young woman who led her to a table while welcoming her to the games and the area.

"I heard the salmon is good?" Carly said.

"The best!" the young woman said. Then she grinned. "Micky is my dad, and I do think we have the best place and food to be found for miles!"

Carly thanked her, and when a young waiter came to her table, she ordered the salmon.

When he was gone, she quickly dialed the number she'd been given for the Krewe "Blackbird" agent who was on his way to her.

He answered his phone on the first ring. When he spoke, she frowned. He sounded anxious.

"Carly. Are you all right?"

"Fine, thanks," she assured him. "I'm out of the castle—that's why I'm calling. I just wanted you to know I'm sure we're on the right track."

"You're sure?"

He sounded doubtful. She gritted her teeth but refrained from an offended reply.

"Yes. Things he says…the way he says them. Yes, I'm sure. But I also wanted you to know I found the stairs to the old dungeons, the basement. But before I could head down, he was suddenly there. You can find them on the first floor if he's not at the registration desk when you get there. He's put up a massive wooden chalkboard-type thing to block them, but they're right behind it."

"Right. I'll check in when I get there—soon, within a couple of hours—and we need to do some slipping around. I don't know this guy, but I know the way a lot of what is being done works. We need to spell each other sleeping."

"You mean—"

"Yes, slip into one room or the other, one sit up while the other sleeps and vice versa."

"Oh."

"Even then, we need to take extreme care. Gas masks—we can't count on avoiding all the tricks, even as two people. We need to use extreme care."

"All right. So, I'm having dinner and then heading back. I'll see you when you get there."

"Driving as fast as I can without a British arrest."

"I'm fine. Take care."

She ended the call and stared at her phone. She hoped he wasn't one of the—albeit few, but out there—agents who didn't think a woman could be as effective as a man.

If so, on this, he was wrong.

A man like Aaron would prey on those he saw as weak, as perfect victims. And she wasn't any fairy-tale princess who needed saving from the tower.

Then again, maybe she was being a jerk, judging him before she met him. And maybe he had the right to be so cautious—she had read the reports. He had been the one to go in and end the reign of America's most recent H. H. Holmes Society murderer.

Her food arrived quickly, along with a delicious cup of hot tea. She chatted with the waiter, smiled and told him she was there for the games.

He was excited and told her he was happy he worked the late shift—he'd be at the games the next day, too.

It was just starting to grow dark when she left the restaurant. When she entered the castle and headed for the stairs, she saw Aaron was at the registration desk.

"Best meal ever! Thanks for the advice!" she told him.

He nodded and smiled. "Local food! And reasonable."

"It was great."

With a wave, she headed for the stairs. She hesitated. She and Luke had talked about guarding one another in the bedrooms.

Still, she needed to go in.

She studied the room, glad she had set her trap.

He had been here. Her things, so carefully laid out, had been moved. She quickly looked at her luggage, digging through her clothing, hoping he hadn't gone that far.

It didn't appear as if he had found her gas mask, carefully wedged between her heavier clothing. He was damned good if he'd almost gotten everything back to the way she had set it up before leaving.

Well, he could just be a voyeuristic creep, she reminded herself.

No, this all fell into place too completely. His mention of Chicago, whether he was really from there or not. The way that he talked, even the way he had looked at her while he talked. The castle. The fact his name didn't come up anywhere...

And he thought that mentioning Chicago, buying a castle, was so tongue-in-cheek, as if he laughed at his own jokes, inwardly certain she didn't have a clue she was being teased by a serial killer—and that, indeed, she hadn't seen the half of it.

Well, he was wrong. All that was left to do was wait.

To that end, she secured her gas mask beneath the covers in her bed, slipped out of her jeans, shirt and shoes and into a nightgown—before lifting her jacket from the supposedly secret camera and frowning as she looked at it, pretending to dust an unseen particle of something from it.

She crawled into bed then, pretending to close her eyes, to draw the covers over her head to protect against the smidgen of light coming into the room from the moon that had risen in the night sky. Of course, there were drapes, but for her purposes, she hadn't drawn them.

She waited.

And she instantly smelled the slightly sickly-sweet odor that began to fill the room. She dipped her head deeper into the bed, finding the gas mask, drawing it to her face.

As she had expected, the door opened. She carefully looked out from her cocoon of covers.

It almost appeared as if a monster had arrived in the room.

Well, if he was all that she thought, he was a monster.

He arrived dressed all in black with a cowl over his head, eyes covered with a mask—and the gas mask he was wearing all in black as well.

He stared at her form as she lay on the bed.

And then he walked closer and closer...

When he reached her at last, he was laughing.

Which was good.

He wasn't ready for it when she sprang up, slugging him hard in the jaw.

He reeled back, swearing, but quickly regained his composure. "Oh, no, oh, no! You bitch!"

She leaped to her feet. But as she did so, her mask slipped, and for a moment, the room began to reel. His laughter cut through her like a knife.

He wasn't quite as weak and spineless as she had hoped. Before she knew it, he was at her side, laughing still as he swept her up into his arms, warning her, "I told you. You haven't seen the half of it, no matter who you really are, you bitch!"

Out of the room, she felt as if the weakness and dizziness that had seized her disappeared. But they were heading out; he was easily carrying her down one set of stairs and along the first-floor great halls until he reached the giant board and pushed behind it.

They were then heading down the stairs she had discovered earlier…but not been able to follow all the way.

She could have fought then.

But she waited.

She needed to see the basement—or dungeon—and just what it entailed.

First, it was huge, covering the length of the one hall.

It contained more strange torture devices than she had ever imagined; he would have done the Spanish Inquisition proud.

Human cages lined the ancient stone walls, along with chains. Scold's bridles were lined on a stone shelf. The room even had a guillotine.

There were three different racks, all equipped with thick ropes.

One was not empty. A once-pretty girl lay upon it, sobbing and screaming as she realized he had returned to the area.

There was a table by the young woman's side that contained every imaginable kind of blade, from heavy curved knives to slimmer shimmering blades that appeared like scalpels.

Several of them were covered in dried and crusted blood as if they had already seen use…several times.

It was time to fight. Her head was clear; they had reached his objective, where he had all kinds of weapons—but weapons she could use as well.

"Now! Now you'll see the other half of it!" he promised.

She bucked hard against him, slamming his jaw with her right hand, startling him this time, since he had thought her knocked out.

A high kick caught him in the groin, and he doubled over in pain. Still screeching, he ran around the table, seeking his trove of knives.

He picked one up, ready to throw it.

She ducked. The missile slammed against the stone behind her.

"I will get you!" he vowed. "No!" he declared suddenly. "I don't need to get you. I will make you so damned sorry and then I will cut you to ribbons, too! But first, watch!"

He grabbed another of the knives, this one a curved blade, like a bowie knife.

"No!" Carly shrieked, praying she could reach him and stop the blade before he could thrust it into the sobbing young woman tied to the rack.

She didn't get a chance to move.

A shot suddenly rang out, a deafening blast of noise against the ancient stone backdrop where they all stood.

She realized her new partner had arrived.

And he had blasted the knife from the man's hands with a perfectly aimed shot, sending him falling to the floor with shrieks of agony.

Carly stared at their rescuer but the light down here was low. She saw nothing but a tall man making his way toward the rack.

"You're all right. You're all right now!" he said gently, and Carly realized he was talking to the young woman on the table.

She kept sobbing, but begging him at the same time, her words barely coherent. "Get me out of here, please, please, please. I'm bleeding. I'm scared. I'm..."

"It's all right!" he said.

By then, Carly was at his side.

"I'll free her—you get him," she said. "Please."

He nodded to her, turning back to the H. H. Holmes Society member known to them as Aaron Miller. But even as he turned to reach down and drag the man to his feet, Aaron let out another deep and terrible scream.

He had another knife.

Special Agent Luke Kendrick instantly began the perfect move to wrest it from him.

But not before the man managed to thrust half the blade into his own chest.

CHAPTER TWO

"Don't pull out the knife!" Luke warned, staring in horror at the man, who now slumped in a seated position on the floor. Carly MacDonald had raced to him, dropping down by his side.

"Help me—please, God—not that monster!" the young woman on the rack cried.

She was a victim; she had to be helped first. But Luke wanted the monster on the floor alive, too. That was the only way they might get more information and stop the ridiculous spread of the murder society.

Carly hadn't pulled at the knife; she was stanching the flow of blood from the wound the best way she could while Aaron smiled weakly.

"I'm like God, man. I make my own choices on life and death!"

That the man could talk was encouraging. There was a chance, a slim one, he had missed his vital organs. And the woman on the table needed to be freed. While Carly dealt with the wound in Aaron's chest, Luke worked at the ropes with one hand and used the other to reach for his phone and dial Emergency.

Ambulances first—their victim deserved desperate care; while

Luke didn't think the man on the floor deserved help, unlike Aaron, the FBI agent was well aware he wasn't God. He also knew he wanted the man alive.

He freed the young woman, telling her she had to remain calm and help was on the way. When she tried to rise, she couldn't. He then realized she had to be in agony, as one or more of her joints had been dislocated.

He was impressed by the speed of help. On the one hand, each second in the dim dungeon area of the castle seemed like hours, and yet sirens blazed through the night within minutes of his call. Soon, medical help and police were pouring down into the basement. He was able to step back and close his eyes for a minute as the young woman on the table was helped, as emergency personnel took over on attempts to save Aaron Miller.

Carly MacDonald was covered in blood. She was wearing a flannel nightgown, and while it covered her completely and was probably warm, he knew they needed to go with the police to fill out reports. They needed to help local law enforcement understand the worldwide alarm regarding the strange new brand of murderer they had apprehended.

He walked over to her, sliding his jacket off and putting it around her shoulders.

"I'm fine," she assured him.

"It will be cold out."

She looked as if she might refuse, as if she was determined she would always do everything on her own.

Not promising behavior in a new partner, but...

"Thank you," she said simply. "So—"

"We can drive in ourselves. Apparently, there is someone from the National Crime Agency arriving to go through all of this with us," he told her.

Both the young woman and Aaron were taken away at last, taken to hospitals in separate ambulances.

The police on duty were looking as shocked as anyone might as they remained at the crime scene awaiting a forensic team.

Inspector Malcolm Finnegan, senior officer among the four who had arrived, walked over to Luke, shaking his head. "Quite well. You stopped this fellow before he managed to finish off the poor lass!"

Finnegan was a tall man, solid in stature and demeanor. His voice was low and his accent seemed to add a solid truth to his words as well. Luke truly respected the man; he'd arrived quickly and handled the situation with admirable efficiency.

"There is that. Saving a life, ah, sir, a good day it is, then. Even…here." The man stretched out an arm, indicating the extent of the torture chamber Aaron Miller had created.

Luke nodded, but even as he did so, he noticed at the far end of the dungeon, there was a massive fireplace, surrounded by stone, but with a metal grate that had to have been about six feet broad and three feet deep.

"Excuse me," he murmured.

It was far past the torture machinery that had been gathered to the area, just beyond a damaged settee and a few plain wood tables.

"Blood."

"What?"

He hadn't realized Carly had followed behind him, observing.

"The table," she said quietly.

"I don't think we stopped this man before he murdered people," he said simply.

She didn't reply. He saw the blood on the table and hurried on to the fireplace with her in tow. He stopped low, balancing on his toes, to move a poker through the ashes below the grate.

Bone.

Human bone.

Just how many had Aaron managed to kill before they'd gotten there? And how the hell had he created such a killing machine of the castle with no one noticing?

That, of course, had been one of the nineteenth-century Chicago killer's points of expertise; he'd fired construction workers constantly so that no one but him knew the full layout of his "castle."

He'd heard Inspector Finnegan come up behind him. "Tattie ower the side!" the man swore.

Luke didn't know the Scottish expression, but he did understand the emotion in the man's voice. They hadn't realized what a disaster they'd stumbled upon.

"Forensic and medical examiners will need to comb through here and sort out what they can," Carly said evenly. "We'll need to compare DNA if we can find it with those reported missing. I'll go up to my room to clean up and change. I will bag my nightgown as evidence for the forensic team."

Luke and Inspector Finnegan watched Carly make her way to the stairs.

"It's glad I am that our man from the National Crime Agency will be meeting with us. In all my years, and they've been aplenty, I've not seen the likes of this," Finnegan said. "Brendan Campbell, the man's up in the ranks, he's a specialist but likes to be referred to as Agent Campbell. He was approached by your people working with Interpol earlier, but…well, to be honest, we didnae think such a thing could be coming here. Though this fellow Aaron is—"

"American. We know," Luke interrupted.

"Not that we do nae ha' our share o' monsters!" Finnegan said.

"The world simply produces monsters now and then," Luke assured him.

"But we ha' stopped this one!"

When Finnegan was emotional, his accent grew stronger.

Rising, Luke looked at him and nodded. "Thank you, sir. We must celebrate our wins because we do face our losses. So—"

Carly quickly returned with the bloody nightgown in an evidence bag. She was clean and dressed and ready to go.

"We should drive on in. Follow me, if you will. We'll leave Forensics to it."

He headed to his car, not thinking to ask Carly if she wanted to drive. But in the car, he glanced her way at last.

"Sorry. I've been on my own for a bit, and I just—"

"You just act. I understand. It takes a bit to get used to being a partner again."

He arched a brow and studied her curiously. He had to admit, hearing he was meeting with Carly MacDonald had made him think she'd be a slender blue-eyed blonde, innocent and fragile looking, as such an undercover operation might require.

He figured she could gush with enthusiasm and appear to be delicate and naive. She was slender but shapely and had the most unusual eyes he'd ever seen, almost golden, bright against the darkness of her hair. She managed to be fiercely feminine, he thought, and purely professional, all in one.

He had to wonder, too, what might have happened if he hadn't come along. She seemed to be wary and well trained, but while he'd received the permissions necessary to carry his weapon, she hadn't been armed when he'd come upon her. Then again, he understood the number of police officers in the United Kingdom—including Scotland, Wales and Northern Ireland—numbered about 155,000-plus police officers by any title and less than seven thousand of those were authorized to carry weapons. Of course, the population of the UK was just short of seventy million, and less than six million of that number resided in Scotland. Then again, he'd learned in the sparsely populated cornfields of Kansas that monsters could operate just about anywhere.

The police station was small. Of course, they were in a rural area that was only huge now because of the love for the games that stretched beyond the country.

As they headed in to meet with their National Crime Agency counterpart, Luke couldn't help but notice that those there under arrest appeared to be young and had most probably been brought in for being drunk and disorderly—perhaps with a charge or two for prostitution thrown in.

They were led to a small conference room.

Brendan Campbell was not seated at the table there waiting for them. With his arms crossed, he was pacing the small area, waiting, shaking his cleanly shaven head all the while.

He stopped to greet them and walked around the table to shake their hands. He was a thin man, about six feet in height, with blue eyes that seemed to blaze against his features and the shiny surface of his bald pate.

"Pleased to meet you, pleased to have you here," he told them. "I've been in contact with your supervising field director." He paused as if he was sometimes as confused by American ranks within agencies as they could be in the UK.

"Jackson Crow," Luke said. "And heading our team in Europe, we have Mason Carter and his partner, Della Hamilton."

"Right, right, thank you. And the good Lord help us! Thank you for finding out what was happening at the castle. Shocking. I've also spoken with Billingham, and he's still working the scene south of London and… Who is this that these people are emulating? And has no one discovered where this is coming from—the dark web?"

"Sir, the dark web is just as it sounds—dark. Our people are working on it, but they follow trails, they have a lead, the site goes down and it pops up again. The dark web is not as much a mystery to me as is the sheer number of those it seems to reach," Carly told him evenly.

"We're field agents," Luke added politely. "Our mission is to get around and stop every head of the hydra that we can while

---

.

those who are geniuses at maneuvering the internet seek out every bit of information they can. Trust me, without the help we've been receiving from our main offices, we wouldn't be finding what we are."

"Well, I'm grateful that perhaps your stay in Scotland is over," Campbell said, and then he seemed to realize the harshness of his words, for he added quickly, "Forgive me! We love having visitors in Scotland. It's just—"

"We understand!" Carly interrupted softly. "And we're hoping ourselves that our stay here is helpful and—"

"You should go to the games," Campbell said, smiling. Then he shook his head and grew serious. "I mean, yes, the Highland Games are wonderful."

Carly smiled. "I've been to them, sir. My grandparents were from here. We came back often enough."

"Ah! Thus, the good Scottish name. Lovely! But for now—"

"Now," Luke said, weary, wishing it wasn't now almost four in the morning. "I'm assuming you want to understand more of what is happening."

"What has happened. Pray God there will be no more here!"

Luke nodded. It wasn't that he didn't believe; he did. He knew there was a God and knew the human soul went on.

But just as good things happened in the world, so did the bad. And monsters would carry out their deeds where they chose whether this man wished them all gone or not.

"All right, then."

"Sit. We'll have tea. Or coffee," Campbell offered.

"Either would be lovely," Carly assured him, glancing at Luke. There was something in her eyes. Was she warning him not to be abrasive?

He didn't mean to be abrasive. He'd just seen what this heinous dark-web society was causing; he knew it stretched far and wide and knew wishing it was gone wouldn't make it so.

Luke glanced at Carly and she nodded and they both sat.

"I would truly enjoy a cup of coffee, sir," he said, as the man joined them, taking a seat on the opposite side of the table.

Luke lowered his head for a moment, wondering why he was feeling like a perp might after being brought in and questioned.

Because Campbell was planning a strange kind of interrogation.

And he could handle it. He was more well-versed in America's first serial killer than he had ever wanted to be.

Campbell smiled. "I'm going the coffee route myself, as it is. Agent MacDonald, for you?"

"Make it easy. Coffee all the way."

He hit a little buzzer on the desk, asking that a coffee service be brought in. A tray with cups, a coffeepot, sugar and creamer was brought in—along with a plate full of scones. He realized he was hungry.

But with a cup of black coffee in his hands, he decided that he needed to start talking before he wolfed down any food.

"There is someone out there—and we have no idea what country he or she is in—who has pulled together a 'society' dedicated to imitating a man whose real name was Herman Mudgett but is better known as H. H. Holmes. His expertise was insurance fraud, but to acquire the benefits from that fraud, he became an expert at murder and an expert at the disposal of bodies."

"The fireplace at the castle, the grate—the bones," Campbell said.

Luke nodded. "Holmes was born in 1861 in New Hampshire as Herman Mudgett and first used his pseudonym Holmes when he headed to Chicago, circa 1885—he abandoned his wife and child to make that move. Neighbors didn't have any bad things to say about the family or Herman when he was a child. All that would be noted later was that he really loved money, and he had probably stolen from his employers and clients at the odd jobs where he worked. Neighbors later also said he was a loner. What may have been a bit of inspiration for what was to come was the story that a number of local boys shoved him into a doctor's office, where he was forced to stare at a skull. It terrified—and fascinated—him. Anyway, he married, wound up going to medical school in New Hampshire and then Michigan. It's believed by profiling minds that it was there he learned first what a skeleton and other body parts might be worth, and he also learned a great deal about dissection. The World's Fair, or, at the time, the Columbian Exposition, was due to take place in Chicago in 1893. Before the event, which would draw tens of thousands of visitors, the man started work on what would become known as his 'Murder Castle.'"

"And that's…" Campbell said, casting his head to the side as if he was confused.

Carly stepped in, saying, "No one really knows exactly when he started killing. But many people in psychology and criminal profiling believe he first murdered for profit. As Luke said, he discovered in medical school just how much corpses were worth. He was most probably involved in grave robbery at the time. He went into insurance scams—finding ways to have policies written out to him under various names, and then having the victims die. He got money from insurance—"

"And then from selling the corpses," Luke told him. "In his Murder Castle, he even arranged for vats with acids to remove flesh from the bones, and other vats were filled with bleach to totally prepare them. The skeletons were worth a great deal."

"Then," Carly added, "around 1892, he went into the phase that some call his sex murders. He was apparently charming and could easily sway women. There were four women he was supposedly married to at one time or another, and three of them wound up disappearing, along with the child of one and the sister of another. No one really knows exactly what he did or didn't do. He wrote his own confession, but he lied so often in life no one knows what was true in it. Some people he claimed to have killed were alive after his execution, which finally came in 1896.

"For another fraud, and something truly heartbreaking, he pretended to have come up with a scheme that involved one of his partners, Benjamin Pitezel. Pitezel would leave behind a large insurance policy, and they would pretend he had died, with Holmes producing a corpse from elsewhere. Except he really killed the man. Then, pretending he was helping the man's widow, he traveled with three of the Pitezel children, murdering a young boy first, cutting up his body and burning it, and then gassing two of the sisters and burying them in Canada, where their bodies were found. It was for the murder of Pitezel that he was finally condemned to death, although his arrest was initially for insurance fraud, and it was the Pinkerton Agency that finally caught up with him because he had a talent for moving around to avoid the law.

"But...the Murder Castle was Aaron Miller's inspiration for what he did with his castle here. Again, experts believe Holmes first killed because he was a 'homicidal entrepreneur.' He killed women because they provided money or because they were getting in his way or refused his advances. He killed children because they might be witnesses. The thing is..."

"That there is now a society dedicated to this man?" Campbell asked disbelievingly.

Luke sighed and grimaced. "Sir, we've seen what can happen in human society. Many people may hate others for reasons of sexual identity, ethnicity, religion or race—but they keep it to themselves until someone in power or adored by the public for some reason makes horrible behavior seem all right. Something to go ahead and speak on or act on. At any time, there may be those out there harboring fantasies of murder. For them, the H. H. Holmes Society makes those fantasies seem acceptable, something someone might act upon."

"There just can't be that many people out there who would...

who would act out murder because others were doing it!" Campbell said.

"Let's hope not," Luke said. "What we have today that didn't exist back then is social media—people across the globe in massive numbers can be reached. Even a small percentage of that number is more than we want out there. But what we also have today is far more in the field of forensics—the same media that may reach monsters also reaches law enforcement. We got Aaron and we will keep investigating until we've got the site down—and every adherent to H. H. Holmes."

Campbell shook his head again. "So, this castle Holmes created had a dungeon? I've not been, but I have heard there are castles in America. There's a Hammond Castle, right?"

"Yes, in Gloucester, Massachusetts, built in the early twentieth century," Luke said. "But the Murder Castle wasn't a castle. Holmes just called it a castle. It was a new building he had constructed several years before the World's Fair. It didn't have a dungeon but a basement that was used for torture, murder and body disposal. And here, Aaron Miller had work done—just as someone did south of London—to re-create some of Holmes's killing machines. Rooms where gas could be piped in. Vaults where people might be asphyxiated. Chutes to dispose of bodies, fireplaces that burn at tremendous heat, vats with acids..."

"No one will easily get away with selling bodies these days in Scotland!" Campbell said indignantly. "This is a contemporary world and we are a part of it. Scotsmen were indeed a great part of the industrial revolution, and we continue to make and use all that technology and communications avail us."

"Of course," Luke agreed politely, glancing at Carly again, trying to assure her he knew how to play decently with local law enforcement.

"Do you believe more of these maniacs might be working in Scotland? I can't imagine many Americans might have purchased castles in Scotland," Campbell said.

Carly stepped in quickly, as if afraid his patience wouldn't last.

"Sir, it doesn't need to be a real castle, and another killer might not even be American," she said. "The problem with today's technology is that people *can* reach out across the world and find what I believe in my heart to be a small percentage of human beings capable of being so truly evil. Our people at headquarters are studying everything they can that might be suspicious and are searching for the site again. And if Aaron Miller lives, he may give us information we need."

Campbell studied his phone for a minute. He looked across the table again at the two of them, nodding. "This is the third incident we know about, though one is suspected in France, where your coagents are looking into the situation. But there is one event we know about that took place in the States, one south of London, and now here. Do you want to be part of the crew ripping apart the castle now? Finding out just how far this horrid event went on before your arrival?"

"There is one thing I want," Luke said, "and that's to speak with Aaron Miller, if he survives."

"I will see that it happens," Campbell said grimly.

"Thank you," Luke told him.

Campbell sat back, shaking his head. "They don't call us 'Bloody Scotland' for naught. Our history is rich with wars, betrayals, martyrs and triumphs. But…wars were fought for kings, for country, for power and, sometimes, for ideals and freedom. This sickness is different, heinous, and we cannot abide it. We are grateful you are here, and I swear we'll avail you of every effort of Police Scotland and the National Crime Agency to stop it!"

Campbell had grown suddenly passionate. For a moment, the older man reminded Luke of one of the great warriors of old, a modern-day William Wallace.

"Thank you," he said again.

Campbell grimaced. "For now, paperwork. Agent MacDonald, you're in agreement with all I've said, and I believe—"

"We're grateful, sir," Carly said. "We will await whatever help is still needed from us. And as far as Aaron Miller's castle goes, we trust in your people. I just need to retrieve my belongings. And I'm with my partner on his request."

"Aye. That be fine and good. Scotland is no different from America in one regard," Campbell warned them.

Luke almost smiled at that. "Paperwork?"

"Indeed."

"Then we shall get to it," Luke said, looking at Carly.

"Always," she said, nodding in turn.

When they were at last ready to leave, Carly asked, "Do you mind dropping me? I don't need to be there when they discover the victims or speak with those who will need to vacate the castle. But everything I travel with is in the bedroom where I was staying."

"I have no intention of just dropping you. I'll wait while you retrieve your belongings," Luke assured her.

"And then I'm assuming that we'll join Mason and Della in France and see where they've gotten with their investigation. They know that people have disappeared in the wine region where they've been working with the local police and Interpol, but—"

"We're not to leave," he told her, studying his phone.

"But—"

"Check your phone. There's a message from Jackson Crow," Luke said. "'Blackbird needs to continue soaring over bonny Scotland. More when we have specifics. Arrangements made for a B and B off the Royal Mile.'"

She pulled out her phone, read the message herself that had been sent to them both and nodded. "Okay. Well, I do love the Royal Mile, and I was afraid we'd be sleeping in an airport."

He grinned at her. "You're new to the Krewe of Hunters."

"I started with the Bureau three years ago—just three months ago with the Krewe," she told him.

"Well, we'd never have to sleep in an airport unless horrendous weather was grounding everything. Adam Harrison has afforded the Krewe a lot of what he sees as necessary benefits. He'd have made sure we had a flight—just as someone in power has seen to it we have rooms. We do the work, and we work for an agency within the Bureau created by a man who never took a personal tragedy to a bad place but rather wanted to use his amazing financial expertise to help others. We're incredibly lucky."

She was smiling oddly.

"What?" he asked her, curious.

"Lucky. We deal with so much awful."

"But we do our best to stop it, too."

"Right. I saw your face," she told him. She was staring at the road ahead, not at him.

"My face—"

"You didn't want Aaron Miller to die. Many people would have felt he deserved death."

"We need him alive."

She turned to look at him at last.

"You were one of the agents who found the first copycat murder castle, so to speak. In America."

"In Kansas," he said flatly. She was watching him.

She wanted to know him, understand him. Not something terrible, of course. But he felt that, somewhere inside, he was still raw. He had received the best training possible for an agent; he had worked with many different branches in the Bureau. He would always put professionalism above emotion. But right now...

And still.

He was stuck with her. Could be worse. She was capable, professional, and had seemed to have the looks and ability to slip into just about any role. She even smelled good.

But since Kansas, his undercover work there and the horrible discoveries they'd made, he'd really turned into a loner. Maybe even a bit of a jerk or a bastard, and he probably needed the time with a therapist that hadn't been mandated because field action was so urgent. He was now assigned to work this together with Special Agent Carly MacDonald, with Interpol and all local agencies there to help at a moment's notice.

Carly had drawn out the monster of the castle; they had taken him down. And Campbell could be right. The danger in Scotland could be over.

And then again, it might not.

He had to try to be decent.

"Hey. Are you with me?" she asked softly, and he knew that her words meant more than simply for the moment.

"Yeah. In Kansas," he repeated, shaking his head. "It was bizarre, being that Gary Houghton, the Society member, was from such a rural area. He started out with a typical farmhouse, completely surrounded by cornfields. Then again, due to tornadoes, he had a large basement built deeply into the ground. But there is a major Kiowa museum and several decent-sized towns fronting the farm there, enough so that during festivals he was easily able to attract visitors as a B and B, not too many at once, which managed to work to his advantage for quite some time." He paused.

"When I got there—pulling a lot of what you did at Aaron's castle—I slipped down to the basement at night. I had no choice. He had the point of a knife about to slide into a woman's throat. One of our team members who'd been awaiting my signal arrived with perfect timing and had to shoot him. We found out he'd followed the entire Holmes manifesto—acid baths, bleach, massive incinerator and human remains that are still being sorted out. Some in better condition than others, a recent victim still lying in a pool of blood... The man liked knives. Holmes may have first become a killer after becoming a grave robber for the money that could be made on bodies and bones, but I don't think money meant anything to Gary Houghton. He liked knives."

"It must have truly been far beyond awful," Carly said. She was looking at him evenly.

He sighed, giving her a grim smile. "And here is the problem. We are looking at a society of people with sick urges, all making their sicknesses seem fine because they have others they can share with, making them feel as if what they want to do makes them special and powerful."

"Like you told Campbell—we have our advantages, too!" she said, her tone a little fierce.

Luke felt a real smile curl his lips.

"We do!" he agreed. He felt his phone vibrating again, but hers was in her lap and he didn't need to reach for his.

"I've got it—message from headquarters," she said. "And it reads, 'Have a rest tonight—organizing intelligence and working out travel plans for tomorrow.' Okay, so…"

"We're here," he said quietly, turning into the drive to the castle that was still filled with law enforcement vehicles.

Finnegan greeted them somberly when they entered the castle.

Naturally, the registration desk was now empty, as were the great halls stretching in either direction.

"We have no idea what we've got. We're digging up floors, digging out his firepit… 'Tis a horror museum," Finnegan told them. "I was below but needed…"

"A break. We're human," Luke said.

"Have you—" Finnegan began.

"We've just come for my things—we'll be right out of your hair!" Carly promised sweetly.

Finnegan smiled at her. It was obvious she did all right with their British counterparts. That was good. Luke needed to accept her as a partner—and maybe even relearn how to be a bit more like her.

"Finnegan," she continued. "Irish?"

He laughed softly. "Well, going back, y'know, tribes from all over moved on up or over in the British Isles. The Romans referred to the Irish as the 'Scotia' around 500 AD. Came to be a name for Gaelic peoples, and then again…count the centuries! People have been hopping over the island for years and years."

"I've just always loved the name," Carly told him. "I took a class on *Finnegans Wake* back when I was in college. Loved it! I'll just be a second, or a few seconds, I promise!" she added.

She left them, hurrying for the stairs to the second level.

"Yer a lucky bloke, my friend," Finnegan said. "In this…well, someone of good cheer and optimism can help clear a few o' the dark clouds!"

Luke gave him a friendly nod.

But Finnegan was staring at him, somber again. "Such a situation found south of London and yet there may still be more?"

"We don't know. Let's celebrate discovering and ending this horror show, shall we?" Luke asked.

"Yer right, of course. But—"

"Ah, wow! My partner is speedy!" Luke said. He was glad that Carly was already heading down the stairs; she traveled light. She had one roller bag that would fit in the overhead bin in most commercial airplanes and a second over-the-shoulder one, and that was all.

She was quick and adept. It was the gentlemanly thing to do, of course, to reach for a bag, and he did so.

Again, he thought she would rebuff him, but she released the handle of her roller bag and gave him a quick smile and thanks before turning to Finnegan.

"Thank you for being so prompt!" she told him. "Arriving with law enforcement *and* the medical help we needed." She offered him her hand.

"Special Agent MacDonald, a pleasure," Finnegan assured her. "And it's with sorrow that I hope we do not meet again."

"Understandable," she said.

"Unless it's over a pint or a wee bit o' our best whiskey!" he said.

Luke decided to rescue his new partner by stepping forward to reach for and shake Finnegan's hand.

"A pint somewhere, sometime!" he said. "We're heading for some sleep, sir. I haven't been to sleep since delving through two of these sites, so..."

"Looking forward to me own bed!" Finnegan said.

Luke placed an arm around Carly's shoulders, aiming her toward the door.

They were out.

He set her bag in the truck and slid into the driver's seat, then frowned as he saw she was walking away.

"I've got a car here, too!" she reminded him. "Thanks for helping with the bag—I'll meet you at our little motel or B and B or whatever!"

He smiled and nodded. He hadn't lied, he realized. It had been hours and hours since he'd slept.

Or eaten.

Past lunch, before dinner. But Edinburgh was an amazing city and beloved by tourists; something would be open for a meal, and then with any luck, he thought grimly, they'd get to sleep.

He was about to set the car into gear when he felt his phone vibrating again. He pulled it from his pocket, glancing down at the text he'd just received.

It had been sent to both him and Carly and had been written by Mason Carter.

Had hoped to see you. I believe you heard from Jackson Crow. Great croissants here. Maybe not, too busy to enjoy. Get some sleep in Edinburgh. You may be heading a 'wee' bit north, between Urquhart Castle and Inverness. Details in the morning, still gathering intel.

Urquhart Castle sat on Loch Ness, with the city of Inverness about twenty miles away.

His phone rang as he held it. Carly, of course.

"We may have a bit of a stay in Scotland," she said.

"We'll be heading to Loch Ness, so it seems."

"But not to find the monster."

"Not *the* monster. But *a* monster, nonetheless. You hungry?"

"Hey, sure, all that talk of monsters, really revs up the appetite."

Luke grinned. "See you soon."

He ended the call. They weren't far from where they'd spend the night before heading out deeper into the center of the country in the morning.

But it was going to be okay. They'd get something to eat. They'd get some desperately needed sleep.

And Finnegan was right.

He was lucky.

He wasn't sure how, but in her way, Carly MacDonald did help when it came to tamping down the demon monsters that plagued his mind.

CHAPTER THREE

The B and B that had been reserved for them had exactly what was necessary. A great place to park, a soft bed and a shower in each room. It had been a long day and it felt like it was later than it was—almost dinnertime.

Carly saw Luke's car was already parked when she arrived, but she found him inside, speaking with the owner of the house, a lovely woman in her sixties with one of the softest, sweetest burrs to her voice Carly had ever heard.

"We're just—"

"Tossing stuff in our rooms," Luke said. "We'll eat right down the street, a place called Clarabelle's that Mrs. Douglas here recommends very highly."

"Perfect!"

Still, Carly took a moment to jump on the bed in her room and test it out. She hesitated a minute, thinking if she was still on her own, she'd pop out and buy a box of energy bars, eat in the room and enjoy the bed.

But she felt that she understood some of her new partner's strangeness. He'd been at the beginning of this nightmare.

Maybe given a chance, he could prove to be a team player. So—dinner!

She sprang out of bed and hurried back downstairs. Mrs. Douglas was nowhere to be seen; Luke Kendrick was standing by the door.

"Clarabelle's. I've never been there before, but I'm sure Mrs. Douglas knows what's good around here."

"You know a lot of other places here?" he asked her, opening the door.

"Yeah, well, most of what I told Aaron Miller when I was checking into his castle was true. My father's parents are from the area. Actually, they're from a little place close to where we'll be going. It's called Drumnadrochit."

"You've been there?"

"Of course. I'm an only child but I have three cousins. My grandparents took all of us when I turned ten, and I've been back since. Not for a while now, but…"

"And did you see the Loch Ness Monster?"

She grinned. "No. Nessie evaded me. Of course, there are great theories about the creature. Okay, it's definitely not a plesiosaur—he'd have to breathe, and he'd be seen. Also, with a neck with eighteen million vertebrae, he couldn't get his head out of the water in the way some 'eyewitness' reports suggest he could do. But maybe he is a huge fish of some kind. Sturgeon can be up to fourteen or fifteen feet…or something else."

"There's a great story that there's some kind of monster in a lake in Sweden, and maybe they're one and the same. Maybe the creatures come and go—and really enjoy Loch Ness during the salmon season."

"Storsjöodjuret," Carly said. "Apparently, both lakes connect to the North Sea. But! A big creature couldn't make it over some of the rocks that would connect the water to Loch Ness, but then again, some researchers believe it could use the Caledonian Canal."

"Of course," Luke said. She was grinning, and he seemed relaxed at last, something that made her glad. As partners went, once he seemed more at ease, he was going to prove to be okay, she thought. He was an imposing figure—a good six-four, she determined. He was a crack shot; she'd seen that. And his first determination seemed to be to save lives. Of course, they'd needed Aaron Miller alive, but she felt it was more than that. Sometimes, it was easy to think they should shoot to kill. Sometimes, they had to shoot to kill. But killing was never her first choice, and she was glad it wasn't for him, too.

She'd known he'd been one of the agents involved—the lead agent—on the first case. Naturally, this would dig into him.

But when he smiled, he was striking. He had a handsome face with sharp green eyes, lean cheeks, but a solid jaw. He was clean-shaven, and his dark hair was short, but not buzzed. He was good-looking, she realized—once she wasn't feeling defensive, as she had at first, or worried, as she had been when she'd seen his tension working with other law enforcement.

"And what do you think?" he asked her, indicating a door that was just up the street.

"Well," she said honestly, "since most of the world would think that I'm crazy if they knew what I do to begin with, I try to keep an open mind. Do I think it's possible there's some kind of a creature? Well, we know that creatures exist everywhere. The tuatara—looks like a really creepy iguana—lived along with dinosaurs, and so did a few other animals. And the whale shark has been swimming around for twenty-eight million years."

"Okay. I'll keep my eye out," Luke promised. "If we're sent that way."

"Whether there's a creature or not, the area is beautiful."

"And the ruins of Urquhart Castle are fascinating," he said.

She smiled. "So, you know the area, too."

"I only have one grandparent from Scotland and she was born

in Glasgow," he said. "But, yeah, you know, your parents bring you places, and if you like them, you get back."

They'd reached the restaurant. She almost opened the door but decided he wanted to do so and allowed him.

It was charming inside. There were several booths and tables, all offering little vases with flowers. A window opened to the kitchen and the chefs and cook could be watched.

"Going to have some haggis?" he asked her, noticing it was on a placard by the host stand that offered the daily specials.

"Salmon!" she said.

He laughed. "I'll be going with the salmon, too."

They were quickly seated. The salmon was served with potatoes and broccoli, and they both ordered it. And to her surprise, they both ordered coffee.

"You know, we're going back to get some sleep," she reminded him.

"I'm trying to stay awake long enough to get there," he said. "And you?"

"Same."

"Sleep will be amazing," he said. He shook his head, frowning, looking down at the table.

"Is there an ant running around or something?" Carly asked him.

He smiled, looking up at her. "No, I guess I'm just disturbed. This 'H. H. Holmes Society' thing. Scotland is a relatively small nation within Great Britain. How long has that site been out there? And it would be one thing to believe it was only hitting the English-speaking world, but Mason and Della are in France following up on disappearances there."

"It's disturbing, but there's hope! First, at headquarters, Jackson, Adam, Angela and others will be working their magic. Law enforcement across the world will know what's going on, our country will be covered and we are working with amazing people. Luke, we will get it shut down. And for tonight—"

"Sleep."

"Right." She was silent a minute and then shrugged and smiled. "St. Columba was the first one to notice a Loch Ness Monster, you know, way back."

He laughed softly. "Back to Nessie! As if history wasn't enough."

She winced. "Good old history. Man and his determination on bloodshed. And the greater the history in an area, I'm afraid we find a greater legacy of violence. In 1544, there was something called the Battle of the Shirts. It was basically between Clan Cameron and Clan Fraser, and Clan MacDonald supported Clan Cameron. And then in 1544 and 1545, they raided Urquhart, which was held by Clan Grant at the time. The place was wiped out—cattle, sheep, you name it, and... Anyway, none of my ancestors was executed, to the best of my knowledge, but it didn't go well for Ewen Cameron, who was executed in 1546."

"Do you think they'll blame you now?" he inquired, grinning.

She laughed. "No, I've been there before, and all went well."

He shook his head. "Like Campbell said, Bloody Scotland. If I have my history right, they can trace people dating back to about 3,500 BC. God alone knows what happened until the Romans came and defeated the Caledonians at the Battle of Mons Graupius in 83 AD, but the Romans decided the Scots were too wild, rowdy and violent, so they built the Hadrian's and Antonine Walls in 122 AD and 143 AD—give or take a year or two. Tribes come in from Ireland and other places. Your St. Columba arrives in 500 something. Battle, battle, battle, the Vikings arrive. Iona is burned. In 1124, David I becomes king and introduces the feudal system. Then in 1128 David I founds Holyrood Abbey."

Carly stared at him, frowning.

"What are you? An encyclopedia?"

He laughed. "Trouble really came after William I swears allegiance to Henry II of England in 1174—that causes war and violence for years and years to come because Edward I will then give the crown to John Balliol in 1292, which leads to the days of the hero, William Wallace, beating the English at the Battle of Stirling Bridge. Of course, Wallace will eventually be captured and executed, drawn and quartered, with his 'quarters' being shipped about to be displayed so that others won't follow his lead. But instead, while Robert the Bruce has been forced to play both sides at times due to his father's close friendship with the English king, he will rise up at last after his father's death, win battles, lose battles, but eventually prevail and become Robert I of Scotland."

Carly leaned back, laughing softly. She hadn't figured him for a man who would know history so well—and seem to love it.

"Very good."

"I'm sure you could have told me."

"I know basic history, but I couldn't have rattled off those dates! Let's see… Robert's son, David, will succeed him at the tender age of five. After David II, Robert II will become the first Stuart king, and we all know what eventually happens to Mary Stuart, Queen of Scots."

"But her son will wear the crown of Scotland and the crown of England."

"I feel sorry for Mary, but she should have been much smarter!"

"It's hard to judge, hundreds of years later," he told her.

"Battle, battle, battle—but the Acts of Union passed by both the English and Scottish parliaments that put them together."

He grinned. "And to this day some Scots are nationalists, and some want to hang tight to the financial status quo. Who knows what the future will bring?"

"They won't go to war again—I'd bet my life on that!" Carly said, smiling.

"The world is a strange place." He shrugged, but he was

smiling, too. "Think about it—we bet our lives on humanity every day."

"Nope," she told him. "I count on those I work with. I count on the fact that, despite what we see, the vast majority of human beings are good! What, you're going to argue that?" she demanded.

"Nope!" he said.

Their food arrived. It was excellent. They'd both consumed their coffee; they both asked for more.

"Think we're pushing it?" Carly asked him.

"Maybe you, not me. I'm going to crash like a lead balloon!"

"Yeah, I will, too, I think. Tonight—"

"I've trained myself to wake up at just about anything," Luke said. "But honestly, I know Jackson and Angela—and I know we wouldn't be where we are tonight if they hadn't thoroughly checked it out. That's the incredible thing about the Krewe. We have such an amazing backup team. When they say you need rest, they mean it. And when you go into the fray, you know what you're up against."

She smiled and nodded, and soon they were heading back.

"Thank you," he told her.

"For what?"

"I think you would have bought a deli sandwich somewhere and just gone to bed. I was really hungry. Thank you for going with me."

"Hey. Partners," she said.

He paused a second, looking at her, smiling.

"Yeah. Partners."

He started walking again, and they headed on down the last block to their B and B, not pausing again until they were inside.

"I have an alarm set for whatever time Jackson or whoever wants us to get info," he told her. "Turn your phone off—you had the worst of it. Get some sleep. I don't intend to crawl out of bed until I have to."

"That's a plan! Thanks."

She thought she could argue; he'd been at two crime scenes where horrible things had happened.

But she just didn't feel like arguing. She smiled and they parted ways on the second floor and made their way to their own rooms.

She was afraid at first she'd be so overtired that she wouldn't sleep. But after a long, hot shower, she fell into bed.

And sleep came almost instantly.

Luke woke as his phone rang. An instant tension filled him; he'd set it so that only a call from headquarters or Mason Carter would come through.

It was headquarters, and glancing at the time, he realized that Jackson or Angela had spent the night working—it had to be about 3:00 a.m. in the United States.

It was Angela.

"You've taken the site down?" he asked her hopefully.

"No, we don't have it down again. But there is an internet café not far from you, and we know someone there accessed the site. I'm thinking the two of you might want a good strong cup of coffee to get the day going," Angela said. "We're on it from that advantage. We're pulling all the security footage we can from the area. But if someone is on the site, and you can see who—we may be able to nip a problem in the bud."

"We'd love a good cup of coffee to get the day going," Luke assured her. He laughed softly. "And you'd be surprised by the Brits who want to get their day started with a good jolt rather than a fine cup of tea."

"Be careful, be charming, and when in Scotland, use the term Scot. The trend for nationalism is growing, and they may prefer to be called Scots! Scotland is a country, but a country within a nation," Angela reminded him.

"Got it."

"And you will be getting a call from Campbell soon, I think. Aaron Miller is stable—they believe he might be able to talk by the afternoon."

"Good. Maybe we can get something from him."

"Don't be too hopeful, Luke. These people are users—they are using the site. Somehow, we've got to figure out how it goes up so quickly after we get it down and how this person is routing things around the globe so that we have such difficulty finding the origin. No one wants to believe such a monster comes from their country—"

"But every country out there has produced a monster now and then," Luke finished. "You know we all studied serial killers," he reminded her quietly. And they had. Every country from A to Z, such as Abdullah Shah, who had killed twenty travelers in the '90s, to the infamous Andrei Chikatilo of Russia, who had murdered at least fifty-five people between 1982 and 1990. "No country, no ethnicity, is immune—because however different customs, cultures and languages there might be, human beings are one and the same. Most want to live their lives being decent, if not good, people, working, playing, raising their families, finding the comfort of love for those families to be the driving goal in life."

But there would always be those with hearts and brains not quite wired properly, and they could occur anywhere in the world.

"What about heading toward Urquhart, Loch Ness or—" he said.

"Still on it, nothing solid. Campbell is supposed to be getting back to me shortly. He's having to deal with the media, play the right note between warning others and not playing into any kind of panic—or letting a monster know law enforcement might be on to him. Or her. I don't think there is a gender bias working here. Be warned. He's very carefully kept the two of you out of any information given to the public, but there was no way the public wasn't eventually going to find out about a cache of bodies in a castle."

"Right."

"Enjoy your coffee," Angela said dryly. "Check in with Campbell in a few hours."

"I'll get Carly up and we'll be right on it."

"She's a good agent—make sure you play fair," she warned.

He frowned. "Angela, you know—"

"I know that finding the first of our Society's victims was hard, Luke. But Carly is top-notch, and she has a Scottish connection. She has the charm to play just about anyone, and you need to make use of that. She's clever—"

"She's the brain and I'm the brawn?" he asked lightly.

"Don't kid yourself. Give her an edge and she'll knock your socks off. Seriously, our power is in the fact that we can share what we learn from the dead who have stayed and are anxious to help us when they've seen something or know something. By the way—"

"So far, the only spirits we've seen on this have been in whiskey bottles," he said.

"Keep an eye out. Someone has seen something."

"Angela—"

"Sorry about that one. Yes, you always have an eye out. So does Carly. Just remember to back one another as partners, use all our hidden talents and all we've learned through training and criminalistics."

"Yes, of course. I will be a team player. Carly is already proving to be a partner I would have happily chosen myself."

"Great. I haven't lost my touch, then, at studying living human beings!" Angela said. "Well, you were the right people who I could get into the right place at the right time. Stick to it. We are working around the clock here, I promise you."

"Right, and maybe you should try this thing called sleep tonight," Luke told her.

He could almost see her smile.

Luke had been in the military. He'd been a cop for six months before entering the FBI Academy. He'd never imagined that there could be such a thing as the Krewe of Hunters until he'd received the strange call from Jackson Crow. And while their work remained brutal, he'd never thought he could work with people who were so decent and respectful, never asking of others when they weren't ready to give of themselves to a case 100 percent.

A group of people who didn't think he was crazy, with whom he could share some of his strange methods of deduction.

Rising, he made a call to Carly. She answered on the second ring.

"You slept?" he asked her.

"Soundly until about five minutes ago," she assured him. "So…"

"No movement yet. Except for coffee."

"That sounds wonderful—"

"At a café where someone has accessed the H. H. Holmes Society site," he added.

"Oh, well, uh, still…coffee along with the job. Better than it could be," she mused. "I'll be out there in five minutes."

She was. Luke wasn't sure he'd ever worked with anyone, man or woman, who could promise five minutes and hold to it.

"So, how are we playing this?" she asked him.

"I thought we'd start out by ordering coffee," he said.

She grinned as they walked, following the GPS to the address Angela had texted them.

"Café. Hmm. They may have full breakfasts, which shouldn't be so bad—"

"Probably at tables, maybe separate from a bank of computers."

"An internet café may well be an internet café, wherever it is in the world," she commented.

They found the place easily. It was just 9:00 a.m. when they arrived, but the place was crowded, booming with a breakfast crowd and a group dedicated to doing whatever each individual did on the web.

Edinburgh was one of the most beautiful capital cities to be found anywhere and drew tourists from all over the world. It wasn't surprising that the café was crowded, and Luke could only imagine how busy it would be during festival season.

"No desk spaces," Carly murmured.

"But a table just opened there," Luke pointed out. He gave the hostess a charming smile, and she assured him they could have it as soon as the staff had a chance to clean it.

They were seated in just another minute.

There were long tables at the far end of the room with computers. Twelve of them, Luke counted. Every computer was taken.

He thought back to the time he'd spent studying with the Behavioral Sciences Unit. Whoever they were looking for was probably midtwenties to midthirties and male. Someone who believed, at least, that they might emulate the charm that H. H. Holmes was rumored to have had, allowing him to create friendships and prey on the women he had married—two of them bigamously—and/or seduced.

A middle-aged woman was at one computer, two teens who should probably have been in school were seated next to each other on one side of her and a fortysomething businessman sat on the other. Two more computers were occupied by young women and six were occupied by men in their twenties to thirties.

"Someone is getting up," Carly murmured. "Right between the two men."

Luke knew Carly would appear less a danger to the men.

"Go," he said quietly.

She rose to go over to the computer. As she did so, he called out to her, "I'll order for you, and make sure you tell your mom hi for me and that we're having a great time!"

"She'll just be so happy we're here!" Carly called back to him.

She walked over and took the seat between the two men. She smiled in a friendly manner as they each looked at her, and then made it appear she was giving her complete attention to the directions on the screen. She logged in with her credit card and searched for her mail carrier.

She could be seen, just as he could be seen. He smiled, certain he knew what she was doing.

Writing to Angela as "Mom."

Then again, maybe she would email her real mom. He knew her parents were alive; he'd done a bit of studying on her when he'd been told he was going to meet her. He'd discovered what could be learned online.

As she sat at the computer—and he was sure she'd switch from mail to information on travel in the area—their waiter arrived. He put in their orders for breakfast and asked for the check at the same time in case they needed to leave quickly.

She stayed long enough to look up a few sites and then logged out, smiled to the two men again as she rose. Both said something in return, smiling, their eyes appreciative.

She was a stunning woman, whether playing a role or not.

She slid back into her chair opposite his at the table.

Smiling still, she leaned forward as if she was excitedly giving him information about some special spot they might visit.

"The fellow with the reddish hair, thirties, watched me hardest when I left. He logged out when I glanced up at him, but I got a quick look. I think he was on the site, Luke. What do we do from here? He's off the site unless he logged back on."

She fell silent, sitting back and smiling and then saying thank you as their waiter appeared with their food, and their check as Luke had asked. He pretended to give his full attention to the amazing display before him, that included tattie scones, eggs, beans, bacon and tomatoes.

The man was a redhead with a full, impressive red beard. He appeared to be in his late twenties, thirty or thirty-one at most. He was dressed as if he was ready to head off to work in a casual blue suit with an open-necked tailored shirt beneath.

"This is delicious. Try to eat some of it. We can't do anything to the man for sitting at a computer," Carly murmured.

The food was great and he was hungry. He pulled his phone out to put a call through to Campbell while chewing until the man answered.

He didn't need to describe their situation—Angela had been in touch with the agent. He and Carly would follow the suspect when he left the café, but law enforcement needed to be ready to head in and check out the computer and find the adherent's identity.

He spoke quietly and Carly nodded, assuring him that he wasn't being heard beyond their table.

The man who had accessed the H. H. Holmes site logged out and rose, grinning.

They hadn't quite finished their food.

No matter. As he left the café, they rose to follow him the minute the door had closed behind him.

"Back up—let me get ahead alone," Carly said. "But be on my tail!"

"Oh, you bet," Luke promised.

She hurried ahead. Luckily, the man then seemed to be obsessed with his phone, and she was able to pass him on the street and then pause in front of a shop window in time to cause him to almost crash into her.

Luke kept a careful distance, but he could still see what twist she was using to draw his attention.

She appeared to be distressed, trying to smile, to be a pleasant human being, while pretending she'd just had a terrible fight with Luke, her travel companion.

The red-haired man smiled and just talked at first.

Then he set a comforting hand on her shoulder and indicated a walk they should take. Luke quickly realized they were heading far down the street that paralleled the Royal Mile, away from the castle and toward Holyrood Palace.

But then they turned off the street, as if they were going for a stroll.

It was hard to hold back. They were easing away from the busy area off the Mile and heading for Canongate.

Luke frowned and realized they were indeed going for a walk. A long walk.

They were headed in the direction of the highest point in the city that was geographically filled with rugged rock and peaks.

Arthur's Seat in Holyrood Park was part of one of four historic hill forts dating back about two thousand years and built upon the remains of an extinct volcano.

The park was beautiful and was enjoyed by locals and tourists alike.

It was also where a man might find many a place to be alone with a young woman and do what he would with her.

Luke quickened his pace.

Luckily, others were on Canongate, but crossing the street where he wished didn't prove quite as easy. He was afraid he might lose the duo as he stopped, giving heed to the traffic. But his moment came and he sprinted across and was soon sliding easily into the land that was the beginning of the large and beautiful park.

Edinburgh was fantastic if just in its geographic history, the volcanic remains giving it great crags, cliffs, heights and valleys.

The red-haired man wasn't interested in a gentle stroll through the green grasses. As Luke had suspected, he had apparently convinced the lovely American tourist in his care she needed to head all the way to the highest point, Arthur's Seat.

He knew he had to keep his distance. He was glad he had done so when his phone vibrated—it was Campbell.

"We sent our team into the café. The bloke at the computer was Peter Bond. He has a record for petty theft—and for assault, attacked a young woman just outside a pub and the arresting inspector wrote in his report that he believed it to be an attempted rape. He's currently unemployed, but he's done all right dealing in Bitcoin. Most importantly, he was on that H. H. Holmes Society site—and it disappeared just as our techs saw it. Your people are trying to capture a source when it reappears. Don't treat this fellow lightly."

"Don't intend to, sir!" Luke assured him.

The pair had disappeared just beyond a bend in the path.

Luke hurried after them with all speed.

"This is lovely of you!" Carly said sweetly. "I thought my day would turn to pure disaster, with me sitting alone in my hotel room, wishing I was home. But here you are, taking time out of your day, being gracious to a rather pathetic tourist like me!"

"Not at all, not at all!" Peter assured her. "Such a lovely tourist as yourself! I am sorry it's in a foreign land that you've had such a blowout with your fiancé—"

"Don't even use that word, I beg you! I shudder to think I even considered marriage to such a rude bore!" Carly told him.

"I'm just glad my secretary called and said my Belgian client had been delayed by travel concerns," said the man who had introduced himself as Peter Bond. "It's such a perfect time to be here. On the weekends, we'd not have a second of privacy, but…still, this morning, work for the adults and school week for the wee ones, so…" He paused, giving her a mischievous smile. "We should have some delicious time to savor the sights just on our own. The heights are terrific, the old hill forts—"

"Are so fascinating!" Carly said. Again, she employed the truth as she told him, "I'm just in love with old and historic places and things. I mean, the Spanish did settle St. Augustine in the 1500s, and it's actually the oldest city in the States settled by Europeans, but…hey. I grew up in Daytona Beach. It's a great beach, but nothing as cool as all this! I mean, wow. Edinburgh is so, so old!"

They were moving higher and higher.

Instinct told Carly he intended something. Privacy? For him to toss her from a great height? Or privacy so he could throttle her or rip her to shreds? Perhaps both.

But just as instinct warned her he seriously meant an attack, it assured her Luke was close behind—should she need help.

Peter Bond was going to be surprised if he believed an American tourist had no means of fighting back.

"Ah, St. Margaret's Loch lies there, if we veer off a wee bit. Shall we take a look?" he asked her.

"Of course! With your kindness and being such an incredible tour guide, I will follow where you lead!"

He was leading them over a slope of grasses, toward the water.

And toward a rich grouping of trees.

And when they were behind them…

He turned suddenly, drawing her hard against him and pulling something from his pocket. At first, she couldn't fathom what he was about. Then she realized he had a rag in a baggie that he was ripping open, and the rag was doused in something.

She held her breath, kicking him as hard as she could with a solid knee to the groin as he tried to cover her mouth with the cloth.

He let out a startled grunt of pain, doubling over but dragging her with him. She wasn't even sure what he called her then, his muttering grew so dark, but she had to twist hard to avoid the rag. He was a big man, and she knew she had to maneuver against his weight as well as all else.

"I'll have you now, whore! Fight, fight, fight me! I'll best you yet!"

And he would if he could get the rag over her mouth and nose.

She couldn't let that happen.

Carly ducked, causing him to slam to the earth, but he was up again quickly.

He caught her again, and she slashed out with a move of her arm and elbow learned in one of her martial arts classes, balancing her weight carefully as she did so. He cried out in pain, furious, swearing, obviously not caring in the least if anyone heard anymore.

If she could just get the rag to his face…

He moved toward her again, doubled over, screaming in pain, but not to be stopped. He was hurtling the whole of his body at her, ready to slam her down to the ground in order to trap her beneath the bulk of his body.

She was prepared, ready to slip to the side, but…

He never touched her.

He was ripped away.

Ripped. Literally. As if he was lifted from her by a superpower and cast far across the ground, where he went crashing into a tall tree.

Luke Kendrick was standing before her, staring at the wounded man screaming on the ground.

"You seemed to be doing okay," Luke said. "But…" He shrugged. "Just seemed like we might as well get it over with and get Campbell out here as quickly as possible. I got the call. We are going to be able to question Aaron Miller—though I was thinking we might want to have a more civil conversation with this fellow right here."

CHAPTER FOUR

Luke sat across the table from Peter Bond with his hands folded before him. Carly wasn't next to him. They'd decided that first Luke would question the man with Campbell sitting next to him, and Campbell would be ready to dive in whenever he chose.

"I don't know what I'm doing here," Peter Bond protested. "That horrid woman attacked me. I was trying to be kind—"

"I wouldn't try that!" Luke said impatiently. "Your finger-prints are all over the plastic bag that you were using to carry your chloroform."

"Self-protection! We're not gun-toting wild men like people in your country," Bond said.

"Then again, there's a record of you reading from a chat on the H. H. Holmes Society website that carrying chloroform in a plastic bag protects you—and renders any victims pliable for whatever your plans might be. Since there is such a record…"

"No! No—if I found anything on the dark web, it was by accident—"

Campbell spoke up, looking at Luke. "I didn't say a thing about the dark web, nor did I hear you do so."

"Anyone can read anything!" Peter insisted.

"With great interest," Luke said, leaning toward him. "Let's get the truth from you. I'm not the one charging you here, but Interpol and the Scottish authorities are very interested—"

"Very interested, indeed," Campbell assured him.

"All right, all right, all right! I was seriously approached by the young woman. Yes, I stumbled on that stupid website at the café. But—"

"You've been on the website before. That's how you know to carry chloroform in plastic," Campbell said.

"But I didn't do anything!"

"You assaulted a young woman. Which, by your record, we know to be something you've done before. I'm afraid that will stand against you," Campbell informed him. He looked at Luke. "We don't have a death penalty, but we are capable of putting people behind bars for many, many a year."

"Oh, I know you do. I don't know the ins and outs, but our legal system is based on yours," Luke said easily.

Peter Bond sat back.

"I am asking for counsel," he said flatly.

"As is your right—even I know that!" Luke said, rising. "It's just a pity. If you were to tell us what you know, the charges against you could be tempered."

"Don't you understand!" the man raged suddenly. "I don't know what I can tell you. There's a website. You know that. I went on the website!"

"You don't know who keeps creating the website?" Campbell asked him.

The man shook his head. "It's just a stupid website. I didn't want to hurt anyone. I thought that ridiculous American woman wanted sex."

"Interesting. Women who want sex don't usually need chloroform," Luke said.

"She wanted it!" Peter raged.

Campbell shook his head and stood up, indicating they should go on out.

Luke agreed. They weren't going to gain anything from the man. He was a follower and not a very bright one.

He had greater hope they might discover something by visiting Aaron Miller in the hospital.

Carly met up with them as they exited the interrogation room.

"He's no great leader," she said, having been watching the questioning from behind the glass.

"I think we're all agreed on that," Campbell said. He looked from Luke to Carly. "You probably saved another young lady from a situation she might not have left quite so easily. Though if he meant rape *and* murder, we will never know. Thankfully, he will face charges, and no counsel is going to work to get him to walk free."

Carly shook her head. "But we didn't get anything out of him."

"Neither did we let him get away with anything," Campbell said. "Go on to the hospital, if you will. Perhaps you can gain something from Aaron Miller. I could not. I believe the fellow has lost his mind completely. How he managed to keep anything going in his state of confusion, I'll ne'er understand."

Luke frowned. "He—he struck himself in the chest. I have no medical degree, but…would that loss of blood have such an effect on his brain?"

"He missed his heart and major organs," Campbell said. "That's the extent of my medical understanding. Perhaps the pressure has gotten to him. Let's face it, there is something psychologically wrong with a man to do as he was doing."

"Only a true psychopath can dispose of human remains as if they were nothing," Luke agreed. "And yet…"

"Holmes kept his mind sharp right up to his execution?" Carly said.

"Of course, these people are not Holmes. And Holmes didn't

need his Murder Castle to commit several of his murders. He dismembered Pitezel's son and gassed his girls in a trunk in a room in Canada. He killed for money and he killed for sex, with no compunction whatsoever. But he never became incoherent."

"We have to remember these people are not Holmes—they simply want to emulate him," Carly reminded him. "We'll go and see what we can discover from him, if anything. Thank you, sir," she told Campbell.

The man nodded, studying her, then glancing at Luke.

"Thank you. We will remain grateful for the intelligence you and your group have brought into these investigations and remain ready at a moment's notice to assist."

Thanking him again, they left.

"You doing okay?" Luke asked Carly. He was driving again. She'd assured him that she really didn't give a damn who did the driving—as long as they were doing a decent job.

He was pretty sure he did a decent job driving.

"I'm fine," she said, glancing his way. "I'm a little angry with myself."

"Why is that?" he asked her.

She shook her head. "I knew he wasn't armed because he wasn't expecting me to be any kind of a problem. And I have my gas mask, ready for all we know about what goes on at any of these 'murder castles' or houses or places owned or operated by any of these website users. I screwed up. I never thought he'd have chloroform in his pocket!"

"But you were holding your own just fine."

She glanced his way. "I like to think so. But I'm also grateful you were there."

"Partners," he said simply.

"I think we should both go in to talk to Aaron," she said.

"Agreed."

"I need to admit, too, I was disappointed—although I didn't really expect we'd get much out of Peter Bond. First, aren't you kind of an idiot to access that kind of site at an internet café where police can come in and trace whatever was going on?"

"Not the brightest, no," Luke agreed. "He wasn't one of the castle owners, and I think he may have been telling the truth—other than the fact that if you had wanted sex with him, he wouldn't have needed the chloroform."

"Do you think he intended to kill me?"

"I'm actually glad we don't get to know," he said.

She grinned, but her smile faded when her gaze fell to her lap.

"I keep thinking I could have played it better."

"I don't think you could have."

"Thanks."

He drove into the parking lot of the hospital where Aaron Miller was being treated in the criminal wing. As they exited the car, he told her, "I mean it. He hasn't given us anything more because he doesn't have anything to give us—and we stopped him before he could do something horrible to someone."

She smiled. "We've just got to get a grip on this thing."

"It's not just us," he reminded her.

"I know. We have a great crew. Or k-r-e-w-e."

They went in and saw the right people to get in to speak with Aaron Miller.

He was chained to the bed and attached to an IV and a monitor. When he saw them, to Luke's surprise, he smiled.

"Well, visitors. Alleviate the boredom!" he said.

"You could alleviate it for us, that's for sure," Luke said, taking chairs from the end of the room to draw by the bed.

He took the chair closest to the man, allowing Carly to keep a distance, sitting next to him and closer to Aaron Miller's feet.

"You're bored? Hey. Not everything can be as great as staying with me," he said, amused.

"Yeah, great! But, you know, I'm still curious," Carly said. "You know, about the other 'half of it' that you kept talking about. Torture, murder…"

"Hey. I could have gone on forever," he protested, frowning.

"No one goes on forever," Luke assured him.

"I had tutelage from the best of the best," Aaron said.

"Oh? And who would that be?" Carly asked.

"Who do you think?" Aaron asked.

"You got me," Luke told him.

"Ah, come on! Guess!"

"Whoever is running the site, and you know who it is. You need to tell us. Maybe you'll get out of prison before you die," Luke said.

He stared at them, shaking his head. "You know who is running it!"

"No, we really don't," Carly told him.

"H. H. Holmes!" Aaron said, annoyed.

"H. H. Holmes is dead," Carly pointed out. "He was executed in 1896."

"That's what he wanted everyone to think. He was the coolest man ever. He could charm anyone, including the executioner's assistant. He slipped away, and another corpse was substituted for his!"

"Even if he escaped, he'd be..." Luke looked over at Carly, lifting a brow.

"Born in 1861 as Herman Mudgett. He'd be well over a hundred and fifty years old now. I just don't think anyone is walking around at that age," Carly said.

"Hey, you asked, I told you!" Aaron said angrily.

"Okay, so someone is saying they're H. H. Holmes," Luke said.

"And I'm telling you it *is* H. H. Holmes!"

Carly stood. "Come on, Luke. He doesn't know anything."

"Hey! It's not just the site! He came to the castle!" Aaron told them angrily.

"He came to the castle?" Luke asked doubtfully. "When?"

"Right before the little dark-haired bitch checked in," Aaron said. "Hey. You just missed him!" he added with a smile.

"Whatever," Carly said. "Luke?"

"You don't know! You had to have heard he was probably Jack the Ripper. He could move like lightning, sweep any woman off her feet, be so cool that other men liked him!" Aaron said.

"There was a TV series on Holmes, starred a relative, a man I believe—oh, who thinks that his ancestor was Jack the Ripper, too. But thanks to him and others, the grave of H. H. Holmes, Herman Mudgett, was dug up and DNA from the corpse was tested... Your hundred-and-fifty-plus-year-old guy is not running around Scotland today," Luke said. "Carly?"

"Let's go."

"He was at the castle. I'm trying to tell you the truth!" Aaron swore.

"Okay, well, we'll see about it," Luke said.

Carly was already halfway to the door of his room, ready to knock on the door for the guard outside to let them out.

"He'll get you, he'll get you, he'll get you yet!" Aaron screamed, straining against the cuffs and chains that kept him tethered to his bed.

Luke resisted the urge to hit him and joined Carly at the door.

In another few minutes, they were out.

She shuddered in the car as they started out, looking over at Luke.

"What is it about that guy? I never touched him, and I feel like I desperately need a shower!"

"Campbell said he was crazy," Luke reminded her.

"It's a—different kind of crazy." She hesitated but then shifted in her seat, placing her hand on his shoulder. "Luke... I... We haven't talked much. But I never came across a remaining soul, spirit, ghost...that was evil. I've come across moms who have stayed to watch over their kids, soldiers who watch over battlefields, victims hoping to help catch their killers or abusers. I have never come across anyone evil!"

Luke was thoughtful.

"And I don't think we will," he told her.

"But he believes it!" Carly said.

Luke smiled and nodded. "Someone out there is pretending to be H. H. Holmes. While he used the pseudonym H. H. Holmes, the man's real name was Herman Mudgett. By either name, he was executed in 1896. I don't have answers to the ever-after—no one does. But I've gotten to meet several of the Krewe members. We've talked. No one has come across an evil spirit. Maybe they really are sucked right down to hell. As we've seen, there are plenty living each decade to replace them."

She smiled at last and nodded.

"Hang on," he told her. "I'm going to call Campbell. I want to make sure no one who isn't us or other law enforcement—and that's limited—is allowed to see him for any reason."

"You think whoever it is might try to get to him?" Carly asked. Then she frowned. "Wait—wouldn't that be a way to lure whoever this is into the open?"

Luke paused and nodded slowly. "But no one sees him without one of us in the hospital, and there must be law enforcement in the room with anyone who comes. If someone is playing Holmes, and they decide they want to see him—"

"It could be to make sure he dies so he can't talk anymore?" Carly asked.

"Exactly," Luke said.

"Wait. No, I mean, don't wait on that. But I want to go back in for a minute."

"Oh?"

"Let's get a description of the H. H. Holmes who visited Aaron—right before I came."

"All right. And after...we can do better than that."

"You're right. We'll have the footage from all the man's hidden cameras. The police have access, right? What he was doing was illegal—filming people when they had the right to expect privacy?"

"Yes, guests have the right to expect privacy, other than in the museum, registration desk and public areas. In those areas, being as he was the property owner, Aaron had the right to film. I'm not sure about all the legalities, but—"

"Whatever they are," Carly announced, "I'm going to get around them."

She reentered Aaron Miller's room and Luke followed her.

"Back for more torture?" Aaron asked Carly. She had walked right to his side and was smiling down at him.

"No. I came to tell you I believe you."

He frowned, doubting her.

"I'm serious. Not that I really know you, but we did have a few very human moments." She gave him a smile. "And because of that, I believe I know when you're telling the truth. And you told me H. H. Holmes visited you himself. I want you to tell me about him."

He stared at her curiously. "Well, he looked very normal. Not a particularly tall man, medium build, dark hair, great mustache. He wore a suit and he had me laughing. Told me he usually wore a really cool derby hat, but he didn't want to bring attention to himself. He said only the cream of the crop—those who could really imitate his genius—got to know who he was. I figure you might have even called him a handsome man, one with a great smile."

"Thank you. Maybe I'll get to meet him, too," Carly said.

"Oh, he will meet you!" Aaron promised her solemnly.

"And me," Luke promised, stepping up to the bed and offering Aaron his best smile. "Trust me, he will meet us both."

"Oh, he won't mind meeting you, too," Aaron said. He shrugged but winced as he did so. "He'll dispatch you quickly, I believe. Because his true genius is with women."

"Such a genius he managed to get himself hanged," Luke said. "Oh, but he escaped that, right? And then he found Ponce de León's Fountain of Youth, I take it, since he's still walking around."

"He's immortal. As I am, so it seems."

"No, you just have really bad aim," Luke told him. "Carly."

He headed for the door again. She followed him.

He didn't put through all his calls until they left the facility and were out in the car. There he put the phone on speaker so Carly could contribute when needed and put a call through to Jackson and Angela first, and then to Campbell.

Their Scottish counterpart was going to see to it that all the footage they'd discovered at Aaron's castle could be studied, along with all the footage from security cams at the café.

"Have they discovered anything else about people disappearing in the Loch Ness region?" he asked before ending the call.

"We can't pinpoint anything. Naturally, there have been some preposterous headlines—'Does Nessie Dine on Tourists?' being one of the latest. We have reports of four missing persons near Urquhart Castle, a couple from Brussels, an American woman, and a young student from Calais. None had made overnight reservations, and family and friends just became concerned when they couldn't reach them by cell after several days. We're still looking into the situation because there had been one other 'missing' person who turned out not to be missing at all. She'd gone on to Inverness, but she'd lost her cell phone and hadn't managed to pick up another. We don't have a specific place, so…"

"Keep us posted, please."

"We'll gather what you've asked to view. Give me an hour or two, if y'will."

"Thank you!" Carly told Campbell.

When they ended the call, Luke shook his head.

"'Does Nessie dine on tourists'!" he said, shaking his head.

"Well, if he is a prehistoric beast, he presumably has a massive appetite," Carly said.

He turned to stare at her, but she was grinning.

"Touchy, touchy!" she teased. "So—"

"We wait. I didn't get to finish breakfast."

"But we did have breakfast."

"And half the time we forget to eat," he reminded her. "Or we don't have the time. I say let's get a good lunch, and then we can study all the different footage—and find Aaron's H. H. Holmes."

She nodded, grinning. "Fine."

"You know," he murmured, "we can't go too much by a physical description. The real Holmes only stood about five foot seven. A fairly small man by today's standards. But mentioning to Aaron something about his derby hat…this man, whoever he is, has studied H. H. Holmes. He's gone through the stories and legends—and the facts. He won't be trying to appear like Holmes when he's out on the street. But I figure we are looking for someone who is maybe five-ten or so, medium in build, and a good-looking man capable of great smiles and charm."

"Like Peter Bond?"

"We know better than most that monsters don't necessarily have scales and fangs. What supposedly aided Holmes during his years of scheming and murder was his ability to draw just about anyone to his way of seeing things. Our modern Holmes will be the same. And, yes, like Peter Bond and Aaron, he may be selecting a certain type of man when he helps or encourages his followers through the website. So. Lunch?"

"As you wish."

"There's a place near the castle I'd like to try. Can't help it. The restaurant is called The Devil's Advocate."

Carly groaned softly but smiled and said, "Sure. I've been there. It is great."

"We'll drive back, park the car and do a little walking. Then by the time we've eaten, we should be sustained and ready again for the road."

"Again, as you wish!" she told him.

Though it was past the restaurant from their parking spot, Luke found himself walking to the entrance of Edinburgh Castle.

"I don't think we've been invited to lunch here or Holyrood," Carly said dryly.

"Yeah, sorry, sorry. I just wanted to see the entrance, and the statues of William Wallace and Robert the Bruce."

She grinned. "Cool history here in Bloody Scotland, but we need to know all we can about a different history."

"Agreed. Let's eat."

They entered the restaurant. Carly suggested their charcuterie board to start and any form of their fish. Their waiter was great, with descriptions of everything on the menu, and the place was charming.

"You know," she told him, taking a sip of the tea she'd opted for at lunch, "you're partial to Robert the Bruce!"

"What?"

She laughed. "When we talk. I admit, great book and great movie, and so most people admire Wallace the most."

"I do admire Wallace. A man who fought not for a crown, but for his country and his people. But remember, too, that history usually has a spin put on it by those who recorded it. I happen to like Robert the Bruce, too. So human." He grinned. "A conflicted man. A politician of his day, and God knows, politics have not gotten any cleaner. Did he murder John Comyn? But, hey, do you know that the term 'Braveheart' was a title that was given to Robert the Bruce back in the day? Sir James Douglas carried Robert's heart in a silver container when waging war in Spain against a surprise attack by the Muslims there. He supposedly threw the case at his enemies, shouting, 'Lead on, brave heart. I'll follow thee!'"

"You are just full of fascinating trivia." She shrugged. "But," she added, "if ever I read about a historical character who might have been easy prey for the H. H. Holmes Society, I'd say Edward I!"

"Careful. I don't think the English would like you much for that."

Carly grinned. "Just Berwick—just Berwick! Historians say he massacred half the city after the Scots there protested and fought against his rule. Women were brutally raped before being brutally murdered. Children were murdered. They say the river truly ran red with blood."

"I don't think Edward I was even there."

"He ordered it—the killing was done for his benefit. A benefit of power, kind of like a benefit of finances, very much so an H. H. Holmes thing. Edward I was brutal—he wanted to be king of everything and everyone."

"Well, his subjects didn't love him but they respected him."

"They feared him!"

"True. Still, I totally admire Wallace, but my boy Robert the Bruce was truly Braveheart! Seriously, think about it. Writers have praised Rob Roy and vilified the Marquis of Montrose. Rob Roy wound up pardoned and lived out his days in freedom. The Marquis of Montrose, like many others, fought for Charles I, wound up captured and brutally executed—as a traitor. Charles II came into power, had the marquis dug up, and he rests now in a fine tomb at St. Giles', a hero! Spin is everything, you know."

"Other than the facts—as in we know the Marquis of Montrose was brutally executed."

"Have you ever seen him walking around?"

Carly grinned at that. "No. I imagine he was pleased when Charles II returned triumphant to reclaim the throne, and he went on."

"What?"

She spoke and frowned. "I wish that there was someone who could help us!" she said. "Bloody Scotland, and we haven't seen a single—"

"We are trained FBI agents first and foremost. We can only hope for other help," he reminded her.

She nodded. "You're right." Carly shrugged and smiled at him. "When, um…?"

He sat back, appreciating their conversations were easy and just how much he was coming to like her. In their situation, of course, it was perfect to have such an attractive woman capable of switching characteristics, tones and attitudes like a Broadway actress as his professional partner. But he realized it was growing to be more too quickly.

And still he answered her, knowing what she was about to ask.

"When I was very young," he said softly. Then he hesitated and shrugged. "I was twelve. I adored my aunt Jillian, my mom's sister. She was fun, she was single, no kids, but knew how to be with a kid, to play, color, draw—teach. She came to every Little League game I played. Then…she was murdered. She was found in her apartment with her throat slit. She was well-liked. My mom and dad, her friends, coworkers—everyone was devastated. And no one knew who would have done such a thing. The police didn't have a suspect. No prints, no DNA.

"I didn't see Aunt Jillian at first—it was at her funeral and she tried to comfort me. But she told me to have the police look at her boss. I told my mom…and she told me she'd already suggested the man to the police, but…no evidence. I went back to the cemetery and found my aunt, and she told me she was sure he had tossed the murder knife in the dumpster next door where a restaurant unloaded their trash. I did some dumpster diving myself. And since there are a million crime shows on TV, I knew that I needed to call the cops the moment I dug through a bunch of rotten food and found it. Chain of evidence. The cops came. They didn't know what a kid was doing in the dumpster, so I told them the most logical place to get rid of a murder weapon would be with restaurant refuse that might be contaminated by animal blood and… Anyway, his prints were all over the murder weapon and he wound up confessing. And apparently since what goes around can really come around, her killer was killed in a gang war in prison."

"Do you still see her?" Carly asked.

He smiled. "No. She thanked me, and she went on. But before she did, she said I would be a great investigator. Of course, I reminded her she was the one to tell me to check out the dumpster. The thing was, in her mind, I had done it right. And she said, too, she had never been seeking revenge. She just wanted to make sure it never happened to anyone else."

"And that's what made you—"

"I went into the military first. I didn't know what I wanted, and I figured after high school it would give me time to figure out my future. I went to college after—and because of Jillian, I did major in criminology. Became a cop for a few months, applied to the FBI, went to the academy, and then you know the story after that."

"Jackson Crow found you," she said.

He nodded, smiling. "And I happened to be on the case in the States and… Seemed logical for them to send me here. The Blackbird division is still gearing up, but…"

"Right. With Mason and Della in France—"

"We're both familiar with Scotland," he finished. "And you?"

She smiled. "For me it was easy!" she said softly. "I was on tour in Key West when I was about twelve, and the guide got some information wrong. There was a man next to me who was infuriated. Had to do with the age of piracy and salvage. So I told him he should just say something, and he told me that I needed to do it for him and I did and…"

"And?"

"The tour guide asked me to leave. But later on I was with

my folks having dinner, and a couple who had been on the tour came by and told my parents I was a brilliant kid and that I had been right. They had made sure the tour company got it right from then on as well. His name was Captain Jack and he showed me where he'd lived in the 1800s."

"You were never scared?"

She grinned. "By the time I realized I'd been prompted by a ghost, I knew he wasn't scary and he wasn't going to hurt me."

"Nice. Still, pretty brave for a kid."

"Brave—or slow!" she said lightly.

"And the FBI?"

She shrugged. "College and straight into the academy. And in several situations, I did get a few leads, and it was awkward to try to explain, and difficult and…"

"And then Jackson found you."

"I think it was Angela. We were both at the wedding of mutual friends and wound up talking—just talking, not about the dead or anything. I was suddenly called to the Krewe offices, and it was the best thing that ever happened to me. Luke, thanks to the Krewe, we get to feel sane!"

"So, in other words," he teased, "there really is a Loch Ness Monster?"

She laughed softly.

"I try very hard to keep an open mind on all things!" she told him.

His phone was ringing. He answered it immediately, listened and ended the call.

"We're now invited to spend hours and hours going over video footage. They'll be doing the same back at our headquarters. By the time it's all over tonight, you're going to be very grateful I made you go to lunch!"

CHAPTER FIVE

"There's the museum at Aaron's castle," Luke noted.

"He had other guests, of course. Then, I believe, he truly made the effort to appear to be an open book. He let locals and those who had just heard about the place in to enjoy the 'museum' part of his castle. It made him look like a local hero, I guess? He didn't charge for people to come in," Carly said thoughtfully. She lightly bit her lip, shaking her head. "Do they know yet just how many victims he had in there?" she asked Luke quietly.

They were alone in one of the conference rooms with a large screen and video feeds from the castle, from the café and from any other security cameras that had been found and handed to the police by other businesses on the street nearby.

"At least six as it stands now, but—"

"There will be more," Carly said sadly. "He was probably so generous because he could chat to those he just let in, too—and decide who might disappear without being noticed."

"Probably," Luke agreed. "Anything?"

"Well, people," she said. "Aaron said Holmes had left right

before I checked in. When I got there, I put my things in the room, looked for the camera I was sure he had hidden."

"And you found it," Luke said approvingly. "There are hours of blank film from your room, just opening up when you headed to bed."

"Hey, modern-day. Have to watch your prey if you want to attack at the right time," Carly reminded him.

"So true. What about the museum?"

She kept studying the footage and tried to remember walking through the museum. Her focus hadn't been on other visitors, but she remembered a mom with her two boys, a young couple, and, yes...

"There was a man studying some of the shields," she said, frowning. "Could have been someone," she added.

"Close your eyes. I'm no hypnotist or therapist, but let's try the go-back thing. You're upstairs in the museum at the castle with your intent being to discover anything you can about secret rooms, doors, possibly tubes that could carry gas, chutes to the basement below..."

She looked at him for a minute and then closed her eyes.

"Is it cool in the museum, temperature-wise?"

"Pleasant. The air was just comfortable. Not cold, not hot. And I'll give our heinous killer this—he created a pretty cool museum, too, with all kinds of shields, weapons—I'm sure the police are testing them all now—and articles used in medieval days. Toiletries, dishes, beautiful, jeweled chalices—all in glass-covered display cases. The museum stretched across the entire hall, the walls—all the ancient stone—covered with displays, and..."

Yes, there had been a few men, one with a girlfriend and one alone. And the one who had been alone had been medium in height and size.

Dark-haired.

"No mustache," she said aloud.

"What?"

"Oh, you were right, closing my eyes… I remember the mom and her kids, a young couple, and a man, medium-sized, height and build, dark hair, no mustache."

"Did he pay any attention to you?"

She shook her head. "No, he was intent on studying paintings on the walls. I don't remember him paying the least bit of attention to me."

"That's suspicious in itself."

"Pardon?" she said, confused.

He grinned. "Somewhere along the line, I'm sure someone informed you that you're a beautiful young woman. Capable of a wonderful smile and natural charm—which you are great at laying on thick, by the way. If he made a point of not looking at you, that's suspicious."

"Well, thank you, I think."

He laughed. "It was a compliment. Take it." After his laughter, he frowned.

"What are you seeing?"

"He knows where the cameras are. He keeps his face averted."

Carly studied the screen. "Run it back a bit."

He did.

And he was right. The man was purposely keeping his face toward the wall.

"What do you remember about him?"

Carly pursed her lips and shook her head, angry with herself.

"I wasn't paying that much attention. I was focused on what Aaron Miller might have built into the castle and where everything was and… I think I was more worried about what other young women might be staying there."

"You don't remember his face at all?"

"He kept his back to me—and pretty much to everyone else there—the whole time, just studying everything that was on the walls. What I can remember is…average, I guess? He was nowhere near your height, medium in build, good posture…"

"There has to be a better shot of him. I'm going back to the hours before you checked in. There should be a shot of him in the office somewhere, too."

"Aaron said he was there. He didn't say he was in the office."

"True. Okay, but he had to have gotten up to the third floor somehow."

"You know where I don't think Aaron had any cameras?" Carly asked.

"The stairwells. The cops didn't find any."

"Right. He probably came up to the hallway by the stairwell."

Luke rewound the tape, going back to the hours before Carly had checked in.

"This is going to take forever," she murmured.

"We can see who is there by fast-forwarding—"

"But not too fast fast-forwarding," she said.

He grinned. "Right."

They went through the footage of the registration area first. Nothing.

No sign of the man at all, though they could see Aaron chatting with the young woman with her child, the young couple and Carly herself as she arrived.

"He didn't come by the front entry," Carly said.

"There's another entrance. Somewhere. There has to be."

"The walls surround the courtyard. You only have entry there if you're a guest—in one way or another—because I assume if you ask to go to the museum, you could also get out to the courtyard. But you're right—there has to be another entry somewhere."

"The basement."

"But the police have been crawling all over the place—"

"But they haven't been looking for another entry. Still, other than figuring out how our Holmes got in and out—"

"We don't know that's the man who pretended to be Holmes. Like I said, no mustache."

"Oh, come on, Carly! You glue one on, you peel it off!"

"True!"

"All right. Let's say we think that's him," Luke said. "Let's move on to the café footage."

"Sounds like a plan."

Luke hit different keys on the computer they'd been provided.

"Here we are, the café."

"But we are going to need to go through days and days and—"

"Fast-forward," he said, grinning. "And remember, we're not the only ones going through all this. And still…"

"Still?"

Luke looked at her. "If you see the same man who was at the castle, even though you didn't get a good look at him, you might recognize him here."

"Okay, so…fast-forward."

He started doing so.

She laughed. "Slow down!"

"Not so fast fast-forward," he agreed. "We do need to look at days of footage, but I want to start with when we found Peter Bond on the site. Right before the site disappeared."

"It hasn't come back up, right?"

"Not that we know of, and Jackson or Angela would have informed us all."

"If this Holmes character really exists and he was in the area, how would he have taken the site down?"

"This guy knows what he's doing," Luke said. "All he would need is the right tablet or even a phone, if he's as good as I think he is."

"Are you good with computers?"

"Decent—but not on that level. Angela might be, or others here or back home, but…"

"Decent. That's the best I can say for myself, too, I'm afraid,"

Carly admitted. "Schoolwork, of course, social media when I was a kid, lessons."

"It takes a special kind to manage the dark web," Luke murmured.

"Earlier this morning—let's start there."

The café opened early—very early. They'd headed out around nine that morning—the café had opened at seven.

And people were in and out.

"Stop!" Carly said.

"You mean…the guy in the hoodie?" Luke asked, looking at the screen and frowning.

"Luke! Like you said, a mustache goes on and off. A suit goes on and off, and if you're running around trying not to appear to be the same person—"

"Okay, okay. And you just may be right. He keeps the hood of that thing pulled over his forehead. He slouches, as if he's trying to look younger, like one of the kids who might come in before school, or…"

He paused, finding a point where the man in the hoodie was at the register, ordering.

For a minute, he had to look up.

He was of medium height and was of medium build. His face was attractive, his smile, as he ordered, pleasant and charming.

"Luke."

"Yeah."

"I think that's him. I couldn't swear it on a stack of Bibles, but…"

"So, he was there this morning."

"And go forward. He drinks his coffee at the computers. He…"

"He's just going through motions there. Playing the part. Look, there he goes. He's getting up, heading out. I need footage from the street!"

Carly realized her phone was buzzing. As Luke moved to

reach for his own from his pocket, she saw they were both receiving texts.

They automatically looked at one another and then their phones.

Luke read aloud, "'Arrangements being made for two tonight at small town near Urquhart Castle. Still on footage, please report, work facial recognition/other ID on this end. Contact again in an hour when final info coordinated on this end.'"

"We're leaving again," Carly murmured.

"But not right away. Carly...look."

Luke was staring at the screen. He'd drawn up the footage from a bank across the street from the café.

And they could see the man in the hoodie leaving the café.

Taking out a small tablet and quickly working away at it.

"Could that be our pseudo-Holmes?" Carly murmured.

"We'll point out our man to headquarters and head back to retrieve our things," Luke said.

He was already on the phone.

"I'll get Campbell," Carly told him, rising to do so. She found the specialist in his office, busily studying his screen as she entered.

"Special Agent MacDonald," he said. "We've taken away easy access to guns here, and I was thinking it wouldn't be such a bad thing if we could outlaw hoodies!"

Carly nodded. "We've informed Jackson, and, yes, sir, I think I recognize the man in the hoodie from having been at Aaron's castle as well. Jackson has—"

"I've received the info as well. I'll be following you. I believe you'll be going to Gordon House—not a castle but a Georgian estate. It's near the ruins of Urquhart Castle, and we've still got a young man and three young women unaccounted for in the area."

"We haven't received the address yet—"

"There's many a place near enough. Inverness is still a bit

of a drive, but many people stay there when they're going on to the loch or to view the ruins." He looked up at her. "As I said, I'll be following you. Inspector Billingham is on his way to join me. Not to worry—we won't be obvious, but we'll be near when we're needed."

"That sounds fine, sir—"

She broke off. Luke had joined her.

"We've a place," he said briefly. "Sir—"

"I'll be following," Campbell assured him. "Discreetly."

"Sir, I now have you as the number one on speed dial," Luke told him. "Carly?"

She turned to follow him, and they headed out, ready for their next murder-castle assignment.

Luke had the phone on speaker as he and Carly drove to Gordon House.

"We have you going in as a couple," Jackson Crow said over the phone. "Not married, just a couple. We think a young couple disappeared there, and there has been some paperwork we're following up on, cash disappearances, and we think this fellow is playing on Holmes's ability to get people to 'invest' in his wild schemes. So, play the couple mostly in love, but with the possibility of a breakup. Holmes managed to make mistresses of his marks' wives. And, Carly, you need to play it as you did with Peter Bond, as if you might be available."

"I can be a jerk," Luke assured him.

"No stretch there!" Carly said, laughing.

"Hey!" he protested.

"All right, sounds like you're well on the way," Jackson said. "And needless to say, but I always say it, take extreme care. I'm going to suggest that you—"

"Sleep in shifts," Luke said.

"That and never be anywhere when the other isn't aware of exactly where you are and what you're doing."

"Of course, Jackson," Carly said.

"And Campbell and Billingham are headed your way," Jackson said.

"Yes, Campbell informed us."

"Police in the area are aware of what's going on. They've been perplexed by the disappearances that have happened—and annoyed that headlines like to stress the fact the Loch Ness Monster might be responsible. There's a lot going on in the area—monster hunters searching for Nessie at an unusually high scale."

"That works in a way. Good reason for tourists to be pouring in."

"We're working on an identity for the man who might be the founder of this Holmes Society," Jackson said. "Good work on following the man from the castle to the café."

"Thanks," Carly murmured, glancing at Luke. He knew she was hoping she was right.

"We don't believe the owner of Gordon House is the man, though, correct? This has been something ongoing?"

"You're after one of his followers, we believe. And trust me, we've followed every disappearance and looked into every guest list at every guesthouse, hotel, hostel, you name it, anywhere near the last known locations of those who are missing."

"Jackson, we know how good you are," Carly assured him.

"You'll be watching on two fronts. Clayton Moore, owner of the property, and Ben Pratt, manager. Moore is married, but his wife is in England most of the time, while he stays in Scotland. Pratt is from Boston and he was married, divorced, and strangely enough, no one has heard from his wife in six years. She disappeared from the face of the earth," Jackson informed them. "The briefs on everything we know are in your emails."

"Could they be working together?" Carly murmured.

"They could be," Luke said. "Before he murdered Pitezel, Holmes had him convinced they were in on a scam together."

"That would make me wary of being anyone's partner," Carly murmured.

"It is always difficult to fathom the human mind," Jackson said. "And our reality is different since social media reaches the entire world we now live in. We need to get to the heart of this, and we'll be working our hardest here, I promise, but we also need to value every human life. Oh, value every human life—that means your lives, too. But we have every safeguard in position, so just play it carefully. There are the best blueprints we can find in your briefs, but they've played out another of Holmes's methods. They have work done, fire people, then have more work done so there's no one out there who knows everything there is to know about the place except for the two men. Someone make sure to report every few hours—we have our teams working through the night here, as always."

"Of course, Jackson. Thanks," Luke said. "And," he added, glancing at Carly, "remember to give us a bit of time—it's about a hundred and seventy miles from Edinburgh to our destination."

"Of course. But I've driven with you, Luke. You'll be there in no time."

Carly stared over at him.

"Hey, I'm a good driver!"

"Good and fast. Take care—remember you are on the other side of the road," Jackson reminded him.

"Got you, Jackson. And don't worry. I will follow all the legal limits!"

They ended the call. Carly was looking out the window.

She felt him glancing her way. "You are moving fast—but safely," she said, grinning. "And the drive is kind of cool. It's such a beautiful country!" she said. "The way the land rolls, the hills, cliffs, waterways! The nature here is incredible."

"It is," Luke agreed. He flashed her a smile. "We are supposed to be acting like tourists. We can enjoy that part of it. We'll stop somewhere along the way to stretch and breathe, okay?"

She smiled and nodded. He found himself thinking again that he'd been assigned to a truly decent partner. She could roll whichever way they needed.

She could make him laugh.

And she wasn't hard at all on the eyes.

"One hundred and seventy miles. Sure. We can take a break! Maybe we should have opted for a chopper or—"

"Nope. We're American tourists. And driving from Edinburgh is something many tourists look forward to doing. We're just exploring. We're a lovely American couple about to have a tiff."

"Now, that's quite understandable," she said sweetly. She was grinning, and he found he was laughing.

Not a bad partner at all.

He pulled off about halfway through their drive, having checked with his GPS for a place to see one of the fantastic waterfalls that fell along the cliffs and magnificent ridges that fronted Loch Ness.

It was good to get out of the car.

They walked on the rugged terrain to see the sight.

"Playing tourist isn't half bad!" Carly announced.

"One day, maybe again, we can just be tourists," he mused. "The beauty of the waterfall is spectacular."

"We do have beauty, too, in America. In fact, there's so much history and beauty just about everywhere I've been…"

"Yep. And if only the world can be peaceful so we can all share all the beauty and wonder," he murmured.

"Back to the car," Carly said. "Right now, there's peace all around us here in the beauty of the Scottish Highlands. Except for any intended victims."

"Back to the car," he agreed.

He stopped for gas as they went along, and then it was truly on toward their destination.

"I think it gets prettier as we travel along," Luke noted.

She nodded. "I have always loved the area. Of course, I came
first as a child with grandparents who loved to tell the tallest
tales."

"Did *they* ever see Nessie?"

She laughed. "Of course! Well, at least in the tales they told
they did. She was really a creature with gills—she didn't need
to get air—that's why she can go deep and disappear and only
be seen when she wants to be seen."

"Well, their tall tales had logic," Luke said.

"We're near Drumnadrochit," Carly murmured. "From here
just a mile or so to Urquhart."

"Near your ancestral lands?" he asked.

"Something like that," Carly said.

"Spectacular glens and cliffs," Luke murmured. "And there,
ahead, our Georgian manor should be down that road and
around a curve or two."

"Nothing much out here, though we're not far from a few
small towns," Carly commented.

"You know the area well."

She shrugged. "I love the nature here, like I said. The glens
are so peaceful and beautiful. And they can be…"

"Private and you can walk a long way without encountering
another human being," Luke offered. "Though I believe we'll
discover whatever they're up to, it's happening in the manor.
That is a true page from Holmes's book—hiring and firing
workers."

"There! I see it," Carly said.

The house appeared to be at least ten thousand square feet, the
typical rectangular structure with symmetrical windows, shut-
ters and columns. A grand entrance embellished with a handsome arch. The structure itself was composed of brick.

"Built in 1755, after the Jacobite Rebellion," Luke murmured.
"Strange. I would have thought such a place would be sur-

rounded by a national park or…or it would be owned by a historic society or the like."

"Remember, we're not in America. The ruins we'll see at Urquhart date back to the twelfth century, with more building having been done up to the sixteenth century and, of course, some beyond. Supposedly, St. Columba visited here in the 500s and—"

"Saw a monster, yep," Luke said.

Carly shrugged. "Seriously, Scottish history is really cool. And as you said, it always depended whose side you were on, who the victor was, hero, traitor, all wrapped up with all kinds of people coming in and…"

She broke off.

All kinds of people. Heroes, traitors, and now, when swords and shields had been laid down, just the occasional human monster.

Luke pulled into the horseshoe drive. Looking around, he saw the house was surrounded first by a lawn, and then by woods that stretched into darkness, the trees and greenery were so dense.

"Come, my love!" he said. "Time to check in."

He looked up at the grand Georgian architecture, and he couldn't help but remember Jackson's words.

These places were like Holmes's Castle, indeed, so it seemed.

And like the great Eagles song "Hotel California."

For some…

You could check in.

But you could never check out.

CHAPTER SIX

"Some people claim that they see Nessie and some don't!" Luke announced as they walked through the grand entry to the Georgian manor.

"Hey!" Carly argued. He had spoken as he had on purpose. In public they needed to appear as if they were a couple in a relationship who could still get testy with one another.

She let out a sigh of aggravation. "I'm not even sure why you're with me! You're such a doubter."

"Well, no one has proven there's a monster after all these years."

"Hey, a cop, a dedicated cop, swore he saw it," Carly argued. "That's not the point. The point is that—"

"Carly," he murmured, interrupting her. They had almost reached the registration desk beneath the great stairway leading to the second floor of the house. Naturally, he was trying to make it appear that they were civilized, just having a "wee" bit of a spat.

"Hi!" he said, greeting the man at the desk. "We have a reservation. I'm not sure if it's in my name or Carly's, but my friend said this was the best place in the world to stay while visiting Urquhart, and he made the reservation for us."

"First, welcome, and, yes, I have a few reservations for tonight!" the man said. They'd seen pictures of both men possibly involved in the local disappearances in their briefs.

This was Ben Pratt, manager of the house, thirty-three years old, the American who was divorced with an ex-wife who had apparently disappeared off the face of the earth. After the divorce, of course, when the two had been living in different cities, no children involved.

And he was certainly fine for the part, just short of six feet with a head full of dark auburn hair and bright blue eyes, pale, of medium build, the wiry strength in his arms apparent in a short-sleeved tailored shirt.

The better to strangle you with, my dear, she couldn't help but think.

"What name shall I try first?" he asked.

"Jackie probably put it under my name," Luke said. "Lucas Kendrick," he said, smiling as he glanced at Carly.

"Let's see. Yes, I have your reservation. I have you down for five nights. Is that right?"

Luke was still smiling at Carly. "Five nights, right? Maybe we'll see everything there is to see by then!"

She smiled at him and turned to Ben Pratt. "Maybe and maybe not, but we'll start with five nights. Oh, is this a busy time of year?"

"Indeed, it's very busy," Pratt said, shaking his head. "Apparently, some people have said that they're heading in this direction, and then no one hears from them. As soon as something like that starts, some idiot goes on and on about them being eaten by the Loch Ness Monster, good old Nessie. Well, as you can imagine, a place like this has high taxes and some keen upkeep, so…whatever the monster does is good for business and for us."

"Yeah, go figure," Luke said, looking at Carly again. "A monster is eating people, so other people rush to see. They might as well wear caps that say, 'Chew me up next, monster.'"

"Ah, so you're not here looking for the monster?" Pratt asked.

Carly was looking at Luke.

She smiled. "Oh, who said we're not looking for a monster?" she inquired innocently.

"Well, as you can see, my *beloved* here would *love* to see Nessie," Luke told him. "I, on the other hand, am fascinated by the history here and Urquhart Castle."

"The ruins of Urquhart," Pratt reminded him dryly. "But! That said, I can recommend a great guide for you."

"Cool!" Luke said.

"Has the guide seen Nessie?" Carly asked sweetly.

Luke groaned.

"No, seriously, and this is secret—well, kind of secret," Pratt told them. "The guy who owns this place, Clayton Moore, loves history. He is a descendant of the original owners through a convoluted marriage thing. I'm not all that big on ancestry and the like but, anyway, Clayton loves the whole thing, and he does tours now and then. I think he was planning on one tomorrow, so I'll look into it. Getting late, you know."

"It is," Luke said, smiling at Carly. "It's been a long drive."

"You came up from Edinburgh?" Pratt asked.

"We did."

"Well, I'll get your keys, you check in, get some rest...and remember, Urquhart is a set of ruins. Wear appropriate shoes!"

"Will do and thank you," Luke replied.

Carly made a point of giving him a charming smile. "Yes, thank you so much!"

He handed them keys—actual solid metal keys, not plastic cards—and told them, "Just upstairs and to the left. Oh, feel free to explore the great hall and the dining room. There's a library immediately to your right facing the house, the dining room just behind that, and the kitchen a little farther back. There's always water in the fridge and you're welcome to enjoy the library anytime. The kitchen is always open and breakfast is served in the dining room between seven and nine."

"Wonderful," Carly told him. "I do love starting my day with a great Scottish breakfast."

"And a library! I love a good library. Some of us prefer fact over fiction!" Luke said, looking at Pratt and shaking his head slightly—as if letting him in on a joke.

That was, broadcasting the fact he tolerated Carly's silliness for the benefits he derived from their relationship.

"To each their own!" Pratt said. "The best amenity we offer is individual bathrooms. They are small, but decent little shower stalls and somehow we have great water pressure."

"Wow, wonderful!" Carly said. "We'll enjoy."

"What about the other side of the house?" Luke asked.

"Oh, that would be the office and the owner's private quarters," Pratt said. "No entry over there but enjoy the rest of the house. Oh! The Wi-Fi password is 'Urquhart 1.'"

"Okay, thank you!" Carly said. She looked at her key. "Let's see the room!" she told Luke.

"Let's see it. Then the library. Or..." Luke began.

"There are several restaurants a short drive away if you're hungry. Or believe it or not, you can order pizza! All the info is on little brochures in the rooms."

"Hmm, let's think on that, shall we?" Luke said to Carly.

"Okay, our room first!"

They left the desk and Pratt called out to them, "Sorry, there's only a tiny lift for any visitors who need assistance!"

"We're good with stairs," Luke assured him.

They didn't speak until they had reached the room, and even then Luke made a warning sign. They both began to casually search the room, looking for listening devices or cameras.

"Great room. Look at the window—it gives us a great view of the forest beyond!" Carly said.

"Wow. Much better than TV," Luke said.

She laughed. "But there is a TV and cable access and everything."

"If we should want or need it," he said, stepping toward her and drawing her into his arms. He whispered directly in her ear. "He may have a camera in the TV itself. You're going to have to give me a hug anytime you need to say something important."

"Gotcha," she whispered back.

She spun away from him, twirling around the room and then hopping backward onto the bed.

"This is wonderful, Luke, so wonderful!"

"And it's late!" he reminded her, sliding in next to her. "It's been a long, long day."

Curling next to her, he asked, "First shift or second?"

She smiled. Playing the loving couple might not be so bad. She wasn't sure why, but she was exhausted.

She didn't think anything would happen to them that night, but nothing seemed out of the realm of possibility. "Second?" she inquired in a whisper.

"Go for it," he told her.

He pulled her against him. They hadn't found a camera, and he might be right that it was hidden within or was part of the TV. Maybe there wasn't a camera. Holmes had committed his murders without having to watch his victims 24/7.

But times had changed. And she didn't doubt his followers would admire all that had been—and also note how it could be improved with the technology now afforded them all.

She closed her eyes. The bed was comfortable. It was more comfortable feeling the warmth of his arm around her. She shouldn't think that way. They were playing a game.

It was a good game. She'd never been involved with a partner, and she'd played such games briefly before in swift under-cover situations.

But...

She'd be a liar if she tried to tell herself she had never thought that he was an attractive man. Of course, she had thought so platonically.

Or had she? Just physically, he had every appeal. He was muscular without being too muscular. Tall, broad-shouldered. Striking with his coloring, his laughter, his smile…

She winced inwardly. How was she going to sleep now with his arm around her? Her thoughts were veering in this direction, when she could feel the warmth of his body emanating next to her own.

Work could be a very good thing in many ways.

She was tired; there never seemed to be the right amount of sleep.

She wondered briefly if he was feeling any of the same thoughts as she drifted into the sweetness of a dark and restful sleep. Because besides the thoughts that teased at her mind and body, there was also the thought of something equally sweet.

She was safe…

Because he was beside her.

Luke had let Carly sleep until 4:00 a.m., way later than he should have. But in turn, she didn't wake him until eight. It had taken him a while to sleep, though he had closed his eyes and feigned it, resting at the very least.

But this was a hell of a lot harder than he had imagined and there were certain things that weren't easy to hide—all he could do was find the right position in which to suffer.

It was simple biology, of course.

Except that it was more. Still, they were working on one of the most horrible, complex and heinous cases possible. It was necessary to play it professionally to the hilt.

It was more than physical. He'd known her a matter of days. But already…

He could barely remember himself before he had met her.

She made him smile, she made him laugh, think…care. She had simply and swiftly slipped into the soul of his being.

Circumstances, he reminded himself firmly. And circumstances demanded pure professionalism.

When he awoke, she called him sleepyhead and informed him that she'd been up a few hours, but luckily had showered and dressed and now the bathroom was all his. And she was ready, dressed for a day of hiking, exploring and seeing the wonders of the region in jeans, knit sweater and jacket.

As he crawled out of bed, there was a tap at the door. He slid quickly into the bathroom, nodding to Carly to open it.

She did so. With the door just slightly cracked, Luke listened.

It was Ben Pratt at the door, happy to tell Carly that when they'd had a chance to have their breakfasts, they could join Clayton Moore's little tour. He had already planned to take a couple of friends out that day and he would be more than happy if they wished to join in.

"We'll be right down!" she promised. "In fact… Luke!" she called. "I'm going to go on down. Hurry and join me!"

He heard the door close, checked the room with a frown, grabbed his own clothing and headed back into the bathroom.

Even there, he was careful to keep his Glock hidden until he could slip it into the small holster at the back of his waistband.

He wondered if Carly had headed out with Ben Pratt to keep him from feeling uncomfortable. Polite, but not what they needed to be doing.

He believed that she was safe, that Ben Pratt really planned for them to take a tour with Clayton Moore.

He just wondered if there would be other people on the tour—or if it had been designed especially for the man to have time with the two of them.

Dressed, he headed down. There was an older man seated next to Carly at the long table that almost stretched the length of the dining room. There were no private tables here, just the one.

Carly was engaged in conversation, but when he arrived, she smiled and said, "Herr Grunewald, this is my boyfriend, Luke Kendrick. Luke, please meet Gunther Grunewald. He's a German national, but truly loves Scotland!"

"How do you do, sir?" Luke said, sliding into the chair across from him.

"Quite well," Grunewald said. *"Danke."*

"He's been here for several months already!"

Grunewald might be German, but his English was excellent. He smiled at Carly's words and told Luke, "I'm afraid I've little to go home to. I lost my wife last year. We never had children and I'm what's left of my family except for a few young great-nieces and great-nephews. I'm truly enjoying it here—I love just walking out in the afternoons. And my host, Mr. Moore, has let me know that, of course, I may leave anytime I wish or stay as long as I wish." He waved a hand in the air. "This isn't like a hotel where one must pay a penalty for leaving early."

"Ah, almost like a vacation apartment," Luke said.

"Except that I don't need to make my own breakfast!" Grunewald said, shrugging happily.

The man almost resembled a great animated character. He had a full head of thick, curly white hair and a beard and sweeping mustache to match. He wondered at the man's age.

He didn't need to wonder long.

The man shrugged. "I'll be ninety soon enough. My pleasures are simple these days, and I find them here. Miss Carly tells me you'll be staying about five days."

"Well, we're on vacation. And to pay for more vacations, I'm afraid that means that we're required to go back to work," Luke said.

"Ah, yes," Grunewald said. "Indeed, work makes the world go round, it does."

If the man was almost ninety, he'd been a small child during World War II. He was probably a fascinating person to talk to.

He'd also just admitted that he was old and had no one. Was Clayton Moore intending to push his exit from the world once he'd gotten whatever the elderly man had turned over to him?

He wondered if Carly had found a way of asking the man. But maybe not—she had just met him and she wouldn't want to push too hard.

And yet there was always the question: How much time did they have?

Ben Pratt appeared, bringing in a tray with coffee and plates that contained eggs, bacon, tomatoes, potatoes, beans and biscuits.

"Whoa. Now, that is a real breakfast! Great, thank you," Luke said.

"Eat up! Clayton should be down in a minute or two, and his friends couldn't make it, so it will just be the two of you. Though he does have an appointment later, so he'll want to get going," Ben told them. He grinned at Grunewald. "Great company, eh, sir?"

"Great company, indeed," Grunewald said.

"I'll be at the desk if you need me," Ben told them cheerfully, leaving the dining room. He came back in right away. "Hey, just leave things. I'm a one-man show except for the maids who come in about eleven each day. But I'm good at it!"

He left them again.

"A little piece of paradise!" Grunewald said. "Maybe I'll go back one day and die in the fatherland. But it's nice to have good company and so many of one's creature needs attended to by such fine gentlemen."

"They've become good friends, I take it," Luke said.

"More. They're family," Grunewald said.

The food was excellent, and with forensic science being what it was, Luke doubted that the men were poisoning their breakfast fare.

If he was wrong, he and Carly were already in trouble. But

it wouldn't pay for the men to do anything to him or Carly yet—not if one of them was "Holmes" and this was a murder-for-money castle.

"Good morning, one and all!"

Luke saw the man coming before he entered the room.

Clayton Moore was about five-eleven, medium in build, and a good-looking man with a thatch of blond hair and bright blue eyes. He gave them all an energetic smile and paused at the end of the table. "Morning, Herr Grunewald, and you two, of course, are Luke and Carly—my tour for the day, I understand. And I warn you, I love the place!"

"That's great," Luke said, rising. "And thank you so much. We understood from Mr. Pratt that you love history and do this for us for that reason. We're truly grateful."

"History buffs, not monster voyeurs!" Grunewald said.

"Well, Carly really does want to see the monster!" Luke said.

"Hey, nice to meet you, and if a monster was to pop up from the lake, I wouldn't mind!" Carly said, rising as well and coming around to shake his hand. "Forgive Luke—he doubts just about anything I say might be possible!"

She gave Luke a charming smile, but there was a slight sting to her words.

"Well, we'll see what we see, eh?" Clayton Moore asked. "When you're ready, meet me out by the car. It's a bit of a hike and I'll have you doing some hiking around Urquhart, so…"

"I'm all set," Carly said. "Luke?"

"One last bite!" he said, taking that one final mouthful of biscuit and washing it down with the last of his coffee. "Ready to face the day."

"Tell me all when you come back!" Grunewald said. "I shall look forward to it. That lovely young lady, Miss Mary Nelson, I believe her name was—she's headed on out?" he asked Clayton.

"Ah, yes, she said that she was going northward, John o'

Groats, and then the Shetlands," Clayton said. "I wished her a lovely journey! So, shall we?"

"Yes, indeed!" Carly said.

Clayton Moore's car was a new SUV, parked in the drive, and as they walked out to it, he was already in tour-guide mode. "A brooch found in the ruins suggests something was going on back in the early years, and St. Columba did indeed travel through the area," he told him. "Urquhart has been described as the defender of the loch, and one thing is certain—Urquhart saw much action, changed sides dozens of times and witnessed the various Scottish wars for independence. But, my friends, archaeologists believe that the area has been inhabited since about 2,000 BC. There would have been rich areas to farm as agriculture flourished, as well as fine hunting fields full of deer and boar to feed the people. Some say that William the Lion had a fort here, though that has never been proven. The origins of the castle ruins we see today date back to a time when the MacWilliam family rose against David I and his descendants. The last rebellion was put down circa 1229 and Alexander II granted the land to one of his key men, Thomas de Lundin, who then left it to his heir, Alan Durward—it's believed that they then built the first fortification here. When Durward died, the castle and land were granted to John Comyn II, the Black. Now, of course, he—like John Balliol and Robert the Bruce—had a stake in the crown of Scotland, which would become important after the death of Alexander III and then his young child."

"Alexander III!" Luke said. "From what I understand, the man brought about his own death, riding against all advice from his men into horrid weather—and dying when his horse panicked and threw him or trampled him or whatever."

"Well, he died, and then so did the grandchild he'd named as his heir, Margaret, the Maid of Norway, and then there was no direct heir to the crown of Scotland. So, in fear of civil war if they went against one another, the Scots made the grave mistake of asking Edward I of England for help," Moore said.

The owner of Gordon House nodded as he continued. "Bear in mind, the ruins are those of the original fortress and changes that were made through the centuries. Most important regarding the castle, though, is of course the fact that it was a key part of so much that had to do with the history of the country itself. The country, curious as it is, where we are now. Not a nation—our nation is Great Britain. And for all the blood that was shed, it was an act of union and lines of succession that brought us all together!"

Clayton Moore had no problem talking. He barely took a breath during the drive, though he did glance at Carly several times as he drove and spoke—she was seated next to him while Luke was in the back seat.

Behind Carly. This kind of killer wasn't going to strike when he was appealing to them for their admiration and friendship. Still, Luke would be ready to protect her—back her up, rather, he reminded himself—should any form of attack be attempted.

They reached a parking lot and started up the trail when Moore waved to a man in a red cloak.

"One of the guides," he murmured. "Dressed in red because Urquhart was once a Comyn stronghold and John Comyn III of Badenoch was known as the Red," Moore explained. "Always remember that facts are few and must be followed and all else is often in the minds of those who follow. But here...let me try to go in order of time!"

"Comyn—murdered by Robert the Bruce, right?" Carly said.

"No one knows what went on in the church when the Bruce stabbed him," Luke said.

Carly shook her head. "He thinks the world of Robert the Bruce when William Wallace was the true hero of Scotland!"

"Children! Don't argue history!" Moore teased. "Bear in mind, the ruling class changed sides several times during the wars for independence. Balliol, Bruce and Comyn were all in line for the throne—Edward gave it to Balliol, as long as he could be overlord and he swore his fealty to Edward. That all went badly. Balliol was captured, Wallace picked up the fight—oh! And it's most likely that he and Robert the Bruce never even met one another. But it's true—Wallace being captured, hanged, drawn and quartered, with those quarters put on display, enraged the common man. Bruce was able at last to lead his men onward to the Battle of Bannockburn. Didn't really end things—fighting went on for years after, but Bruce did hold Scotland, and the country went on to his heirs, and then, eventually, everything came together through the matrilineality—tracing kingship through the female line. Back to Urquhart! Let's walk!"

They did. It was fascinating to see the various stages of the castle, where the great hall, great kitchen and "great chambers" living quarters for the family in charge might have been.

During the wars for independence the castle changed hands several times, Edward taking the castle, Edward losing the castle...

They saw another guide speaking to a crowd and listened.

"But it had been the Jacobite Rebellion that had spelled the end for Urquhart as a fortress. When James II, a Catholic, was deposed for William of Orange and Mary, supporters of James went into a series of rebellions. Were such wars over religion? People did believe, and it was important, but we can never forget that power and finances have been important through the centuries. But have we Americans here? Many of the Scots captured at the Battle of Culloden in 1746, often considered to be the last major battle on the British themselves, notwithstanding bombs, were given a choice—prison, death or service in the British military across the seas, keeping those nasty colonists in line. They were always causing trouble and the English military was always busy over there until... Well, you know, that nasty little thing that occurred in 1776. Oh, did I say that? No offense intended, my fine friends. As we've noted, history and victory can change everything, and the Yanks are now among our best friends!"

He was greeted with laughter. But his words were true.

Carly laughed softly with the others, looking over at Luke. He nodded. It was so true. History and *victory* changed the way one might remember all that had occurred.

There remains the great George Santayana saying, Luke thought. *"Those who cannot remember the past are condemned to repeat it."*

He looked at Carly and wondered if they were both thinking along the same lines.

History long past, and history remembered and perverted.

They knew about and remembered H. H. Holmes. They couldn't allow a repeat of his career of scams and horrific murders.

"We need to see the sights!" Carly said. "To get up high—if we could take those stairs!"

"She wants to look for the Loch Ness Monster," Luke told Clayton Moore.

"That's fine," Moore said.

He was still talking, showing Carly something in regards to stone balls that had been used as weapons.

But Carly was only pretending to listen, too. He saw she was pointing something out on the stretch of lawn that spanned out behind the castle.

There was someone standing there. A man in a kilt with a swath of tartan wool held over his shoulders by a brooch. There was something about him, other than the fact that no one else seemed to see him.

The man was looking at him.

Luke turned to Carly and nodded.

"Mr. Moore, I think I'd like to wander a bit more here. Would you be so kind as to accompany Carly on her monster watch?" he asked.

"Please, call me Clayton! And I am delighted to be of any assistance to Miss Carly, aye, that I am!" the man assured him.

He smiled, appearing to wander and then heading straight toward the man on the lawn.

The dead man.

As usual, the ghost was skeptical and wary at first.

"Y'see me, man?" the spirit demanded.

"I do," Luke told him. He indicated a section of the woods rising beyond the castle and said, "If you would, sir."

"Oh, I am no one's 'sir,' my friend. Hamish of Inverness."

"Hamish, thank you. I'm Luke, and I believe that you were watching us, looking at Mr. Moore, my friend, Carly, and myself."

"Worried for ye, I be," Hamish told him. "I have wondered for many a year why I remain, except to watch over this beloved land. It was near here I died, with my fellows seeking the protection of the forest after the fighting near Inverness at the Battle of Culloden. We dared not ride forward, not to Inverness, and we knew that we might find help or at least hide out in this direction. But..." He paused, studying Luke. "Time has buried my bones. And those of all who fought that day."

"Hamish, the battles that tore your land and your people apart are now long over, so—"

"You are a colonist?" Hamish asked him.

Luke tried not to smile, remembering that the Battle of Culloden had taken place almost thirty years before the American Revolution.

But the ghost shook his head. "My pardon. You are an American. I watch that telly thing whenever I am able and...ah, well, it may be that here, where I fought, peace reigns, but the world... well, perhaps men will always go to war."

"Unfortunately," Luke agreed. "But—"

"You mustn't leave her long with him!" Hamish said.

"Do you know something? Have you seen something?" Luke asked him.

Hamish frowned, looking at him. "Are you a sheriff?"

"Something like that," Luke told him. Then he shrugged. "You watch TV and I know there are many American programs you may see here. I'm FBI."

"Ah, but with no power here—"

"I have the police behind me."

"Then you are investigating that man!" Hamish said.

"We are. We have nothing against him. He has a home near here—"

"Aye, that I know."

"People have disappeared. And the media loves to speculate that it's the Loch Ness Monster."

"'Tis a monster, aye, all right, but not old Nessie. I saw him with her. Out here, where we are now. And then I saw him go back...and she wasnae with him and I searched for her and couldnae find her!"

"Her, who, do you know?"

"A pretty lass, a pretty lass indeed. They came a few times, laughing and a-playin' as they roamed the ruins. But then they came this way...and I never saw her again."

"When was this?"

"Two days, I believe. You will do what you must to find her?" the man demanded.

"I will. If you could be more detailed—"

"Would that I might, lad. Would that I might. The grounds here are deep and craggy, the forest can be rich. But she did not come out. I watched and waited and watched and waited. I believe she is there, that her flesh will rot, that she will be torn at by birds and creatures of the earth. She did not fall to Nessie! As I say, lad, another monster, of a different kind!"

"Thank you. I promise you, I will do what I can. We are trying to capture this man, and we believe that there is..."

Worse.

He almost said the word, but the spirit of Hamish of Inverness was disturbed as it was and he didn't want to add to his distress. "Hamish, we're working with the National Crime Agency and with Police Scotland and I will talk with them. They have a greater ability to search the woods while…we are worried that other events may be taking place at the house where he welcomes so many visitors. We're also afraid he might be working with another man—"

"Aye! Aye, I've seen the two of them about, talking, plotting! They were here together with her the day before the one took her into the woods. Laughing and all, they were, and the one pretending that he was so in love yet stepping aside for the other!"

"Interesting," Luke murmured. "Either they are truly good friends or working together on this, as we suspected. You don't know the young lady's name, do you?"

"Name, nay, I fear not. Wait, maybe, perhaps… Marion. Mary."

Miss Mary Nelson. Herr Grunewald asked about her this morning, and she is supposedly on her way to John o' Groats and the Shetland Islands.

"Hamish, I promise you, we're going to find out what happened to her," Luke said, hoping that he could keep that promise.

"Get back to yer lady lest she find herself in the woods, too," Hamish said gravely.

"Right. Thank you."

Luke started away but turned back. "Hamish, I don't know these woods. My friend does, somewhat. She had family who came from Drumnadrochit. But none of us can search through these woods the way that you can. If—"

"I will be here, lad. I will be here," Hamish promised.

"Thank you."

Luke felt a strange sense of urgency then. Clayton Moore

wasn't going to pull anything now—not unless he'd had his partner kill Herr Grunewald in their absence and not while they were still in proximity to so many tourists. He knew that.

He still wanted to be back with Carly.

He hurried back to the area within the sprawling ruins where he had left Carly and Moore to walk up to the heights—to see their surroundings better and look for the Loch Ness Monster.

He was gratified to see they were just coming down the stone steps they had started up earlier.

"You've got to go up, Luke! It's fantastic, the view. This is just a beautiful, beautiful area!"

"But no monster?" he inquired.

Carly gave him an icy smile. "One day, someone may prove you a jerk," she said sweetly.

"Well, I guess I should head back. I need to return, but of course, you two can stay and walk around more—the ruins are quite large," Moore told them.

Carly looked at Luke. "A little longer? We can get a rideshare here, right?" he asked Moore.

"Yes." He laughed. "Scotland is a civilized country within the civilized nation of Great Britain!"

They both smiled and laughed. Moore waved as he headed out to his car. Luke thought he eyed Carly with greater speculation.

When he was gone, she asked Luke, "Did you—"

"Meet Hamish of Inverness. He died soon after Culloden, heading this way to avoid the king's troops," he said. "His injuries were too severe to survive, even though he escaped the main battle, is what I think from what he told me. And he saw our good friend Clayton Moore disappear into the forest with the young woman Herr Grunewald asked about this morning, Mary Nelson. He said they went into the woods together. But when Moore came out, he was alone. And now Moore claims Mary Nelson has headed north. How well do you know these woods?"

"Not very," she told him. "I know Urquhart, the walk along the water. I never came out here to play in the woods."

"That's what I thought. And I'm trying to figure out a way to ask Campbell to have the local authorities check it out."

"I'll work on that," Carly said, drawing out her phone.

He listened as she lied. A good lie.

"Sir, I lost the tourist who was just talking to me, but she insists she saw Clayton Moore disappear into the woods with a woman he claims left Gordon House to head to John o' Groats and the Shetlands. Perhaps she's fine and we might reach her... Oh. Well, we were hoping... I don't know her name. My witness disappeared on a departing tour bus. She was distraught, but seemed to want to warn me about being alone with Clayton Moore... Yes, sir, thank you."

She ended the call and looked at him.

"Come on," he told her. "We'll slip a few feet into the woods ourselves, and I'll introduce you to Hamish and let him know the authorities will be searching for Mary Nelson."

He reached for her hand. He wasn't sure why. She took his easily. They were playing a part, of course, but there was no one watching them and...

He decided to quit overanalyzing himself and led her toward the point where he had met Hamish, stepping behind the cover of trees, although a conversation would look much more natural now that there were two of them.

Hamish stared at Carly in amazement, pleased to take her hand, and Carly knew to move it as if she could feel the pressure of his touch.

"Two in a day! I am stunned. It's been decades since I've met a seer!" he exclaimed.

"And I am extremely pleased to meet you, Hamish of Inverness!" she told him. "And I want you to know the right people will be out here soon to comb the forest."

"I cannae believe this!" he said, still studying her incredulously. "And I am e'er so grateful!"

"No, we're grateful," Carly replied.

Hamish turned back to Luke. "The lass is…"

"FBI, too," Luke told him.

"But ye must take extreme care!" he warned.

"We will, I promise!" Carly said. She looked at him. Luke was afraid that she was going to suggest that they begin exploring the forest themselves. He spoke quickly.

"I wanted you to meet," Luke said. "But I think we need to get back. There's an elderly gentleman at the manor and I'd like to see to his welfare, too."

He realized by the way Carly looked at him that she immediately understood his apprehension.

"We will meet again," Carly assured Hamish. She turned to Luke. "Perhaps we should hurry!"

He nodded. "Check for a ride. I'll get info to the right people and…"

"Someone will search the woods," she finished softly.

"As I will be doin' meself," Hamish promised.

CHAPTER SEVEN

When they returned to the house, everything seemed as usual. They were both relieved to see Herr Grunewald was sitting in the library.

"Ah, my friends!" he said, waving as they came through the main entry. "How was your day?"

He obviously wanted company. Carly looked at Luke, who nodded and smiled. They were both simply glad to see him. He had a drink sitting next to him, perhaps a shot of good Scot's whiskey, but he didn't seem to have touched it yet.

"Our day was intriguing," Carly said. "It was filled with beautiful scenery, but you know that."

"You're home early, and I'd have thought you'd be exploring till dark. Glad to see you for a bit, though, my friends. I do miss our dear Miss Nelson! She would so often join me here," Grunewald told them.

"She sounds lovely," Luke said.

Grunewald reached for the drink at his side. Carly looked at Luke and then made a dive to take the drink from the man's hands.

Maybe she hadn't thought it through, but she reasoned if

Moore was following a Holmes's design, he might have had the elderly man with no family sign over his estate to him already.

Clayton Moore has already come back here. He said he had an appointment. Grunewald didn't expect us to come back so quickly. Likely, Moore didn't, either. And if we're back and there is something in the drink...

It will look as if an elderly gentleman naturally passed away, his heart just giving out!

"My dear girl!" Grunewald said, confused. "I assure you—"

"I'm so sorry, Herr Grunewald. But there was a bug or something floating on the top. I'll just see about getting you a new one."

"Drinks are in the kitchen on an honor system," Grunewald said. "Of course, Clayton and Ben always see to my comforts, so—"

"Since I'm here, I can see to them!" Carly said, smiling.

"I'll give you a hand," Luke said.

He followed her into the kitchen, and she wasn't sure where they'd go from there. The contents of the glass needed to be tested, but without being obvious and perhaps destroying any chance of discovering the truth, she wasn't sure how they were going to make that happen.

"Give me the glass," he said after he'd followed her into the kitchen.

"But—"

"Seriously, just hand it to me."

She was surprised when he took the glass from her after pulling a vial from his jacket pocket, carefully ducking down low and indicating she should shield him since there might well be cameras in the kitchen.

She did so. "I'm telling you, there is something floating in the glass!" she said in case they were, indeed, being filmed or recorded.

"I'm looking at it, but I don't see it. But then again, you've *seen* the Loch Ness Monster."

"Oh, will you stop!" she said angrily.

"Right. I'll stop. Now I need to pay for another drink!" he said, setting the glass in the sink and reaching to the cupboard for another one.

"I can pay for it! I'm employed, too, you jerk!" she snapped.

"Stop! I'll just pay for it! Now, as to the liquor…"

"If you'd bothered to read the brochure, you'd know it's in the cabinet next to the refrigerator," she told him.

He found a bottle of whiskey and hesitated, saying, "You may be right. It might have been the bottle, but here…here I've found a new one, and I shall open it."

She noted he had found a sealed bottle of whiskey far behind the one in front, and he studied the seal as he opened it and poured another shot into a glass.

He turned to her. "Okay, ye who read the brochure, where do I leave the money?"

"Right there," she said, indicating a dish on the side of the sink. Luke dug into his pocket and looked at her. "Five pounds," she told him. "Hey, you don't have to leave a tip."

He made a face at her and headed back to the library with the drink in his hand.

Carly thought she should pour drinks for herself and Luke— except that she didn't trust anything in the kitchen now, despite the fact she had watched Luke break the seal. And they didn't need to be impaired in the least, not that one drink should do so, but under these circumstances…

Still, it was more than likely they would soon be joined by either Clayton Moore or Ben Pratt, and she wanted to give the appearance of the two of them joining Herr Grunewald for his nightcap.

She brought out two empty glasses and added a bit of water to each, the perfect stand-in for a clear liquor.

She had barely made it back into the room, handing one to Luke and keeping the other for herself and finding a seat in one of the library's comfortable stuffed chairs, before Ben Pratt came in, smiling away. "Everything fine with everyone? Ah, wonderful. I see the two of you have availed yourselves of the bar. There you go, Herr Grunewald. Companions to drink with again! Enjoy."

"I shall enjoy and allow this lovely couple to escort me to my room," Grunewald said. "I feel the need to rest, but I do enjoy my sip of whiskey each day!"

"And we will be delighted to walk you up to your room!" Carly assured him.

Grunewald finished his drink. "Shall we?"

"As you wish, Herr Grunewald!" Carly said, rising. She took the glasses. "I'll just run these back into the kitchen. We want to be good guests!" she told Ben Pratt.

"You don't have to do so, lass. I can take care—" Pratt began, but Carly was already rushing through the library and dining room. In the kitchen, she quickly rinsed the glasses as if there had been something in them, left them in the sink and hurried back.

Ben Pratt was watching Grunewald, but he made a great pretense of smiling at her as she returned. "Well, I offered my services, but the gentleman is quite smitten—and I'm not at all surprised. Mr. Kendrick," he told Luke, "you are a lucky man."

"Indeed, I am," Luke said, "most of the time!"

"Jerk!" Carly said sweetly. "Come, Herr Grunewald. I would love to take your arm!"

She did so. Smiling at Ben Pratt, she began to escort Grunewald from the room and toward the stairs.

Luke, she knew, was right behind her. Thankfully, Grunewald's room was just two doors down from the one she and Luke had been given.

"Sir," Luke told him. "If you need anything at all..."

"Ah, son, not to worry. These men tend to me well."

"But we're here, too. And just down the hall. Shout if you need anything at all. I sleep very lightly," Luke offered.

"As do I," Carly promised.

Grunewald was pleased and he smiled as he nodded his thanks.

"Lock up, sir!" Luke said.

They left Grunewald after hearing the click of his lock.

Carly swirled into Luke's arms to whisper to him, "Does that do any good? They have keys to every room."

"Time to bring in the troops."

"We don't have anything yet."

"We have your vial."

"And it may be full of good Scot's whiskey."

He smiled at her. "I have it covered. It's only about eight. We haven't had dinner, and for youngsters our ages, it's early."

"But what if one of them—"

"We'll only be taking a chance of a few minutes."

"That's all they'll need."

"No, conjecture, yes, but I believe they're expecting the man to drop dead of a heart attack. The police will be advised he died during the night. No one had any idea he was having a heart attack. They'll leave him until morning," Luke whispered back, holding her head close to his, running his fingers through her hair.

She smiled at him. "What's happening in the library?"

"We have a friend coming by to see about a room. Someone we can meet and with whom we can have a lovely chat while we're turning the vial over to him. First, our room."

She smiled, nodded and suddenly admitted to herself that even amid all this, she really liked the man and liked the closeness they were playing now. First it had been just fine on her part, and now it seemed as if things had moved on to good.

"Right. Our room," she murmured.

They headed down the hall.

"Looks fine, right?" he asked softly.

But Carly had a feeling, though nothing looked disturbed, that Ben Pratt had been in their room. Of course, maids were employed to clean the rooms; their bed had been made and fresh towels had been brought in.

Maids didn't play with a guest's luggage.

They weren't supposed to, at least.

She had left her bag a certain way, and she was sure that Luke had, too. She had put her gas mask in her shoulder bag along with her Glock when they'd left that morning, but she was certain Luke had also come prepared for a gas attack and she wasn't sure how he could have hidden his mask.

Looking around the room, she determined to just ask him. That meant coming close again.

She slid into his arms, locking her hands around his neck. "Gas mask?" she asked.

"Smallest available on the market. In my jacket all day. And yours...?"

"I think he's been in my luggage, but I had mine with me as well. Someone was in my luggage. I know because some clothing has been moved but certain clothing hasn't been disturbed."

He leaned back slightly, arching an amused brow to her. "Ah, you don't think that man would enjoy pulling apart a wee bit of lacy underwear?"

She smacked him lightly, but she almost laughed aloud.

"Trust me. I know my packing."

He nodded, his expression sobering. "Library."

She curled against him again. "Isn't it late for a guest to arrive?"

"Nope. Not really. And not someone who didn't realize they were going to need a room after they became fascinated by the sights at Urquhart Castle." He pressed his lips against her temple and whispered, "Campbell is on the way himself. He sent people out immediately, and I just received his text that he's on his way here."

"I keep feeling…" she murmured.

He looked at her, arching a brow. "Feeling…"

"I know that we're not from here, that—"

"You think we should be out in the woods," he said.

"They know the area. We know Hamish. What I'm afraid of, of course—"

"Is that there is no hope for Mary Nelson and we might yet save Herr Grunewald? We'll get on both," Luke promised.

She believed him. She smiled at him then with determination. They'd known what they were coming into; they'd studied the infamous career of H. H. Holmes while knowing that the site on the dark web would attract different types of twisted behavior within sick and criminal minds.

"Library!" he said. His lips moved near her ear again. "Glock and mask?"

"Still on me," she assured him, patting her bag.

They headed out, Luke pausing to glance at Herr Grunewald's door for a minute. They couldn't just break it down and drag the man away. Even if they told him the truth of what they were after and suspected, he was so enamored of his hosts he probably wouldn't believe them.

"Library," she reminded him.

He nodded, looked at her, grinned and offered her his hand.

She took it.

They went down the stairs together, walking into the library.

They were just in time. The door to the grand entry opened and Brendan Campbell—out of his usual business attire and wearing a pair of jeans and a sweater—came walking determinedly into the hall.

"Hello? Please? I don't have a reservation, but I need a room for the night, if you can help me, please?"

Ben Pratt was at the registration desk and he quickly replied to him.

"Sir, over here. We usually require reservations—"

"Please, young man, if there's anything available, I truly need a room. I should have gotten a driver for the trip! This has really been too much for me."

He was playing the part of an elderly or sickly gentleman well. Carly was impressed. She left the library, heading quickly to the desk.

"Sir, you look as if you could indeed use some rest." She looked at Ben Pratt and grimaced, appealing to what she would naturally think was his kind and decent nature.

"Ben, maybe, if there's nothing else, we could let this gentleman have our room," she told him.

"Oh, no, no, that won't be necessary. I believe we have a room free and cleaned—" Pratt began.

"I'll take a dirty room!" Campbell told him earnestly.

"No, we had a vacancy the other day. I'm sure it will be fine. Room four. Sir, just up the stairs. Oh! There's a small lift."

"Thank you, thank you, young man," Campbell said. By then, Luke had joined them by the desk.

"Hello, I can only imagine that you are with this kind and lovely lass, sir. Would you be so good as to go to my car for my bag? I parked the car a bit close to the road, but my bag is a wee one, not much trouble!"

Carly lowered her head to keep from smiling. Luke would surely place his evidence vial in Campbell's car and the contents of the vial would be tested.

An inspector would be near, ready to take the vial from the car and test the contents. Meanwhile, Campbell would stay and hopefully make sure that no one approached Herr Grunewald to strangle him in dismay that the poison hadn't worked.

And they could head out to the woods and subtly engage the help of their new spirit friend, Hamish of Inverness, and find Mary Nelson.

"Not a problem at all, sir. Happy to oblige," Luke said, heading out.

"I can do that—" Ben Pratt began.

"No big deal. I've got it!" Luke assured him.

Carly turned to Brendan Campbell and offered him her hand. "Carly MacDonald, sir."

"A Scot?" he inquired, as if puzzled.

"An American of Scottish descent, sir," she said. "We're happy to meet you. And you will so enjoy staying here! The house is wonderful, as are Mr. Pratt here," she said, inclining her head toward Pratt and smiling, "and the owner, of course, Mr. Clayton Moore! Luke will get your bag for you and bring it to your room. We were thinking of heading out for a bite to eat, if you'd like to join us," she added.

"Ah, lass, thanks. I'm a bit weary. I do appreciate the invite," he said.

"We'll see you at breakfast, then, sir," she said, heading to the door and waiting while Luke brought in Campbell's bag.

"I'll run this up!" he told them all.

"Thank you—I'll hop in the lift," Campbell said. He turned to Ben Pratt. "And thank you, thank you, so much. I do need a rest. No family, you see, and I should have hired a driver with my…wee problems," he finished.

He was, beyond a doubt, playing the part of a man with one foot in the grave—and Carly had to admit, she hadn't expected it from the staid and überprofessional Brit!

"Night, sir!" she called.

She and Luke were out of the house. He paused as they stood at the entry, pointing toward the trees that surrounded the castle.

"We're not by the area behind the castle," Carly reminded him.

"No, but we are in the Highlands. Roads around twist and curve to create the best routes through the rugged geography."

"You're thinking that there may be a path—a long path, but a path—that leads from the castle area here?" she asked.

"It's possible."

"It is, yes, of course. But if so—"

"It's accessed through the basement—where we haven't managed to be yet, or even find, for that matter. I couldn't find stairs when we've walked through the ground level. I believe that they want to kill Grunewald not for the enjoyment of it, but because he's probably left his property to them, or to Clayton Moore at least, or maybe the other way around."

"The lift," Carly said.

"Pardon?"

"This is a Georgian house, not built as a castle or fortress of any kind. There wouldn't have been a dungeon, but, yes, there would have been a basement. The lift has been installed in the past ten to thirty years, perhaps, whenever the home was first used as an inn or a bed-and-breakfast. Luke, we haven't been in it—it may be the only access to the basement now."

"There must be something else somewhere, but you're right—the lift might well lead down," Luke said. He was quiet for a minute. "Let's take this from the opposite side. Go back, be anxious, really anxious—that is, if Ben Pratt is still down there alone. Get him to follow you out here and into the woods."

"What?" She stared at him quizzically. "I know upon occasion it would be cool if we could just beat the crap out of a suspect, but—"

"I'm not going to beat anyone. But we can lie—and trick him into telling us the truth."

"You mean offer him something so that he'll turn on Clayton?" Carly asked.

He nodded. "Time is not on our side," he said. "Carly, think of the terrain. Mountains, hills—even caves, possibly tunnels, natural or man-made. Ben is the weaker of the two, or so it appears from his personality and the fact that it's Clayton Moore who owns the property. See if you can draw him out—I'm heading due east of the property, toward the woods around Urquhart. I'll text Campbell so that he knows what is going on."

"Right. Go!"

He ran off into the woods surrounding the house. Carly gave him a chance to disappear and then raced back into the house. As she had hoped, Ben Pratt was still behind the desk alone, doing something at the computer. When he saw her, he shut it down.

Very quickly.

"Carly, what's wrong?"

"It's Luke! Oh, Ben, I don't know what he's doing! He said he saw something in the woods, and I don't know where he went—it's like he thinks he's a cop or something. He said people had been disappearing around here, and he could see something that might lead to why. He has me terrified, and I don't know how to find him. It's getting dark and I know that it will get even darker and I'm so scared—"

"He thought he saw something?" Pratt demanded.

"Yes! Something that has to do with people disappearing! I don't know what he thinks he's going to do. He's not... I'm scared, so scared! I mean, we fight all the time, and there are days when I wonder what the hell I'm doing with him. But I don't want him hurt. I don't know what he saw and what he thinks that he can do—"

"Nothing!" Pratt said, and he couldn't disguise the anger in his voice. He quickly collected himself, though, and said, "I'm so sorry, Carly. Of course I'll help you. We'll find him."

He came around the desk, offering her a reassuring smile.

"Which way?"

"This way!"

She started ahead of him, leaving the house and heading toward the eastern edge of the property and the trees that surrounded it on ground level, but then became part of a rising slope that joined into the higher rises around them. He chased after her and she wished she knew a little better which way through the almost nonexistent trails Luke had chosen to go.

"Which way, which way," she murmured aloud.

"He said that he saw something. What did he think he saw?"

"Blood on a tree, I don't know! He was suddenly convinced that he saw proof of something bad happening, and he's such a fool!" Carly complained worriedly.

He stared at her for a moment and turned, and when he began walking, she saw that the path he was following was more of a trail than the ground on which she had earlier taken some of her twists and turns. She wondered how far they were from the castle and thought that it couldn't be more than a couple of miles.

She dug in her bag for her phone.

"What are you doing?"

"I was going to try and call the idiot—"

"No service here," he warned her.

"Oh!" She slid the phone back in her bag.

In truth, she hadn't been making a call. Just setting her phone to do what she needed it to do!

This was a trail that had been recently used. Ben Pratt knew it well.

Had Clayton Moore taken Mary Nelson from her tour of Urquhart and the surrounding grounds back through the forest? It was easily walkable for anyone who was in fit shape, and from what she understood, Mary Nelson had been young and certainly fit.

"Get up here with me!" he snapped.

She looked at him with surprise, and he quickly changed his tone. "Sorry, this ground can be rough, rocks beneath trees… mountains have faults, and there are holes in the ground everywhere, and you must be very careful."

"Of course!"

Minutes later they came upon a jagged outcrop of rock and Carly instantly noted that there seemed to be a black gaping hole beneath it.

Darkness was coming on. She thought that it might be time to simply draw out her Glock.

But to what end? She had nothing on the man as of yet.

"Is he the exploring kind?" Ben Pratt asked her.

"He's stubborn as they come. If he thought that he was on to something—"

"Okay, come on. I'll help you down."

He was looking at her differently now. There might have once been a plan, get a fight going between her and Luke, the angry couple taking off in different directions, no one knowing where they were going after the murderous duo had gotten from them whatever they wanted.

But Luke had been on to something.

And the way that Ben Pratt was behaving and speaking...

He was taking it on himself to get rid of them both now, before they could cause trouble. Maybe he had tried to contact Clayton to let him know that a few of their guests had gotten unruly and he needed help, but she hadn't seen him draw out a phone.

Maybe he thought that Clayton would blame him for the situation and, therefore, he needed to handle it himself as quickly as possible.

"I'll help you down there."

"Oh, I don't know! Luke is the exploring kind—"

He took a step toward her. "I can help you," he warned her, his voice different than it had ever been, "or I can throw you!"

"Rude! Rude, rude, rude!" she muttered.

"It's dark down there."

"I have a little penlight—just go!"

She still had nothing on the man, but she was entering a stygian darkness with him, and the biggest mistake an agent could make at this point was not to be wary and aware that he might strike at any minute.

But Luke was out there—close. He was either watching what was going on...

Or maybe he was in the hole already.

"All right, all right! I don't know what is going on with you, but you are being rude!" she snapped and, turning quickly, held her bag close to her chest, slid down on her rear and then the last few feet down into the absolute darkness of the hole.

Luke heard the shifting of the earth as someone slid into the dark cavern within the cliffs and heights and rocks of the terrain.

He quickly turned out his own light.

He couldn't be seen, not yet. He might need to move quickly, but he wanted something that proved positive that Ben Pratt was involved in this...

Whatever exactly *this* was.

He hadn't been down long. And he wondered if he ever would have found the small dark opening in the rise of rock and wood so close to Loch Ness if it hadn't been for Hamish of Inverness. He'd been startled to run into Hamish almost instantly when he'd left the house, curious that the ghost was so far from where they had met.

"Ah, laddie, not far at all, the way the crow flies," Hamish had told him.

"Ah, well, I'm grateful to see you. I think there must be something here, something that perhaps connects to the Georgian house—"

"A tunnel?" Hamish asked him curiously. "But wouldnae such a thing be seen?"

"No, it would just be an opening in the rock and appear to be nothing more than formation. Do you know about—"

"There is a rise o' rock this way, my friend. Come, follow me."

Hamish hadn't known exactly where the opening was, but once they had reached the area, it hadn't been hard to find.

And they had barely come down into the darkness before he heard Pratt and Carly—and heard the way that Pratt was now talking to her.

He intends to kill her, Luke thought.

But not happening.

Hamish was silent, which didn't matter, of course. If he spoke, Pratt wouldn't hear him.

But he could let Carly know that they were in the cave, near, and that he was ready to step in when needed.

A second disruption of the earth sounded, with bits and pieces of rock and earth falling. Then there was light; Ben Pratt had a penlight on him.

Luke flattened himself against the cave wall, but Pratt didn't turn toward him. "I believe he's this way. Come on, my luv. We'll find him."

"I don't like this. It's a cave and—" Carly broke off. Her dismay was real.

There was a smear of what appeared to be blood along the cave wall.

Pratt instantly pulled a knife.

"Shut up and move!" he told her.

She shook her head and looked terrified—not a hard stretch in the damp and eerie darkness of the cave—though Luke knew she was likely faking it.

"Wait, what are you doing?" she asked.

"Making you come with me."

"With a knife?" she cried. "I thought—I thought that you liked me! Clayton is going to be furious. I know he likes me. He'll be down here and he'll stop you!"

That brought a flow of laughter from Ben Pratt. "Are you kidding me? He likes you all right. He wants to play with you awhile before…"

"Before he kills me?" she whimpered. "Oh, my God! You did kill that poor girl, that woman that Herr Grunewald was talking about."

"Oh, she may not be dead yet," he said, shrugging. "Clayton liked her, too. Oh, you want to meet her? I can arrange that."

Hamish suddenly spoke softly.

"Lassie, we're here! The lad and me, we're here!" he said.

Ben Pratt suddenly shivered, as if he'd felt something, but he apparently shook off the sensation. Carly didn't move a muscle.

She had heard.

"Come, luv. I'll introduce you!" Pratt said.

"Why would I come with you to be tortured before you kill me?" Carly demanded.

"Oh, let's see. Because you think that lover boy is around somewhere and will save you."

"Wait, wait…others! You killed them, or Clayton killed them?"

"We are true partners—we take turns killing. You're just going to disappear. Poor Herr Grunewald. I'll be calling the police myself when the boy is found dead of natural causes, heart attack, poor old bugger! But…come on. You're a lively lass. Play the game, and you may live awhile. You may dream of escape! A chance is better than me stabbing you in the heart right this moment, eh?"

"You'll introduce me to Mary," she said bitterly.

"Aye, if she's still breathing, that is. But she's young and strong and…maybe."

He gripped her arm.

Luke thought she lowered her head and smiled.

She knew Luke was behind her, and he had amazingly found help from a long-dead Scot. She let him take her and lead her…

With any luck, to Mary Nelson.

Who might, hopefully, still be alive.

But Luke didn't trust the man in any way, shape or form.

His Glock was out as he silently followed the two through the tunnel, the furious spirit of Hamish of Inverness right at his heels.

CHAPTER EIGHT

The path they traveled at first was winding and distorted, a natural formation of rock as old as the geological shift of landmasses.

They didn't travel far, though it felt like they moved forever. At one point, Ben Pratt stopped, gripping Carly's arm tightly, looking back.

He threw his penlight over the distance they had walked, but apparently, he saw nothing. He started to pull Carly forward again.

She thought that they had come to a dead end because she saw a rise of what appeared to be ragged gray stone before her, but a shift to the left showed her that there was an L-shape in the earth's tunnel, but that L-shape led to a door.

Still holding her tightly, Pratt pushed on the door.

They were back in Clayton Moore's Georgian manor.

And she was in the basement—not the way she had intended to find it, but they were finally there.

And Luke was right behind her. They were doing what they had set out to do—finding everything that they needed to find.

In a room beyond a room, she imagined. Through another door—one that looked like part of the wood paneling in the regular basement, she determined, seeing the paneled section across from where they stood—there would be your typical, normal facilities, like a water heater, a washer and dryer, storage.

But here…

There were shelves filled with a strange assortment of tools, surgeons' knives and scalpels, pliers, sharpened sticks, an acetylene torch…

Those are vats filled with acid, she thought.

Acid that accounted for the various skeletons kept on shelves there, some articulated, some just in piles of bones.

And there were four tables or gurneys of steel with leather straps with which to bind a person…

Where a woman lay. Silent, eyes closed, spots of blood upon the clothing she wore, here and there, where one or more of the "tools" had been used upon her.

"Ah, my lovely lassie, welcome to our true guest welcome area! Choose a table!" Ben Pratt told her.

"No."

"I can cut you before you lie down, if you choose," he warned her, smiling. "It's better when you're lying down. You just bleed. If I cut you while you're standing, you could fall and break a bone. That would really hurt."

"No, I really don't think so," Carly told him.

It had gone far enough; they had found what they'd hoped, except that…

It appeared they were too late.

Mary Nelson had been a beautiful young woman, a brunette with a sweeping length of dark hair that fell around the whiteness of her face.

"Down!" he ordered.

"No, no, I really don't think so. Luke?"

He'd been standing right behind the door and stepped in, his Glock aimed directly at Ben Pratt's head.

The ghost of Hamish of Inverness came in behind him, rushing over to stand by Mary Nelson, his distress and sorrow apparent as he set a ghostly hand upon her forehead.

"Get your hands off her, Pratt," Luke said.

Ben Pratt stared back at Luke with incredulous anger. "I should have known!" he raged.

"Let her go!" Luke snapped again.

Pratt did. In that second, the manager of Gordon House obviously decided to play it a different way.

"I had to!" he cried out, dropping Carly's arm. "I had to! Clayton was going to kill me if I didn't play his game, if I didn't help him with this…this thing of his. He wanted to be the one who excelled above all others, and he knows where my family lives, and you don't understand. I had no choice!"

"That's not true at all. There's always a choice, I'm afraid," Carly told him.

"No, whatever I said—" Pratt began to protest.

"I'm afraid you're cooked, my friend," Carly said. "I wasn't calling Luke—I knew he was right behind us. I set my phone to record everything you said."

"I had to, I had to say those things. I had to get started on torturing you or else he would kill me, and he taught me that scaring a person first was the beginning and—"

"Maybe there could be some clemency for you if you were to be a witness for the prosecution," Luke said.

"I'll tell you about him, I'll tell you anything you want to know, anything that I know, I swear, I was forced into this, I was—"

"You bloody ass!" they suddenly heard.

They knew where the lift landed now; the door to the regular basement had opened, and Clayton Moore himself was standing there, brandishing a gun and staring at Ben Pratt with a fury that seemed to have turned his entire body red, if the color of his face was any indicator.

"I don't know whether to shoot you or them first!" he raged, staring at Pratt.

"They were on to us!" Pratt cried desperately. Two guns were aimed at him then. Clayton Moore's and Luke's.

"Wait! Clayton, think about it! We don't know who or what they think they are, but they have no power here. They're Americans!" He stared at Carly. "Bitch, your lover boy can't save you, you have no power whatsoever, he has no power—"

"I do have a gun," Luke reminded him.

"And so do I," Carly said. With Clayton Moore now brandishing his weapon at them all, it seemed time to produce her Glock.

"But I *will* kill one of you before I go down!" Moore vowed. "You have no power—"

"Ah, here you all are!"

They were joined by another living soul as Brendan Campbell burst through the door to the torture room, his own weapon aimed at Moore.

"They have no power, eh, my man?" he taunted. "Other than that the two of them are great shots and, wait, I do have the authority to arrest you both. Though if one of them was to shoot your bloody arses first, it would be totally understandable."

Despite Campbell's words, Carly knew Clayton Moore had meant what he had said; he might go down, but he didn't intend to go down alone.

She fired, close enough to catch his right shoulder, and though he screamed and tried to keep his hand on his weapon to pull the trigger, he could not.

His gun fell from his grip.

Campbell was staring at the man; he didn't see that the spirit of Hamish of Inverness managed to use whatever ghostly strength he had to kick the gun toward Luke.

Luke stooped to retrieve it before Ben Pratt could.

As Hamish straightened, he cried out to them.

"She's breathing! The lass is breathing! We need help, now!"

"*I* need help now! Brutality, I will sue you to the ends of the earth!" Moore screamed.

"Watch them!" Campbell ordered as he pulled out his phone. It was best that he called it in; he was the local authority and help would respond immediately, Carly knew.

She glanced at Luke, who nodded, keeping his gun trained on Clayton Moore while also having an eye on Ben Pratt.

She rushed over to the table where Mary Nelson lay bound and began to work on removing the leather straps. They were tied tightly and she had to swing around to grab one of the scalpels from a shelf and begin to cut furiously at the leather that held the woman to the table.

They heard sirens almost immediately. Carly knew that law enforcement—and emergency services—had been alerted to be ready at his signal.

Even as Campbell cuffed the two men, Moore was still screaming about brutality while Pratt was still screaming he had been forced to do what he had done. He wasn't a killer, not a killer himself.

Campbell left the two of them watching over Mary Nelson and the cuffed killers so he could head up and bring other police and medical personnel down to the hidden torture chamber in the basement.

Carly assured herself that Mary Nelson was breathing and she was. But when she searched for a pulse, she found that while the woman had one, it was weak.

Over her days in captivity, she had probably had little or no water—just enough for them to keep her alive to continue the torture—and she had lost a great deal of blood.

Hamish was at her side. It appeared the ghost was weeping.

"There is hope!" Carly assured him, just before help reached them. She stepped back instantly for medical personnel to begin work on Mary Nelson.

Finally, Mary was taken away; Campbell was giving directions to everyone.

At last he came back to Carly and Luke and studied them appreciatively. "My friends, I cannot tell you the depths of our appreciation. We have laws, of course, against illegal search and seizure—"

"Again," Luke reminded him, shrugging. "As in America."

Campbell nodded. "Aye, thankfully, the colonies learned something from the motherland!" He managed a smile that faded quickly as he looked around. "Mary Nelson has a chance. As for those who are here…"

He swept out an arm, indicating the skeletons and random bones that lay on the shelves.

"As for those here, it will take some time for our forensic and medical departments to put the pieces together. Ah! Bad choice of words," he said, shaking his head in dismay. "But they will be taken to a national facility back in Edinburgh. If you would be so kind—"

"We'll get our things and be at your disposal as you wish," Luke assured him. "But—"

"Herr Grunewald is fine. I saw to him."

"You're sure? He was in his room—" Carly began.

"I'm sure. I handled the situation in a very simple way. I knocked on his door for a quick chat. After I had spoken to him, I checked on Mr. Moore and knew, of course, when he hurried to the lift to reach the basement that I needed to follow. Also, I have asked our emergency teams to check on him and see that he is taken elsewhere, wherever he might choose to go. But since he was so concerned about Miss Nelson, I believe he'll want to be near the hospital."

"Let's pray she has a chance," Carly murmured.

"She does," Campbell assured her.

"We'll head up to get our things and start back for Edinburgh," Luke told him.

"Aye and thank you. And fear not—we'll have you assisting with questioning, though it seems they are both determined to speak against the other." He hesitated. "I almost believe your Clayton Moore might wish your shot had been into his heart. Moore is so obsessed with this…this horrid H. H. Holmes Society!"

"Perhaps," Carly murmured. "Though I must say, I'm grateful you are authorized to carry that weapon, sir—and that in our situation, we were granted the authority as well."

He nodded. "I prefer anything other, but under these circumstances…well, we are all alive. And Herr Grunewald is alive and well, and the horror here has been stopped. We'll move onward."

"Right," Luke murmured. "Carly?"

"I'll take my leave," Hamish told them.

The chamber was busy; Carly looked at him and said, "Luke, perhaps we get to the car and pause a minute."

Hamish managed to smile. "Aye, then, I'll see you at the car!"

She nodded, and they went through the door to the regular basement and saw the lift was there and the door was opened and ready.

They took the lift to the second floor and saw that Herr Grunewald was in the hallway with a local policeman at his side.

He excused himself and came over to them, reaching out to take their hands and thank them profusely.

"They'd have poisoned me! I thought them the kindest men possible. My property is left in their hands should I die. My first act on the morrow will be a call to see that my papers are straightened out. I will be near dear Mary, and I will use my resources because now I know… Well, I believe I know what is real and what is not. I cannot tell you how grateful I am!"

"Herr Grunewald, we are equally grateful, and we're praying for Mary," Carly assured him.

"Indeed, sir," Luke agreed.

The policeman cleared his throat. "Herr Grunewald. We need to get you—"

"I am ready, good sir. I just…"

"Of course," the policeman said, nodding at Luke and Carly.

He politely led Grunewald down the hall, and Carly and Luke went into their room to retrieve their things.

She paused, zipped her small suitcase and looked at Luke. "This was…very, very bad. But we're still not at the bottom of it all!"

"Carly, they've been studying all the footage from the café and beyond, both here and in the US. And now we have all the computers from this place. There will be a way to stop what's going on," Luke said.

She shook her head. "The original H. H. Holmes practiced his scams and murders for years," she said. "They don't even know when he began."

"The original Holmes, while a monster, was also a brilliant man. Top of his class all the time when he was a child, and a graduate from medical college when so many people dropped out. Granted, he learned all about dissecting the human body there, grave robbery and the manipulation of providing a corpse when need be for an insurance scam. But he was smart—if he hadn't had his psychotic tendencies, if he'd directed his brilliance and energy in a different direction, he might have been a great man."

"I will not admire a long-dead serial killer!" Carly protested.

Luke shook his head. "Of course not. The point I'm making is that whoever is running this website is more like Holmes. Clever, cunning and probably a psychopath, but not all psychopaths turn into murderers. Holmes might have gone in a different direction, but that's not the point. Clayton Moore is charming and clever, but far from brilliant—in my estimation, at least. He was a true copycat. He had the property and the ability to create a Holmes-style 'castle,' but he never graduated from medical school and his methods became sloppy at the end. We will discover that Herr Grunewald's drink was poisoned when the lab finishes with the vial—he should never have been so careless with others around."

"Maybe Ben Pratt was responsible for the mistakes," Carly said. "Maybe he was Clayton Moore's Pitezel, a man to be useful while needed, and then done away with when the situation demanded. Pitezel was even in on the insurance scam that he believed Holmes was perpetuating. They headed to Philadelphia, where the insurance company was located, and they were supposed to *pretend* that Pitezel died accidentally while substituting another body so that his wife could claim the insurance, and then they could all split it. Of course, that's not what Holmes had intended at all. But he had long befriended Pitezel and his family before murdering the man for his insurance scams—and then murdering three of his children as well."

"Well, then, lucky for Pratt he'll spend the rest of his days in prison," he said.

"Still, it's so frustrating! This is the fourth Society situation you've come upon and the second for me, and it's so frustrating. Whoever is creating this website over and over again is truly a monster—getting others to lead a life of torture and murder—and probably not caring in the least when one or more of his Society members is arrested. He'll keep at it and we'll keep putting bandages on the situation while he gets away."

"But they didn't have the forensic science then that we do now. We've also got some of the best computer technicians in the world working on all this." Luke grinned. "We're not alone."

She nodded, aware that his words were true—they were in the field. But others had been working with all the footage from the café while they had been at Clayton Moore's Georgian manor house. And others were even with them out in the field.

"Campbell did make a timely entry tonight," Carly said.

"Both suspects are still alive, and we may still learn something from them."

"We may, so there you go," he said. "Come on. I want to give Hamish my most sincere thanks."

Hamish was waiting by the car, and Carly hurried to him, forgetting for a minute that she might be seen by one of the many professionals now busy in Gordon House.

"Thank you, thank you so much!" she told him, reminding herself she couldn't really hug a spirit. "Thanks to you, we had the best possible outcome—"

Hamish shook his head. "Thank you. War is one tragic and horrid thing—the murder of complete innocents is abomination. But to be honest, I don't think of meself as a bloodthirsty man, but I'd have loved to see the two of them shot to pieces or chopped to bits, sent straight to the hell where such men deserve to be!"

"Hamish, we are law enforcement, not judges or juries," Carly reminded him quietly. "And perhaps, for such men, rotting in prison while alive may be a greater punishment than death."

"I understand," Hamish said. "And I thank you, and I will watch over Mary."

"We'll be praying for her," Luke said.

"I heard one of the medical men speaking. Her pulse was already growing stronger. There is hope for her, though for so many others..."

"Hamish of Inverness, you have been wonderful, and maybe one day there will be a way to let Mary know how grateful we were for your help. Now, sir, we need to get to Edinburgh."

"Aye. I will be here, should ye need me."

"Thank you!" Carly said again.

Hamish nodded gravely, stepped back and watched as they got in their car and drove away.

They hadn't driven far when Luke's phone buzzed. He glanced

at her while keeping one hand solidly on the wheel as he pulled his phone out.

"Campbell," he told her. "We need to report in to fill out paperwork, then take the night—though it will be morning by then—and let our prisoners be processed. He has spoken with Jackson—they both say we get to rest and let them stew. Also, they've been working together from across the pond and are narrowing down information on facial recognition and timelines to possibly have a suspect again for our dark-web guru. Naturally, you are the one who saw the man, if only briefly, so they'll want us studying what they've discovered."

She turned to him. "There may really be a suspect?"

"Getting there."

Carly leaned back. "I may sleep on the way to Edinburgh."

"Go for it," he said.

She closed her eyes. She opened them.

"I may not sleep," she said wearily. "Too much adrenaline, I suppose, after what happened. You, Hamish, Campbell...it all fell into place!"

"I believe you would have been fine with or without us."

She smiled over at him. "Thanks. Maybe—I'd have shot Ben Pratt if I'd been forced to without blinking, especially after seeing Mary Nelson bleeding on that table. But then Clayton Moore arrived and, though I am a good shot, that might have gone either way!"

He smiled over at her. "That's what I keep telling you," he reminded her. "We're not alone."

She leaned back. "Okay, I'll just close my eyes." It was remarkable that, despite the fact she didn't believe she could possibly sleep, it was still...okay. She was almost resting. There was a comfort and security about knowing Luke was awake and aware, and that he was a man who could almost sense any danger coming their way.

Comfort, security and...

Other than the fact they were after heinous killers, it had been fun playing that they were a loving couple who still might argue like cats and dogs. And acting like she might have been open to a scam if approached by a solicitous and charming other man!

Not good. They were partners.

But in the Krewe, partners often became so much more. Maybe it was simply that they didn't have to hide the strange talent that would make most others think them crazy, or...

Then again...

Okay, so Luke was simply *hot*, and she'd be a liar if she were to deny that touching him had ever been anything other than their mission.

What if he had only been playing a part? In her mind, even calling him a jerk had been something that might have been real. Playing the argumentative couple had been almost surreal, playing so naturally in tandem as they had.

Easy, easy and, yes, evocative, to be with him.

But maybe he was just immersed in his role. They had both worked undercover before; they were both good at their jobs.

And maybe that was it and nothing more.

She was startled into opening her eyes as the car came to a halt.

"You're smiling!" Luke said.

"I am, must have dozed—"

"And enjoyed a pleasant dream at last?" he asked.

She shrugged. "We're here."

"Paperwork."

"Paperwork."

Campbell hadn't arrived yet, but they were led to his office to await him and were given tea and applauded grimly by the staff who greeted them.

Campbell arrived shortly after, and they went through all the necessary items and finished the paperwork within the next few hours.

"By the way, that was an excellent act, sir," Carly told him when they were done, and she and Luke were free to leave for the few hours that remained of the night.

Campbell smiled at them. "Ah, old and stodgy I look to you now, eh? I spent my youth climbing the ladder to arrive where I stand today. I've done enough undercover in my past. Oh! The lab report came in. And thanks to your due diligence—"

"*Our* due diligence. You were there when we needed you, sir," Luke corrected.

"They were going to poison Grunewald. Something called aconite was found in the vial you gave us, and it's very difficult to detect unless one is specifically looking. The idea, of course, was that he would die of a heart attack, one seen as a natural death, and then Clayton Moore could scoop up his holdings. It seems that Holmes murdered for murder. But his 'safe' where victims could be suffocated was also found, and while hundreds of names of those who had disappeared in Chicago came in, very few had anything to do with money. Of course, not all were victims. So, it appears the members of the H. H. Holmes Society may kill for both profit and pleasure. I believe we are getting close. Now we must figure out a way to stop this completely and forever. But that's for tomorrow. Please, we have you at one of my favorite places just off the Royal Mile, a great two-bedroom suite with a full kitchen."

"Thank you," Luke told him, accepting the card with the address from Campbell.

"In truth, I wish I'd been the one to think of it!" Campbell said. "Special Agent Angela Hawkins made the arrangements, and I heartily agreed. By afternoon, if you are ready, we'll see to it that you're able to interrogate the men."

"Separately, please," Luke said.

"Our intent as well," Campbell assured them.

They left the station and traveled to their new accommodations.

The hotel was beautiful and literally right off the Royal Mile. Marble and wood highlighted the entry, a restaurant faced an expanse of lawn before the Mile; when they headed up, their suite was far more than accommodating. Both bedrooms offered private showers, and the kitchen and lounge areas were expansive and shared a view of the city that was spectacular, with the rise of Arthur's Seat in the distance. Bits and pieces of Holyrood Park and the palace were also visible.

"Wow. Angela is…damned fantastic," Luke said.

"She is."

"You look perplexed," Luke told her.

"I guess it's the calm before the storm and I know that…"

"Yeah. Sleep."

"Maybe I did sleep in the car."

"For at least fifty miles," he assured her. He walked over to her, gently taking her by the shoulders.

"We wouldn't be human if we weren't touched by what we're dealing with, with what we're seeing. But we can't serve the people adequately if we don't shake it off sometimes."

She smiled at him and laughed softly. "Funny, I was afraid that since you were the one to walk into the first murder castle on this case, you were taking everything too much to heart. I'm okay, really. I swear it. Sleep, right? We're going to get to sleep."

He nodded, drew his knuckles down her cheek and said, "Yeah." It almost sounded as if he had said the word regretfully.

As if he were wishing for more. And the gesture was so sweetly intimate, indicating a closeness between them, strong and shared and…

Or she was putting something into his tone just because she wanted it to be there.

"We'll get to speak with Moore and Pratt when we wake up," he reminded her.

"Think we'll get anything from them?" she asked, hoping her voice was cool and casual.

"If they know anything, we'll get it. And if they don't—we've had amazing techs and others going through hours and hours of surveillance footage. We'll get something."

She nodded and stepped away at last. "Yes, sleep and, oh, wow! Shower. After the creepy tunnel, the blood, the bones…"

She flashed him a smile and hurried into the bedroom she'd chosen. Without thinking, she began to shed her clothing haphazardly, only pausing briefly to see that her Glock and its small holster were carefully placed on the nightstand by the plush queen-size bed.

With clothing strewn everywhere, she headed into the shower. She was delighted to discover the place had amazing water pressure, and the water itself quickly ran deliciously hot.

She heard the knock on the door to her bedroom and Luke's voice as he excitedly called her name. Grabbing a towel, she let the water run and raced out, calling "Come in!" as she neared the door.

He opened it.

Wearing a towel, too.

"Oh, ah, yeah, sorry, and me… Anyway, got a text from Jackson. The hospital apparently let the big guys know at the same time—Mary Nelson is going to make it. She's already come to and received a ton of blood, has a strong pulse…"

He stopped speaking awkwardly.

"You took your phone in the shower?" she asked him.

"It was on the sink."

"Oh."

They stood there for a minute, staring at one another. Then Carly found she was smiling and chastising herself.

She took chances.

Being in law enforcement, she took chances—calculated carefully, of course—but chances. With her life.

And here and now, when it came to her heart and soul, she was suddenly the worst coward known to man.

But she wasn't going to continue to be.

"Okay, well, that's great information. Wonderful! And you're here in a towel and I'm here in a towel. We're obviously both rid of bone dust and blood and all kinds of stuff you really don't want to share and..."

"Sex is a truly viable alternative to sleeping to shake off some ill effects of such a day," he pointed out.

"You think?"

"I do. And you?"

"It could work. How good are you?" she teased.

"Ah, well, that's in the eye of the beholder, right?"

"Beholder?" Her eyebrow rose.

"Well, you know..."

Life was filled with chances. And there weren't always second chances to follow a bungled first.

"Okay, maybe. I mean, it was an absolutely horrific day, so it can't be worse!"

He grinned at that. "Yeah, and you know guys—we're into anything that moves."

"So, it could be okay."

Maybe they really were in tune with one another. They dropped the towels simultaneously, and Carly moved flush against his naked body.

Hmm...

And maybe he was right. Guys would go after anything...

But it was good. Good to feel his incredible warmth, a heat that emanated from him and seemed to fill her. She willed herself to stop thinking.

To just feel. To take in the incredible moment, to breathe...

His lips touched upon hers, featherlight at first. Then his mouth formed over hers completely. His kiss became deep and intimate, and she felt his hands...

He knew how to move them, he knew how to kiss, touch, caress...

Drawing away, he smiled and swept her up into his arms.

"This is okay, right?"

"Seems okay so far," she assured him.

"I mean, you know, sweeping you up."

"Well, you know, I was going to sweep *you* up, but, I mean, you are kind of heavy, so I guess this is okay."

She fell back upon the bed with him coming over her. She was still smiling as he demanded while grinning, "Are you calling me fat?"

"No, no, just, uh, big."

"That's fat."

"Muscled, is that better? Everyone knows muscle weighs more than fat! And tall, of course. There's just a lot of you."

He preened as his mouth touched down on hers.

The horror of the day was gone in seconds as she felt an urgency almost overwhelm her, the sweetness of sensation slip into her and rule every conscious thought.

Touch, brush, kiss, caress, sweet and natural intimacy, and somehow not just sex, but...

Making love, intimate, locking together, sweeping to new heights...

And then lying together in an aftermath every bit as sweet.

"Was I okay?" he teased, his whisper falling against her cheek.

And she grinned.

"You'll do in a pinch," she murmured.

And they laughed together and made love again. It really was perfect...

Because afterward, she fell into a deep, deep sleep, one she had desperately needed.

CHAPTER NINE

Waking up might have been awkward. Especially since they had gotten to sleep around five in the morning and his phone went off just after noon.

Luke had entered Carly's room last night with his phone in his hand, but he had dropped it along with his towel when she'd walked into his arms. That meant it was somewhere on the floor ringing away.

He bounded out of bed searching the floor. She was sitting up as he found it, watching him, waiting.

He identified himself and realized, of course, that his caller ID was showing him it was Jackson Crow.

He hadn't needed to identify himself.

"Sorry—long, weird night," he told Jackson.

"I figured," Jackson replied. "But I just heard from Brendan Campbell. They have processed Ben Pratt and Clayton Moore. And since none of us customarily democratic and decent countries practice torture, they've let them eat and sleep. But Campbell expects to interview them himself within the hour and he knows you're anxious to be there and put forth your own round of questions. I hated to wake you, but this thing moves at the speed of light, thanks to the wonders of the web—light and dark. Plus, I knew you were anxious to get to them."

"We are," he said, glancing at Carly. It was cool in the room, and she was wrapped in the covers. She didn't appear to be dismayed in the least that they'd given in to basic desires during the night.

She arched a brow at him.

"I'm more anxious to discover, though, if we have a lead on the person who may be behind this whole thing. Has he—or she—gotten the site back up yet?"

"Not that we've been able to find."

"Wow. It's imperative, then, that—"

"You get to it. We'll video call when you're back with Campbell to interview the men you took down last night. Oh, by the way, Campbell came into this Euro-Krewe thing quite unhappily, obeying orders from above. But he's now had nothing to say about you two that isn't glowing with praise. So it's still going to be a hard route, but you are doing great things for international diplomacy."

"Happy to make the man happy. And I admit, I first thought he was a bit of a stuffed-shirt desk dictator, but he's proven himself, too."

"Should I wake Carly?"

He couldn't help glancing at Carly again and smiling.

"That's not necessary, sir. Angela arranged unbelievable accommodation for us. We have two rooms in the same suite, so..."

It wasn't a lie.

"Gotcha. Talk on video soon."

Jackson ended the call.

"They're ready for us?" Carly asked.

He nodded. "So—"

"Get out of here! I want to get ready fast, and I don't want to be distracted!"

She was fierce, but she was grinning.

"No showering together, huh?"

She threw a pillow at him. He laughed, let it fall to the floor, retrieved his towel and hurried to his room.

Another quick shower was in order.

And he was quick; but when he emerged from his room, dressed and ready for the day, he found Carly was coming from her room at the same time. Her hair was pulled back, and she was wearing a pristine navy pantsuit with a blue tailored shirt.

"Very pro," he told her.

"Yeah, I decided the miniskirt and crop top wouldn't be appropriate at the station."

"Do you even own a miniskirt or crop top?" he asked her.

"Okay, no. I thought I might be early and start coffee—"

"They'll have it at the station."

"They'll have tea. And I—"

"They'll have coffee," he assured her. "Maybe it will be bad, as it often is in stations across the US, but they'll have it."

She grinned. "As you say."

"You slept well?" he asked her.

"Like a rock."

'You're welcome," he told her, and she laughed. "Let's go!"

When they headed down, Carly cried out with delight. They had a kitchen, but the hotel still had a complimentary coffee/tea/cocoa station. She instantly veered away to brew herself—and then him—a cup of coffee for the road.

"Okay, cool. This is really good and…thank you!"

"You're welcome!"

Once they were on the way, she looked serious as she asked him, "Where do you think the facial recognition they've apparently pulled from all the video might take us?"

"Well, if the man you saw at Graystone Castle, the man who Aaron Miller told us was there *before* you checked in, was proven to be the same man who was at the café—using the computer that brought up the dark-web site—they might have been able to get an identity on him. If so, we have found our H. H. Holmes Society creator."

"A man who won't have his own castle," Carly surmised.

"Maybe, maybe not," Luke said.

She turned to him. "I don't think he does. Rather, I believe he's playing the role of Holmes at earlier stages in his life. Maybe he's doing some grave robbing—"

"Much harder these days than in Holmes's era," Luke reminded her.

"Or he's scamming the rich for their pensions or their holdings, perhaps hoping to take over some form of castle or, in true Holmes fashion, build his own."

"I think he already has a base," Luke said.

"But then where does he find the time to visit others and the internet cafés?" Carly asked.

"He has management."

"Would he trust people?"

"If, like Holmes, only he knew the true extent of the castle he's created."

"If you hired and fired people the way Holmes was doing in the 1800s, you'd be facing a zillion lawsuits."

"Holmes did face lawsuits and that's how he was finally brought down. After Pitezel's death, the insurance agency hired the Pinkertons to go after Holmes, and the Pinkertons were the ones who found him. He was arrested first for having stolen a horse once—ages before—in Texas, but he'd also made use of an accomplice he'd promised to pay and ended up stiffing, and so the man turned on him. So, he killed Pitezel instead of substituting a corpse as he had promised his accomplice he would do, and told Pitezel's wife that he was in hiding, of course. To 'help her out' he traveled with three of the Pitezel children so that he could eventually reunite them with their mother and Pitezel whenever it was safe for them all to meet. But he cut up the boy and burned his body and gassed the girls and buried them—authorities found them after Holmes was arrested."

"I've seen all the information, too, and it broke my heart to see the reenactment of Mrs. Pitezel on the stand, giving witness against Holmes and crying her eyes out," Carly said. "That's the hardest, I think, even though it was well over a hundred years ago now, thinking that Holmes could have killed those children without blinking!"

"You've read what he wrote from prison, right?" Luke asked.

"Yeah, yeah, the devil had been standing by his mother's side, and as his execution date drew near, he could see his own face expanding as if he was truly turning into a devil."

"'I was born with the devil in me,'" Luke quoted. "'I could not help the fact that I was a murderer, no more than a poet can escape the inspiration to sing.'"

"Whatever! He was truly a monster and one was enough!" Carly said.

They had reached the station and headed in. A pleasant desk officer greeted them and told them, "Campbell is still in with Clayton Moore. But he's had Ben Pratt sitting in an interrogation room, letting him just sit on purpose, so that you could go in whenever you arrived."

They thanked her and walked along a hallway. A guard stood outside the interrogation room, and he nodded to the two of them before opening the door for them.

"Tap, call, anything to draw my attention, should the need be," the young man told them gravely.

Luke thanked him.

He didn't think they were going to need help against Ben Pratt, who had required trickery and a knife or a gun when he meant to take someone down.

And he surely had no weapon now.

"About time!" the man announced as they entered the room.

They sat across from him at the table that offered nothing except rings for chains and cuffs.

Ben Pratt had both wrists in cuffs attached to the rings.

"This is cruel punishment! Complete brutality. I will demand counsel."

"If you demand counsel, we can stop right now," Carly told him.

"What? They've had me chained to this bloody table for hours now, and you think I'm not going to smear your faces in a swath of lies?" he demanded.

Luke looked at Carly and shrugged. She understood his silent decision and stood as he did.

"Wait, what? I have!" Pratt exclaimed. "I've been sitting here for hours!"

"Well, be that as it may," Carly told him, "we just need to hear your swath of lies." She smiled sweetly. "We're not in Edinburgh that often, you know, being Yankees. And there is so much that can be done in the city!"

"What do you want? I'm innocent of everything, everything—except for having been terrified for my own life!" Pratt insisted.

They both stared at him.

"My life, and that of my poor sainted mother!" Pratt exclaimed. "Aye, that's it, the problem, don't you see? He threatened not just to kill me but me mum! And she's a good woman, she is, deserves nothing bad happen to her!"

"Do you think he has a mother?" Luke asked Carly.

She had her phone out, quickly pulling up the police records now accessible to them and then smiling at the man.

"Your poor sainted mother died ten years ago from a heart condition," she told Pratt. "Luke, let's go. This is going to be worthless."

"No! No! Stay here. Talk to me."

"All right," Luke said. "We won't stay long," he promised

Carly. "Talk to us, tell us what else we need to know. Oh, has anyone told you? At the least, I'm afraid, you'll go down all on your own for attempted murder. Poison was discovered in the drink you gave Herr Grunewald."

He sat back, grinning. "Well, Carly, dear Carly! You took the drink from the man. Perhaps you will go down for attempted murder!" he told her.

"Mr. Pratt, I do realize we're Americans, but British criminal law and American criminal law are not so different—" Carly began.

But she was interrupted by a spate of laughter. "What? You're going to take the death penalty off the table. Good heavens, this is a truly civilized nation! No death penalty."

"Maybe you could see the light of day again," Luke said. He turned to Carly. "He really is useless."

"Useless!" Pratt raged. "Useless! I'm the face, man. I'm the charm. I'm the magic man. People see me, they talk to me, they love me, they believe in me!"

Carly looked at Luke. "Wow. Can't wait to tell Clayton Moore he was the useless one!"

"Moore owns the place, Moore had the money to put into the place, to hire the right people—and fire them—when fixing up our tunnel and the chutes and... Moore had money," Pratt said. "But he had nothing, nothing at all, until he found me."

"How did he find you?" Luke asked.

Pratt leaned back, smiling, then allowing a scowl to touch his lips as he was jerked back by the fact he was chained to the table. He snarled and his expression was hideous. "The website, of course."

"It's down now, you know," Luke said with a shrug.

"Even as we're sitting here, it's back up or will be," Pratt assured him.

"But let me get this straight. You were on the website, and you saw a man with a Georgian manor house was looking for a lackey?" Luke asked. Counting him in as secondary now seemed to be the best ploy against him.

"No!" Pratt snapped. "Partner, a partner. I didn't have the finances—Clayton did. He had a way for us to get more and more money if he just had…had the Holmes charm and cunning down. He didn't. He desperately needed me."

"Okay, so you are guilty of multiple murders, kidnapping, fraud and all the rest, then, right? You're recorded here, so… you want legal help, now is the time to claim your innocence. Wait!" Luke said, looking at Carly. "He just said he was a full partner, the charm and cunning and coercion needed for the two of them to operate as true Holmes acolytes."

There was a moment when the man's expression wasn't angry in the least, just betrayed confusion.

Luke pressed the advantage. "Such a fool!" he told Carly, shaking his head. "Poor Ben didn't realize at all he was about to be used just as Pitezel was used all those years ago. There would have been an insurance scam—or maybe poor Herr Grunewald's property was supposed to go in Ben's name, and then Ben, of course, would have everything in the name of his honored benefactor, Clayton Moore. Then…hmm. Interesting terrain so close around here! Ben could have fallen to an agonizing death, broken to bits upon the rocks as he pitched downward from one of the heights."

"Better yet!" Carly added. "He could have plunged straight from the rocks into the loch—and been mauled to death finally by the Loch Ness Monster!"

"No, no, I was a full partner. Clayton was never going to kill me!" Pratt protested.

Luke looked at Carly and they laughed together.

"He wasn't!" Pratt insisted.

"He is the idiot of the duo," Carly said. She turned and smiled at Ben Pratt. "You're a lucky man. You will live. I don't think we can help you. There's murder and conspiracy to commit murder and kidnapping and fraud and, wow, I don't even know what else. There's nothing this idiot can tell us we don't already know, and I believe they really do have life without parole here. Of course, he might worry just a little. I mean…prisoners kill other prisoners here, too, right, just like in the United States? We have gangs, lots of gangs, but then again, we were all founded on the same law and people are people no matter where they are in the world…"

"This is Great Britain! We're civilized," Pratt said. But he was looking worse and worse.

"Sure. Hmm, remember Edward I at Berwick? All those bloody battles… Oh, yeah, everyone here is more decent than in the States. Oh, wait. This is the land of Burke and Hare—"

"Stop it!" Pratt snapped.

"Sure. We're out of here," Luke said.

Luke and Carly stood and he smiled and indicated the door to her. She headed right for it with him behind.

"Wait!" Pratt called.

He was sounding a little pathetic now.

Luke knew he had to be honest. "We can't give you immunity. The charges are too many and too heinous. But we can possibly help when it comes to where you're being held and how you're being held."

Pratt was shaking his head. "He—he did. Clayton. He had me befriend Herr Grunewald so that he would sign over his estates after his death… I was Gunther's friend. His good, his close friend. Then he started talking to Mary Nelson all the time. She was good to him, and Clayton was already intrigued by her. First we had to get her out of the way. Clayton probably wanted her anyway for his table or his rack, and it was easy enough for him to walk her through the forest and intrigue her with the hole in the rock and…"

He stopped speaking. He looked from Carly to Luke and back to Carly again.

"Help me."

"We'll talk to our counterparts and see what we can do," Luke promised him.

He indicated the door again; Carly nodded.

"I can really help you if you really help me!" Pratt pleaded.

"You've just told us what we need, and we do intend to help you to the best of our ability and the law," Luke said.

"No, no…you don't know all of it."

"What don't we know?" Carly asked, sitting again. Luke stood behind her, waiting.

"You don't know about the real Holmes!" Pratt told them.

"The real Holmes?" Carly asked.

Pratt nodded strenuously. "He's alive. He survived his hanging, and he's been alive all this time. And he told us he lives and survives because the members of his society keep blood running, and when blood runs, he draws energy and life from it and sometimes—"

He broke off suddenly, wincing, as if terrified of what he had been about to say.

Carly reached across the table and set her hand gently on his where it lay near the hook that held his shackle.

"Don't be afraid, Ben. You may be a prisoner, but you're a prisoner surrounded by Police Scotland, the National Crime Agency and even the FBI. Someone has lied to you and used you. Holmes is not alive. Years ago, one of his descendants began research on Holmes's life—real name Herman Mudgett—and anthropologists and other scientists were there when Holmes's body was exhumed. DNA proved that it was the real Holmes. He did not escape death. Did you believe you were seeing a spirit or—"

"No! A flesh-and-blood man. He helped Clayton in many of the killings!" Pratt said.

Carly straightened, looking over at Luke.

They'd known someone had been keeping up the website—and that someone had visited Aaron Miller at Graystone Castle.

They'd known a man had been accessing the website at the café.

But now they did know more. They knew that whoever this person was, he most likely did not have his own "castle."

Rather, he was a voyeur on his own website, making use of all those who fell into his trap.

And yet that in itself seemed to be in contradiction to the man who was playing the role of the long-dead Holmes.

His followers should have been men like Holmes, psychopathic beyond a doubt, but a man who had excelled at school even as a child, who had acquired a medical degree and learned how to twist and turn the law in his own favor time and time again and managed to run and elude the authorities for a long time before making his fatal mistake.

Then again, he was operating a "society." Not all members could be brilliant, but they might well have what he didn't, property, the ability to con others out of money.

All things he could enjoy with those who would do his bidding.

"Thank you," Luke said simply. "We'll do what we can."

He and Carly left the room.

Brendan Campbell had been watching the interview through the one-way glass, and he was waiting for them in the hall.

"We must find this man," he told them. He gritted his teeth, shaking his head. "The bloody monster is in Scotland! We now know of several sightings. We've pinned down an image with help from your folk across the pond, but we're still seeking the truth."

"The truth?" Carly asked him.

"The truth. We found an ID for him. He isn't real. We're seeking the truth."

"What was on the identification you found?" Luke asked.

"The false ID by which he entered the country," Campbell told them. "Herman Mudgett!" He shook his head. "How the hell he flew with that name—"

"The entire world doesn't know the names of historic killers," Luke reminded him. "But if you knew his name—"

"And there could be another Herman Mudgett out there. A man named Jeff Mudgett, a wonderful writer, discovered he was the man's descendant when he was forty years old and started investigating and did amazing work on following every trail out there—but the point there is that the surname is a viable surname and I looked it up. There are over a thousand-something people in the United States alone with the surname. So…if our impostor had a passport that went through all checks, he must have bought himself a good one and there's no one to blame for not knowing that the pseudonym might be a play on a historic human monster known as Holmes," Carly said. She glanced quickly at Luke.

"I believe we have come to know the current monster too well—and not well enough at all. You're right. Forgive me my impatience. Just when I saw what our tech pros discovered, it just… I feel that he has so flaunted all this in our faces, and while we've stopped many of his followers, we don't even know how many are out there," Campbell said.

Luke understood. The man was angry with himself and, yes, it was incredibly frustrating and worse to know that the man must truly enjoy the fact that he'd dared to use such a passport—and walked through airports without comment.

"We need Carly to see what we have, but since we ran the facial recognition and came up with a passport matching the facial images we captured off the surveillance footage, it's most likely. But we'll feel more solid, Carly, if you believe it was the man you saw at Graystone Castle," Campbell finished.

"Whenever you wish," she assured him.

He nodded. "Clayton Moore is in another interrogation room.

Ah, and we seldom have our prisoners sit as those two are sitting. But with the body count we're having due to these Society members, we're taking no chances. The expression, I believe, is 'desperate times call for desperate measures.'"

"I can look at the footage that's been singled out first. I don't mind leaving Clayton Moore to sit cuffed and chained to a table," Carly told him.

Campbell started to respond and lowered his head instead. "Come to the conference room, please."

They followed him to a large room where there were a multitude of screens and three computer experts at their station.

They looked up when Campbell entered, asking, "We've what we need?"

"Aye, sir," a young man said, nodding to Carly and Luke.

"I shall introduce you all," Campbell said. "The young lad here is Duncan McSorley," he said, indicating who had spoken, a young blond man with a lean face and visible respect for those around him. "And next to him, Liz Anderson," he continued, pointing out a young woman of about thirty with dark auburn hair. "And, last, never least, the illustrious Ian Muir—we call these three our computer technicians and, sometimes, our superior data analysts, but then, of course, they've been working with your people through Angela and through the group, well, they are quite magnificent."

"Aye, indeed, we try!" Ian Muir said. Like his coworkers, he was young, with a great smile to go with his flaming red hair.

"And you are all deeply appreciated," Luke said, nodding to the trio. He understood computers. He could figure out any phone in a matter of seconds.

But sometimes, the magic he saw others perform on a computer amazed him. He was grateful, truly, for their work.

The young man, Duncan, who appeared to be the head of the trio, rose to point to a screen. "These are the images we've managed to acquire, separate and enhance, along with the capture of a passport bearing the same image—and the name Herman Mudgett."

"Carly, Luke!"

Their names were called from the screen, and he and Carly both paused to look at the one screen that offered a conference call.

A man waved to the two of them.

"Jackson," Luke acknowledged, smiling and nodding. He remembered the words he used so often with Carly—*we're not alone.*

Jackson, of course, was juggling several cases, but he always managed to be on top of everything; Luke wondered how he handled it all.

"Between us, we've gotten good information and, at the very least, a suspect."

"And there he is," Carly murmured.

Luke studied the image that was brought up of their suspect's passport.

The image did not appear on an American passport.

"It's German," he murmured. "A German passport."

"German passport," Carly repeated.

"Which does not mean that the man is a German national, just that he's good at getting passports that pass for the real thing," Jackson said.

"Right, because the name originated in England in the early 1300s and went through many spellings which, according to several sources, meant 'son of Margaret,'" she murmured. "Not that it means he's an Englishman either."

Luke looked over at her, arching a brow.

"I looked the name up when we were studying different aspects of the original Holmes," she said, and she turned to the techs and quickly added, "and, please, just use my given name, Carly!"

"Aye, great, thanks," Duncan said, his *r*'s rolling handsomely.

"And remember, we're Duncan, Ian and Liz. Okay. The man is clean-shaven in every image we've gotten, but according to our understanding, he appeared among his society with a full mustache."

She shook her head. "Yes, this is… I didn't stare at the man forever, so it's not as if his face is indelibly frozen into my mind. But, yes, this looks like him. The eyes. I do remember his eyes."

"All right," Duncan said. "Here's another—artist's rendering done by your own amazing coworker, lovely lass named Maisie."

"She *is* amazing," Carly murmured. "I have worked with her before."

"She is quite wonderful!" Liz agreed.

"I'll make sure she knows that you've appreciated her work," Jackson assured them. "What's important is where it's gotten us."

Duncan clicked a control he held in his hand. One of the images captured on film had been enhanced with the goatee that appeared in most pictures seen of the historical figure.

Carly nodded. "You've found him," she told the group.

"Well, we found a passport for the arrival of a man who is playing a dangerous game with his own identity. He could have run into someone who knew the name," Duncan said.

"But that's half the man's pleasure, considering himself to be far cleverer than anyone around him," Carly mused.

"Any recent sightings of him?" Luke asked.

"Not in the last two days. Apparently, in the café, he put a virus into the computers and then enjoyed a stroll down the Royal Mile," Liz told them.

"I've sent everything we have out to the National Crime Agency and every force we have in the country," Campbell said.

"We've alerted Mason and Della in France and they're following leads there. They've discovered one would-be follower and taken him down, but they're headed to Marseille now, following more disappearances. However, they've been informed, of course, that until the last day or so, at the very least, we believe that the man behind it all is here," Jackson informed them.

Luke shook his head. "Jackson, whoever this guy is, he'll know. He'll know by now that we have his likeness. And he'll change it up. He may even have more passports and show up in another country soon."

"We're all aware that he might move with the speed of light," Jackson said. "But his confidence is amazing. I don't believe he'll have done so yet, but as I've said, we have Mason and Della on alert—and every country out there in and around the EU."

"If only he'd move on!" Campbell murmured. He seemed to give himself a mental shake that sent a slight shiver through his body before he turned to them and said, "Not that I wish him on any other country—nay, I want to stop him here. Jackson, we appreciate your people. And everyone needs to be aware our fine lads and lass here will stay on this in every way possible. I doubt if there's anything more that can be gained from Clayton Moore, but we do have him in an interrogation room, waiting."

Luke looked at Carly, who looked at Jackson.

"Can't hurt, Carly," Jackson said. "We'll all keep anything we learn moving to all parties as quickly as we get it. For now... let's trust in a team effort that will bring this monster down."

"Thank you, Jackson!" Campbell said.

"And thank you. Angela is working it from our end nonstop, and she'll keep in touch with Duncan and his people."

"And you're always just a speed dial away!" Luke said.

Jackson grinned, saluted, and the screen he was on went blank.

"And now..." Luke murmured, looking over at Carly. She gave him a nod and he glanced back at Campbell. "I'm going to suggest that we send Carly in alone and observe. I believe that Clayton Moore signed on to the whole Holmes thing and considers himself superior to all others—and especially women." He smiled at her. "Too bad for him he doesn't begin to comprehend the strength in the 'fairer' sex."

"I'll take a go at him, sir," she told Campbell. "Though I think that we already know everything we might get out of him."

Campbell nodded to them. "Duncan?" he said quietly.

"We are continuing to go through every bed-and-breakfast, inn, hostel, hotel and rooming house in Scotland and the British Isles, sir."

"Thank you!" Campbell told them.

Then he walked them down the hall, indicating two doors. A guard stood before one of them and he nodded solemnly to Campbell.

"Special Agent MacDonald will be going in," Campbell said. "Special Agent Kendrick will be in the observation room. If anything—"

"Aye, sir! I'll be on the alert and wary, sir!" the guard said.

Carly smiled at him, nodded to Luke and Campbell, and walked on in.

Just as Ben Pratt had been, Clayton Moore was wearing handcuffs that were attached to the rings on the table.

He was set up a bit differently, though. She'd shot him in the shoulder. His wound had been treated and was bandaged and his arm was in a sling, making his position awkward with his wrist in shackles.

She saw him a second before he saw her.

He appeared aggravated, weary and perhaps very uncomfortable from the way he'd been sitting for so long, though it appeared that his wound had been given consideration.

He straightened when he saw her, a smile coming to his face but not beginning to touch the hatred in his eyes.

"I should be in a hospital."

"Oh, I can see they treated your injury," she said.

He smiled. The malice in his eyes was almost palpable, and

though he barely moved, he did edge an inch toward her when he spit out his threat.

"You just don't know what's coming, do you? You just don't know. Lady, you are still going to die. You will die because you think you're clever, you think you're good. But you're just another bitch, to be used, tossed out. He will come. He knows you're coming for him, but he will get you, and you are the one who will die, slowly, and in agony. He will see that your blood runs and that you feel every single thing as he chops you up and feeds you to the flames!"

CHAPTER TEN

He was only human. Listening to the threat, the venom, the hatred and the longing that came out of Clayton Moore's mouth struck something deep inside Luke.

Most law enforcement officials were good. Some did get carried away, and anyone toeing the line knew that it was necessary to clean the ranks. Now and then an officer or agent got through who reveled in the power of wielding a weapon, who saw an abuse of power as justified.

Luke knew all that. He also knew that anger was a human emotion.

One that he needed to tamp down at that moment.

But to his surprise, Brendan Campbell, standing at his side, let loose with a string of oaths and turned to him. "Are you going to let—"

"Sir, I'm sorry—even in the United States, I'm not allowed to clock a prisoner under interrogation. Nor am I worried— Carly MacDonald is a top-notch agent who can handle herself."

He was still going in. Just not at that moment. Sometimes, it was best when anger simmered—and allowed a bit of logic to work with it.

And he was right about one thing—Carly knew how to handle herself.

She laughed, shaking her head as she sat down, leaning slightly toward him. "Well, it's my understanding that you may also be tried in the United States—and we do have the death penalty, and this murder conspiracy association of yours qualifies you for it. I won't be delivering your execution, of course, but I will be behind the glass watching as they bring you in, tie you down and put those needles in your arms. I mean, we're not supposed to be cruel and unusual, but knowing what's happening to you, seeing all the steps...pretty grisly!"

"I will not be tried in the United States! This is Britain."

"Yes, but we have extradition treaties, and with what we're discovering about your relationship with the man claiming to be Holmes—"

"Holmes is dead!"

"Oh, come now! You just said he's alive and walking around—and he's going to get me. Your local accomplice has been telling us all about him! And he's an American, from what I understand."

"He is not!"

"That's not what Ben Pratt said."

"Pratt is an idiot!"

"You're claiming he's a Scot?"

"He's a man of the world! He's..."

He paused again, leaning toward her. "He was never just a man. He was always something different. He can't be explained. But he's out there."

"So, you have been conspiring with him. You're making it so easy for me to see that you get a lethal injection. I guess it is more humane than the electric chair. Oh! And more humane than hanging. I read that when Holmes was executed, his neck didn't break—that he was strangled and dangled on the rope for at least fifteen minutes. But rest assured. The lethal injection will be better than that!"

"No! You're…you're going to die. Bloody, awful, terrible!"

"We're all going to die one day. But…"

Carly still managed to appear to be completely amused, which was throwing Clayton Moore into a frenzy of anger, which was in turn causing him to spurt out words he might not be intending.

"You're going to beat me to it!" she promised.

Moore strenuously shook his head. "He is out there and he knows about you and he will find you and it will be the death of you. And I don't care what agents or officers or whatever are with you, or where they come from… He will get you!"

"Really? How does he know about me?" she asked.

"He just knows! He knows that—"

"He was there when we were in the tunnel, when Luke and Campbell and I brought you down!" Carly said.

Moore smiled, thinking he was getting the upper hand again.

"He saw you. He knew that…"

"That you intended to torture and kill me?" she asked pleasantly.

He sat back, refusing to answer.

Luke decided he should go in. He nodded to Campbell, left the observation room, then nodded to the guard, who opened the door to the interrogation room and let him enter.

"So, Carly," he said, as if he hadn't been listening, "did you let him know they intend to bring charges against him in the United States, and we've already started the ball rolling, asking about the governments coming to an agreement? And frankly, of course, I do know how civilized Britain is, but every law enforcement officer thinks that if the death warrant has ever been necessary, this is one of those times!"

Moore frowned. He was growing worried. The man enjoyed delivering death; he didn't want to die himself.

"You're out of your mind! That's not British law."

Luke smiled. "No, it's American law. I suppose there is a way for you to stay in the United Kingdom—it won't get you out of a life sentence, but who knows. With good behavior... I don't know British law that well, so there might be hope. Except that you don't seem to want to serve your sentence here in the UK. I mean, if you did—"

"What do you mean?"

"Well, you're threatening an American federal agent, right? And you do know this guy who created and runs the website, so...maybe you could live by telling us what you know about him."

"No, I...uh... I'm not a rat!"

"Better a live rat than a dead goose!" Carly said.

"No, no, he'll get you—he'll get you and this woman."

They had him confused, and even if they'd been lying, lying was allowed. And they didn't know British law, so...

"I sincerely doubt it. And if he's so immortal and so ethereal and cool, what would it hurt if you told us about him?" Luke asked.

Again, Clayton Moore seemed confused.

"He... You're right. It doesn't matter. He'll kill you both."

"He is an American, right? That's what Pratt said."

"Pratt is an idiot. Yes, he was born in America. But he's lived all over the world, here, in France, in Germany... London. He... he told me that in his earlier years, he was Jack the Ripper— and that he sold the body parts that he took from the whores." He paused to look at Carly. "Maybe he'll sell your body parts."

"Well, that's one thing we won't do," Carly said. "After you're dead, we'll just bury you in a potter's field somewhere."

"I don't know," Luke said. "Maybe his body could go for use in medical science."

"No!" Moore protested.

Carly smiled at Luke. They were definitely throwing the man off—but they needed more.

"You think you've gotten to me. You think that I will describe him—" Moore began.

"Oh, no, we don't need you to describe him," Luke said. "We have plenty of pictures of him. Oh, come to think of it, we even have his passport."

"I guess he's real enough since he needs that passport."

Moore looked completely confused. "No, you don't have his passport—"

"Oh, but we do. We have a picture of it from the last time he entered the country," Luke told him. "And when he tries to board a ship or a plane next time—"

"Don't count on that helping you," Moore said. "He's busy. He is very busy here."

"Interesting. I thought he'd be heading to France, and we'd get him—"

Moore waved a hand in the air. "No. You will not get him through his passport. The man is very busy. And he has everything in France under control."

"Oh, well. Thanks," Luke told him.

"Have a nice rest of your day," Carly said, smiling. "Well, enjoy all the days that you can!"

"No, wait—I helped you. Right? I helped you. You can't charge me in America. I need to stay right here!"

"Did he help us?" Luke asked Carly.

"Well—"

"He's here! He's here. I can tell you that without being a rat because I can't tell you exactly where he is. I know he still has business here and I told you that you were foolish to think that you'd catch him using his passport because he isn't going anywhere."

"I guess he did help us," Carly said. She was at the door but turned back. "Oh, Luke, yes, he did help us, because if he was leaving the country, he might have a dozen passports under a dozen different names, so..."

"Wait, no!" Moore protested, looking down at his hands suddenly. "I am a rat, I am a rat—"

"A live rat and not a dead goose," Carly said. "See you, Clayton."

She was out of the room and Luke gave Clayton Moore one last smile before joining her and thanking the guard who had opened the door to let them leave.

Campbell was out in the hall, waiting for them.

"I wonder that such a being exists in human form," he said, shaking his head. "But I applaud you. I think that you've drawn from the man what he knows. I'm not so sure on that American/British agreement on extradition in such a case—"

"I'm rather sure that since his crimes were committed on British soil that it would be out of the question," Luke said, shrugging with a grimace.

"Aye. But your man fell for it!" Campbell said. "Again, my American friends, hats off to you. And now I have new orders for you."

"Oh?" Carly said. "They've found—"

"Our best—and your best—tech crews are scrounging records. It seems, from what you've gained from this man Aaron, that our would-be Holmes does his best work on the web—finding those who need an outlet for their sick minds," Campbell said. "This man has some means of support since he manages to travel easily enough, though I believe he most probably preys upon his followers for most of his creature comforts—whatever he may be, the man needs to eat. We have some of our best investigators from the National Crime Agency and Police Scotland crawling the streets in every city, but I believe that it's going to be our techs who give us the next big break. They study locations, owners, managers, hotels, inns, B and Bs, anything, including retirement housing, where Duncan suggested such a man might make a financial killing—poor choice of words, but a friendly soul trying to help a lonely person who is half-way out the door..."

"Kudos to Duncan!" Carly murmured. "So—"

"Jackson Crow has suggested you get rest with what remains of the day. In his exact words, you are to 'shake it off' before it gets worse," Campbell said. "Take time to breathe. Field Director Crow has suggested that this is going to get worse before it gets better."

Luke nodded and turned to Carly. "He's right. Let's go breathe."

Carly nodded but turned to Campbell. "If anything is discovered—"

"You will be alerted immediately," Campbell assured her.

He gave them a salute and turned away.

Outside and in the car, Luke noted that it was three in the afternoon.

"What do you want to do?" he asked Carly.

"I don't know," she murmured.

"I have suggestions," he said.

She turned to him, laughing. "Okay... I get your drift, but there is a lot of the day left! Maybe we should stop by the café—"

"There's not actually a lot of the day left, and we've been told to 'shake it off,' but we can stop by the café, see what we see, maybe just wander the Royal Mall or head—"

"We've both been here. We know the sights."

"Ah, but we don't know them together."

She smiled. "That's true. But the café—"

"What part of 'breathe a little' didn't you get?" he teased. "Not to worry. I'll get us parked again at the hotel first—we'll walk to the café and see the sights on the way back, or go somewhere or don't go somewhere, okay?"

"Wow, you are accommodating," she said.

"I try! Except..."

"Except?"

"I think we need to see how Mason and Della are doing."

"Oh, we agree on that! I'll get a text off to the two— I don't want to put them in a bad position if they're…"

"In one hotel or another run by a heinous killer who could be chatting with them?" Luke asked her.

"Exactly."

She had her phone out and put the text through.

Her phone rang almost immediately after she had sent the message and she flashed Luke a smile, answering the phone.

"Mason, we know we're in touch all way round, but— Oh, I'm with Luke and I'm putting you on speaker."

Luke nodded his thanks to her.

"Heading to our fourth little hotel in the wine region," Mason told them. "Della is with me—we're all on speaker."

"Good work, guys," Della said.

"Hey, Della, and thanks. But on your end—nothing so far?" Luke asked.

"We *know* that something is going on down here," Mason said. "A young couple from New Zealand has disappeared in the area, as well as two young women from Paris and an older gentleman from Milan. And so far, since Luke first discovered the Society, we've been to a charming B and B, a larger hotel and a manor from before the French Revolution—we've been to the basements, searched for tunnels, worked with local undercovers, and…"

"But nothing?" Luke asked.

"I can't say *nothing*. We've had some great wine, wonderful French cuisine and seen a lot of beautiful countryside," Mason said dryly. "You two have brought down several members, and thanks to you on the ground and our scientific data folk, we're briefed on everything going on. We'd be up there in a flash if we weren't hoping—"

"To find people alive, we know!" Carly said softly, glancing over at Luke.

"Yeah. We know the investigation called us to the area, but it's popular for all those who are touring the wine region. Some folks like to come in groups, and others are either French speaking or learned enough through classes or online to manage romantic tours on their own," Mason said.

"Like the two of you?" Luke asked lightly.

"Hey, what says romance like a sweet little room in wine country?" Della asked. "Hmm. Maybe not worrying about cameras in the room or gas being piped in?"

"You got a point," Luke said.

"The site is down now but we don't know for how long," Mason said. "And neither do we know just how far this has gone. I understand that Campbell is on your speed dial and that cooperation in Scotland with the local police and with the National Crime Agency has been like clockwork."

"Yes. I thought Campbell might be a stoic jerk at first—" Luke began.

"But he's pretty cool!" Carly said.

"Hopefully, we're on to it here. And if so, we'll be up there before the last ink dries on the paperwork here," Mason told them.

"Well, if you get in trouble there, I think we're a short plane ride to Paris from Edinburgh and we can drive out to that Champagne region pretty fast."

"Luke, we have the two of you looking for the head of the snake—we know he's there. We don't know how many idiots around the world have joined this society. Get the head of the snake. We're good, and Jackson and Angela are covering it all at the top, information central."

"Well, enjoy the wine," Luke said.

"And you have yourselves a good Scot's whiskey," Della said.

"Or enjoy some haggis," Mason suggested.

"I think Carly turned into a pescatarian when we got here," Luke joked. "Well, we are headed back to the café off Royal—"

"Cops are covering it," Mason reminded him.

"Yeah, but we're, um, 'breathing' until the cyber folks get back to us," Luke said. "Except that Carly thinks that if we try the tourist stuff on the Mile we might—"

"See H. H. Holmes walking down the street?" Mason asked.

"He won't be H. H. Holmes, Herman Mudgett or any of the aliases we know," Carly said. "The thing is, I did see him, so…"

"Got it. You won't be happy if you don't do something pro-active," Mason said. "All right, then, make Campbell and Jackson your first calls—make me the third."

"Got it," Carly assured him.

They reached the hotel and Luke parked the car. "So, you want coffee that badly?" he asked her.

"Maybe I'll have tea. And a scone. They do have delicious scones," Carly said.

"You know, we should be looking for a good restaurant. We're really messing up the sleeping-and-eating thing here—dinner is the next meal on the plate," Luke said.

"You don't want to go to the café?" she asked.

He smiled and shrugged. "Actually, I do. They have sand-wiches, too, so…"

They headed to the café. Luke walked to the counter to order. Carly found a seat at the long table where computers were set up for use. He waited for their tray while she slid a credit card into the computer and began working on it. He watched curi-ously; she was online, but she seemed to be giving her atten-tion to the table.

He found a little dining table and set their tray down and walked over to her. He placed a hand on her shoulder.

No one in the café remotely resembled the man who might have created the H. H. Holmes Society.

But you never knew who might be one of his Society members.

"Hey, got the food," he told her. "You never said tea or cof-fee, so I went with tea, have milk and sugar on the side."

The middle-aged man at the next computer looked up at him.

Luke smiled broadly. "We're engaged, but it was all so fast—I'm just now learning how she takes her tea!" he said.

The man grinned at him. "Aye, laddie, important to know!"

"You okay?" He leaned closer to Carly, feeling her hair brush his face.

"Yeah, got it, ready for food!" she said. "Wait, why don't you sit down and read this page, too?" she suggested.

She, too, turned to the man at her side. "We're tourists—I guess that's obvious."

"And great to have you to our beautiful and fair city," the man said. "You must start with the castle—"

"Oh, we've done the castle and it is wonderful. And the whole city is as you said. It is beautiful!" Carly agreed. "It's often considered to be the prettiest capital in all Europe—maybe in all the world!"

She stood so that Luke could take the chair.

"We've done so much here and we love it all and could do it all, but I was just reading about the vaults—it all sounds fascinating!" Carly said.

She was on a web page that offered tours—including tours of the Edinburgh vaults.

He read the page, though he already knew most of what it could tell him. Ghost-tour enthusiasts loved the vaults—Scotland was really good at ghostly, ghastly, history. So many wars through so many years. Clans banding together, clans at odds. Of course, the tunnels came comparatively late in Edinburgh history, but they offered myriad stories about criminal empires. Then entered the modern world…

And perhaps offered a place where monsters slipped in.

He carefully erased their work on the computer—although knowing that anything on a computer lasted forever in the ethernet somewhere—and smiled at the gentleman who was seated next to him.

"Now, you can't possibly ha' done all that there is to do in our beautiful city without going underground. There's the Surgeons' Hall Museum, Parliament House, The Writers' Museum, the National War Museum of Scotland and so, so much more!" the man suggested.

Luke smiled again. The man was probably about fifty with graying auburn hair, deep blue eyes and a kindly smile. As outgoing and friendly as he seemed to be, Luke thought that he was a little nervous.

He decided to keep an eye on the man.

"Thank you! We'll look into it all," he said, and headed over to the table to find Carly.

"Making friends wherever we go?" she teased.

"Hey, he was your friend. I think he was much happier with you, and I don't think that he's keen on the vaults. So, what caused your fascination with them?" he asked her quietly.

"Someone was on that computer earlier today looking up the history of the vault, and then witchcraft in Scotland, geography and more," Carly said, speaking softly as well. "Luke, I've been down there before and it is a fascinating history. The vaults were created in the nineteen arches of South Bridge around 1788, and at first, supposedly, it was great. They were used for shops and all kinds of aboveboard enterprises—there were taverns, tradespeople—but it was also an enclosed space, and in time, you probably had air so rank it was just about impossible to breathe. Anyway—"

"After about thirty years, the homeless found a place there, criminals found a place there, and it was all…not good. Water came in—it was never properly sealed. All in all, there are about one hundred and twenty arches and—"

"Hey! You do know that Mason and Della went down to the arches—in search of the last serial killer assigned to the Blackbird division of the Krewe?"

"I read their briefs before I was officially transferred to the

Blackbird division," Luke said. "But why your fascination? We were talking about a stroll down the Mile and—"

"Luke, someone wasn't just looking up information about the vaults. There's an impression in the table—someone was writing it down."

"The word *vaults*?"

Carly shook her head. "I don't know if it's important or not, and you can go look—but it's as if they were writing on a piece of paper, something they needed to know or remember or pass on, and they pressed so hard that it etched into the wood."

"Okay. There are ghost tours down there every night of the week and possibly every day—I just know that they're offered by every tour company in the city."

"But only some of the vaults are open for tours—we can call Mason and Della and find out what they found out. There are rumors—"

"Right. *Rumors* that Burke and Hare used the vaults for some of their murderous activity, but no scholars say that there's any evidence that points in that direction," Luke reminded her.

"You don't think it's possible that a would-be H. H. Holmes is using the vaults?" Carly asked him.

"Oh, I didn't say that at all," he replied. "I'm just playing the devil's advocate. I came here with a college buddy, Peter, just before we both enlisted in the military. He was a major sports guy and was big on the vaults because one of his rugby heroes had something to do with the excavation, and we spent a couple of nights there. The vaults were closed, if I remember right, between about 1835 and 1875. Here's why my friend Peter knew so much. A tunnel was found leading to them in the 1980s by a rugby player, Norrie Rowan, and it's a cool story because he used the tunnel he had discovered to help a Romanian player escape the Romanian Secret Police before their revolution in 1989. Rowan pressed forward with an excavation and tons of rubble were removed, along with all manner of fascinating artifacts, a door to the past—and, of course, the vaults were open again and became big business."

"And now the tunnels are used for tours, parties and whatever else the city decides they should be used for. Luke! They were rediscovered because someone found a tunnel. They know of about one hundred and twenty vaults. Someone here, in this café—"

"Might have been a tourist really intrigued and wanting a ghost tour of the tunnels," Luke warned her.

She gave him a serious frown and he smiled, saying softly, "I told you, I'm just playing devil's advocate. But, with everything that goes on down there, it's hard to imagine that someone has created their own little dungeon in the vaults when the vaults are in use, not always, but known to the city, known to the police..."

"I know that."

"And still?"

She nodded. "I know. But if we could understand the vaults—"

"We might get a better understanding of what's around them. Carly, there's no real reason to suspect that this man is using the vaults in any way. Remember, they were excavated over thirty years ago," Luke reminded her.

"I do know that. But the violence of geography in the past is half of the reason why this city—and this country—is so beautiful. The rising cliffs, the dipping green valleys, the rugged rock, the rich forests. All right, Arthur's Seat in Holyrood Park is the highest point, by the extinct volcano, but it's all rugged and up and down and mountains and..."

"And there's plenty of room for all manner of things going on below the ground," Luke agreed.

"Which makes it all so hard," Carly said. "We can't dig up the entire city. But! Like the natural tunnel was something that Clayton could use—creating a man-made tunnel from his house to join it—it's hardly shocking when you do think of the terrain," Carly explained.

"Well, our H. H. Holmes Society creator does need a real base," Luke said.

"Maybe we could take a ghost tour anyway! We are tourists," Carly reminded him before looking up, smiling and falling silent.

The man who had been next to her at the computer table was walking over to them.

"This isn't rightly my place, but you seem like a decent couple and...there was a lad sitting at that computer before you came in. He was getting angry, looking for a site he couldn't seem to find. Then he got a message in his email and he seemed happy again and he pulled up everything that he could find on the vaults, just like you were doing. And he was whispering under his breath, 'Bloody vaults, bloody vaults!' and he seemed so happy I thought that he was going to crow like a rooster. I called the cops before you came in. But I don't know if they understood... The kid could have meant nothing. The kid could have meant something. I had a feeling that he was looking for that site on what they call the dark web and couldn't find it, but..."

He lifted his hands.

"I'm sorry. I mean, you're a couple, but... I watch the news. I think you should be careful."

"Sir, thank you."

They both stood and Carly said softly, "Sir, could we have your name and information? I'm sure that the police do deal with young people being young people and chatter on the web that might not mean anything. But..."

She broke off, glancing at Luke.

"We know the right people for you to talk to, sir," Luke said, looking at Carly.

"My family is from here—we've been in the States awhile, but my grandparents still have friends and family here," she said.

"And one that we know is with the National Crime Agency," Luke offered.

"We can give him a call."

The man looked around nervously. "I don't know—"

"He'll keep you out of it, sir, I promise, but he may want to speak with you."

Carly was looking at him.

They'd also want the security footage from the café, and fast.

Carly had her phone out. When it was answered at the other end, she played it perfectly.

"Uncle Brendan! Met a friend at the café and I think you might want a word with him. Can you come and, you know, act like a normal human being greeting friends?"

On the other end, Brendan Campbell apparently agreed.

Carly ended the call. The Brit crew at headquarters had kept their link with the café cameras so they could easily find whoever had been next to the older gentleman earlier.

There would also be a tech in shortly to go through the computer again.

"May I get you some coffee, sir, tea?" Luke asked him, offering him a hand. "Luke Kendrick, sir, and this is my girlfriend, Carly MacDonald."

"Pleased," the gentleman said. "Michael MacDuff, and…yes, lad, I may as well have me a cup of coffee and sit."

There were four chairs at the table and Luke indicated that MacDuff should take his seat while he went to purchase the coffee.

Carly gave him a smile and he sat. He was evidently nervous. Buying more coffee, Luke kept an eye on the table. Carly was doing her best to put him at ease—without mentioning the fact that they were American law enforcement.

As Luke returned to the table, MacDuff was speaking nervously to Carly.

"I don't… I mean, I don't suppose that this man is a danger in the world when we're surrounded by others, but I have seen the news and we're on the nervous side. I believe that the media everywhere in the world can seek out the sensational, but in this… Police spokesmen and women have been on the air, warning everyone just about everywhere about the website. Maybe the very warnings put those with sick and evil minds on the hunt for the dark web, but the warnings are taken to heart by others. Of course, we all have that thing wherein we think, aye! Sad, tragic, but though it happens to others, it wouldnae happen to me. But this. Even the young lads and lasses, they've taken this to heart, not slipping off to quiet places for their naughtiness."

"Sir, I believe you'll be fine."

"And I may have been talking out of line, but…" The man hesitated. "I may be maligning a youth who is just excited about the vaults or…"

"How do you know he was looking for a site on the dark web?" Luke asked.

"He kept muttering beneath his breath, but I could hear him. He kept saying he knew what the hell he was doing and how he could get anywhere he wanted to go, there had to be something wrong with the site and that it had to go back up. Then, like I said, he got an email that pleased him, he stopped his angry muttering and banging on the keys!"

"And still…" MacDuff said miserably.

"It's all right, really. I know that my uncle Brendan is going to be grateful for any lead," Carly assured him.

She had barely spoken when MacDuff sat back in his seat. He was facing the door, which opened.

He stared at the man who entered.

Who was staring at him.

It wasn't the would-be Holmes. It was a man in his early twenties, barely past his teenage years. He was wearing a band T-shirt and jeans and a denim jacket.

He smiled at MacDuff and pulled a weapon from a holster beneath his denim jacket and took aim at the older man.

"Nosy old bloody bastard!" he cried.

MacDuff just stared.

"Down!" Carly shouted.

Screams echoed throughout the café.

MacDuff hadn't moved; Carly jumped on him, bringing him to the floor.

And Luke drew his Glock and fired. There was simply no choice.

The sound of the bullet exploding sounded like thunder in the small confines of the charming café.

CHAPTER ELEVEN

Carly winced inwardly.

Chaos. Absolute chaos.

People were screaming in the café and people were screaming out on the street.

She had managed to get MacDuff down beneath the table, and while the screaming went on, he lay there, staring up at her.

Thankfully, the young man was not a hardened criminal savvy in the way of guns; Luke had fired quickly and the man never had a chance to pull his trigger.

But like others...he was screaming.

But thankfully, the café had been under police observation since they'd discovered that their suspect had used one of their computers. Two officers in plain clothes immediately arrived, urging that people remain calm; EMTs arrived for the man who had threatened to shoot MacDuff.

Carly was trying to calm MacDuff down when one of the officers came to her. "Special Agent MacDonald, we need to get you and Special Agent Kendrick out of here right now—news media personnel are out in the street. We've been informed that we can't let you be seen, not if you're to continue to investigate undercover. If you'll come this way..."

"Ah, lass, don't—" MacDuff began.

"Sir, we'll get you out with them," the officer said.

He ushered the three of them out through the back. Carly wondered how they were going to manage the reporters but remembered that only MacDuff had any inkling of what he'd been warning them about—and why a deranged young man would want to shoot him. And yet it was insane. He had stood on a well-traveled street with many witnesses around while brandishing a gun he surely wasn't allowed to possess.

They might get answers. He was being rushed to the hospital, but an EMT had told them it didn't appear that his vital organs had been struck.

Campbell had arrived on the scene himself; he had dealt with the reporters both anxious and horrified that someone had attempted murder—with a gun—at the café.

But he returned to his station soon after they did and asked that Carly and Luke—and MacDuff—join him in his office.

"Guns have been banned here since 1997. We had the Dunblane Massacre and the amendment was passed... A lad like that shouldn't have had a gun. I mean, this isn't America—it's not the Wild West!" MacDuff said, sitting in a chair in Campbell's office. "That kid...he had a gun. A gun! I was certain I was a bloody goner. I mean, the lass had said that she was your kin, not...and..."

MacDuff broke off, shaking his head. "He came back for me as if he'd gone out and then...then thought that I might know something and..."

"Mr. MacDuff, we're grateful that you were worried about a couple when you heard someone muttering about the vaults," Campbell told him. "And sorry that you were noted by a criminal, one brandishing a weapon."

"I heard them mention the word *vault*, and then after what

I had heard the bloke muttering, I just felt that I had to warn the couple. I'm glad I did! He came back, but if I would have walked out on the street instead of taking the time, he would have ambushed me and there would have been no defense for me!" MacDuff said. "Lad," he began, turning to Luke, then shaking his head with confusion. "Sorry—Special Agent. I understand—I am grateful for my life!" he told Luke. "And…" He paused and turned to Carly. "…you…you saved my life as well. If he'd gotten a shot off… Why? Dearest Lord above us! Is he part of this terror plaguing us now, terrorizing so many places now?"

"We believe he might have been seduced by the website that had been up, aye," Campbell said. "You did humanity a service, sir."

"And," Carly assured him, "your actions are the kind that remind us all that while there are those who have criminal intent, there are way more good and decent people in the world."

He smiled at her. "Thank you."

Campbell cleared his throat. "What we need from you, sir, is any tiny scrap of information he might have given you."

"I can't tell you much more than I have, I'm afraid," MacDuff said. "He just kept muttering. He was annoyed." He frowned for a minute. "I enjoy a good cup of tea and checking my email at the café, but I'm often surprised by the people who talk to themselves when they're online, softly and muttering most of the time, and innocuous. But this fellow…he was annoyed, shaking his head, hitting keys and hitting them harder, as if that could change the internet. But then he found something in his email, I believe, that seemed to make it better. Maybe the 'creator' has cameras, or has hacked the security system… I don't know. But I believe, as I told the agents here, that he muttered the word *vault*."

Campbell glanced at Carly and Luke. "None of that made the news. And, sir," he told MacDuff, "thanks to you, we are forewarned and will take measures to discover whoever else might be involved in whatever it is that is going on. We'll see that an officer gets you home, sir."

MacDuff smiled and nodded and turned to Carly and Luke again. "My dear Yanks, please know that you will be forever welcome in my home, should you ever need a place in Edinburgh."

He stood and Carly, Luke and Brendan Campbell stood as well.

A uniformed officer from Police Scotland was waiting to escort the man safely home. But at the door, MacDuff turned back, hugging Carly, hesitating, and then giving Luke a hug as well. Luke grinned and nodded at the man and he left.

"Sit, please," Campbell said.

They did so. "The vaults are an active part of the city. During festivals and holidays, many are in use, and as you know, there are many tours—ghost tours, mostly," he said, as if disdainful of such things. "Ah, well, they do deal with history, and the history is intriguing. I don't see how anyone could be using the vaults—"

"We don't think that anyone is using an actual vault. As you know, sir, the city has heights, streets have sometimes been built over ancient streets, and that…"

"Underground Edinburgh. Aye, there is a great deal to be discovered below ground level," he said wearily. "But—"

"What we're thinking is that there is a tunnel or chamber that might be accessed through or near the vaults," Luke said.

"I believe that it's more than possible," Carly added. "We know that the man who appeared in the museum at Graystone Castle was at the café. The man Luke had to shoot—"

"His name was Brian Blackstone," Campbell told him. "His ID was on him and the lad has led a troubled life and a sad one, I fear, though that is no excuse to harm others. But one can see how this man's mind might have been warped. He's from London, father strangled his mother when he was about four and he bounced around from family member to family member, got into some deep trouble with drugs in school, managed to graduate, but did some time for theft. Oh, there was an incident when he was seventeen—other lads beat him to a pulp in a toilet at a concert."

"I'm not a psychologist," Carly said, "but in this case, I do imagine that he could have been easily seduced by a site that, in his mind, helped him find revenge against all who wronged him."

Campbell nodded. "We have our people searching for the email that promised him power. Oh, by the way, Special Agent Kendrick, you are quite the shot. You saved everyone from harm by catching the man's shoulder in a manner that wouldn't allow him to get a shot off himself while still keeping him alive. He may, when stabilized, provide us with a lead, and any lead now will be of great service."

Carly leaned toward him. "I believe it's late now for any of the tours, but—"

"You needn't fear. We have discreetly as possible placed law enforcement throughout any area being visited." He hesitated, leaning back. "The vaults—underground. I believe your own people were involved in an incident last year, Agents Carter and Hamilton. Again, the modern world!" Campbell said, shaking his head. "Perhaps they—"

"They're in France, sir," Luke reminded him. "There is someone who has joined the H. H. Holmes Society there in the wine region."

"Of course. Of course. I know that. Well, for this evening, again, you've done us great service. Please, rest, get some sleep. We are staying on the wary side, my friends. You've yet to get caught up. Trust in our National Crime Agency and Police Scotland. We'll let nothing happen with the rest of this night!" Campbell promised. "And the hospital assures me that you'll be able to see our young would-be assassin in the morning—they have him sedated now, but you may question after rounds in the morning. Again, for tonight…my people will be vigilant and in mass."

"Sir," Luke assured him, "I have seldom worked with finer forces."

With a smile, Campbell nodded.

They'd come in with the police and were driven back to their hotel in a police vehicle, but Luke asked that they be dropped off a block from the hotel. They were still just tourists.

When they arrived at their hotel and passed through the lobby, they could see on the large-screen TV at the far rear of the room that it was still tuned in to the news.

And the news was about a young lad taking a gun to customers at a café, and someone else with a gun taking down the young man, presumably one of the few officers authorized to carry a gun, but there had been so much chaos and confusion that eyewitness reports conflicted. The police had announced that, thankfully, an officer had been enjoying a cup of tea when it had gone down and he'd been able to stop the perpetrator before any of the customers in the café could be hurt. The young man with the gun was recovering at a local hospital.

"Another one," Carly murmured to Luke as they headed to their suite. "Is he going to be able to tell us anything that we don't know? That kid isn't our real website creator."

"I don't know. I am curious to speak with him. I don't think that this young man is our usual psychopath. I believe that he even wanted to kill Mr. MacDuff, but that he was afraid that he had given away too much of himself while he was at the computer. He may be our best link. Then again, I doubt he has money or a castle or a manor with a dungeon, so he wouldn't be someone for our website creator to use—either as a voyeur or participant in torture and murder. Still…" Luke said. "I just feel that there may be something he can say."

"He couldn't find the website to 'chat' with others—but he

appeared happy, according to MacDuff, when he got an email. Do you think that the head of our snake actually emailed him?" Carly asked.

"I know one thing."

"What's that?"

"I'll be better at answering questions after a little more sleep."

"Just sleep?" she teased.

"Well, we got some walking in today, but not a lot of exercise. And they say…"

"Hmm. Exercise."

They headed to the suite. When the door closed, Carly turned into his arms. "They do have a gym at this hotel and it is available 24/7…"

"Now, that's true," he agreed, slipping his arms around her and her jacket from her shoulders.

It fell to the floor.

He shrugged, a teasing light in his eyes. His own jacket fell to the floor.

"But…ah, we'd have to get dressed again, and that just seems like such a hassle!"

"Oh, so true! I guess we could find something to do right here."

"Well, walking a few more steps. Easier to exercise on a mattress than on a hard floor! Oh! Wait, your place or mine?"

Carly laughed, swirling around and heading for the first bedroom, her bedroom in their suite, and he followed. They kept laughing, fumbling with one another's clothing, buttons and zippers, and she laughed again as he keeled over when his jeans caught in a tangle and he landed hard on the bed.

She joined him.

And it was…sweet, gentle, urgent…

The kind of exercise that could sweep away the day, leaving her basking in impossible physical comfort and release, then just loving the act of lying beside his hot, damp body, feeling his arm around her as she rested against his chest.

His fingers moved through her hair but neither one of them spoke. They just lay there, "exercise" kicking in and allowing for sleep...

But Carly dreamed. She saw the young man at the door to the café again. Saw the strange look on his face, and then forgetting that look, knowing that from their positions, Luke would be the one to draw and she had to get MacDuff down before a bullet soared through him...

...over a *vault*.

The vaults?

Or another form of vault. It was true—there was so much of Edinburgh to be discovered on what was now street level. Mary King's Close, where victims of disease had been shut in, left to survive or die because the city had to stop the deadly spread...

Foundations, basements...

So many, many places...

She was surprised to waken with a jolt, suddenly convinced that *vault* didn't mean what she'd thought originally.

They needed to see Brian Blackstone.

She didn't realize that she'd jolted herself awake until she heard Luke speak softly to her.

"Remember, if we're going to be any good at this, we need to let it go sometimes."

She turned to him, grinning weakly. "I did let it go. I exercised like crazy! But I guess in my sleep that my mind went back to it and...we need to talk to Brian Blackstone."

"I believe we can do so in just a few hours," he reminded her.

"I don't think he was talking about *the* vaults," Carly said.

Luke sat up on an elbow, looking down at her with a curious frown.

"You were convinced that we needed to go to *the* vaults."

"Now I'm thinking that the term *vaults* might be to throw

anyone off if they weren't part of the Society but became aware of information going around."

"Possibly. I still think…"

"What?"

"When the site goes back up, I need to become a member."

Carly arched a brow.

"I need to be someone like Brian Blackstone. A man who has been used and abused by society. Maybe my mother poisoned my father and I was pushed around and made fun of by the other boys at grade school—my mother wasn't caught because she learned poisoning that wasn't easily detectable at autopsy, but I knew what she had done and I hated her and I started to think that all women were alike and deserved to die before they killed others," he reflected.

"The site is down."

"And since we haven't caught him yet, it will go back up."

"He won't be using the café anymore," Carly said.

"No. We could try the library," Luke said. "I should say 'libraries.' There are several, including several that are dog friendly."

"As great as I think that is, we don't need to worry about a dog right now."

"You do like dogs, right?"

"Of course. But we don't—"

"I'm just curious," Luke said.

She paused, grinning at that. "What? If I didn't like dogs, this was going to be a quick affair?"

"Hmm. Well, neither here nor there. I knew you liked dogs. You have tremendous compassion for people, and when someone can be that empathetic, it's extremely unlikely that they're not going to like and care for animals."

"I know great people who would never purposely hurt an animal, but they don't particularly want one. Wait! Do you have a dog? Now, that's just cruel when you're going away all the time!"

He smiled. "I had a fantastic German shepherd named, cleverly, of course, Heinz, such a good German name for a wonderful dog with a thousand talents. I was in and out of the military and, like so many of us, spent a year with the police force before entering the academy. I could be with him, but in that time, of course, he grew older."

"Oh, no! He passed away?"

"No, he's having a remarkably wonderful life with my young nephew, Mark. Heinz is old for a German shepherd now, but my nephew adores him, and he's in the best of hands—my brother Sean is a veterinarian."

"Oh!"

"At this stage of his life, Heinz gets me when I'm in town, and he gets more love than you'd ever imagine from my brother's family."

"Hmm. One FBI agent and one veterinarian," Carly said. "Your parents did well."

He grinned. "And a professor of archaeology and, a bit different, a successful actress."

"What?"

"My sister, Justine, is in Hollywood. She's been in several movies but the theater is her true love—she's great at it."

"Justine Kendrick," Carly murmured.

"You've heard of her?"

Carly smiled. "Believe it or not. A few years back, she was with a traveling Shakespeare troupe, right?"

"She was."

"Incredible Lady Macbeth!"

"Thanks! I'll let her know."

"A veterinarian, a professor, an actress and an FBI agent— now, that's different. Intriguing choices in very different careers," Carly said. "Okay, wait, actress and FBI agent. Maybe not so different—not after hearing about the person you're going to become when we find a connection to our Holmes Society creator!"

He smiled, leaning back. "I think I might put a call through to one of my siblings for help."

"You may need help as an actor," Carly said thoughtfully.

Luke laughed. "No, I was thinking about my brother the professor. When Andy and I were visiting the vaults way back when, he was already heading into archaeology. He may have some insights for us. I'll give it a few hours. It's, um…" He paused, looking at his watch. "It's close to six in the morning here, which I think makes it something like midnight in Virginia, so I'll give him a chance to get sleep since he probably has a full agenda."

"He teaches. Does he still—"

"Yep, every few years he goes on a dig somewhere," Luke told her.

"It must be cool to have a family like that," Carly murmured.

"Mostly. Oh, we could fight like cats and dogs when we were kids—drove our parents crazy. But now, yeah, it's pretty cool. I was torn about Heinz when Jackson wanted me to head to Europe for Blackbird, but there was my brother, assuring me. Or rather, informing me that at his age, Heinz was going to be a lot better off with him and his family. I had to agree."

"Nice."

"You're an only child?"

"I am. Thankfully lots of cousins."

"The best of both worlds. People to play with who go home when you get tired of them!"

She smiled, curling into his arms. "It's 6:00 a.m. here. Time to rise and shine!"

"Or exercise quickly and then rise and shine."

"Minuteman, eh?" she teased.

"When the minutes call for it!" he assured her.

Carly laughed, and moments later, though she was tempted to hold close to him, she sprang out of bed, heading for the shower.

She dressed quickly and discovered that he'd returned to his own room and showered and dressed just as quickly.

He even had coffee going.

"Coffee and tea downstairs," she reminded him.

"Carly, it's still not even seven. They're not going to let us into the hospital—"

He broke off, frowning, pulling his phone from his pocket and studying it.

"Luke?"

"Ah, yes, well. So, we can head to the hospital. Apparently, young Mr. Blackstone was sedated from the time he went in, slept well through the night, and woke switching between bouts of screaming at himself and sobbing. They're anxious for us to come in—I believe the hospital wants the man charged and transferred to a facility better able to cope with his mental condition as soon as possible. But while those arrangements are being made, we're more than welcome to speak with him."

"Let's go!"

Because the young man had been wounded in an incident still in the paperwork region of being resolved, he was allowed to be in a general facility. That being said, Luke and Carly found that two Police Scotland officers were watching over his room and were informed that an officer accompanied every doctor, nurse, aide or orderly who entered. Despite his injury, Brian Blackstone could be wild. He hadn't threatened violence toward any of them as yet, but in his stages of self-loathing, he "flopped like a fish," and they wanted to make sure that no one was injured by his flailing. One of the officers was older, probably close to retirement, but he was straight and strong and, Carly imagined, very capable. The other was younger, but as tall and sturdy looking as the older.

"We're good," Luke assured the officers.

"So, we've heard!" the older man assured him, grinning.

"Well, thanks so much," Luke told him. "I meant we are good to go in alone."

"Aye, then," the younger officer told them.

But Luke hesitated then, looking at Carly. "Maybe we should take this in two shifts. This time, we are talking about someone with some serious issues in his life."

"I take first?" Carly asked.

"Should one of us accompany her in case he becomes—" the younger officer began.

But Carly smiled as Luke laughed and assured him, "If he gets rowdy in any way, I promise you, we'll all feel badly for the guy!"

She nodded, lowered her head, then glanced at Luke, grateful for the pure confidence he had in her—and knowing it was real. And returned.

"Wait!" the older of the two officers said. "We can give you a mic so that we can capture whatever is going on in there—"

"That is fantastic," Luke replied.

"Here, there's a truly wee pin, if you just—" the younger officer began, producing a tiny wireless microphone and earbuds.

Carly took the microphone from him, smiling and setting the little pin under her jacket and hiding it from sight.

"Perfect," he told her. "We've two sets of listening devices—"

"Give him mine," the old officer said. "And the two of you pay heed!" he warned his junior and Luke.

"Thank you," Carly said to them, and entered the hospital room.

She was growing accustomed to interviewing people when they were attached to IVs or some other medical apparatus, but something about this young man seemed to speak to her heart. Maybe she knew too much about his past.

And maybe the past didn't count. She had known of many

people with horrible childhoods who had used their pain to rise above others in kindness and in their chosen fields.

And yet this was more understandable than the human beings without any kind of a sordid past who found it amusing to watch others suffer and die.

"You!" he said.

"Yeah, me."

She walked over to the bed. He laid his head back.

"You took over my computer next to that blabbermouth!"

"Blabbermouth?" Carly queried. "The man simply welcomed me to Scotland."

The young man on the bed shook his head, staring at the ceiling. "No, no, he was paying too much attention to me and he's not—" He stopped.

"Not what? Not a member of the Holmes Society? But, hey, the website is down, so maybe there is no more Society—"

"Oh, lady! Just because a website is down—that's no indication that something doesn't exist!"

"You're being used," Carly said flatly.

He wasn't looking at her; he still stared at the ceiling. He shook his head again.

"No. For once in my life, *I* wasn't going to be used. I was going to be doing the using. He promised me…"

"Well, who is 'he' and what did he promise you?" Carly asked.

He smiled finally, turning to look at her. "'He' is a genius, going by Holmes these days or, sometimes, Herman Mudgett. He knew about my past and he promised me that we'd get our hands on Geoffrey Culpepper and Joan Wakefield. Once I helped him, I'd be in and he'd make sure that I was able to repay everything that happened to me!"

"So, you've met this man going by Holmes or Mudgett?"

He grinned at her. "I'm not giving you anything against the man. He's a genius. He is the only person who cares and cares deeply for those who have been so tragically wronged in life."

"He's promised to help you get even with people who wronged you? But you were born in London and many of those people—"

"How do you know?" he demanded angrily.

"Because I'm basically a cop and—"

"You're an American!"

"This is true," she said patiently. "But—"

"Oh, bloody hell! I get it, aye, we know! He started in America, but his message is so resounding that he must cover the world!"

"His message to sick killers?" Carly asked.

"No! I am not a sick killer. You don't understand. Look at you! From the time you were a wee one, people likely fawned over you, telling you what a sweet and lovely child you were! No one would hurt you and men fell over themselves to gain a smile from you!"

"No, not exactly," Carly assured him. "And you're not a bad-looking man at all. In fact, one might consider you to be handsome."

"Me?"

He wasn't faking his surprise. Again, Carly couldn't help but feel empathy for the man. He truly had no self-esteem whatsoever.

His eyes lowered and he said, "Well, apparently, I wasn't such a charming bloke as far as Joan Wakefield was concerned."

"What did she do?"

"Teased me to the ends of the earth and then walked away right into the arms of that bloody bastard Culpepper. And they both looked back and laughed and laughed at me. He said, what was I, a total fool? I thought that a woman as beautiful as Joan could care for a worthless nothing like me? But it doesn't matter. Even with me here. It doesn't matter because *he* knows about them, and one of the things that the Society is sworn to do is to protect all members, carry through when someone fails."

"Interesting. I've met a few Society members. They weren't striking back at people who had wronged them. They were more like the original Holmes, into scamming money, making bodies disappear and murdering for the simple fun of it upon occasion," Carly informed him.

"I don't care about others. I care about Holmes!" He smiled suddenly, looking at her again. "You will never get him, you know. He's not just a man. He's—"

"Yeah, yeah. He escaped execution and is over a hundred and fifty years old and still wandering around looking like he's in his late thirties."

Brian Blackstone looked at her as if she was the one having mental problems. "You are so off! He isn't just a man. He's so much more than that. He's the memory of things that need to be done, of the fact that revenge can be sweet, that it's a way for a man to become a man. He's an ideal!"

"An ideal who murdered children?" she asked.

"Not this Holmes."

"I told you. I've met his followers who murder for the simple pleasure of watching other human beings suffer."

"And they are just the riffraff and will fall by the wayside. Holmes is testing them all, and those, like those you have met, mean nothing."

"Well, they mean nothing once they've been caught."

He shook his head again as if she just didn't get it—and maybe never would.

"Fools will get caught. He gives them a chance. He observes their operations. And, if he discovers that they don't understand the true meaning of the Society, he moves on, and whatever happens to them at that point, well, it happens to them."

"Hmm. First, you let yourself be caught, but he... Okay, I think I see. He's testing people. He visits those who are creating murder castles, be they just rooms underground somewhere—or even aboveground somewhere—but if they aren't the true recruits he's looking for—like you—he moves on, and if they get caught, well, they get caught and there's just nothing he can do about it," Carly said.

"You're beginning to get it," Brian said, smiling grimly and nodding.

"So, in other words, someone has a vault somewhere—" Carly began.

"A friend," he interrupted, smiling.

"And that friend is the one who emailed you and finally made you smile when you couldn't find the H. H. Holmes Society site on the dark web."

"Yeah."

"So, there's a vault somewhere not too, too far from the café—between there and the Edinburgh Vaults—where you were going to head, and this friend of yours was going to help you get even with people who hurt you?"

"A friend, and Holmes himself!" Brian assured her.

"So, you've met him."

"I would have met him," he said bitterly. "I...ruined it. I was almost there but I panicked and then I... Then your idiot friend shot me!"

"You were about to shoot an innocent man," she pointed out. "By the way, where and when did you get that gun?"

He started to laugh. "You think I should give up a gun dealer? Someone would shoot to kill if I was to do that!"

"I think the police will find the truth whether you help or not, and if they know that you're in police custody, well, they'll assume that you gave them up. And you know what? As against the law as it is to be dealing firearms illegally, I don't care so much about that. The police will find the truth—don't ever underestimate that. I've gotten to meet several of the men and women of Police Scotland and the National Crime Agency. Bright law enforcement. I—"

He interrupted her with raucous laughter. "If they're so bright, why do you need me?"

She shrugged. "Okay." She turned to leave the room.

And again, it worked.

"Hey!"

She spun around and walked over to him. "Where did you intend to go when you left the café?" she demanded, standing right over him.

"I don't know!"

"You don't know where you were going?"

"That's just it—I panicked and I went back to shoot the old man and... I never received the final instructions on how to reach the vault!"

He was distressed, obviously telling the truth.

"All right. Thank you," she said.

He suddenly burst into tears. "He should have killed me! Your friend should have killed me. I am worthless. I couldn't even do that right."

"No one is worthless," she told him. "No one. You are not worthless. You led a hard life. You almost killed a man, but thankfully you didn't. You have a chance. A chance at a real life if you learn to ignore people who think they're better. Brian, please! You have a chance."

He had almost killed a man. He had longed for revenge, real revenge, against those who had wronged him.

But he was a broken human being and she couldn't help but feel sorry for him.

"My—my cell phone," he said.

"Do the police have it?" she asked.

"It was a burner and I tossed it in the trash when I left the café. If...if you bring it to me, I can show you the email I finally received."

She took his hand gently and squeezed it. "They'll search for it. And the help you give us will be noted—if you're that scared about turning people in, there are agencies that can help you. You can have a new name—and a new life. And you are a fine-looking young man. Don't let rude, cruel people who think that they're superior slip into your mind again. Forget revenge. Don't think about the past and concentrate on the future. Brian, seriously, you have a chance at life, at a real life."

"Will…will you see me again?" he asked. "I know that you're with that other bloke, but…"

"I will see you again. People can be friends," she told him.

"Still? Even though I was going to shoot that man?"

"I'm not so sure you were certain that you were going to pull that trigger at all."

Maybe he would have pulled the trigger.

She would never know.

But maybe there really was hope for him, too.

"I need to get the information about your phone to the police," she said. "But I promise, I will check on you again. So will Luke."

"The fellow who shot me."

"He couldn't take a chance."

"He didn't kill me."

"He hates killing, avoids it any chance he can."

He was thoughtful, staring at the ceiling, not sobbing, but still crying, tears slipping down his cheeks.

"Maybe he should, though. Maybe he should. If he finds Holmes…"

"If law enforcement finds the man, we will do everything in our power to arrest him and bring him to justice," she promised.

"He'd kill you in the blink of an eye," he reminded her.

She smiled. "He's a criminal—we're law enforcement," she said.

"But don't let him kill you."

"Brian, we're taught that if we're in imminent danger of death, we are allowed to save our own lives, so thank you, but don't fret on our account. Take this time to get better! Watch fun TV, sitcoms, or history pieces about great discoveries. I can arrange for you to have books if you like."

He wiped the tears from his cheeks and gave her a smile at last. "I'd best stick with comedies for the time, I imagine. Or books about space… Once upon a time, I thought that I might be an astronaut!"

"How old are you?" she asked him.

"Twenty-three."

"The years stretch ahead of you," she said. "I'll talk to our associates here. I believe you may be required to do some time, but even then—you can start on a real education. Brian—"

"I could have a life," he whispered. "I'm young, and…"

He seemed confused.

"There are people out there who will help you," she said firmly. "Take care. Rest, get better and, please, help us, help Police Scotland and the National Crime Agency with anything that you have."

He nodded and said, "A computer geek could find it, but the password on the email is banshee1097#, username BBStone," he told her.

"Thank you! Thank you!" she told him.

He nodded gravely. She smiled and managed to escape the room at last.

Luke and the two men from Police Scotland were staring at her as she came out of the room.

She had become so engrossed in her conversation with Brian Blackstone that she had forgotten they were listening.

"Wow!" the younger officer said.

She winced slightly. "I really feel sorry for him—we heard about his past. But—"

"We already have people searching the rubbish for the phone," the older man assured her. "We'll have something from it. And we have an expert at the café—he's been trying to trace the history on the computer and find out what they can about this man's email and other emails that might be in his contacts."

"Thanks," Carly said. She looked at Luke. He was gazing at her, smiling very proudly, and it felt good.

"You okay?"

"I am. I just hope I'm not a liar," Carly said.

"You're not," the older officer assured her. "We do have agencies where he can be helped, and what he's done will help at his sentencing. And—"

He broke off, frowning, and Luke glanced at Carly—both their phones were vibrating and they pulled them out as the older officer looked from his partner to Carly and Luke.

"The website. It's back up!" Luke said.

CHAPTER TWELVE

Carly stared at the computer screen in front of her; she was with Duncan, Ian and Liz while Luke made a call to his archaeologist brother, Andrew Kendrick.

They'd gone through Blackstone's email without any issue—as anyone might have done with his sign-in information—but the three in the computer room could trace locations and times as the average person might not do so easily.

"Carly, I wonder if we need to get you in to speak with Blackstone again," Duncan said, sitting back. "Earlier emails seem to have come from the Galway region, others are from here in Edinburgh and a few are from the Stirling area."

"Well, we know that until a day or so ago our Holmes Society creator was in Edinburgh," Luke said. "Did either of you find mention of vaults in any way?"

"No, but as I'm sure you've read, there are some freaky emails from someone calling himself 'BVLT' on the server—BVLT. Could be—"

"Bloody vaults?" Carly asked.

"I've heard stranger," Duncan said. "There is something here, one more place, and our man Blackstone was supposed to be involved in it. Maybe he was caught because this man—the head of it all—just doesn't care which of his followers falls by the wayside. But Galway..."

"Galway?" Luke asked. "Galway, Scotland?"

"Oh, come, you've heard of Sawney Bean?"

Luke frowned. "Yes, I've heard of Sawney, but isn't most of what people claim to be truth mostly legend?"

"Legend usually comes from something," Duncan said.

"And that is true," Luke agreed. "So—"

"Sawney Bean, born Alexander in East Lothian in the sixteenth century. He wasn't good at any of the trades and decided to find his own manner of survival. He met Black Agnes Douglas, renowned as being a vicious creature, accused of witchcraft, and together they left home and created a place in a deep cave on the coast between Girvan and Ballantrae. The story gets very creepy in several ways. They had six daughters and eight sons and thirty-plus grandchildren, the grandchildren being the result of the children in all ways—"

"Incest, if you didn't get that," Liz supplied, amused.

"Got it," Luke assured her.

"Anyway, they managed their great clan for well over twenty-five years, surviving off the land in a unique way, as in attacking unwary travelers, robbing them and—the really disturbing part—eating them. There are estimates that as many as a thousand people disappeared through the years until they attacked a man who was a warrior returning from a fair with his wife. The poor wife was sliced to ribbons by the women in the clan while the husband survived when others came upon the road. He went to the magistrate, and they believe that it was King James VI who arrived in a fury with dogs and a small army. Sawney and the clan were taken, and you can imagine that they weren't dealt with kindly. Supposedly the women were burned at the stake and the men met a similar fate, but in addition their reproductive parts were hacked off and they were slashed almost to death, left just alive enough to feel the burn of the flames."

"And it's all a legend," Liz reminded them.

"Excuse me," Luke said, gazing at his phone. "Call I need to make," he added, stepping out of the room.

"Legends, legends, legends," Liz murmured, watching Luke go.

"And legends are based—" Carly began.

"Usually, on some kind of truth," Liz agreed, grinning. "Different people tell the stories different ways, but in the end, it's about an incestuous clan that included a witch that resided for decades on ill-gotten gains and human flesh. So far, I've not heard of any members of our Holmes Society being cannibals."

"No, there was never a suggestion of cannibalism in any of the records we've gone through, and trust me, there were many, not to mention the research done by investigators through the years, one of those researchers who enlisted professionals being none other than a descendant," Carly murmured. "And yet—"

"*Toll-fuaraidh!*" Ian suddenly announced.

The others stared at him, but, apparently, Ian knew what he was saying.

"*Dungeon,*" Ian said. "Gaelic."

"Does he mention anything specific?" Carly asked. "Any basement can become a castle dungeon. Except..."

Duncan shook his head. "I've had many a friend who has worked at the Edinburgh Dungeon. Yes, it's one of our rather spooky attractions and not for the fainthearted, but they do a great job with both history and entertainment. For anyone into good, clean, spooky fun with a dose of our bloodier history thrown in, it's fantastic."

Carly grinned. "I've been there. And, yes, I agree—fun place, great 'scare actors' when I've been, and, yes, they do a great job putting the 'bloody' into Scottish history." She shook her head. "This man wouldn't be using a place that was constantly in motion. What I was thinking is that this place might be between the vaults and the tourist attraction. Places that are underground. At some point in time, there might have been other tunnels and rooms—or vaults—between them."

"Possibly. In your jargon, there's a bit more than a mile between the two, along the Carlton Road," Ian offered. "But I understand that you struck on something inside Blackstone and maybe he knows where—"

"I think he was expecting to receive further instructions when he left the café, but in his twisted mind, he thought Mr. MacDuff was a terrible threat to everything, and he had to do something about him. And thanks. For the conversion—I'm still horrible with kilometers!" Carly told him, smiling. "I wonder..."

"If it isn't just possible Blackstone might give you more?" Duncan asked.

At that moment, the door opened and Luke walked in.

"I've got something," he said, almost simultaneously with the four in the room saying, "We may have something!"

"Oh," Luke said. "You first."

"There's the Gaelic word for *dungeon* in one of the emails," Ian offered. "But, of course, we don't believe it's a reference to a pretty great tourist attraction—"

"But it is a reference to the underground, and the underground between a few of the tourist attractions and the Edinburgh Vaults," Luke said.

"How—" Duncan began.

"His brother is an archaeologist," Carly explained.

"But—" Liz began, confused.

"He's an American, yes," Luke said. "But he was here about seven years ago when the university sponsored a dig. There was only so much money, but they did find another street-beneath-a-street, some empty rooms down there that had artifacts dating back to the early 1700s. They stopped when they ran out of funds. The entrance was sealed off with the city council and university agreement that they'd get back to it, but funding, life and other things got in the way. According to Andy, there's a vennel or alleyway behind a small dress shop and the entry can be found there."

"No one watches it?" Carly asked him.

"Supposedly sealed—at the time of the dig or excavation, all three little shops that front the alley were just empty buildings, caught up in a recession, and the alley backs onto the walls of a major bank, and when I say 'walls,' I'm talking stone about ten feet high—Andy said that it was probably erected in the 1700s, too."

Duncan laughed, looking around at the others. "Well, here we've been half the day searching desperately through emails and web connections, and Luke made one phone call."

Luke grinned and shook his head. "Not true. My phone call might not have meant so much if it didn't seem that, at the very least, our information appeared to agree. Carly—"

"We're headed to the tunnels?"

"We are, and we'll be joined by Campbell and a few members of the old excavation team from some of the institutes of higher learning in the area," Luke told her.

"Okay, well…" Carly rose to join him, turning around to the computer trio to say, "Thank you!"

"We'll keep at it in every way," Duncan promised her.

"In every way!" Ian echoed, with Liz nodding her agreement in silence.

"Thanks," Carly murmured again.

She followed Luke out and they were soon in the car.

"How long before we're joined by the others?"

"They're getting it all together. Probably an hour or so."

"But we're heading out now?"

"I thought you might want to go dress shopping," he said, giving her a grin.

"Okay, why?"

"Because, according to Andrew, they found the entrance by

doing a lot of digging. And it's amazing how much things can change in a few years, but I think there might be more to it than that."

"Oh?"

Luke glanced her way again. "There was construction done on all the shops recently. Really recently. Within the last year. And it seems that part of the dress shop was built out a couple of feet into the vennel."

"Within the last year? Someone looked up ownership of the shop, right?"

He nodded. "It's owned by Margaret Crowley. She looks great on paper. Thirty years old, college degree in design, worked for an international chain store before she bought this place herself."

"Just this last year?" Carly asked.

"Right before the construction started," Luke said.

"So…you think that she's part of this?" Carly asked.

"Yeah."

"Okay, so—"

"I had Police Scotland check it out. The police and the National Crime Agency are clear to search the vennel, but since she owns the shop it's considered private property and, well, laws here are similar to laws in the United States when it comes to searching without a warrant."

"Maybe she would just agree."

"But if she didn't, we'd have no plan B."

"You want to break some laws?" Carly asked him. "We're guests in this country. If there's an angle, there's got to be a way to work it."

"Imminent danger," Luke said. "Also, I talked with Andy for a while—there are steps in the vennel leading to a higher 'ground' area. And as is evident in about the whole city, there might be anything just about anywhere, so many levels, so much that was topside that is now beneath the ground level as we know it."

"You think something from the store may lead into the area beneath the old stone steps?" she asked.

He nodded.

"So, your plan is…?"

He shrugged. "You look at dresses. I'll look around. And if I find something, I'll hope that our shopkeeper is distracted and I'll figure out how to get where I need to be."

"And if you find something?"

"Then you won't see me and you'll know to disappear into a dressing room and find me. Underground, I'm not at all sure we can text, so it may be a little blind. Anyway, grab some clothing. And if someone has been using an entrance to the tunnels from the store for illegal activities, well, it won't matter if Miss Crowley is missing a dress or two."

Carly smiled.

They parked and started walking to their destination. The storefront was like any storefront—mannequins were on display. The store was small, offering only one window. Carly paused to study the clothing offered.

"Well?"

"It's too bad our shopkeeper may be a criminal. She has good taste."

"Oh, good. Then you won't hate looking around too much."

They walked in, hand in hand, but Carly let out a gasp and walked over to a handsome denim pantsuit.

The shopkeeper, presumably Miss Crowley, was behind a counter at the rear of the store. The little shop was in two sections, a half wall separating them. The dressing rooms were at the back of one side, while there appeared to be an office behind the counter.

As she studied the pantsuit, Luke walked to the counter, smiling and greeting the young woman. "Hello. Lovely place you have here."

"Thank you," the young woman said. "May I help you? What are you and your lady looking for today?" she asked politely.

"I'm not sure," Luke said. "My girlfriend just fell in love with your window display. She says you have excellent taste. Oh, I'm sorry. I mean, whoever owns the store or creates the window displays—"

"That is me. I am Margaret Crowley, proprietor, and thank you very much," she said, returning his smile.

Carly studied the woman as she pretended to hold the pantsuit up, viewing it from different angles.

Margaret Crowley was attractive with auburn hair bobbed at her neck, frothy bangs and a slim, pretty face. She was about five-seven and built nicely, slim but shapely.

She looked like someone who might be a Holmes Society victim—not a member.

But then again...

"What's on the other side?" Luke asked. "Sports, evening wear?"

"I have some gorgeous dresses over there. Some are brand names and some are by local designers and seamstresses."

"Nice!" Luke told her. "I'll wander over!"

As he did, Carly approached the woman with the pantsuit, catching her attention lest she watch what Luke was doing.

"Hi. I just heard my boyfriend telling you I was in love with the display window. I was! You have the neatest stuff in here. I'm one of those people who really like the unusual. And, yes, this is a denim pantsuit, which should be ordinary, but the cut is great, the angles in the front of the jacket, the embroidery on the back... This is really lovely!"

"Ah, pantsuit—trouser suit, my dear, here in the UK. But by whatever name... Thank you! I take it you would like to try it on?"

"I'm a six in the United States and the one that I picked up would be too big. And I'm terrible at the UK sizes, I'm afraid. Would you mind helping me?"

"No, no, of course not. Let me find the equivalent of a size six for you," Margaret Crowley said. "I love that piece myself. And it is one of our local designs. You'll note the fabric is thin enough for comfort, but if you have a sweater on underneath, it's quite warm as well—which we do need now and again around here."

"I live in Virginia. We can get chilly, too," Carly said.

The woman was heading to the front of the shop. Luke could explore in the other area all that he wanted.

Margaret Crowley seemed happy to find Carly the right size. She produced it with a flourish. "There were only five of these made, so you should enjoy it!" she told her.

"May I try it on?" she asked politely.

As she did so, the little bell at the door rang. Carly couldn't have asked for better timing as two women, already bearing shopping bags, walked into the store.

"Of course, of course," Margaret Crowley said. "Please, back of the store just behind the wall there, and, as I told your boyfriend, there are some lovely gowns over there, too! If you'll excuse me."

"Of course!" Carly said, and Margaret Crowley gave her a quick smile and moved forward to welcome the new arrivals.

Carly hurried to the second section, looking for Luke.

She frowned, not seeing him anywhere.

"Psst! Carly. Here!"

She swung around. He was in the last of the fitting rooms. She arched a brow but he was reaching out to her. She headed in.

The little dressing room was crowded with the two of them in it. There was a hook for hangers, a small chair in the corner and a mirror.

"What are we doing in here?" Carly whispered.

Luke smiled at her and turned to the mirror, gripping it by the right side and leaning against the wall to pull at it.

The mirror opened and exposed raw wooden steps leading down to darkness.

"Okay!" Carly whispered.

She dropped the pantsuit on the chair and, as Luke held the mirror/door for her, started down the steps.

Into darkness.

But he was right behind her, drawing out his penlight and throwing its light over the steps—to the stone level beneath them.

"Was this where your brother came with his excavation team?" she asked, still whispering.

"I don't know." He trained the light on the long tunnel stretching before them, one that appeared to have been carved out of rock, with nothing there but darkness stretching ahead for what seemed like forever. But then Luke's light fell on an opening leading off toward the left, and another, one that led to the right.

"Left, right?" he queried.

"I'll take right…leading toward the street," she murmured.

"Left—might take me to an excavated area," he said.

Carly drew out her own light and cast the glow to the right, following her path into what seemed to be a side room, vestibule…

Or vault.

It was perhaps twelve feet by fifteen feet or so. Toward the rear of the room there was a large set of drawers, the kind that might be found in an office.

They weren't historic pieces but might have been found in an office shop that offered specialized sizes for different businesses.

She walked toward the drawers curiously, wondering what might be found inside. She opened the first and frowned, gritted her teeth and shook her head.

It was filled with different sizes of knives.

The second offered rope and tape.

She opened the third and froze.

There had been a smell in the tunnels, naturally. Beneath street level, no fresh air circulating...but...

The third drawer offered a body.

It had been there a long time. Wrapped in white sheeting, it appeared to be partially mummified and partially rotted. Swallowing hard, Carly moved the sheet from the face.

The flesh was sunken. Stretched too tightly over the bones. But an abundance of rich auburn hair surrounded the remains of the face and skull, making Carly think that the body had belonged to that of a woman, a young woman.

A perfect Holmes Society victim.

She turned to call out to Luke.

But she never let out a sound.

Margaret Crowley was standing there, pointing a gun at Carly's head.

"Where's the boy toy?" she demanded.

"I—I don't know," Carly said. Her reply was honest to a point. She knew he had gone in the opposite direction; she just didn't know where he might be right then.

She could draw quickly. She knew that she could.

But before this woman could fire her piece?

"I thought there was something about you two!" Margaret Crowley said. She shook her head. "But you did look like a loving couple out to shop and what man doesn't want to see his woman in nice clothing—before she takes it off, of course. Who are you? Police Scotland?"

"I swear to you. I am not Police Scotland."

"And I thought you were. I thought you were using an atrocious American accent to throw me off!"

"Sorry, it's the only accent I have."

"So, why are Americans delving into places where they shouldn't be?"

"I, uh, just tripped when I was putting my bag on the chair,"

Carly said. "I grabbed the mirror to steady myself and…well, it opened, and who could resist a staircase that leads underground? Listen, I didn't see anything—"

"Are you blind?"

"No!"

"Then that's obviously a body. Too bad you just had to trip and too bad you're so curious! I'm afraid I can't let you back up the steps now."

"Wait, wait, wait—we wanted to be part of it!" Carly claimed.

"Part of what?" the woman asked suspiciously.

Carly stood tall and stared at her. "What you're obviously part of. The H. H. Holmes Society!"

"What?" she demanded furiously. "No, no, I'm the only woman in this thing and I am so sorry—"

"You will be sorry! I spoke with *him* myself. I just didn't know that you were part of it when we came into the store."

"Sorry, I don't believe a word you're saying!"

Margaret Crowley was going to shoot. Carly had no recourse but to draw her own weapon and duck, hoping Crowley didn't really know what she was doing.

But she never had to fire herself.

Because Luke had appeared silently behind Margaret Crowley and set the barrel of his Glock hard against her temple.

"I really suggest you drop your weapon," he told her.

"No!" the woman screamed, her hand shaking, but her grip still strong. "No, no, I can't, I can't, I will not, I…"

Looking at Luke, and at the gun still pointed at her, the way that the woman's hand still shook, Carly didn't dare take a chance.

Dropping low, she took careful aim, making sure she avoided Luke and catching the woman in the hand with which she held the gun.

With a horrific scream, the woman dropped her weapon, grasping at her shattered hand and staggering back. She would have fallen to the floor had Luke not caught her and lowered her gently.

She sat there screaming vindictively, promising they would still die.

Luke had his gun still trained on her, but with his free hand, he had his phone out.

"You have to see what's in the drawer," Carly said, kicking the woman's weapon from her and stooping to retrieve it.

"You need to see what's in the rest of the place," he returned dryly before speaking to the receiver of his phone call. "We need a medic—" he began.

But a second man walked up behind him. Brendan Campbell.

"What is it with you Americans?" he demanded. "So much gunfire!"

"Well, I am sorry!" Carly said. "But I couldn't help but feel it was better I shoot her hand than she put a hole in my gut!"

Campbell was grinning. "All right. I'll let it go. Ambulance on the way. But, Miss Crowley! I am with the National Crime Agency and you are under arrest."

In between her screeches of pain, the woman began to laugh.

"I don't know what you're laughing about," Campbell said. "This place is riddled with bodies and you're—"

"Oh, you idiots!" she said.

"I don't think so. There are bodies down here," Luke said politely.

"A body in a drawer right here," Carly said.

"Miss!" Campbell said politely. "Lass, you're the one on the floor. My dear Miss Crowley, you're under arrest—"

He was interrupted by the violence of her laughter and then her words. "Miss Crowley? You go right ahead and arrest Margaret Crowley and have fun while you do it! She's the one in the drawer over there!" the woman announced.

She started to laugh again, and then to sob in pain.

Carly walked over to stand above her. Even below the earth, they could hear the blare of sirens. And other footsteps.

Campbell, of course, hadn't come alone.

"We're good here. We need a forensic team and an ME down here—several discoveries have been made. We need the medic here for this harpy as soon as possible," he told the two men who had come to the arched stone doorway of the cubicle or vault.

"Witch, ugly witch!" the woman on the floor screamed to Carly. "You'd look like a true pile of *shite* in that pantsuit."

Carly shrugged and walked over to her.

"I didn't really like it that much anyway," she told the woman. "But if that's Margaret Crowley in the drawer, just who are you?"

The woman laughed and laughed.

And then she managed to smile at them all, though tears ran down her face.

"Who am I? You haven't figured that out yet?" she demanded.

"Well, an impostor, obviously," Luke said.

"Who the bloody hell are you?" Campbell demanded, his tone impatient and angry.

"It's obvious!"

"Who?" Campbell roared.

"Why, sir, I am none other than H. H. Holmes himself!" she announced proudly.

Campbell stared at her with disgust, stepped by her and left the vault.

His foot caught her leg and she screamed again in agony.

"I am H. H. Holmes!" she screamed again.

"No, no, no, you're not," Luke said. He glanced over at Carly, indicating she should join him.

She did so. They walked out of the vault with her screaming after them.

"I am H. H. Holmes! I am! I am H. H. Holmes in the flesh!"

The woman was carrying on so loudly that for a minute, Carly thought the other sound she heard was an echo…

But it wasn't.

There was someone, somewhere in the underground, who was screaming as well…

Screaming desperately for help.

She looked at Luke.

"Get the troops searching!" he shouted.

Carly turned, stepping back into the vault. She ducked down by the still crying and shouting woman who had claimed to be the victim in the drawer.

"Where is she? Who do you have down here? Where is she?"

The woman began to laugh again.

"Where is she?"

"In the dungeon!" the woman said, sobbing and laughing. "She? Just she? Dear, dear. She's obviously in the dungeon! Dying, and *she* will die, trust me, before you can find her!"

CHAPTER THIRTEEN

Once, Luke thought, scientists had explored this section of the underground, discovering history, discovering the day-to-day lives of those who had lived centuries in the past. They had done research to improve contemporary knowledge of the past, of society, of history.

It seemed that in that long-ago day, there had been many little rooms off what had once been vennels between shops, homes and now…

The rooms, even those discovered by his brother's archaeology team, were being used as if they were part of a Holmes "castle." He'd discovered one room with vats of lye, another filled with gallons of bleach, another with a pile of bones.

But he hadn't found anyone living.

And though he couldn't blame Carly for trying, he knew the woman who had taken on the role of Margaret Crowley wasn't going to tell them anything.

And he understood Campbell's disdain. She wanted to be Holmes. She wanted to convince them—and perhaps herself—that she was the brilliant mind behind everything that was happening. There was something about her, though. Just something about her that would be pathetic if the crimes she had probably committed hadn't been so horrific.

She wasn't the mind behind all this. When they caught the man claiming to be the modern-day Holmes, the reincarnation or immortal spirit of the man, he would be calm. He wouldn't scream, he wouldn't respond with anything other than calmness and disdain. Like the original Holmes, he would tell lies about his innocence—and lies about his guilt.

He wouldn't scream, and even if he was shot in the hand, he wouldn't cry.

But she was part of this. Part of the Holmes Society even before it had taken root in the United States. She did know him; he had arranged for the death of the real Margaret Crowley, he had arranged for this woman to take her place, and then, through her, he had made use of the old tunnels and then those he had created through the construction on the shop.

"Luke!"

It was Carly, about twenty yards down, standing by the stone wall, head close to it.

"Luke, I can hear her...someone. The crying is coming from behind here, but it's solid stone and I can't see a path to get around and through here," Carly told him, frustrated.

"Campbell!" he shouted.

The agent quickly joined Luke, with another dusty man in what had been a neat business suit walking quickly behind him.

"Professor Wynn Grantham from the university. He was on the dig," Campbell said, introducing the man. "Special Agents Kendrick and MacDonald from the States," he finished.

They all nodded to one another.

"Glad you're here," Luke said. "Carly heard someone crying for help—if you stand here in silence, we'll hear her again. We can't figure a way through."

Grantham frowned. They were all silent. Then they could

all hear it—the woman's now soft sobbing, as if she believed all was lost.

"Hello, hello, where are you?" Luke cried. "We're trying to find you!"

"Here, here, here!" the woman cried, but the sound just bounced and echoed off the walls, not giving them the direction that they needed.

Campbell pulled his phone out. "I'll get some heavy equipment down here, but this might take time. Professor Grantham?"

Grantham had the look of a professor. He was a tall, slim man of about forty with a lean face and spectacles, along with an air of determination.

But even Wynn appeared to be at a loss.

"We worked on the corridors to the left," the professor replied. "I'm not sure—"

"I can get Andy on the phone again. Maybe he has another insight," Luke said.

"Andy? Ah, Professor Kendrick, of course!" Grantham said. "You are related?"

"He's my brother," Luke said, pulling out his phone. As he did so, Carly looked back to the stairs that led to the dress shop's fitting room.

"Maybe there's another mirror, or something else from the shop. I'll head back that way."

"I'm with you," Campbell told her.

Andy answered the phone on the first ring.

"Did you find anything?" he asked, knowing it was Luke on the other end.

"Lots of dead bodies. But we're hearing someone crying desperately behind a thick wall of stone—I think we need to get to whoever it is fast."

"Bodies to the left—where we excavated?" Andy asked. "You don't mean—"

"Bodies from the 1700s, no. These were cleaned with acid and bleach. Andy—"

"Okay. Which side of the corridor?"

"Right side. And by the way, Professor Grantham is here."

"Put me on speaker," Andy said.

"Got it."

Luke did as his brother asked.

"Wynn, no pleasantries—I understand there's a life at stake. I can only think of one possibility," Andy said over the phone. "Remember the old stone stairs and the half level? There seemed to be an opening there that we never explored—it looked like it led to more rock, and before we could contemplate where it might lead, we ran out of money. But it seemed to twist up. Twist, slant, curve. Maybe it twists up and over. I'll keep thinking, but that's what comes to mind first."

"Thanks, Andy," Luke said.

"Right. Thanks, I remember. We're on it, Andy," Grantham said.

"I'll keep studying the maps I still have," Andy said. "And, Wynn, watch out for my brother. He can lead you into some of the damnedest places. How—"

"The gentleman from the National Crime Agency called me. He said that there were lives at stake. We managed to excavate history so that a monster could relive it," he added bitterly.

"Don't ever think that," Campbell told him. "You're not the guilty party. We're grateful that you're here."

"Thank you, and I know what your brother is talking about. I'll take the lead," Grantham said. He looked at Luke. "You're going to get a little rock dust on you."

"I've worn it before," Luke assured him.

"This way, then."

Luke followed the professor away from the wall. He'd seen the stone steps off to the right earlier but it appeared that they led to a dead end of solid rock.

"There's a crevice," Grantham told him. "Come on. You got a light?"

"I do."

"I'll let you lead."

At first, Luke thought the man's memory was off. Heading up the worn and ragged stone steps, it looked as if they were going nowhere. But Grantham was right. The crevice wasn't visible easily because it was at an angle that made it appear that the stone merely continued.

Luke turned on his penlight again, shining it forward. The corridor was narrow—but not that narrow. A human body fit through easily enough, but it appeared, again, that it just led to another stone wall.

"We came this far and we would have gone on, but…digs are financed. And our financing ran out. But— Wait!"

Grantham stooped down, picking something off the ground. Luke shone his light back and asked, "What is it?"

The man was hunched down on the balls of his feet but he looked up at Luke. "A cigarette butt, with lipstick on it. New. This wasn't here before."

"So, our shop owner was here—and maybe with someone else. Let's keep going," Luke said. He started moving forward again. Once more, the corridor angled, but he realized that they were going up—and perhaps they had risen and twisted enough to be near the area where they had stood before, listening to the desperate cries.

"Steps!" he announced.

They led downward, and in minutes, he was in another dark corridor, one they hadn't been in yet. He began to move more quickly seeing more vaults, these a little smaller, a little tighter, than those he hadn't traveled through before.

Luke had never tended to be claustrophobic, but being in the strange tunnels and vaults off the vennel gave him a tight feeling. Maybe it was the smell.

It seemed that here, in this particular set of twists and turns and ups and downs, the scent of death and the ages seemed to permeate the stale air.

"There!" he said suddenly. "Wynn—sorry, Professor—an archway, right ahead of us!"

They moved quickly. He heard movement and the soft catching sobs but something else as well…a scraping sound.

It wasn't just him. Wynn Grantham looked at him with a worried frown, and he motioned for Luke to hold back.

Luke pulled his Glock as he eased around the small archway leading into the little room within the maze.

"Luke!"

He lowered his gun quickly. An ironic grimace twisted his face as he saw Carly and Campbell had reached the room already.

This one offered tables, one with something that resembled a medieval torture rack.

Carly was busy trying to untie the bloody woman who still sobbed as she was released; the other table held a man who appeared to be unconscious.

Campbell had his phone out.

"Well, it seems your way of getting here was much better," Luke told Carly. "How long—"

"We stepped in here a minute before you did—I was right. Well, you were right. You found the first entry through the mirror. And we almost didn't get it—that one had a secret spring and it was by feeling around the thing that we found it by accident. This place is a maze."

"Is the man alive?" he asked.

Carly nodded. "It's hard to tell…" She broke off, glancing at Campbell. "He has a weak pulse and he's breathing. And this lady…"

The woman was still just lying on the table, though she had been released. He saw that she had been covered with a sheet, but to free her, Carly had removed it. She was clad in nothing but underwear, and blood had dried on several surface wounds that had been etched with a blade across her skin.

"Do we know who they are?" he asked.

"The gentleman is out cold, the lady thought Carly intended her harm, but…"

Luke drew the sheet back over the length of her body and stood by her head, trying to reassure her. "Ma'am, we're here to help you. Please, try to calm down. Medical help is on the way, and you'll be at a hospital in no time. Could you tell us your name, please?"

The woman tried to form a word with her lips. It came out as a whisper.

Carly moved closer, saying softly to Luke, "I think I know who they might be. Is your name Joan? Can you nod if I'm right? Joan Wakefield."

The woman managed something of a nod. As she did, they heard the emergency medical team heading their way.

"Help is here," Carly assured the woman, and she looked at the others. This vault was small, very small. She imagined it might allow for two people to practice their forms of torture on two bodies tied to the tables, but for help to come in…

They all knew it. Wynn Grantham was the first out, followed by Campbell, Carly and Luke.

"They are going to need all possible help fast," Campbell told the young medic in the lead.

"Yes, sir, we'll make sure there are no bleeders or lethal breaks and see that they are transferred immediately. The hospital is already apprised we'll be on our way."

Three of the medical crew managed to get in the room; Luke paused in case they needed help navigating their patients out of the small space.

"Carly, you said that the woman's name was Joan Wakefield. That was the woman Brian Blackstone believed did him so wrong along with the man…"

"Culpepper. Geoffrey Culpepper. These two are what truly cemented Brian Blackstone's affinity for the H. H. Holmes Society," she said. "They're probably extremely lucky that Brian panicked and wanted to shoot MacDuff, thinking he might have known what he was up to. Whether it is the shopkeeper herself or someone else—the man we believe to be the head of the snake—they had managed to kidnap this pair for him. Brian probably wrote in a chat session about them, giving information, allowing for someone to do further research, kidnap them and bring them here, expecting Brian to deliver the finishing touches," Carly explained.

"You don't think Brian Blackstone knew that they were already here?"

"No, sir," Carly said, looking at Luke.

"Again, whether the shopkeeper with her stolen identity or the man playing Holmes, one of them had these people here, hurting them but saving them for Brian. Then, once they couldn't reach Brian, one of them would have finished them off. This is a maze—they knew about the area. My theory is that our man 'Holmes' arranged for a newcomer to the city—the real Margaret Crowley—to be a victim here to expand the operation and allow the easier access that Carly and Campbell discovered through the second mirror. It would have been her operation under his direct supervision."

"And he managed not to be here now," Carly said.

Wynn Grantham was looking at Luke and Carly, shaking his head. "Your brother told me you were something," he said.

Luke grimaced. "Something good, I hope."

Grantham nodded, wincing. "You, uh, would have been fine without me."

"Professor, no. We are in your debt. Without you, we found the dead. With you, we found the living. And they'll have hope," Luke assured him.

"Well, these two came through a mirror," he said, indicating Carly and Campbell.

"But we almost didn't," Carly said. "And..."

"We'll have teams down here searching every possible nook and cranny—and slot, hole and opening. We may have need of you again, Professor," Campbell said. He turned to Luke and Carly. "Go home."

"To America?" Carly asked, puzzled.

"No!" Campbell said, almost smiling. "To the hotel. Greater numbers of officers and professionals, including a few of Professor Grantham's colleagues and forensic anthropologists, are arriving as we speak to tear this place apart. The torturer and the tortured are on the way to the hospital. Go to your hotel. I am going home. These days are long—everything of importance will be found, trust in others. We can interview our fake Margaret Crowley in the morning and her victims as well. Hopefully, we can acquire a few more leads on the web creator of the Society. Today was, at least, one battle's victory, though the war continues."

Luke nodded. "Yeah. We need to, uh, shake off some of this."

"Bone dust," Wynn Grantham said in agreement. "It was good to meet you," he told Carly and Luke. "Andy talked about you a lot—and the rest of your tribe. Good to see you have a hell of a partner, too," he added, giving Carly a nod.

"Thanks," she murmured.

"Want us to walk you out?" Luke asked him.

Grantham looked at him with a somewhat sheepish look. "Uh... I'm among the experts staying," he said.

Luke almost laughed. "Hey, it's okay. We don't know this place in any way similar to you—I'm sure you'll continue to be of great help. Okay, Carly—"

"We'll walk you out," Campbell told Luke. "Carly and I know the best route, I believe."

They left by way of the second dress-shop mirror.

And it was a hell of a lot easier. A very large Closed sign was already on the door—along with ribbons of police tape.

"I'll be back into the office crack of dawn," Campbell promised them. "Carly, I believe it might be best if you speak with Brian Blackstone again. Then our victims—"

"Assuming they live," Carly said quietly.

"Assuming they live, but I believe they will. But conversations with Brian and then the victims may help when seeking what line to take with our fake Margaret Crowley," Campbell finished. He paused, suddenly, frowning as he looked at his phone. He returned his attention to them with a smile. "You'll be glad to know that our computer people have gotten the website down again! They're running a trace and they'll have more soon. Legend or fact, I'm not sure. But Robert the Bruce was known to have been a great leader when it came to guiding men into battle. A victory was celebrated because each step had to be honored in a war. Please, think of it that way. Each triumph brings one closer to true victory."

Carly grinned. "Great speech," she told him. "And unnecessary. I'm ready for a shower! Except—"

Campbell groaned aloud but waited.

"I really do need a shower. But, sir, yes, others who have a greater understanding of the vennels, vaults and the excavation will be working here. But the woman who had claimed to be Margaret Crowley and now the head of all this was not so seriously wounded. I know how good your hospitals are. In an hour she'll be under sedation, but there's no reason she won't be able to talk. It's growing late, but—"

"She's right—time isn't on our side with this thing," Luke said. "We'll give it a few hours and talk to her."

"But the victims are in sorry shape," Campbell said.

"And I understand that life itself is always most important," Carly assured him.

He looked at Luke, who said, "She's right. While our would-be Holmes is on the loose, time is everything."

"I'll meet you at the hospital in an hour and a half," Campbell told them.

"Yes, sir!"

They parted ways. Luke glanced at Carly as he started the ignition.

"Do you think that this woman is going to give us anything? She is determined that we believe she's Holmes."

"She's a wild card. But she's so violently determined to appear to be the head of everything... I'm wondering, Luke, if she's another party with no self-esteem, that claiming to be the head of it all is something that isn't true, but makes her feel as if she is superior, perhaps, even to the man who is the actual head," Carly said.

Luke nodded. "All right. This time, let me start."

"Because I shot her?"

"That, and because she's determined to show she's important and she will fight that harder with me. At some point, you come in and tell me what to do—that will draw a kinship with her. She doesn't want to believe that she answers to anyone, and she might become even more wordy if she feels you don't answer to anyone, either. That behavior—in her twisted mind—might elevate you."

"Playing the gender angle."

He glanced at her. "Yeah. And I hate doing it but hate the idea that more and more people are dying as well."

"You're right. We'll play it to the hilt."

When they reached the suite, Carly told him sternly that he had to use his shower while she used her own.

"Afraid I can't resist if we're both all wet, hot...surrounded by steam?" he teased.

"Nope. Afraid *I* can't resist," she responded sweetly, causing him to groan, making his response dramatically loud.

She laughed and he was glad. Morgue humor. He had worked with many medical examiners in the past and he found their jobs harder than his own. But he had learned as well that there were few people more determined to look for the good in life than those who dealt with the results of violent death.

In twenty minutes, they were both ready to head to the hospital.

"We'll check in with Campbell and, of course, the woman's doctor," Luke began.

As he did so, his phone rang.

"Campbell," he said, handing her the phone to put it on speaker.

"Yes, sir, we're on our way. ETA ten minutes," Luke said.

"Yes, the bullet is out and she's bandaged up, some sedation, not enough to put her out," Campbell said. "We have her true ID. Her name is Mildred Mayer. She was born in Wales, lived in Berlin, London and Perth throughout the years, with Perth being the most recent. There is a warrant out for her arrest—she indulged in a bar fight that cost a man his eye.

"The first body we discovered is that of the real Margaret Crowley. She was English by birth but had a dual citizenship with British and Canadian passports. Her mother died recently in Canada. She used the inheritance money to purchase the shop via an online sale, and thus no one knew what she looked like. So, of course, no one knew that Mildred wasn't the real Margaret Crowley when she took over ownership of the shop. Exactly how and when they managed to take the real Margaret, I don't know."

"Interesting. Apparently, whoever our real Holmes is, he conceived the idea of the vennels and vaults right after the excavation ended due to lack of funds," Luke said.

"Their timing had to be tight," Carly said. "Once the plan was in motion, they must have pulled a scam on Margaret Crowley, perhaps convincing her that they were part of the sales team, or neighboring shop owners."

"And, therefore, they were able to pick her up from the airport, bring her immediately to the shop and dispatch her before she had the least concept of what was going on," Luke said. "Theory, at any rate."

"Sound enough," Campbell said. "Two of Police Scotland's finest are on guard by the room, and as you know—"

"There are still guards on Brian Blackstone," Carly said.

"And our victims?" Luke asked.

"Indeed. Undercover officers are also on the job—we don't want any of our suspects or witnesses to suddenly have reversals in their health," Campbell said. "I may be a minute or two behind you. Get started as you like."

They reached the hospital, where they spoke with the medical personnel first, and then met the two guards watching over Mildred Mayer's room.

This time, Carly took a pair of earbuds while Luke took the tiny mic.

He knocked softly at the door before opening it. Mildred Mayer lay there much like other patients. An IV bringing her fluids—antibiotics and painkillers, he assumed—stood on one side of the bed while her arm was slightly raised in a sling.

She gave him a baleful look as he arrived.

"What do you want? I have no intention of telling you anything at all that will bring harm to my followers."

He started to laugh softly.

"You think all that I have managed is amusing?" she queried.

"No, I think you're amusing. If it had served the original Holmes, he would have ratted out his own mother. Also, you're just capable of everything that went on through the real Margaret Crowley's shop."

She stared at him, about to insist that she was Margaret Crowley, and he decided to speak first.

"We know you're Mildred Mayer," he said with a casual shrug.

"You don't know—"

"Well, here's the thing. Today is a new day full of forensic science and you can say anything at all that you want—judges and courtrooms go with science. So, you see, your fingerprints are on file with a few law enforcement agencies, and, therefore, scientifically, we know that you were born as Mildred Mayer."

"You don't understand anything," she said impatiently.

"Wait, let me see—an idea doesn't die. Men die, but ideas can live on forever. So, you have an idea about a man who once lived known as H. H. Holmes, or Herman Mudgett."

"Maybe I'm God," she told him.

He allowed himself to laugh. "My dear Ms. Mayer, you are so far from any kind of a god that it's laughable. Hey. I've got something for you."

He pulled out his phone, producing the enhanced picture of the man Carly had first seen at Graystone Castle, created using various video footage and the artistic endeavors of Maisie, their artist extraordinaire back at headquarters.

He stuck it in front of her face.

"There's Holmes," he told her. "There's your god!"

"He listens to me!" she hissed.

He allowed himself a spate of laughter again. "So, he is the leader of the pack and you are just his lackey. Tell me, who had the brilliant idea to recruit Brian Blackstone? Do you always go after people who are seriously paranoid? I mean, he was a wild card, but he told you about the people he felt deserved to die on the website and you two managed to snag Geoffrey Culpepper and Joan Wakefield. That was clever of your master—"

"I don't have a master!" she snapped.

"Oh, that's right—you think you are the master. Thing is, whoever he is, I do have to hand it to him. Man, does he know his way around a computer!"

"He doesn't know anything about..." she began, but then she stopped. "Oh, no, no, no."

Again, Luke chuckled softly. "I got it. You were the one with all the finesse. Somehow, you were the one to lure Geoffrey and Joan to the store. Once they were there, well...they had the two of you to contend with. I'm sure the police have found a gun by now—"

"Guns are outlawed in the UK."

"Yeah, but just like in the good old US, criminals have a way of getting hold of a firearm or two," Luke said, shrugging. "Like I said, we know you had one, and Police Scotland and the men and women from the National Crime Agency have found it by now. Of course, I've seen your handiwork. You prefer a blade. Wow, woman, you are heartless! All those vats of acid. What made you such a sick and pathetic puppy?"

"I am not pathetic! Or sick."

"No, seriously." Luke moved one of the chairs in the room closer to the bed and straddled it. "Did your daddy beat you? Wait. I know what it was. The kids in—what do they call it here, secondary school—did they make fun of you? Oh, wait, sorry, I haven't studied your dossier completely. Don't know where you went to high school or whatever. But that's where kids can be cruel. Oh! I know. Some teacher took advantage of you!"

"No one takes advantage of me!" she snapped.

"Oh? But they did," he said with confidence.

She tried to sit up. She fell back but tried propping herself up on her side to stare at him. "Once, just once, and back then, I taught those bloody bitches a lesson and I have never, never let myself be ridiculed or taken advantage of again. And that's why, since I don't think you're entirely stupid, I felt for Brian Blackstone when I saw his chatter on the web. And no matter what you do to me, I made sure that those two horrible people would die, blood draining from them bit by bit. I'm talented with knives and razors, very talented. I wanted to make sure that they knew that the way they treated someone else caused what was happening to them and—"

She broke off. Luke was laughing again.

"What? What the hell do you see as so damned funny?"

He smiled very pleasantly. "Well, you aren't the head of anything," he told her. "You see, a lot of us have had a chance to study just about every record there is on H. H. Holmes, the man who lived in the 1800s, who was executed—with DNA proving he is the fellow buried in his grave—and you never really understood a thing about him."

"What are you talking about? I know the man! I worked with the man."

"You worked with *a* man. But you don't know anything about the 'idea' you think you've cultivated here and now in this century. Where is he? He sure as hell never sticks around when his so-called Society members face arrest. And life sentences. Not one of you will ever be free again. He runs. He runs like a scared rabbit."

"He doesn't run like a scared rabbit! When he knows he has a master in charge, he moves on to teach the discipline to others!"

Carly entered the room, laughing. "Oh, my God! I am so sorry, but I have been listening to some of this. Miss Mayer, you are so, so off! Revenge? Holmes doesn't go after people for revenge—that would be stupid and risky. He started off as a grave robber—*to make money!* He went into insurance scams *to make money.* Then again, there was that occasional person he had to get rid of. And in *his* Murder Castle, he probably screwed up a few times, killing people who might not have had what he thought they might to steal, but, hey…he felt no remorse. He wiped out women and children without a thought. He practiced some torture, I believe, but for entertainment! And still, even when he did like someone, he didn't feel a second's remorse. Oh! My God, woman, you were such a screamer! Holmes never, ever screamed. In fact, his last words were to his executioner, and you know what he said? He said, 'Take your time, old man. Don't bungle it.' Well, sad to say—or justly, perhaps—the 'old man' did bungle it and the fellow struggled and kicked, strangled for about twenty minutes before he could be pronounced dead."

"You shot me! And I will sue—"

"Oh, Luke! It's not just Americans who are litigious! She wants to sue me for stopping her when she was trying to kill me. I don't think that flies in a Scottish court!"

"You are going to die!" the woman promised her.

"We're all going to die one day," Carly said agreeably.

"No! He will know all about you—"

"Oh? How?" Carly asked.

"He—he knows things!" Mildred informed them. "He—he just knows things!"

"The guy must have ESP," Luke said to Carly.

"Well, that's good since you won't be seeing a phone or a computer for a long, long time," Carly said. She looked at Luke. "I guess they get to call an attorney or solicitor or barrister for counsel, but that's the only call she'll be making."

"Yeah, and Campbell will be watching over that!" Luke said, smiling grimly and nodding at Carly.

"You will die, trust me! He's always watching, always seeing!" Mildred said.

"Really? He saw what was happening and he didn't try to help you?" Luke asked.

"Oh, Luke, that's the thing! He never goes back to help anyone because anyone who follows him is expendable! All that matters is him. And he must make sure that his devoted followers know that if they are captured, they must spew threats at those who capture them. It's part of his modern mantra!" Carly said.

"He— No! He would have helped me, he would have—" Mildred protested.

"If he were around," Luke said with a shrug. He leaned close to her. "We have it on good authority that he's already left the country. France, from what we've been told."

It was Mildred's turn to laugh. "That's what you think? You are such fools and you don't understand. He knows. He knows things when they happen. And he knows who deserves to die in one of his dungeons after being tortured for hours on end! He—"

"He's still here, in Scotland," Carly said to Luke.

"Yep. Well, thanks, Mildred, you've been great. Very helpful," Luke told her.

She suddenly looked like a rabid dog, screaming and slamming upward in the bed, trying to rip out of her cast to lunge at him.

Luke quickly caught hold of her arms and pressed her back to the bed, glancing at Carly, but she was already in the hallway, calling for medical assistance.

Nurses and a doctor hurried into the room. A sedative was shot into the woman and she fell back, eyes closing.

"I'm not so sure you should be talking to patients," the doctor told Luke.

"Sir, we're trying hard to see that you don't get any more patients like this," Luke told him. "And trust me, we're trying to keep as many bodies out of the morgue as we can."

The doctor swallowed and nodded.

"And she'll be all right—we aren't going to need to speak with her again," Carly informed him.

They left the room. Campbell was in the hallway himself.

"Two things," he told them.

"And they are?"

"Duncan and his people want to see you at the station when you can get there. And then it turns out that while Mr. Culpepper is still touch and go, Miss Wakefield is sitting up and she wants to help us in any way possible. Along with something a bit odd," he added.

"And what's that?" Carly asked.

"She wants to speak with Brian Blackstone."

"Oh?" Carly asked.

Campbell shook his head. "Must have hurt like bloody hell. That woman gave her dozens of flesh wounds, rubbing salt into them while she waited for Blackstone to reach her—and then just for her to bleed out. But you'll never guess what she wants to do."

"Probably not," she said, glancing at Luke. "What does she want to do?"

"Apologize to Blackstone for having treated him so badly that he felt so horrible," Campbell said. "And, get this, it's sincere. Occasionally, even in our line of work, you get to see the goodness and decency in humanity."

Luke smiled back at him. "Yeah. Because it is out there, 99 percent of the time."

Campbell laughed softly.

"I'd not be giving it quite that great a percentage! But, aye, maybe 97 percent of the time. You may check in now with Miss Wakefield. Just in case."

"We'll stop by. But once again, we think we got what we needed," Luke said.

And at his side, Carly nodded. "Our H. H. Holmes—the creator, if you will—is still in Scotland."

"That bastard just won't leave," Campbell said. "Well, that's what we thought, and that means you better catch that bloke, and fast. But, hey, Duncan just might have something for you, so get to him and the rest of my computer team as soon as you can. Oh! Then you should get to your hotel and sleep. I mean…"

"Yeah," Carly said dryly. "Thank God! We've all showered. At least we're all clean people who just need a little sleep now."

"Amen to that," Campbell said. "Because we believe you'll be on the move again come the morning."

CHAPTER FOURTEEN

Brian Blackstone had already improved. He was sitting up in his bed as Carly and Luke entered. He was watching an old sitcom and seemed to be enjoying it.

He turned to them, his smile broadening as they entered.

"Hello! And thank you!"

"Thank you—well, you're welcome, of course, but for what?" Luke asked.

Tears suddenly stung his eyes. "They wheeled her in here today. They wheeled Joan in here today. The poor thing. She has slashes all over her body, but she told me that they were waiting for me to kill her and...well, she doesn't realize, I guess, that I did intend to go until I was afraid that I might give Mr. Holmes away, and...she apologized to me! She said that she was so sorry, that no one should ever treat anyone like that. And she said that she wasn't mad at me. She was worried about Geoffrey, but...she said that her behavior had brought it on, and...it was a pretty severe lesson, but she was so sorry for the way she had behaved toward me, the way that they had laughed at my pain."

"Well. That was nice," Carly told him.

"I..."

His eyes remained wet as he told them, "I don't know... I don't really understand how I became so obsessed, so sure that I wanted revenge, that revenge should have been so much worse than the wrong that was done to me. I was so sure that it didn't matter that the revenge was..."

"Deadly?" Carly asked him.

He nodded.

"Brian, this is important. I think that I understand this. When you left the café that day, you came back, convinced that Mr. MacDuff knew what you were doing. But Joan and Geoffrey were already taken. Did you know?" Carly asked.

He shook his head miserably. "I was supposed to leave the café and wait for a call. All I had done until then was chat on the website."

"Did you have a number to call?" Luke asked.

Brian Blackstone shook his head again. "I was just supposed to wait. I had been promised that all the retaliation against those who had wronged me that I had ever dreamed of was just about to happen. I was a loyal member of the Society and all would be taken care of for me—and with me."

Luke cleared his throat. "Brian, I'm just a little curious. The H. H. Holmes Society is a fairly telling name. You didn't suspect—"

"Aye, I did wonder," Brian admitted.

"And you'd seen the news. You knew what had happened in other places. So, what did you think?" Luke asked softly.

The man looked as if he was going to cry. "I guess... I don't think that it was real to me. I mean, I wanted someone to slap my enemies around, humiliate them...but you're right. I should have known. And...maybe in a sick way I did, but when I saw Joan now...she was so sorry, and because of me, she might have died, and she's covered in bandages and they're afraid that her wounds could turn septic and... I deserve whatever happens to me."

"Brian, you have cooperated," Carly reminded him. "We—we're not judge and jury and we are Americans learning about the law in different countries. But you have a chance—"

"I'm better most of the time. They've given me a good psychiatrist!" he told them.

"That's great. Don't mess with your medication, okay? It's important that you take it consistently as it's prescribed. Check with the doctor if it needs to be adjusted and never screw with it yourself!" Luke said.

Brian Blackstone nodded. "I will not!" he swore. He frowned suddenly. "I don't know this...but I think that the creator has... Well, I don't think that he started with the H. H. Holmes Society. He is like the wind. He can come and go. I believe I might have seen him if I hadn't been arrested. I think he would have been where I would have been told to go...a dress shop, I understand from Joan. A dress shop that led straight to hell."

"We do believe he is still in Scotland," Luke said.

"That's not what I'm trying to tell you...what I think. Someone on the chat one day was talking about fake IDs and passports, and the creator chimed right in," Brian said.

"We know he has a fake passport, an ironic one," Luke said.

"No, no, I mean, I think he has a lot of passports. And he had to have money to have started this thing—I think that he must have spent some time in jail or prison and made a lot of connections to lead him to stashes of money or those who can create passports and all, though I have no idea what country that might have been in. English speaking, though. That does seem to be his language," Brian said. "Thing is, in a chat room, you don't hear accents, so..."

"Did he use words that suggest a country?" Carly asked.

Brian was thoughtful for several minutes. Then a light came to his eyes and he looked at them excitedly. "Once, he wrote that he was going to go and watch 'footy on the telly.' I mean, I guess that could be Britain—but it sounds like Australia. Maybe even New Zealand. But..."

"Not American," Luke murmured, looking at Carly.

She shrugged. "Unless he purposely uses different regionalisms."

"Well, we need to see Duncan," Luke said. "Brian, we wish you well. And of course—"

"Thank you," Brian said. "I will make sure to reach you if anything else comes to mind, I promise!"

They left his room. Campbell was in the hall; he'd been speaking with one of the officers but excused himself when he saw them.

"Get to headquarters—I think Duncan can set you up. How is Mr. Blackstone? Anything else from him?" Campbell asked.

"I believe he's trying," Carly said. "He might have been someone who should have been on the right medications years ago."

Campbell nodded. "That's the assessment of the psychiatrist we have seeing him."

"And still," Luke warned. "He could be a hell of an actor, trying to weasel his way out of some major charges. But, in my gut, I am pulled toward believing he regrets the way that his lack of self-esteem took him."

"Well, I'm going to say that it's different with Mildred—our fake Margaret Crowley. That woman goes beyond the bounds of insanity."

"And yet she managed to run that shop," Carly said.

"I didn't say that she wasn't smart. Believe it or not, in my experience, many smart people wind up becoming members of cults or falling for the lies of politicians and others, sometimes because the lies benefit them, and sometimes because the human mind is a maze itself. But Duncan believes that he's cracked a way into the website as an adherent. Best get to him."

"On our way," Luke told him. "Oh, by the way, if our poor, madly deluded Miss Mildred comes up with anything else—"

"You will know immediately," Campbell promised them.

They headed out. As they did so, Luke turned to Carly and said, "Let's get in touch with Jackson. They'll be working in both places to keep the website down. We need it up until I can get on it."

"You're going to re-create your past?" she asked him.

He grimaced. "I'll do a good job—I promise you."

"I can be the sickie, if you prefer."

He was thoughtful. "I think he kills men for money, more than for the need to torture. He prefers his associates to be male."

"What about our psycho, Mildred?"

"He had to have a woman to take on the identity of another woman, but I wonder if even he didn't have a few concerns about her mental state. She provided what he needed, and I have a feeling that if we hadn't come through when we did—and he'd had a chance—she might have been a true victim rather than an accomplice," Luke said.

"Maybe. But—"

"He kills without compunction or regret, but he does take on the Holmes role very seriously. He also kills for money. Anyway, let's get a hold of Jackson."

Carly nodded and pulled out her phone, putting through the call and announcing again that she had the phone on speaker.

"I know you're working on getting the site down again," Luke said.

"Angela believes we're almost there," Jackson said.

"Hold off about thirty minutes?" Luke asked.

"Luke, there are already a few—"

"I know, I know, and we'll hurry. But we have to get to the real thing before it continues to get worse and worse. I believe that I can set up a meet," Luke told him.

"Oh?"

Luke explained that he wanted to go in as an "assistant," with Carly showing up right after to become an intended victim.

"You'll be playing with fire," Jackson said.

"Aren't we doing that already?" Carly asked him.

"Point taken. Be careful," Jackson warned. "And updates—"

"Every step of the way," Luke promised. "Angela is on the site?"

"She is."

"She'll see what I'm doing. I'm going to be John Smith—already have a false ID in that name." He frowned, glancing at Carly.

"I didn't come supplied with fake IDs—it wasn't in the job description. But he doesn't know me, so my own passport should suffice."

"He's seen you, Carly," Jackson reminded her. "If you saw him in the museum at Graystone Castle, then he's seen you."

"And I don't see that as a problem. That's something I'd talk to him about right away, if I got to meet him," Carly said. "Jackson, we'll both be there. If he befriends Luke, Luke will be there. That's why we're partners, right?"

"I wish I could send in a squad," Jackson muttered.

"You need warrants, Jackson. We don't know where we're going yet, and if we did, we still couldn't just demand that the local authorities go in and search a place. This is our best option," Luke told him.

"Buy a new burner phone, now," Jackson advised.

"That's right," Carly murmured. "If you can catch his attention, he'll play the same game he did with Brian Blackstone—get you on the line, then somewhere alone, and he'll call."

"Got it," Luke said.

"Fine. We'll watch your chat," Jackson said. "Go for it."
They ended the call.

Luke glanced at Carly. "I'm more worried about you."

"What? No lack of faith in your own abilities?"

"Hey, that's putting me between a rock and a hard place!"

She smiled. "I have infinite faith. And I'm just dying to see your chat."

"Not dying is the whole point," he reminded her.

She smiled. "Hey. Aren't you supposed to have infinite faith in me, too?"

"I do. I just…"

"Hey!" she said, turning to him. "This is what we do, remember? And me failing you, losing you, is something that scares me, too. So, we trust in our training, in our abilities—and our guts!"

Luke nodded, grimaced and changed the subject. "Place up ahead. We'll get new phones and report back."

"Yep."

They quickly acquired the phones they needed and returned to the car. Carly sent their numbers to headquarters and Campbell as Luke drove.

They reached the offices where the computer crew was waiting.

"All right," Luke said. "Showtime!"

Duncan was waiting for them with the rest of his team. His computer was up—on the H. H. Holmes Society site.

"Can't he trace the computers back here?" Luke asked.

"Not with the tangle around the world we've managed and all our firewalls… Trust me. Come on—we're computer geeks," Duncan told them.

"Sadly, nerds," Liz said. "That made life a little hard in secondary school, but now…now it feels like we're on top of the world."

"And you are," Carly assured her. "Today's world, hell yes! You are on top of it!"

"Let me get to it," Luke said.

"Set you up right over there," Duncan said, pointing to a pair of chairs and a computer. "Just hit the key—join chat. I've already set up a fake profile."

Luke glanced at Carly. She smiled grimly and took the seat next to him.

She watched as he hesitated a second and then typed, starting with his admiration.

Tough world we're in, and we need people like you! he wrote, using the handle *Slashsmith*. He glanced at her. She shrugged and nodded and he wrote again. And you have mastered it. I humbly offer up my greatest praise!

Means to an end, eh? someone wrote—handle *Creepy Crawler*.

Wish I could have used this as a means to an end, Luke put in.

What was your beef? Someone else, *Death-Toll*.

Wish I could have taken my old man to a 'castle.' The bastard continually beat the shit out of me, alcoholic son of a bitch. Then there was Gordie from the soccer team. Thought he was God. I didn't get big until my early twenties. Time in a gym helped with that.

Another person entered the chat. *Homeboy*. So, where is your old man? Don't feel regret—go for the kill before it's too late.

It is too late. The old bastard died from a rotten liver. But Gordie is still out there. I wish…well, hell, I want to get him one day. I could use some practice. Man, if I can ever get to that creep, I want to… I want to make him suffer. Real pain. For hours. All the while him knowing that it's all over, that when the agony ends at last, it's lights out.

Silverware. Test out some silverware. You got a number? Homeboy wrote.

Yeah, yeah! Luke wrote in the number of his new burner.

Eleven. Tomorrow, opening. Alone. Moo, Homeboy wrote.

Homeboy left the session. Luke did, too.

"What the hell did any of that mean?" Ian asked, shaking his head.

"We know where and when," Carly said, looking at Luke.

"Come on, you guys. This is Scotland!" Luke said lightly. "Silverware, often sterling silver, so..."

"Stirling," Duncan said. "Stirling, Scotland. That's where he'll meet you. At 11:00 a.m. tomorrow."

Luke nodded.

"But...'moo'?" Liz asked.

Duncan was already tapping away at keys. "Yeah, there's a place there called The Spotted Cow. I'm assuming that's the meetup spot."

"Thanks for all your help!" Luke said.

He looked at Carly. "Plan in action," he told her. "So..."

"Let's go, eat, get some sleep," she said.

"Take her down?" Duncan asked Luke, referring to the site on the dark web.

"Take her down," Luke agreed, nodding his approval. "And thank you, the three of you—you are on top of the world," he declared.

Liz laughed. "And sitting behind a computer is a lot less dangerous than what you do!"

"And may save more lives," Carly assured her.

Carly waved. And they were out.

In the car, Luke looked her way and asked, "Room service?"

"Hell no, I want to eat."

"Meaning..."

"We really need food. And I'm afraid that—"

"I'm that irresistible?" he teased.

"You're that—"

"Irresistible!" he crowed.

"No, I was going to say pushy and forward."

"Oh, that hurts! I may deny you the pleasures of the flesh," he laughed.

"Like hell you will!" she said, grinning. "Seriously, I'll bet the restaurant is still open. We order dinner, we eat... No interruptions."

"Fine. Be that way." He smirked. "Want to report in?"

"Jackson and Angela were watching the chat."

"Still. Check in. Just so they know that—"

"They'll know the site is down. But..."

Carly dialed again. Jackson answered immediately and informed them that Police Scotland and members of the National Crime Agency were already alerted.

"Stirling is another popular spot for visitors and they come from all over the world. Stirling Castle is one of the most important in the country. Stirling Bridge is where William Wallace defeated the English. It's also just beautiful countryside and we're talking Highlands."

"So lots of earth beneath the earth," Carly murmured.

"Exactly," Jackson said. "To get to the point, visitors have been disappearing—and it hasn't been because they headed back home. It's one of the locations—Stirling and its outskirts—that's been brought up as the destination for a teacher who went missing—unmarried, no children, parents deceased—who didn't appear for a never-miss lunch meeting with a friend. Also, a young artist who was looking for locations to paint. Folios coming your way. There are a couple of other possibilities on people being in the area and then disappearing. Angela and Duncan have been conferring on where in the area our Mr. Holmes might have found a willing subject with the right property for a base, and they're down to two possibilities, doing some research on the owners and operators as we speak."

"Thanks, Jackson. We'll be heading out in the morning," Carly told him.

"Stop by to see Duncan again—he'll get GPS tracking on those burners," Jackson said.

"Will do," Luke promised.

They ended the call just as they reached parking for the hotel. As Carly had hoped, the restaurant was still open, but was about to close. They ordered quickly.

Luke shook his head, looking at her. "I'm not so irresistible, huh?"

"Luke, we barely made it in here."

"Ah, yes. I see which hunger is first in your book."

She grinned. "Okay, pay attention. This place is only open a little bit longer. To the best of my knowledge—and from what I've experienced—you're a 24/7 gig."

He laughed softly. "Okay, but where's the romance? One night left alone before we plunge into the fire. Now, a true romantic would have run up the stairs—"

"Why? They have an elevator."

He groaned softly. "Run up the stairs, made mad, passionate love, called down for room service, which, like me, is available 24/7 here. Then—"

"Then they'd have had to have gotten dressed—"

"And then dined and gone into mad, passionate disrobing again!"

Carly laughed. "Eat your fish!"

"I guess. Pretty much all we've eaten is fish."

"You don't have to order what I order," Carly reminded him. "You can get a steak."

"All I can think of is the long-haired cows. Those damned things are cute."

"Lamb," she suggested.

"Babies. I don't eat babies."

She grinned. "Well, if you finish your fish, I'll be waiting. Romantically, I promise!"

She hadn't really finished her meal but she'd had just what she wanted and needed. Grinning as she left him, she opted for the elevator.

Much easier and faster than the stairs. In the room, she hurriedly set her Glock in the bedside drawer, stripped and flew into the shower. Her intent was to be so quick that she could be posed and awaiting him.

But she hadn't counted on the speed with which Luke could sign a tab and she was so focused that she jumped—and might have pulled her Glock from the drawer when his shadow suddenly appeared on the other side of the shower door.

"Hey! That's a great way to get shot!" she warned him.

"Oh? Not for me."

"You shower with your Glock?" she asked him.

"I keep it closer than you do."

"Ah, well, I wasn't planning on shooting you and you were the only one I was expecting."

"Well, that's good to hear!"

As he spoke, he moved closer to her. His body was against hers before his arms came around her.

"Last night," he whispered.

"Hmm."

"Hmm?"

"*Last night.* How does a woman take *romantic* words like that?" she asked.

"Well, we're supposed to be a pair who have just met one another and…"

"Right. And people who have just met never have sex? What are all those bar-pickup one-night-stand guys famous for?"

He laughed. "Guys?"

"Okay, sorry, I meant young people, both sexes!"

"I was thinking about cameras."

"Sorry. Too kinky for me!"

"Me, too." He managed to laugh. "But we have to be careful since there are probably cameras everywhere. Well, you know, careful, but we still really want a good performance, but not *that* good a performance. And once we think we're on to something…"

"Oh! Yeah, of course!" Carly murmured. He was soooo right. They wouldn't be together, not like this. Not for the next several nights. It would be too easy if everything just fell in place once they arrived—wherever it was exactly that they were going.

"So, tonight…"

"Yeah," she murmured, lips against his.

There was something about a shower. Steaming water enhancing the slide of lips and fingers down flesh, the hot, damp heat of the human body…

Then, of course, there was laughter and urgency when the shower became too small to accommodate everything that was wanted.

Emerging, halfway drying, stumbling a wee bit, making it to the expansive comfort of the bed…

The night wore on. They slept, woke and slept again.

Morning's light began to filter through the room. One last chance…

And they took it, and for just a few minutes, they held together in silence. Then…

"Okay," Carly began.

"Nope, nope, I got it, know the drill!" Luke assured her. And, rising, grabbing his towel, he headed out of her room and to his own.

They met out in the kitchen but Carly didn't bother to brew coffee; they knew they could get it downstairs.

"It makes sense that we stop by and see Duncan with the phones," Carly said.

"And you and I can't drive together," he reminded her.

"I know that. But I'm also hopeful that he'll have an idea about our phones. I mean, what if Homeboy demanded to see your burner and he saw my number on it?" Carly asked.

"Well, we both need to keep our regular phones handy somewhere that's not obvious and somewhere that—"

"Can't be found? That's impossible. Have you ever noticed

how many times crooks find things that are supposedly so hidden no one could find them?" she asked.

"Somewhere that would be difficult for a criminal to find, at least. Mine is going to need to be in the car," he said thoughtfully. "The man isn't stupid, obviously, and he'll check everything."

"It's been a while since you've been frisked, huh?" Carly teased.

"Define *frisked*," he said. "Frisky, frisked…"

She gave him a punch in the arm. "Let's get to Duncan. And figure out my transportation."

When they arrived, Duncan assured them he could fix the phones up with GPS tracking and brought them out to another technical employee who worked with cars. His name was Justin Ellery and he told them Luke needed to switch cars; he had the perfect little SUV for him, with a cell phone planted deep in the driver's seat, one only accessible when a button in the back of the steering wheel was pushed. Also, the car was new in the line for law enforcement vehicles and not possibly known by any criminal element. But if needed, it could be found quickly since it was their vehicle and they would have all the GPS coordinates.

"Second problem," Luke said. "Getting Carly to Stirling."

"That's easy."

They were out in the motor pool, and Carly whirled around when she heard Liz speak.

"Easy?" Carly asked.

Liz grinned. "I'm driving you. I'm taking you to The Spotted Cow. I'll have one drink with you and need to drive back. But then Luke can see you sitting at the bar by your own little self and he'll be like, *Hmm, maybe that's an easy pickup*, and you'll be on your way to conversation and flirting when our suspect watches and measures up Luke, deciding if he's right for a higher position in the H. H. Holmes Society."

Carly looked at Luke.

"It's a good plan," he said.

She glanced at her watch and smiled. "Liz, you're not supposed to be—"

"In danger. But I am supposed to be smart," Liz said. "And I will be in and out of there before I appear on anyone's radar. And we need to get started. Driving time is about an hour and a half and it's after nine, so..."

"Let's do it. We'll go get Duncan—" Carly began.

"Right here!" Duncan called, coming out the door and over to the car Luke would now be taking. "Phones ready. Carly, you should get your bag. Lust at first sight isn't going to play well if Luke already had your overnight bag."

"How true!" Luke murmured, and they all grinned. "Okay, so, let's do this... Oh, and my new passport identifies me as John Smith."

"That's pathetic," Duncan told him.

Luke grinned. "Not if you're after a guy whose passport lists him as Herman Mudgett."

"He's right," Carly said. "This man we're after might find it funny—and clever. John Smith has to be one of the most common names in the English-speaking world.

"Give Liz and me a head start, about ten minutes?" Carly suggested.

Luke nodded. "You two be careful."

"I'm just going to teach my friend from America a lesson in good Scottish whiskey!" Liz said.

Carly nodded and grabbed her bag from Luke's car, then waved and followed Liz to another little SUV. She started to slide into the car when Liz said, "Wrong side. I'm driving."

"Sorry, I forget."

"That's right. You Americans drive on the wrong side of the road."

Carly smiled as she got into the car. "Would you mind if I had a Guinness?" she asked.

"Ah, lass! That's an Irish beer! You'll be ordering an Innis and Gunn," Liz informed her.

Carly sat back, grinning. "They don't serve Irish beer in a Scottish pub?"

Liz gave her a stern look and Carly laughed, "I'll be ordering an Innis and Gunn!"

They drove for a while, chatting casually. Carly noted that Liz was an attractive woman; she wondered if she'd really been teased at school.

"It's hard to imagine that you were ever…"

"Mocked as a nerd?" Liz asked her.

"Um, yes."

"Some. Because I was in love with computers from the time I could reach a keyboard. And, besides that… I have a husband and a child now and being a nerd kind of seems to have paid off…" She broke off and took a deep breath. "I wanted to matter. But I'm also your basic coward. And I have seen amazing inspectors and constables who were injured or killed. And I want to go home every night. I'm in the perfect place." She glanced at Carly. "I don't see how you do it."

"I…don't know. I knew I wanted to be in law enforcement. I was never bullied, but I saw bullies and I read enough and I like stopping the bad guys."

"And Innis and Gunn will help!" Liz promised.

"Let's hope. So, how old are the kids? What does your husband do?"

Her kids were little boys, five and seven. Her husband was a teacher. They talked and did a lot of laughing for the length of the drive.

They arrived in Stirling and the GPS sent them down the right streets to reach the pub.

"You've been here before?" Liz asked her.

"I've been all over Scotland," Carly said. "My grandparents, my dad's folks, were born here. They wanted me to see Stirling

Bridge. They wanted me to see where a common man took a stand that changed the course of a history."

"You do know he was hanged, drawn and quartered," Liz said.

Carly nodded. "Of course. But that very face enraged the people and encouraged Robert the Bruce to pick up the battle. Also, Randall Wallace wrote a great screenplay and Mel Gibson was pretty darned cool in the movie."

"Just remember, movies are fictionalized."

"Sure. Some. It was still stirring—just as the man must have been in real life!"

"We can keep arguing movies," Liz murmured, "because we are here."

Carly nodded, and as they walked to wooden doors at the entry to the pub, Liz reminded her, "Okay, when it's a movie about the American Revolution and it's filmed in the colonies—"

"The colonies?" Carly asked as they entered the pub.

"Well, still the colonies to me!"

"Come on. That was over two hundred years ago. We're the best of allies now," Carly told her. "But, of course, we all know that history can be in the telling!"

As she spoke, she turned slightly. Stirling Castle sat high on a crag, with steep inclines on three sides. It was truly magnificent from where she stood.

"Not sure history needs to be enhanced," she murmured.

"I'm pretty sure this building must be nearly as old as the castle!" Liz marveled, opening one of the massive wooden double doors to the establishment.

It was a charming place, paneled and warm. A massive hearth was toward one side of the establishment where there were numerous tables. The place had just opened; there were two patrons sitting at the bar and two groups of four had just claimed tables in the dining area.

They sat at the bar and a handsome, sandy-haired young man walked over to them. "Ladies! What may I get you this fine day?"

"Well, I shall have your best Scot's whiskey, and my American friend here is an ale lass. She wanted a Guinness but I insisted she have an Innis and Gunn!"

He grinned. "Welcome to Scotland," he told Carly. "A whiskey and an Innis and Gunn—though we do carry Guinness, if that's what you'd really wish."

"No, thank you. I'm going to humor my friend and try a new drink!" Carly said.

She had barely ordered before she saw that someone was sliding up beside her.

Luke.

"I think I just heard a fellow Yank was in the pub!" Luke said.

Carly smiled at him. "I am here to see Stirling, but my Scottish friend told me we should start with— What did you call it, Liz? A wee dram?"

"I don't think that Innis and Gunn comes in a wee dram," Luke said. "Would you mind if I joined you?" he asked.

"Not at all," Liz said, looking around Carly.

They all heard Luke's phone buzz.

"Excuse me, ladies," he said, walking away toward the hearth.

As she stared after him, Carly saw there was a man in one of the groups of four who was also on his phone.

She didn't recognize him as the man she had seen at Graystone Castle...

At first.

Now his hair was longer and blond. And he was clean-shaven.

But...

The bartender delivered their drinks.

Carly picked up her glass, and as she took a sip, she told Liz, "Drink up. In the words of one of the literary world's greatest detectives, I believe that the game is afoot."

CHAPTER FIFTEEN

Luke answered the phone without his name, just saying, "Stirling."

A soft laugh was his reply. "Join me. I'm with a few friends. Turn to your left."

Luke did so. He saw the man with the clean-shaven face and tousled blond hair, but it was the same man, the man in all the video images from around the internet café, the man Carly had seen at Graystone Castle.

"Only four chairs," he said.

"I'll draw one up," the caller told him. He laughed softly again. "Though I did see you talking to that cute thing at the bar. Maybe you should chat her up for a minute or two."

"Well, I wouldn't mind doing that, except I did come to meet you."

"You're an American."

"I am."

"Find out if she is—and find out where she's staying. And if her friend is hanging around, too. Then come and join me. As if we're old friends. Call me Harry. I go by Harry Green. And I'll call you?"

"John Smith."

"Seriously?" There was soft laughter at the other end.

"Won't your friends know we're not old friends?" Luke asked.

"Ah, you see, we're new friends, too. These people are visitors to Stirling. Go have a chat with your girl at the bar, see what you can see. I mean, you look like you can manage yourself well enough these days."

"Oh, yeah. I learned a lot along the way. Doesn't mean…"

"That you don't still wish you could put an ice pick through your old man's eye?"

"Oh, you bet," Luke said. "And…my first assignment seems to be an easy one!"

The call ended. Luke grinned and walked up to the bar, glad it was still early and the seat next to Carly remained vacant.

He tapped her on the shoulder and gave her a smile. He kept his voice low but just in case asked softly, "This seat still vacant? I may still join you."

Carly returned the smile and made a sweep with her hands to invite him to take the chair.

Liz, at her side, leaned in. "We know that's him!" she whispered. "Can't we just—"

"Liz, we have nothing on the man other than the fact he was in a café, accessed a website and was in Graystone Castle. Liz, you know the law."

"Well," Liz said, "you don't think you can get him to draw a gun on you so that you can shoot him?"

Luke gazed at her, grinning. He didn't know if it was intentional or not, but Liz was playing a part well—the part of a second girl ready to get into the flirting game.

"Lizzie, not sure how to do that," he told her. "And if he has people near here…"

"I know, I know," Liz murmured. "We have to find out where he's holding, torturing and killing innocents in this area."

"And take him down for good," Carly said, sipping her drink.

"I'm supposed to find out where you're staying," Luke said.

"Either Vicky Inn or the Glen Hotel," Liz said. "That's the best we've come up with in our research. Those...they're old places that have been renovated in the last year. And they were on travel itineraries by some of those who haven't been heard from since they headed to this area."

"We can say that I'm trying to figure out where Liz should drop me before she leaves."

"Perfect," Luke said, laughing as if they joked about something sweetly amusing. "I can ask my new friend—Harry Green here, by the way—which place I suggest for you to stay. If you are staying in this area. Oh, and remember, I am now John Smith."

He left his bar stool and stood again, setting a hand on Carly's back. "You will have lunch with me, then, eh?" he asked her, letting his voice carry.

"As long as I can have another of these!" Carly said, letting her voice carry and lifting her Innis and Gunn.

Luke grinned and headed over to the table where the man who was calling himself Herman Mudgett on his passport—and Homeboy on the website—was sitting.

And, of course, here he was Harry Green.

There was an older woman, perhaps seventy or so, sitting at the table along with him, an attractive woman of about forty and a man who might have been her husband or partner, older than her by a decade or so.

"My friend!" The man calling himself Harry Green stood and welcomed him. "My friends, this is John Smith."

The older woman arched an amused brow.

"Yeah, I know!" Luke said. "With a surname like Smith, my folks might have given me a more unusual first name, but my dad was John, his dad was John..." He let off with a grimace. "And you all are?"

"Kaye Bolden," the old woman told him, offering a hand.

"And this lovely couple here are Terry and Jim Allen. We've

been remarking on your friends at the bar. Old friends, new friends?"

"New friends. Carly and Liz. They're up from Edinburgh, Liz hosting an American friend and just dropping Carly up here so she can see Stirling, but apparently she still hasn't decided where she wants to stay."

"Oh!" Harry Green said, gazing across the table at the couple. "I think we can help there."

"We own Vicky Inn," Jim Allen said. "It's a bit out of the city proper, but still close enough that she can easily see the castle, Stirling Bridge, the kirks…and, of course, if I do say so myself, we're a perfect place for a foreigner who truly wants the local feel!"

The local feel, yeah!

"I need a place to stay myself," Luke said.

"I have already made a reservation for you," Harry Green told him. "Why don't you bring the young ladies over?"

"I will certainly give it my best shot!" Luke said.

He thought Green moved his head in to speak softly to the couple, who seemed to be concerned.

He couldn't hear the words, and he wondered what he dared say with the older woman at the table—could she be in on it, or was she an intended victim, someone rich, alone, and ready to hand over her assets to those giving her a comfortable home and a decent life for her later years?

"Vicky Inn! Let me go make the suggestion," Luke said.

He walked back over to the bar, touching Carly on the back again and smiling as he leaned against the bar.

"Vicky Inn! The lovely couple over there own the place and it sounds great!"

"Great. I'll go on and head home—" Liz began.

"Don't you want to have a bite of lunch with us first?" Luke asked her.

"No, I'm afraid I should get back to work," Liz said. "But,

Carly, enjoy! Stirling is wonderful, so much history, you're going to love it!"

The women stood and Liz hugged Carly as if she was a great friend from across the pond.

"Let me walk you to your car," Luke said. "And I'll be right back!" he told Carly. "I can drive you since I've decided to stay there myself."

He accompanied Liz to her car. "Get out of here. Fast," he told her. "Don't stop for anything until you're back at work, right?"

"I have petrol, I'm fine, I won't stop," Liz promised. "Duncan has a burner phone that can't be traced—I'll get hold of you and let you know when I'm there."

"Good plan. I don't want any number assigned to any law enforcement agencies coming through on us. Drive!"

"You got it! You know we're far smarter than that, right? Planned from the get-go!" She grinned, got behind the wheel and waved as she left the pub's parking lot behind.

Luke walked back in. So far, so good. Or, so far, worrisome. But they were on course.

In the pub he saw Carly had wasted no time; she had introduced herself to Harry Green, the older woman and the "hospitable" couple who owned Vicky Inn.

He joined them.

"I was just telling your new friend we're going to need to leave and won't be able to have lunch with you, which I believe you were planning?" Harry asked Luke.

"John was kind enough to ask me," Carly said. "And to tell me about Vicky Inn. I'm so glad. I'd looked up a dozen places and just couldn't make up my mind! But getting to meet Jim and Terry Allen and Kaye…it's wonderful."

"I told her I was sure she'd truly love it!" Terry said.

She had a soft, faint brogue and Luke smiled and asked, "Terry, where are you from originally?"

"What? You knew I wasn't a Scot?" she asked.

"No, I couldn't tell—"

"But you nailed it. Terry has been here about ten years now, but she's originally from Alberta, Canada," Jim told them.

"Ah, nice. Two beautiful places!" Carly said.

"Well, we've got to get back. Now, you two enjoy your lunch. The lamb chops here are quite wonderful," Terry said. "We'll have nice rooms ready when you get there!"

"Vicky Inn," Luke said, grinning at Carly. "Built during the Victorian era, and thus—Vicky!"

"Do you think she would have minded?" Jim asked.

"From what I've read about Queen Victoria? Not in the least," Carly assured them.

"Well, I've a few things on the agenda, too," Harry Green said. "You two, whatever you choose from the menu, it will be great. People come from all over to dine here!"

"Thank you!" Carly told him, wide-eyed and excited. "I mean, the local experience is so wonderful. Thank you!"

"Thank your friend there, Mr. Smith," Harry Green said. Waving, he left the table.

"And we are out, too," Terry Allen said. "Kaye, are you joining us?" she asked the older woman.

"I do think I should. But I'm delighted to hear that you'll be joining the Vicky Inn family!" she told Carly and Luke.

"Harry Green" hurried out, followed by Terry and Jim Allen and Kaye Bolden; Terry solicitously held Kaye's arm lest she trip.

Kaye seemed to walk along just fine.

Carly sank into a chair at the table and Luke took the chair across from her.

"Well?"

"We're in," she said.

"All right, different rooms now. As soon as you're in—"

"Cameras, hoses, anywhere gas might enter a room… I know the drill, Luke, remember? And may I remind you—"

"Learn as quickly as possible what the architectural situation is, if anyone is belowground—alive."

She nodded. "So, no lamb."

"More salmon."

"Think we'll still like salmon once we're home?"

"Sure. I'll just take some pasta or a taco now and then as well."

Carly laughed softly. "You do know that other places offer a variety of foods."

He looked up at her, smiling. He'd actually been studying a menu that had been left on the table.

"You'll never guess what they have," he told Carly.

"That would be?"

"Tacos! All kinds of tacos, beef, chicken—and fish."

She grinned. "Hmm. Tacos."

"Which are great, I'm sure," Luke said. "But I'm going with the shepherd's pie."

"Okay, we'll both go with the shepherd's pie," Carly said agreeably.

"Now, just because *I* ordered shepherd's pie—"

"Oooh! Thinking a little too highly of yourself," she informed him, smiling. Except, suddenly, she wasn't smiling.

"What's the matter?" Luke asked her.

"I'm not sure. I just…" she murmured.

"What?"

"Should we be worried about Liz?"

Luke frowned. Liz had been the natural choice to bring Carly—a young woman dropping off her friend from America who wanted to see more of Scotland. And she'd left right away…

And was in a car alone with killers having just seen her.

"You know what I'm worried about!" Carly said.

He nodded.

"It's a long shot," Carly said. "But…we're an investment to them. They're not going to kill us right away. You need to make them believe that I have money. If they're eager—"

"If they want a victim quickly, they'll go after Liz. She came up, she left you. So she could have disappeared anywhere between here and her return to Edinburgh.

"All right," he decided. "I'll drop you at the Vicky Inn—and catch up with Liz, get our info through to Campbell and see that she gets an escort for the way home."

"But then they'll know—"

He smiled at her. "Not the way I plan to do it!"

"But—"

"Kaye Bolden, an older woman, but you never know. Probably an intended victim, but, hey, we've seen some surprising things. Terry and Jim Allen—couples have murdered before. Harry Green, our friend who comes with many names and faces."

"Or hair colors," Carly said with a shrug. "But Harry Green or one or two of the others might have headed back to the hotel—"

"And someone might have gone after Liz," Luke said thoughtfully.

"Maybe I should go after Liz, and you—the new good friend—should head to the hotel," Carly suggested.

"Let me warn Campbell."

"Make sure you use the right phone!"

Luke grinned. "Gotcha!"

"It's a good thing we didn't get to order tacos, shepherd's pie or anything else!" she said, rising.

He did the same.

He called Campbell and informed him that their meeting up with the suspects here had left them worried that someone just might go after Liz.

Campbell assured them that he'd get patrol out; Liz wouldn't be alone.

"I will get men out, but if you can… Liz isn't trained as an officer or agent. So, just watch out all the way around until we've officers everywhere and it's all in force!" Campbell said.

"Still," Luke began, "Liz is gone. Carly is here—"

"Luke! You're worried about me, and I guess I'm thankful for that!" Carly said, smiling. "I'm a good agent. Top of my class. And…"

She paused, frowning.

There was a man staring at them from the bar. He was seated where a middle-aged woman had been a few minutes before. An empty glass was before him.

He was dressed very oddly. He wasn't wearing a kilt, but he was wearing a strange gray tunic-like wrap. His hair was dark, curly and long, and he had a solid, thick beard of the same color. He watched them curiously and with concern.

Luke realized he was, of course, a dead man.

"I think there's someone we need to talk to," he murmured to Carly.

"No," she said softly. "One of us needs to talk to him. And one of us needs to go after Liz!"

"All right." He dug in his pocket for his keys. "Vicky Inn can't be far from here. I'll get there. Go after Liz."

Carly nodded. Before she left, however, she turned to the ghost at the bar. She approached him quickly, pretending to have dropped her phone by the stool she had taken earlier.

Luke smiled as he listened to her.

"Dear sir, we see you. My friend and I see you and would so desperately appreciate any help that you could give us!"

Then she turned and hurried out the door.

Luke approached the bar—and the man who had apparently been dead for a very long time—ready to learn what he could from the "remnant" or "remaining spirit," as many preferred over being called "ghosts."

But the ghost wasn't going to have it.

He rose before Luke could reach him, shaking his head. His

accent was different: a Scottish burr, but one that was deep and guttural. English hadn't been his first language, Luke thought.

"Kenneth, clan Menzies," he said briefly. "I'll be takin' m'self to join the lass on her way—she knows not the danger!"

He was gone before Luke could attempt in any way to stop him.

CHAPTER SIXTEEN

Carly had barely keyed the engine before she realized that someone was sliding into the passenger's seat and she smiled. Only one soul she had seen here could slide through a closed door to join her.

"Hello," she said softly.

"Yer goin' after yer friend," he told her.

"I am," she said determinedly, setting the car into Drive.

"Then I am with ye, lass! Kenneth Menzies, at yer service. I'm not much with me fists, but I've eyes that ha' seen the evil of centuries, and thus can warn one well of danger in the offing!"

"Thank you, then. Luke meant to talk to you—"

"And talk later, we can!" he assured her.

"Do you believe that Liz is in danger?"

"Aye! They watch. Now, yer friend might not fall for a scam, but…they ha' nails aplenty in the parking out there, unknown by the pub, mind ye, but they're there."

"Ah, they puncture tires of the unwary? And if they puncture the tire on a car full of brawny men, they just let them call for a tow?"

The ghost at her side nodded. "I've been tryin', but…until this day…well, none saw me."

"No one?" Carly said, surprised. "But I had assumed that—"

"Oh, that I died many a year ago? Indeed, lass, I did. The Battle of Stirling Bridge, and a fine and nobly glorious way fer a man to give his life! Wallace was a true friend to Scotland, no braver or more loyal a man to his people e'er lived, and, as I am now, I saw the Bruce, and while imperfect as all mortal men, he rose to the status of countryman as well."

"The Battle of Stirling Bridge!" Carly murmured. "But, sir—"

"That was the year of our Lord 1297, a lovely September, and we set the stage! Only so many of the enemy could cross the narrow bridge at a time and our Wallace had us wait until a number were over and then we attacked and they were cut down and led into the marsh. Their companions watched from across the water and ran, broken…and it was brilliant the way it was taken and…" He paused, shrugging. "One day, one day soon, when my time is done, I will join my brethren from that day and my sweet Jane, lost ere the battle began."

"But you've been here…since?"

"Aye." He shook his head. "William Wallace was not so poor a man, not elite, yet educated by monks and supported by an important bishop. And it was true that he murdered the English Sheriff of Lanark and led men to take the entire garrison, but, lass, you kin, the sheriff killed the Wallace's wife and deserved all that was done. Alas, I saw the battle lost at Falkirk, and knew of the betrayal by Sir John de Menteith that led to his capture, and then…"

"I'm sorry," Carly murmured. "And I do know that the wars for independence went on for almost sixty years, which must have been brutal for you to see. But then, and in all the centuries to follow, Luke and I are the first among the living with whom you've been able to speak?"

"Nay, lass, nay! I have met…six of those like you with the

strange and special ability, but none until you and your lad in this century," he told her.

Carly smiled. "Wow. So…" She paused, wincing. "Then, sir, I'm afraid you saw the castle here change hands many times and I'm so sorry. You know about Wallace and—"

"Hanged, drawn and quartered, and yet that very face created a nationalism as perhaps nothing else might have done. Ah, William. The hangin'…they don't let you die. Ye must be alive until they rip yer heart and guts from yer livin' flesh! Aye," he said, shaking his head, "but now the great Wallace rests in peace!"

"I can't even imagine how horrible such an execution might be," Carly murmured. "Or how any human being could do that to another."

He arched a thick dark brow at her. "And, lass, we must keep it that way!" He hesitated. "When it came to the time when the Bruce had been pushed back save for Stirling Castle, it had been sworn that the garrison would surrender if reinforcements didn't come. Now, William Wallace always fought King Edward I, one of the greatest kings and commanders any country ever saw, ruthless, beset, fierce and a warrior like few others. He died as the wars went on and Bruce faced off against Edward II, not so great a warrior! But he sent reinforcements because he darednae lose Stirling Castle, but the Bruce prepared and caught the English at the Battle of Bannockburn. He was far outnumbered, but again, he used the river, he set traps, he forced the landscape. English archers couldnae fire on their own men—he finally found one advantage point, but Wallace sent in his light horse cavalry and continued to fight on the front, and in the end…"

"Edward II barely made it out alive," Carly put in.

Kenneth nodded with a smile. "And thus those wars ended at Bannockburn and Robert the Bruce was truly king of the Scots. Ah, lass. Mankind does not change! There came the Jacobite Uprising, wars over religion, the horror of witchcraft trials, countries always seeking to take other countries, and if that is not enough, you have human monsters preying upon innocents!"

"Such as our would-be H. H. Holmes," Carly said. "But, Kenneth, if you haven't really seen anything happen, how do you know where it might be happening and who might be causing such a thing?"

"I've suspected the Vicky Inn of being...a bad place. I have gone, I have watched, I have waited. But..."

"You haven't seen anything solid yet."

"But those these folks encounter are not always seen again. And as I am...there be little I kin do!"

"Sir—"

"Nor a 'sir,' lass. Kenneth of Clan Menzies."

Carly lowered her head and smiled. "Kenneth, the term in this century is one of respect. But, the point is, Luke and I—"

"Yer not from here."

She smiled. "No, we're from America. Now, if you've been here for hundreds of years—"

"Yer American. Aye."

She smiled and said, "Yep! American. Kenneth, I need to make a phone call."

"Aye, as ye need, lass!"

She gave Liz a call.

Liz answered cheerfully.

"Everything is all right?" Carly asked her.

"Lovely. Beautiful drive."

"Listen, I'm following you—"

"What? Why? I just left you at the pub!"

"We're a bit nervous about the amount of people who may be involved—and that they might know that you're alone."

"Oh, aye, Campbell rang me. Said I'd have a police escort soon. You needn't—"

"I'm following until you're with the police."

"Fine. But you needn't—I'm an excellent driver."

"Just stay on the road until someone is with you."

"Aye, then. I'm slowing down—you can catch up."

"There's a plan. If officers are there to assist you, call me back and I'll head on to Vicky Inn."

They ended the call.

"The lady is with Police Scotland?"

"The National Crime Agency. But she's with the computer—scientific data analysis—department. She's not a…"

"Warrior?" Kenneth asked.

She nodded. "But Luke and I are here working with Police Scotland and the National Crime Agency—"

"Ye've some power, eh?"

"We do. And we thank you for any help. You will know so much about this area that we don't. You've been here many years and seen many changes, I'm sure—"

"Others go. I ha' stayed. Perhaps it is now my place to help end the reign of a monster!"

She glanced at him. "If you haven't seen anything that—"

He laughed softly. "Ah, lass! I'm fond of the pub—they ha' a lovely TV. I see the world around me and I know what's been a-happenin'."

Carly kept her eyes on the road but smiled and nodded to him. It was possible, of course, to find the spirits of the deceased in cemeteries in which they were buried—but she also knew that they weren't bound to those cemeteries and often preferred to be elsewhere.

"Now, lass, what's that mischievous grin about?" Kenneth asked.

"Many friends I've met like…pubs. And their homes, fairs…" She turned quickly to smile at it. "Places where they enjoyed before…"

"Death. 'Tis not an evil thing but the natural end to the life of the flesh," he told her. "Ye need not dance around, lass. I know I'm dead."

He said it in a way to make her laugh and she did.

"Thank you," she told him. "Thank you for coming with me. You are a true delight to know."

"May I return the compliment?"

She smiled. "You may!" She let out a sigh, frowning suddenly. "You have been to Vicky Inn?"

He nodded. "I have been there, other places…through the woods."

"And nothing has happened?"

"Nothing that I have been able to see," he said.

"But you're sure—"

"Lass, I was a scout and a warrior. There is almost something in the air when evil is about. I told ye, I see the telly. And," he added, "I was there, at the pub, when a bloke came lookin' for his lass. She'd told him she was headed to Vicky Inn. But that pair swore they never saw her." He looked at Carly. "Ye rang up yer friend. She knows that there is danger. She wouldnae stop to see the woods, to take pictures?"

"No, no, Kenneth. And remember, members of Police Scotland are looking for her, too," Carly assured him.

They were driving along a lonely stretch of road surrounded by hills and forests. It was beautiful scenery, green and touched by the sun, scattered with wildflowers and rich shrubs.

"Such a landscape," she murmured.

"Some just as it was in me day," Kenneth said. "Aye, the very ground here, the cliffs, the glens, the country. Cool rivers running, and Stirling itself, twixt the Highlands and the Lowlands."

"Stirling itself," she repeated. "And this drive! So lovely."

But it was along that stretch of the road, soon after she had spoken, that Carly almost froze.

Liz's navy SUV was pulled up on the side of the road, parked neatly and clearly on the embankment.

"I told her not to stop driving!" Carly muttered.

She immediately slowed her pace and veered toward the embankment, too.

"Lass? That's the car she took?" Kenneth asked.

"Liz, yes, it's an unmarked police vehicle and it's what we came up in. Kenneth, with all these woods... Oh, my God! Where is Police Scotland?" she wondered, slamming the door behind her as she leaped out of the car.

The spirit of Kenneth Menzies was quickly at her side. He glanced at her. "Is she in the thing? Perhaps restin'?" he asked hopefully. "Ah! There's a tire down. The lass had to pull over. She couldnae drive it farther."

Carly was already by the car, hoping against hope Liz might still be inside.

It was empty. She pulled out her phone and dialed Liz.

She heard the buzz.

Liz's phone was on the front passenger seat of the car.

"There be trails ahead, almost as old as time. Both rise to that mound—one to the southwest, the other to the northwest. Put a call in to the police. Ye may need a good hound or two."

"Thank you," she murmured, dialing Campbell's number and quickly explaining to him where she was to the best of her ability—her directions were probably good enough.

Kenneth helped her as she spoke. She knew she needed to call Luke, but Campbell told her he would do so; he also suggested that she wait for backup.

"Time could be everything, sir. And—" she glanced at Kenneth but couldn't tell Campbell she wasn't alone "—I am a trained agent, sir. I will be careful."

She ended the call and looked at Kenneth. "That is the truth! She had a good head start—a good twenty-minute head start on us," she said to him. "And the others left the pub soon after Liz, all of them, the older woman, Kaye Bolden, and the couple, Terry and Jim Allen, and... Green. That's what he's going by, the man we believe to have started all this and to…supervise and/or partake in all the scams and the killing."

"You know, I am quite amazed, lass. You can hear me so easily, girl? As if I spoke in a live man's voice?" he asked her.

"Yes, I can. It's—"

"A trait, aye, passed through families and generations, a sense," Kenneth mused. He winced and said, "I saw a few condemned as witches, aye, in a very bad time, and those not even so gifted taken for naught. I ask, though we've talked long, because I must make sure that I am loud and clear. I will shout for ye and ye must take care—"

"I really am a trained agent," she said.

"Any man and woman may be taken by a worthy opponent," he warned. "And if anything, me lass, scream bloody murder, for that's well what it may be!"

It wasn't much of a great pep talk, Carly thought. But he was truthful. That was what made a partner who always had one's back so critically important.

This time…

Her partner was already dead. But Liz was a brilliant analyst—not a "warrior." She had never been trained for what might have befallen her.

"Let's move!" she told him. She started to walk and felt his hand on her arm. She felt it strongly, and for a ghost to have such a powerful physical manifestation was rare, but then Kenneth seemed to be incredible and rare already as a ghost as he surely was when he was a living man.

She paused, looking back at him.

"Ye know the legend of the Bruce and the spider?"

She smiled and nodded. "He was taking refuge in a cave on an island off Ireland. He watched a spider as he wondered if he would ever prevail. The spider patiently spun and re-spun its web. And Robert the Bruce knew that he needed patience and never to give up. Don't worry, Kenneth. We don't give up."

He nodded at her and they headed to their separate trails.

Carly moved almost silently, taking great care as she followed the narrow trail that had been forged by foot through the centuries. She left the glen, climbing, encountering a rich backdrop of trees and shrubs. But as she moved, she studied the path itself.

There was no indication that others had been there just before her. No recently broken branches appeared before her and she began to wonder if, perhaps, Liz hadn't been forced into another car, taken…

Back to Stirling?

But as she wondered at her own foolishness in not suspecting that as the first possibility, she heard Kenneth calling out to her.

"Lass, this way, come careful, fer…they may be close!"

She turned quickly, almost at a run as she retraced her steps to follow the path that Kenneth had taken. Once she reached that path, she slowed again, knowing that she needed to take extreme care.

Liz's vehicle had been sabotaged, she was sure. But how many people—and which people—might have followed her? Were there others beyond those they had seen at the pub involved?

She was moving slowly and almost silently again, using the trees for cover, when she saw Kenneth ahead.

She was pleased to startle him when she emerged behind him; he had doubted her abilities. Maybe he would have more faith in her now.

He ignored his own reaction, pointing out ahead.

"She's tied to a tree. The lass. I see one man and the old woman, who seems to be calling someone, waiting for a response, and I don't think that the man has seen her yet, realized that she has a phone out and maybe she's calling for help. Yer lass, Liz, she's there and tied to the tree!"

"Yes, that's Liz. The old woman was introduced to us as Kaye Bolden. She stays at Vicky Inn. Lives there, so it seems," Carly whispered.

"A victim, one would think. With her holdings turned over to the Allen couple," Kenneth murmured.

"Probably. But she is calling someone," Carly whispered.

"Now…the bloke has a gun," Kenneth warned.

"So do I," Carly told him.

If Kaye Bolden was calling for help, help might be there soon. Before Police Scotland could arrive.

Carly couldn't take a chance with Liz's life.

"Can you…?" Carly began.

"Create a distraction? Aye, that I can!" Kenneth shouted.

He moved off through the trees, managing to cause a disturbance with the branches by literally *walking through them*.

"What the bloody hell?" the man shouted. He appeared to be about forty, medium in height and build, but angry when he heard the noise. His accent sounded English.

Kaye Bolden had her cell phone in her hand—but she hadn't managed to dial a number to warn anyone. She was just staring, as if stunned to hear that another person might have been near them.

"Get a hold of him. I was not supposed to be in any cross fire!" the man declared angrily. "They had promised to pick her up. I'll not go down for this! She'll need to die fast if it's a copper out there or if someone sees…"

He shook his head furiously and then rushed off toward the bushes Kenneth was rattling.

Kaye Bolden stared after him. She started to lift her phone.

There was no choice. They couldn't let the call go through.

Carly made a beeline for Kaye Bolden, throwing herself on the woman and forcing her to the ground.

The cell phone went flying and Kaye Bolden stared up at her with a burning hatred so intense that Carly almost felt the heat.

She pushed herself up, ready to rise and ease her weight from that of the older woman below her.

"Thank God!" Liz cried. "Thank God, thank God! Oh.

Carly! Help me, help me, she's down, he's gone. Oh, my God! They were behind me, you had called me… The tire went and I tried to grab the phone but he was behind me so fast and he dragged me from the car. They were setting me up to be taken to be tortured and killed. Thank God, thank God!"

"Shh!" Carly warned.

Liz's words of gratitude had come too soon.

Kenneth had distracted the man and lured him away, which meant Carly had been able to stop Kaye from making a call, but he must have heard the commotion by the tree.

Carly had barely lifted herself from Kaye as she saw him running back, gun out.

Aimed at her.

Carly flew up behind a tree in the nick of time, drawing her Glock from its holster at the small of her back.

The man came running back first firing wildly and then shooting right at them.

Kaye Bolden was starting to rise.

"No!" Carly shrieked. "Get down!" The woman didn't hear her.

And one of the man's bullets found a mark.

Thankfully, not Liz.

And not Carly.

Kaye hadn't heeded Carly's warning. She had kept moving and his shot caught her as she tried to rise, piercing through her back and bursting through her chest into the trunk of a tree. He was, Carly thought, firing a 9 mm loaded with full metal jackets.

He was taking aim again.

This time at Liz.

And Carly had no choice—she fired.

He went down.

She had learned early in her career that just because a suspect went down, he or she might not be disabled. She rushed silently over to the man, retrieved the gun at his side and rolled him face up.

His eyes were open. Now, staring up at the sky. He was dead.

She closed her eyes, thoughts racing through her head. She hated killing, though she wasn't sure how she'd feel if such a time came with the man pretending to be a modern H. H. Holmes, the man who had created the Society that had caused the anguish and death of so many. She couldn't dwell on that. She believed that Kaye Bolden was dead, too, killed accidentally by this man.

At this point, the seriousness of her actions was worrisome. She had fired her weapon and caused a death.

That meant paperwork and an inquiry. She was an American agent and she didn't object to any kind of investigation or paperwork, except that...

She had to get back. She had to return to Luke, arrive at the Vicky Inn...

Set herself up and find the end to all this horror.

"Carly, please! Set me free!" Liz begged.

Of course. The poor woman had been tied to a tree, expecting all manner of horror any minute. Carly rushed over, fumbled in her pocket for her Swiss Army knife and began working furiously at the ropes tying her.

But then the ghost of Kenneth Menzies was at her side, shaking his head. "Ah, lass, ye are something of a warrior, then!"

She couldn't answer him. She wondered if he understood much of the modern world. In his mind, killing someone who would have killed you was simply the only choice. Of course, it was, really, but as law enforcement...

She couldn't reply because Liz was there, still mumbling about both her fear and her gratitude. But Kenneth knew she couldn't reply.

"Sirens!" he said.

"At last," Carly murmured.

"Ye'd best ring the lad back at the pub or the Vicky Inn," Kenneth told her.

"Yes!"

"Yes?" Liz repeated, confused.

"I just remembered—give me a second. I need to let Luke know what is going on," she explained.

She made certain she drew out the right phone and hit her speed dial, connecting her burner to Luke's burner.

As she did, she heard someone was coming from cars that had drawn up to the embankment far below and she shouted as loudly as she could. "Here, up here!"

Luke, on the other end, heard her. "Carly, Carly, what's happening there? Are you all right? Is Liz all right?" he asked.

"I'm fine. Liz is fine—"

"Nay, I'm far from fine!" Liz cried.

"We are alive and unharmed," Carly corrected. "But, Luke, I killed the man who took her. He was firing at us and I had no choice. I don't know how quickly—"

"You'll be fine," he told her.

"Pardon? How can you know?"

Police were coming up the trail. A tall, slim policewoman and two policemen in uniform, along with a fourth person.

Brendan Campbell.

How the hell had the man managed to get there so quickly?

"You'll be all right. Liz was taken by them but—"

"Someone caused a slow leak in one of her tires that became a fast leak, and she had to drive off the road. It had to have been planned by someone who knew she was leaving the pub. Oh! And, Luke, one of the dead is Kaye Bolden—"

"You had to kill the old lady?"

"No, no. I just knocked her phone out of her hand. Her companion was aiming at me, I think, but he hit her and he was going to hit Liz. I had to—"

"Yes, Carly. You had to. I'll see you when you get here.

These places all seem to have libraries. I'll be in the library at Vicky Inn—you'll find it when you get here. Is Kenneth still with you?"

"Yes."

"Good. Keep him with you."

"Uh, if he wishes."

"I guarantee you, such a man will not leave you."

She almost managed to smile. Because she believed him.

"They're here. I'll call on my way," she promised, ending the call. The trio of police officers were nearing her and they paused in front of her; she nodded. They waited and so she did as well.

Then Brendan Campbell was standing before her. But before either of them could speak, Liz had catapulted herself into the man's arms, barely coherent as she explained what had happened to her and then turned to Carly, saying, "She saved me! Oh, my dear bloody hell, but she saved my life!"

"Good to have you here," the tall policewoman told Carly.

"Aye," agreed one of the others. "We might not have made it in as timely a manner. I'll start with photographs," he told Campbell, and Carly realized he was carrying a large camera. "But Forensics and a medical examiner are on the way."

"Observation and notes," the policewoman murmured, walking toward the body of Kaye Bolden.

"Interviews," the third officer said, looking at Campbell.

"I will start and I'll be fast!" Liz said.

And she was fast, explaining how she had suddenly realized her tire was almost flat—and then it was. She hadn't even had time to pick up her phone before the man had dragged her from the car. He and the woman had dragged her fighting and kicking up the incline and tied her to the tree. She'd heard him talking to someone about coming to pick her up. And noooooo! The older woman had not been there to help her; she had been something like a…supervisor. Then there had been a rustle in the bushes, the man had run off, and before the woman could make a call,

Carly had caught her and they'd gone down together and then the man had come back, shooting! But he missed Carly, hit the older woman, kept shooting…and thankfully, thankfully, thankfully, Carly had shot back!

Carly said that they'd feared something when they'd been at the pub in Stirling and she had decided to follow Liz just in case. Campbell, of course, had been notified, police had been on the way, but when she saw Liz tied to the tree and the woman about to make a call, she'd decided she had to make a stand, get the phone from her and free Liz—except that the man had started shooting and she had returned fire.

"I wonder what distracted the bloke from looking after his victim?" the officer mused.

Carly shook her head.

"A bird? Some other creature, a rodent or even a wildcat," Liz offered.

Campbell shrugged. "But you knew the woman?" he asked, looking at Carly.

She nodded. "She was at the table with the suspect Luke was to meet. And you know, of course, that he and Luke connected, that he 'met' me at the bar in the pub, and he took me to the table where 'H. H. Holmes,' who is now Harry Green, was sitting with the woman who was introduced to me as Kaye Bolden and the owners of Vicky Inn, Terry and Jim Allen."

Campbell nodded. "Any idea on the identity of the man?"

"I never saw him before," Carly replied.

"That's fine—we'll be taking care of the scene from here," Campbell said. "Normally, I'd take your Glock but…timing is important. You need to get to the inn." He paused because the officer who had been taking notes had hurried back.

"Sir, we've an ID on the dead man. Beau Simpson, address given on his ID is in London, and he's been arrested numerous times, just freed after a three-year stint in prison."

"Does the name mean anything to you?" Campbell asked Carly.

"No, I have never seen him before and I've never heard his name," Carly told him.

"Just another Society member," Campbell muttered, his voice hard. His mouth was tight for a minute and then he spoke to her again. "We'll be here with Elizabeth," he assured her. "I have another man, Daniel Murray, joining you and Agent Kendrick at Vicky Inn. He'll follow you back at a distance, but with this happening…"

"A third is greatly appreciated," Carly assured him. "But I can—"

"Drive straight back," Campbell told her. "We can't take time with this. People are missing."

"Yes, sir. I am going right now."

"You're certain that the woman didn't start a call mentioning that you were suddenly upon them?"

"I'm quite certain."

"And your dead man—"

"He wouldn't have known me," Carly said with certainty.

"Then go. This spreads like a virus—we must stop it."

"Yes, sir," Carly promised. She waited for a beat and then glanced at Liz.

"Go!" Liz said. Then she hugged Carly tightly. "Thank you for saving my life!"

"I'm grateful as well," Carly assured her. "Then…yes. I'm heading back."

Kenneth Menzies had been standing in silence the whole time.

"I am with ye, lass. Ye'll not go alone!" he vowed.

She lowered her head because she couldn't resist a smile. No, he couldn't do much with his fists and he couldn't lift a sword or shoot a gun.

But he had proved himself invaluable.

With a slight nod that was to him but might have been to

the others, she turned and started back down the incline of the trail to her vehicle.

She slid behind the driver's seat and Kenneth Menzies just glided in next to her.

Starting the car, she turned to him before heading onto the road.

"You were wonderful!" she told him. "Thank you."

"The lass is alive."

She smiled and nodded. It saddened her that Kaye Bolden had died, but then…she had chosen her actions. Or maybe she hadn't. Maybe she hadn't known what was intended for Liz. And still, somehow, it seemed sad.

Worse than that. If she had been alive, she might have saved them all from a great deal of trouble, worry and danger. She might have pointed a finger right at the people who were doing the heavy lifting when it came to kidnapping, torture and murder.

"Lass, yer not happy," Kenneth commented.

"No, no, I am. I mean, they went after Liz. And she is alive. But—"

"Lass, ye didnae set out to kill. They did."

"I know. But if we'd taken her alive…"

"Ye've the heart, girl. Ye've the heart. There are others—if ye had learned more from the woman, police might have rushed in. Some may have died lest they talk, while if y'go in with yer lad and find them…"

He let his voice trail hopefully.

She smiled and nodded.

"You are coming with me all the way?"

"I kin explore where y'mightnae go!"

"And so you can!"

CHAPTER SEVENTEEN

Luke sat in the library at Vicky Inn, a book on his lap.

One he had read so he could pretend he was reading and answer questions about his enjoyment of the novel, should he be asked.

Vicky Inn.

Built in 1842, the house offered a beautiful facade, a sweeping porch, handsome columns, a third-floor attic and, Luke was certain, a deep basement.

The man calling himself Harry Green here had returned to the pub and offered him a ride when he'd heard Luke had lent his car to his new lady friend so that she could stop quickly for something special for her hair she'd read could only be purchased at one nearby shop.

"But—you just met her," Harry had said, frowning.

"Oh, I am certain she's coming back for me. I warned her. Told her I kept a GPS on my car. Of course, she laughed, saying she has not the least intention of stealing anything. I saw her wallet—she has plenty. In fact, of course, I'm intrigued to find out just what she does have in this *worldly* world. She'll come

back. I know my women, Harry. I'll just give her a call and tell
her she can go straight to the inn if she wishes."

"But you didn't go with her?"

And Luke had laughed. "I was still enjoying a good whiskey. I hear that it's the one main export in all the British Isles.
Is that true?"

"I must admit, I know little other than the fact that I enjoy
a good whiskey," Harry had told him. "But come on, then. I'll
give you a ride. If you want to give her a call—"

"Will do. Um, wait! You just came back here. Didn't you
leave and say—"

"Screwed up. My appointment is tomorrow. I was going to
have another drink, but if you're ready?"

"Whenever you are, my friend. But you're welcome to have
your drink."

Harry Green had appeared amused. "They have good whiskey
at the inn. But this lady… Carly. You already got her number?"

"Of course I did. I work fast. And… I'm anxious."

"Tell her not to mention where she's going—someone may
get in first, and while my friends know you're coming and believe she is, I wouldn't want them giving away their last room."

He feigned a call to Carly. He knew at that moment, she
wouldn't be back that soon, but he told her to take her time—as
long as she did return his car. "Oh, and I'll wait for you. There
must be a place downstairs somewhere with chairs—"

"Fantastic library," Harry assured him.

"The library," he said to his phone.

He did need to speak with Carly again. But he also felt he
didn't want her phone ringing if she was in a position where she
was hoping to be quiet.

He would give her time. She would call him.

Of course, he learned exactly what had happened. Thankfully,
he was checked in when he did hear from her and had a moment
alone when he brought his bags to the second floor—and to his

room. Room six. At the end of the hallway upstairs. Rooms one, two and three were next to each other on the one side of the hallway and rooms four, five and six were on the other.

Terry Allen was behind the counter that sat at the rear of the beautifully appointed main parlor of the house, smiling broadly when she gave him his room.

"And we have your new friend right next to you. Room six."

When he came downstairs after speaking with Carly and searching the room, Harry was gone.

He wondered where the man was.

And he wondered what he was doing; they were going to need to move fast. Jim Allen was also nowhere to be seen, and Luke couldn't help but wonder if they weren't in a "vault" somewhere on the grounds, doing unspeakable things.

He knew Carly was not going to be happy that she'd killed a man—or that Kaye Bolden, the woman who might have given them something, was dead. Go figure. Granny had apparently been in on it.

Then again...

Someone in the Society, the dead man, was tasked with stopping Liz. Someone was supposed to then go to retrieve her. Interesting. They'd have planned on taking back a screaming, protesting woman...

No, they'd have knocked her out with something.

Still, they'd have been tasked with getting her in somewhere. He looked up. Carly had arrived. She didn't see him across the parlor where he sat and she walked up to the desk where Terry Allen was busy at her computer. She turned quickly, though, a big smile on her face, as she heard Carly's arrival.

"Hey! You're back. I hear you went to a special store?"

"Oh, not a special store. I was a bit across town. They're known to carry American brands, and as rude as it sounds, I use certain products and..."

Terry laughed. "Not to worry—I understand. Anyway, the

young man whose car you took is in the library, but I'm assuming you want to get rid of that bag. You're in number five—we only let six rooms here, so it's easy to find. Second floor up the stairs."

"Oh, thank you!" Carly said, accepting her key. She frowned, pointing behind Terry and the desk. "Isn't that an elevator?"

"It was, or rather, it is—we just don't allow guests in it right now. Too many mechanical problems, and we can't get the elevator man out here until next week."

"Oh."

"You don't have a problem with stairs, do you?" Terry asked worriedly.

"No, no, not at all. Good for our cardio, right?" Carly returned cheerfully. "So, I will just walk up and dump this. And the library?" she asked politely.

"Right there!" Terry Allen smiled and pointed.

Luke, his book in front of him, waved. "Come on down! The materials here are great. You like reading, right?"

"Of course! I love books," she said. "Back in a jiffy!"

With a smile, she headed for the stairs. As she did, Luke saw their spirit friend from the pub was there, too; he watched Carly head for the stairs, turned to nod at Luke and hurried after her.

They both turned to the hallway of rooms at the top of the stairs. Terry Allen left her desk behind and walked over to Luke.

She was smiling as if they shared a great secret.

"You do move fast."

He gave her a smile and a nod. "I believe she's a tech heiress."

"Or—a liar?"

He shook his head. "Not the way she was speaking. She grew up in various places because of her father's job—Silicon Valley, some time in China, some in Hong Kong… Sounds like the real thing. Her suit is high-quality—clothing seems stylish…and she didn't introduce herself as rich. She did tell me she didn't care what a hotel cost as long as it gave her a real feel for a place."

"Well, keep finding out all that you can!" Terry told him.
She glanced at her watch. "Hmm," she murmured.

"Is anything wrong?" he asked her.

"No, I, uh, just expected Jim back. He and Harry are usually here at around this time. We serve cocktails and snacks about now."

"Ah, man, nice!" Luke said.

He thought he might know where Harry Green and Jim Allen were. They had probably headed out to relieve their accomplice and Mrs. Kaye Bolden of their captive. But they should be back soon. They would have arrived at the area where Liz's car tire had gone flat.

They would have seen the police cars.

And they would have hightailed it back, wondering if either or both of their accomplices had been killed, or worse.

If they had talked.

Carly came back down the stairs while Terry Allen was still standing by him.

"This place is beautiful!" Carly raved.

"Well, thank you," Terry Allen told her, smiling.

But the woman still looked concerned. She was smiling away, but...

She'd known that the two men had gone to retrieve a victim.

"Oh, excuse me!" Terry added. "The phone is ringing."

"Of course. But we can help you if you need to serve something—or we can wait! We were just at the pub," Luke told her.

"No, no, no, I'm, uh, sure that everything is fine and that's a call to tell me they're almost here!" she said, hurrying away.

When she was gone, Carly smiled at Luke. "Think she's getting some strange news?" she asked.

"Oh, yes. Though they can't know everything that happened. But they may be on edge, wondering if someone isn't talking to law enforcement, trying to make a deal. Where's our new friend from the pub? He followed you upstairs."

"He's going where we can't go," Carly said softly. "Heading up to the attic and going through the second floor. Is anyone else staying here now?"

"I haven't seen anyone else," Luke told her.

"He was wonderful, by the way," Carly said. "I don't know how much you know about what happened on the way out—"

"I talked to Campbell after I talked to you. He said he's sending us one of his people to join in on the splendor of the stay."

They were supposed to be playing a flirtatious couple; he dared to pull her close to him, rising, taking her face between his hands and kissing her lightly before whispering, "I'm grateful. So grateful you and Liz are okay."

"Luke, I didn't kill Kaye Bolden. If she hadn't died—"

"No, you didn't kill Kaye. A killer killed her. And you saved Liz. So far, so good."

"But if we had one of them—"

"Liz could be dead, and I don't think I could have lived with that. And I sure as hell couldn't have lived with it if that killer had killed you."

She smiled. They were so close. Whispering. But Terry Allen was headed back toward them.

"Thank you for being such good and patient guests," she said. She was doing the smiling thing, but it was obvious that she was still disconcerted.

"Can we do anything?" Carly asked her.

"No, no, they'll be here any minute. And we have whiskey and snacks in the kitchen, and in an hour or so, we're having fresh salmon, my potatoes—delicious, if I do say so myself—and asparagus," Terry told them.

"It sounds divine!" Carly said. "I know that breakfast often comes with a stay like this, but I never imagined dinner."

"Oh, we do everything possible for and with our guests!" Terry exclaimed. "Excuse me again, though. I'll head to the kitchen to get dinner going."

"Of course," Luke said. "Oh, okay…the library is right here, and…"

"Head to the left," Terry said cheerfully. "Dining room, kitchen, pantry—all that on the one side of the house and you're welcome there anytime."

"Thanks!" Carly told her. "This really is such an amazing experience!"

Terry left them. Carly smiled and came close to Luke; there had been no attempt to hide the cameras in the parlor and reception desk. It might have been natural for any establishment to keep cameras over their business areas.

"Luke, if they're worried about seeing the cop cars and wondering if their people talked, they'll hurry up to get rid of anything."

He smoothed her hair back, smiling, as if the two of them had really made an instant connection.

"I am aware, but…"

The door to the parlor opened and a young man entered. He had shaggy dark hair and wore an AC/DC T-shirt and carried a backpack.

"Hey! I read about this place in a tour book!" he told them. "Is there—"

"The owner is just in the kitchen," Luke replied cheerfully. "And I have no idea if they have any rooms available tonight. But—"

Terry came hurrying out. She didn't seem surprised to see that they'd been joined in the parlor by another guest.

"Hello, Mr. Murray?"

"Yes! How—"

"A lovely lady—I believe your mom—called to make a reservation. Welcome. Come over here and I'll get you signed in," Terry said.

She was still off. Cheerfully off.

"Daniel Murray, yes, thanks, and I did tell my mom I wanted

to come here," he said. He looked over at Luke and Carly. "Hey!"

"We're Carly and Luke," Luke told him. "You'll love your room."

"Well, that's it, then," Terry murmured. "We only let six rooms and I am in the process of renovating one of them. There will just be the five of you. We have Mrs. Bolden—lovely elderly lady, you'll truly enjoy her—Carly, Luke, a gentleman named Harry Green and you, Daniel. So, give me about thirty minutes. I've decided on a true dinner tonight, but give me that bit of time and head on into the kitchen for the evening meal—I am an excellent cook, if I do say so myself."

"Wow! And I'd been wondering where to head out for dinner," Daniel said.

Campbell had told Luke that the undercover he was sending was young but experienced, someone who could play the naive American to the hilt.

He turned to Carly and Luke and said, "Hey, just going to stow my gear. Mind if I join you two after?"

"Of course not," Carly said.

With a wave, Daniel Murray started up the stairs. As he did so, Kenneth Menzies came down the stairs, passing by the newcomer.

Daniel Murray gave a little shiver.

He might not have seen Kenneth, but he'd felt him.

Terry gave them one of her nervous smiles and headed back into the kitchen.

The ghost continued over to Luke and Carly, shaking his head. "I found nothing, I fear. But," he added with a frown, "four of the rooms still have bags in them."

"So, there are people hidden here," Carly murmured. She winced. "Living or dead. Somewhere."

"And they'll kill them quickly and hide whatever evidence," Luke said. He looked at Carly as he spoke, but they knew his words were for their helpful ghost. "Below. There's access to the basement of this place below. And God alone knows what tunnels any underground area might have. Kenneth, if you can check below..."

"I've not found access for the living as of yet. I shall try the kitchen. Most oft, in these new places, that's where one can find—"

"No!" Carly said suddenly. "Kenneth, can you get down the elevator that is supposedly not working?"

"Aye, lass! Of course I can."

"Thank you!" Carly told him.

Luke wasn't sure why, but he stopped the ghost. "Kenneth, wait. Can you slip into the kitchen first? I don't know why this woman wouldn't want us all in there as she prepared things— except for the first so many minutes..."

"Poisoning the food, eh?" Kenneth asked.

"Possibly," Luke said.

Kenneth headed after Terry. While he was gone, Daniel Murray came hurrying down the stairs. "There you are," he announced, walking over to them. As he shook Luke's hand, he bent and said softly, "I found tubes in my room. Gas tubes, I believe. Well concealed in the closet behind a lockbox."

Luke didn't have a chance to answer; the door opened and Harry Green entered along with Jim Allen.

"Hello, there!" Jim said, looking over at the three of them. "How are you enjoying our humble—but charming—establishment? And you, young man—"

"Daniel Murray, sir, of Cincinnati, Ohio!" Daniel told him.

"Welcome. I'm Jim, and this is Harry Green."

"I'm a fixture," Harry said dryly, grinning at the newcomer. "Now, I understand that we're about to have a lovely dinner."

Terry came hurrying out of the kitchen. She was doing her best to play the role of happy innkeeper, but her nervousness was almost palpable to Luke.

"You're back! Good! I may be needing a bit of assistance," Terry said. "In the kitchen."

"Of course," Jim said. "You will all excuse us?" He looked at his wife pointedly. "Mrs. Bolden is still sleeping?"

"Oh, aye! She asked not to be disturbed tonight," Terry said. "That's what she told me, anyway."

"Then we will certainly leave her be," Jim said. "So—"

They all offered their guests quick smiles and disappeared toward the dining room. As they did so, Kenneth returned.

Disturbed. He walked right through Harry Green but the man didn't seem to notice.

"There's something," Kenneth told them. "Not in the food— in the whiskey. Don't be drinkin' the whiskey!"

Luke wasn't sure how to answer him with Daniel Murray seated by them. But to his surprise, the man said softly, "This place is…"

He stopped speaking. Luke and Carly both looked at him expectantly.

"Never mind," he murmured.

"Haunted?" Carly suggested.

The man hesitated again, looking downward. "It's a murder castle, so of course it has a feel. But…"

To Luke's surprise, he stared at Carly and murmured, "I can't *see* as my grandmother did, but I have a sense that…"

"There is someone here?" she murmured.

Luke had to wonder at first if Daniel Murray had been sent not just to assist, but to test them as well. But when the man looked at him, he was suddenly certain he wasn't lying. "Yes, we have it. And, yes, a friend is with us."

"Then he can help us!" Daniel said.

"He is helping us. Somehow, we need to get through dinner without drinking the whiskey," Carly said.

"Poisoned?" Daniel guessed.

"Possibly. Or laced to make us pass out," Luke said. He looked at Kenneth.

"I just saw the wee container by the whiskey bottle. Three glasses were already poured—others waited empty to be filled when you went in."

"So, we need to pretend to drink whiskey and get to our rooms as quickly as possible. But whatever is going on must be down below and we need to find access," Daniel said.

"Our friend Kenneth will find us a way. We'll have dinner, pretend to drink whiskey and head to our rooms," Luke said.

"But what if they think we should drop dead immediately?" Daniel asked.

Luke glanced at the ghost of Kenneth Menzies for a moment. Daniel had a good point.

"I'll be moving faster than air," Kenneth promised.

"Normally, I'd say no, it is going to be something to make us pass out so that we're pliable to be brought down to their torture chamber, wherever it may be. But tonight, they may be desperate. They all know by now that the police found Liz—what they don't know is what might have happened to Kaye Bolden and her accomplice. But they must be worried and maybe even expecting the police here at any minute."

"Maybe we should just arrest the three of them now," Daniel muttered.

"We can't prove anything yet," Carly reminded him.

"We could just shoot the three of them," Daniel ventured bitterly. He shook his head. "Not really from Cincinnati, you know, though I do pride myself on an excellent American accent. What this is doing to *my* country is—"

"The world, Daniel. The world." Luke shook his head. "And we need to make sure that Harry Green is the H. H. Holmes Society leader and that it ends forever. If the police were to come now, he could find a way to put it all on the people he's so easily used because they're sick themselves—Jim and Terry Allen."

"Can that be real?" Daniel asked. "A husband-and-wife torture team?"

"Suzan and James Carson, Fred and Rose West, there's the whole Karla Homolka and Paul Bernardo set of killings—including her sister—and many more, I'm afraid," Luke told him.

"And I was in horror of the bloody deaths I witnessed in battle!" Kenneth murmured.

Luke nodded, worried for a brief second that he should stop now, they didn't really know Daniel Murray, but at this point, they needed to trust the man. "Daniel, the spirit you're feeling is that of Kenneth Menzies. He was killed during the Battle of Stirling Bridge."

Daniel nodded. "Thank you, Kenneth," he said softly. "So, now—"

"I will get below," Kenneth said.

Luke watched him start to walk away. But he turned back.

"There are chutes," he said. "For soiled clothing, one imagines. Two in the hallway. A man would fit in one, a lass, too," he added. "I will see how they fall."

"Perfect, Kenneth."

"I hadnae thought to take one down as yet," Kenneth said. "There are stairs from the kitchen, hidden by a cupboard wall, slides easily, I do believe, but I don't be knowin' fer sure. Now... I will try the elevator."

"Thank you!" Carly said.

Kenneth nodded and headed behind the desk, disappearing from their view. Possibly having made his way through the elevator floor.

Daniel was watching Carly.

"What is it?" Carly asked him.

"I was just wondering if a dead man could save us if this all goes to hell," he said. "But so help me, we must stop them!"

"We will," Luke said firmly.

And he sure as hell hoped that his certainty was real.

Harry Green suddenly returned, smiling. "Luke, my boy. Come on in here, will you? I'd have a word or two before dinner."

Luke gave Harry Green his most serious nod. "Excuse me," he told the others. "My friend—he helped Carly and me decide where we should stay tonight."

"Nice," Daniel said, and Luke knew the man had been filled in on the entire sting, but to Harry Green, Daniel was a prospective accomplice.

Maybe *he* could drink the whiskey, he thought dryly.

At the least, in the kitchen, he might discover the easiest way to discard their shots of the stuff without being noted.

They could always play the magician's trick, change glasses.

And yet they couldn't be seen.

One way or the other, he feared, the killers were going to feel that they needed to up their game.

How?

With the whiskey?

Pity. He'd always enjoyed a good Scot's whiskey before. Ah, well. Onward. Maybe they were going to let him in on just about everything.

After all, they were mysteriously down a few accomplices.

"It's amazing, isn't it?" Daniel asked Carly.

"Um, many things are...?"

He smiled at her. "Your ability." He shook his head. "I saw it, so, on the one hand, it was wonderful. Oh, my granny! I know on the day that she died, she was greeted by many friends, and she left this world in peace. And I could *feel*, but I couldn't see or speak with the ghosts she seemed to be such good friends with. They gave her peace when..."

He stopped speaking, wincing.

"I joined the National Crime Agency determined to stop terrible things. My father was stabbed to death in a robbery when I was thirteen."

"I am so sorry!"

He smiled at her. "It's all right and I'm sorry. I didn't tell you for the sympathy. I am, I believe, just jealous. I've known to work for what I've wanted all my life, but this… One has it, or one doesn't, and I fear—"

"It could develop," Carly told him. "Our founder—our American founder, now Assistant Director Adam Harrison—didn't have it, but his son did and he recognized it in others. At first, he just knew the right people to help others in certain situations. Then—because he's also brilliant and an incredible philanthropist—he managed to put together a special unit of the FBI. Of course, we're supposedly special because we deal with cases that involve the occult and cults, witchcraft, voodoo, anything that's seen as out of the norm by others."

"Aliens?" he asked, grinning.

She laughed. "No. I think there may be a different 'special' unit for that. But there came a time when Adam could see his son, Josh. He'd never had the ability before, but maybe his love was so great, or his commitment to the good in humanity so great, that he developed the ability."

Daniel smiled at her. "Maybe. But as far as earthly help goes, Campbell himself will be standing by—five minutes away—if we give them a call to come in. But…"

"But?"

"Thank God for your ghost. I would have drunk the whiskey."

Carly smiled. "Luke will know more."

"They believe he's a member of the H. H. Holmes Society," Daniel said.

She nodded. "And that he just met me and he's certain I'm very rich. The game played there is that he gains all my property. Although…with the real H. H. Holmes, that meant I would give him my property, and then he would give them the property and then…"

"Then he would die. So, why would they assume he didn't know exactly how Holmes worked? The whole Pitezel situation… He was going to substitute a corpse for Pitezel, and they'd share the insurance money. But, of course, he killed the real Pitezel instead and then lied to the man's wife, saying he was alive, that they'd manage everything and meet up. Then he took three of the children and killed them, the greatest horror, and then, thankfully, he was caught."

"The Pinkertons were involved, hired by one of the insurance agencies. By the way, Allan Pinkerton was a Scot!"

"Ah! So, lass, thankfully, we've got the Scots involved in all of this."

Carly smiled. "Exactly."

"And I'm older than I look," he told her. "Thirty-three."

"You could easily pass for early twenties."

"And sometimes I do. Campbell wanted someone who could appear to be young and dumb!" he said.

She laughed. "Young and naive."

Daniel glanced at his watch. "It's been a bit. How the hell are we going to pretend to drink the whiskey?"

"I think that's going to be the least of our problems. Time is everything now, too. Kenneth has told us that the room Terry claimed was being renovated still had someone's belongings in it. These people have taken their 'guests' down elsewhere and who knows how many other people."

"And you think any might still be living?"

"I do. They like the torture game, from what we've experienced already. And Kenneth will find us a way down, though I am worried about how this will play out. They must know by now that their people aren't coming back."

"Thankfully, Luke is in with them."

"But will they be honest with him—or intend to use him, as Holmes used Pitezel?"

"Well, they won't be able to, will they? Because Luke knows what he needs to know, and if he's a member of the Society, they must be aware that he knows what he knows, too. Hopefully, they'll believe that he's entirely one of their own."

"Shh," she warned suddenly.

Harry Green was coming back for them, smiling broadly.

"All right! The kitchen is set, whiskey is out, and we're about to share a few wee drams and some excellent food."

"Wonderful," Daniel said. "Wow! I was expecting breakfast, but not dinner. Or supper. Or a meal at night, by any name."

"And the whiskey is a-flowing," Harry Green told them. "Let's get this night moving."

CHAPTER EIGHTEEN

They were going to need to play it second by second.

While Harry Green didn't know what had happened to Liz, Kaye Bolden and her accomplice, he did know something had gone wrong. And, in his mind, he had probably played it all brilliantly with Luke.

Harry had, earlier, invited everyone to dinner. Now, of course, "everyone" wouldn't be arriving.

"We're going to do things a bit differently than I had planned," he had started off telling Luke. "Kaye isn't resting—she has disappeared."

"And, wait—you don't know how?"

"She was on a mission. With another Society member. And she has disappeared, and I'm afraid she might have been taken by the police."

"Then shouldn't we all be the hell out of here?"

"We will be. But we've seen nothing yet. And if the police were to burst in here, they'd find nothing. We keep everything close to the chest."

"Then why—"

"I don't believe Kaye or anyone can really do anything, but

it's time to take a bit of a holiday. Easier if Terry hadn't let in that young lad," he said with annoyance, looking over at her.

"Eh!" Terry snapped in return. "I didn't know at the time you and Jim had failed so abysmally at—"

"Watch it!" Harry Green warned her.

"Terry!" Jim echoed.

"We'll have our meal—our guests will sleep. Soon after, we'll remove them to the tunnels, and we'll have some fun on the way out."

"Won't people wonder what's happened to us all?"

"Oh, they'll find us—we'll have barely survived the explosion. But the way the fire we'll set burns, they'll be lucky to find anything that isn't as decimated as if an atom bomb had gone off."

"I did love this place," Jim muttered.

"Indeed. But that's part of the game—moving on when necessary. And the insurance payout will provide a new place and the game is half the fun of it, eh?"

Terry had then moved over to the oven, taking out a large pan with her meat course, and then moving on to scoop her potatoes and vegetables onto serving plates.

"Well, I'll not bother with the dishes tonight," she muttered.

"What about Mrs. Bolden—was there insurance on her? Oh, and what about Miss MacDonald?"

"Mrs. Bolden already turned her property over to me at her death, no problem there. But as to Miss MacDonald—"

"She is rich. Like Midas," Luke told him.

"Ah, more's the pity. But she'll have to sleep with the others. You'll have time to get back to your room. Oh! You can say you banged on the door for Miss MacDonald, but she wouldn't let you in, she wouldn't believe there was a fire!" Harry had said. "You won't fail us, eh?"

"And I was set. I was going to sleep with her tonight."

"You'll have to keep it in your pants. Sorry."

"Bummer."

"I need to know if you're going to mess this up in any way," Harry Green had told him angrily.

Luke had given him a grim smile. "Hell no! There are other broads to sleep with, no problem."

And so Harry had moved on, eager to get moving, bringing Carly and Daniel into the room.

Terry took center stage then, walking over to greet Carly and Daniel.

"Welcome, welcome, one and all!" she proclaimed, lifting her small glass to them as they walked into the room. "We try here at Vicky Inn to be different. To make you feel as if you're one with the beautiful countryside around Stirling. And the people, too, of course. We're honored that you've come here. In my opinion, anyone can stay at a chain hotel, but to really feel Scotland… We're so delighted that you feel the same."

"Ah, man, this is too cool," Daniel said. "And it smells wonderful."

"Ah, I told you, I'm a good cook, if I do say so myself," Terry said. "So, we eat at the kitchen table, just like a good Scottish family. Take your seats. I'll get the whiskey."

"May I?" Luke asked Carly, pulling out a chair at the table for her.

"Thank you," she said sweetly.

"Let me help you," he told Terry, working with her to bring the serving dishes to the table.

Then he took the chair next to hers—Terry Allen was at the end of the table next to Carly. Terry's husband took the opposite end, and Daniel and Harry Green were left to take the remaining chairs next to Jim Allen.

"Whiskey!" she said, reaching for the decanter. Harry, Jim and Luke already had full glasses in their hands.

Terry's sat on the table before her place setting.

She poured for the others.

"All right, then—" she began, about to take her glass.

"Wait!" Daniel said.

"Pardon?" Terry asked him.

"Sorry, old habits die hard. And I know I'm a guest, but… could we say grace? My mother was kind of strict on that and in her memory… I can be fast!" Daniel said.

"Oh, in memory of your mum," Harry said.

"But of course," Jim agreed.

"Okay, just bow your heads and close your eyes for one minute," Daniel said, and when the others had done so, he bowed his own head and went on with, "God is great, God is good, and we thank him for this food. Amen!"

The others all echoed an "Amen."

"Just pass the dishes around, if you will, please," Terry said.

They did so and murmurs of "could you please pass" and "thanks so much" went around the table along with the food. When they all had their plates set, Terry turned to Daniel.

"So, you're a believer," she said.

"Indeed," he said with a smile. "I am."

"Ah! You believe that there is a God, that there is a heaven and that sinners will pay in a fiery hell?" Harry asked him, amused.

"Exactly. Except all that stuff about a fiery hell. Hell is just the absence of God. Then again, no man is without sin, but there is forgiveness."

"No matter what we've done," Terry said. "If we ask forgiveness at the end, we're forgiven."

"Oh, I don't think it's that simple," Daniel said.

"And what is it, then?" Jim Allen asked.

"True repentance," Daniel said solemnly. "But I'm sorry. I didn't mean to intrude on anyone's way of doing things, just my personal thoughts on all…"

"All right, then, to us! And to all that comes in the years that stretch before us and beyond!" Harry announced, picking up his glass.

The others did the same. Carly brought her glass to her lips. She glanced at him and he knew—Daniel Murray had bought them the time they needed.

She had switched her glass with Terry's.

"Hear, hear!" she cried.

And the attention was on her. He didn't see how their British counterpart had managed to dump the contents of his drink, but he was sure that he did.

"I can't wait to get started in the morning," Carly said, taking a bite of her food. "I mean, Stirling Castle, Stirling Bridge—I saw the movie about William Wallace! I can't wait and I hear that the castle has the most amazing displays and wow… Terry! You said that you were a good cook. These potatoes are to die for," she said sweetly.

Terry gave her an immense grin. "Well, thank you, my dear."

"It's not the same bridge that was here in Wallace's day, mind you," Harry said. "That bridge went down with the weight of the English cavalrymen, caught between the one side and the other. Wallace didn't have the men of the great English army, but he knew his terrain and he used it entirely to his advantage. Now the castle! It changed hands and changed hands…and it was often believed that whoever held Stirling Castle held Scotland!"

"Oh," Carly said, blinking and giving up a tremendous yawn. "I am so sorry—I am so rude. I've about finished my plate, and I'm suddenly so tired I feel I might fall asleep with my face in my plate." She winced and glanced at Terry. "My friend and I…we only get to see each other every few years, it seems, and I'm afraid we stayed up a bit late imbibing and…"

"No, no, dear, it's quite all right," Terry told her. "You go on up to bed and get some sleep. You'll want to be fiery bright in the morning."

Terry did think her words might be totally amusing to her coconspirators, Luke thought dryly. But he saw Kenneth was back with them, nodding gravely to him.

And ready to be with Carly and let her know everything he had learned.

She stood and was careful to waver.

"I have cleaned my plate," Daniel announced. "I'll walk you up!" he told Carly. And then, as if he was another guy who might be accused of horning in on someone, he quickly turned to Luke. "I'll just see she's safe on the stairs, and I am going to totally crash, myself!"

"Of course, and thank you," Luke said.

The two of them left the room, followed by the ghost of Kenneth Menzies.

"Let them get up there—let them get to sleep."

"I need a bit of time—" Luke began.

"Hey, it's like a crashing airplane. You can't take it with you," Harry said impatiently.

"I don't intend to—but I do want to make sure I have my credit cards and my travel checks. I mean, we need so much time to make sure they're asleep, right?"

"Yep, but if you're not with us and there's a tap on the door and it's the police who have managed to get here before the boom, you're as dead as they are," Green warned him. He leaned toward him, his tone hard. "This is the H. H. Holmes Society. We play it safe and we play it as hard as Holmes!"

"And that's what I want," Luke assured him. "But we're going to need cash to get by, right?" he demanded.

"We'll need just a few, too, Harry," Jim Allen said. "And… whatever the hell happened. No one has come. Someone would have come by now if Kaye had opened her mouth. Hey, Harry, come on! She was an old broad. Maybe she had a heart attack trying to move and never got anywhere."

"All right." Harry took another bite of his food.

The others did the same, eating quickly then.

"I really do make the best potatoes in the world," Terry said.

She yawned deeply and seemed surprised that she did so.

"Indeed, ma'am, you do," Luke said. He had cleaned his plate—and done so quickly. He wiped his face with a napkin and stood.

"Thank you. I'll be down in a flash."

"Meet at the elevator, and if you're not there..." Harry warned.

"I'll be there," Luke assured him.

Kenneth was back, and as Luke left the kitchen, he smiled. Sometimes, all the help in the world couldn't help—because once they were underground, communication devices might not work.

But for the beginning of this play, at least, they didn't need calls, texts or the internet.

They had Kenneth Menzies.

"I cannae help the lass! We must move quickly!" Kenneth urged as they hurried up the stairs. "She's bound to some strange table like a rack and I cannae undo the binds upon her. Oh, aye, and we must hurry! He's something down there, some form of gas and a control that I think... I think it will explode everything. It looks like catacombs down there, bone set in carved-out sections of the walls, and it's a nightmare, blood on tables—"

"Kenneth, Kenneth, thank you, and please, calm down," Carly said.

They had reached the top of the stairs. Daniel was looking at her, anxious, knowing that she was learning something and not knowing what.

"We've got to get down there," Carly told Daniel. "And fast. He plans on blowing the place up and creating a fire. Luke will buy all the time he can, but—"

"How do we get down there?" Daniel demanded.

"The elevator—you know, that elevator that doesn't work. But if we try that, they'll see us, and God knows what controls they might have up here."

"The chutes," Kenneth said.

"The chutes," Carly repeated.

"Will we break our necks and die?" Daniel asked.

"They curve around and land in giant containers of bloody sheets," Kenneth said.

"No, we'll be all right!" Carly told Daniel. "Kenneth—"

He headed down the hall. Carly glanced at Daniel, who felt the movement. She nodded and they quickly followed him.

Kenneth indicated a panel. She touched it and it slid open.

She grasped the edge and hiked herself up.

"Carly, I should go first," Daniel said.

She gave him a big smile. "Daniel, you're a doll. But quit treating me like a girl. I'm a well-trained agent."

She didn't wait for a reply but ducked the rest of the way into the chute.

Instinctive fear set in for a few brief seconds. It was dark, and it was like plunging down a long, long twisting waterslide.

But she landed softly and caught herself quickly, grabbing the edges of the giant laundry bin into which she had fallen. She'd almost made her way out when she heard the whishing sound of Daniel's movement through the chute and she hurried to move out of the way.

"Carly?" he whispered on landing.

"I'm fine. Penlight coming on!" she assured him.

Of course, he carried his own. And between them, they began to shed a glow around the area where they had landed. At first, it seemed that there was nothing but sheets.

Bloody sheets, as Kenneth had said.

"Here, here, come along!"

She heard Kenneth's voice and scrambled then to hike herself over the rim of the giant bin, followed by her British counterpart.

Kenneth was ahead of them. They ran after him. Carly figured that they had reached the area where the supposedly non-functioning elevator arrived belowground.

There was a sharp twist that led away.

Down a tunnel.

The ancient violence of the earth itself had provided here—the underground was deep and long and had been used by mankind for eons and eons...

The tunnel seemed to stretch forever.

But, of course, it did not.

Harry Green meant for himself and his close associates to get out—and for their guests to perish in an explosion or fire or something caused by old gases, perhaps, or human error, or... would it matter to him, because in his mind, he'd be gone, moving on, starting over.

But Luke never closed the door to his room as he supposedly gathered just the things that he needed. And he believed that the man still thought that Luke was a crazed follower; he hadn't argued when Luke said that he'd just get out of the house. If Luke was going to make things difficult in any way, Harry Green would happily let him perish, too—something that, of course, he wasn't going to explain.

He had told the man he'd meet him at the elevators. Green wouldn't care if he did or didn't.

Carly and Daniel would already be deep in the bowels of the place, and they should have been left alone, but...

With his door just barely ajar, he saw Jim and Terry head toward the supposedly nonfunctioning elevator; just a few minutes later, Harry Green followed.

Luke waited.

Giving them all time...

Then he followed as well. They were possibly getting ready to get whatever they needed from below and then get out.

With or without him.

But he had to get down there. If there was going to be an explosion, they all needed out. He had to find Carly and Daniel.

Down below, he winced at the size and scope of the underground. Then he frowned, noting that there were strange metal spikes here and there along the way.

He paused and realized that they needed out—he didn't dare take the time to study the various aspects of Harry Green's "safety net," as time was of the essence. He had a feeling that with or without a main detonator...

The place could blow sky-high at any time.

With Daniel, Carly followed Kenneth, and she saw something similar to what she had seen before, that there were vaults cut into the tunnel. And she realized that at some point in history, perhaps soon after the Romans had left Britain and Christianity had arrived, the place had been catacombs. Many of the dead were decayed beyond anything that could have been recent.

"They could have had an archaeological discovery of immense importance down here," she muttered.

"They wanted to make their own," Daniel said dryly.

"There. In there!" Kenneth said.

They turned, and on a table that resembled a medieval torture rack lay a young woman. She was covered with a sheet, but when Carly checked for a pulse, there was a faint beat.

"She's alive."

"I told ye so," Kenneth said. "Get her out!"

"I will, I will. What about the explosives?" Carly asked.

"Down the next tunnel," Kenneth said.

"I'm on it—I'll get to the explosives," Daniel told Carly. "I hear Kenneth, clearly," he whispered, amazed and awed despite their situation. He looked at the ghost.

"I'll take you with me, sir, and you can show me where you have discovered them," Daniel said.

The two hurried on.

Carly dug in her bag for her knife, flicked it open and began working at the heavy ropes. Harry Green had been busy helping his Society members; the victim was tied in much the same way Carly had seen before. In a matter of minutes, she had the young woman freed, but she couldn't draw a response from her and she figured that, as before, the woman had lost too much blood.

She would need medical help fast.

She tried her phone. Nothing. What she had expected.

But she carefully lifted the young woman from the table, sliding her over her shoulder and hoping that she wasn't causing more harm. It wasn't easy, balancing her load and trying to keep her light trained ahead lest she further injure the young woman by banging her into the heavy stone walls of the underground.

She walked out of the little vault within the tunnels, determined to reach Daniel and Kenneth as quickly as possible and get the young woman out.

Some of the bodies in the niches along the walls were as old as time; some were certainly newer since she was sure that vats of acid and bleach and more could be found down here as well.

She had just moved slightly down the tunnel when she heard a scratching sound.

It didn't come from ahead of her.

It came from behind her, from the area where the elevator set down.

She kept moving forward, focused on reaching the two ahead of her.

But she was startled into freezing when she heard a tremendous rush of laughter from behind her.

"Leaving us so soon, Miss MacDonald? And demanding that other guests go with you? How very rude of you. Well, let's hope you have young Daniel's faith, and you haven't been too vigorous a sinner. Because, Miss MacDonald, if you'd repent on anything, the time to do so is now."

She turned.

Of course, the speaker was Harry Green.

"Well, I do like having friends with me," she told him.

He had a gun aimed at her. She didn't know what it was in the dim light, but it didn't matter much. If a bullet struck her at this distance of five feet or so, it would be deadly.

"How on earth did you come to be here?" he demanded. "Oh, you can put your friend down if you like. We have a few minutes, and I am supposing you will want to bare your poor soul."

"I'm fine holding her. But I am curious. How crazy are you? Do you really believe you are somehow the real H. H. Holmes reincarnated?" Carly asked.

They could hear her; they had to be able to hear her. Daniel Murray was just down the tunnel.

And Luke had to be close.

She needed to keep him talking. She had her own Glock. There was simply no easy way to draw it without him seeing what she was doing.

"Who knows? Maybe I am a reincarnation. All I know is he was a brilliant man—he excelled at medical school."

"And at stealing corpses."

"Yes, and his dissecting methods...amazing! But this is an expensive world we live in and his ability to survive and prosper...truly amazing."

"So, you do it for the money, not the joy of killing?" Carly demanded.

"Money, money, money! It does make the world go round," he said.

"Then why the torture rack?" she asked.

He shrugged. "It's fun. You know, Holmes killed the Pitezel children because, well, because they were just an annoyance. I don't think he tortured them. And the pregnant mistress who was bugging him—he knew he could kill her easily in a botched abortion. Others...oh! The rack. He wondered if by using the rack he could create a giant race of human beings. I mean, that was medical science. Okay, I think he enjoyed killing, too."

"Can't get your rocks off any other way?" she taunted, knowing that she would anger him. She needed him to be off. Maybe to even come up to her and...

"Drop the gun!"

The man had been about to take a step toward her. He stopped dead in his tracks. She realized Daniel Murray had backtracked and was right behind her, his gun leveled at Harry Green.

"You want me to drop my gun?" Green demanded.

"Now," Daniel said.

"Fine!"

Harry Green dropped the gun. But as he did so, he drew something out of his pocket and showed it to them.

It looked like a little black box.

No. It was a remote control.

A remote control for whatever explosives he had planned to destroy all evidence of there ever having been any evil done at the site.

"You'll kill yourself, too," Carly told him.

"Well, your friend can drop his gun, and we can all take our chances."

"Not going to happen," Daniel said.

"Oh, yes, it will!" came another voice.

Jim's. Jim Allen was down here, too. And now he was standing just behind Harry Green, his gun leveled at Daniel.

Carly gritted her teeth, knowing they had to keep it together—there had to be a way out.

And there was.

Luke was there. Luke was...

"Ah, lass! Maybe if ye shift the lass yer carrying, ye've a gun, too, eh?"

Kenneth was at her side.

She nodded. "Where's Luke?"

She was speaking to the ghost, but the others thought she was speaking to them.

"Luke? Ah, sorry, girl! Luke is planning to save himself. Pity, he would have enjoyed you so much. In fact, his only regret is that you didn't get a night in!" Harry Green told her.

She let out a groan, shifting the weight of the young woman she carried, and while laying her down as gently as possible, she drew her Glock and took aim, blowing Jim Allen's gun out of his hand.

He screeched in pain, and Harry Green roared in rage and lifted the black box above his head.

"Well, then, welcome to hell, lady! I will now blow us all up sky-high!"

CHAPTER NINETEEN

Will he do it? Can a man with an ego like his, with such extreme narcissism, do something that will end his life?

She didn't know. And for the moment, perhaps, she wouldn't need to.

Because someone else was suddenly there.

"Wow! You really want to be blown up, all that genius of yours reduced to atoms floating around in the great nothing?"

They were all startled by the sound of another voice, but inwardly, Carly smiled with relief.

Luke had been there, following, watching, awaiting his cue.

But it was still true that Harry Green held a remote that could ignite an explosion that would decimate the entire house, the tunnels and the landscape around them.

But Luke seemed unconcerned. He had his gun out, trained on Harry Green as he casually came up from behind, almost nonchalant as he joined their group.

Three against three, with what should have been a clear advantage for them—they were the ones with the gun trained on the others.

But then again...

"I will be blown sky-high, but so will you and your precious little…whatever she is!" he snapped, looking at Carly.

She looked over at Luke. "Not really little!" she protested.

"No, fair-sized!" Luke agreed.

"What is the matter with you people?" Harry Green demanded. "You're about to die."

"Except I don't believe you want to die," Luke said casually. "I mean, seriously, come on—think about it. You are H. H. Holmes incarnate. There would be absolutely no sense in blowing yourself up. You stop that, we arrest you, we arrest your friends here, there's a trial, you receive life sentences. But! What would Holmes have done with a life sentence? He'd have found a way to escape—and a way to pick up again where he'd left off. Of course, you'd have to leave these two rotting in jail because they're just not as clever as you are—"

"No!" Jim Allen screamed in protest. "No! No, no, no, no, no! I was the one who found this place, still equipped with tunnels from centuries ago. I used my inheritance to buy this place, to be the incredibly genial innkeeper—I am more Holmes than he is!"

"How dare you?" Harry Green countered. "The website is mine. The concept is mine. You were nothing but a builder until I taught you the way."

"And you were both worthless. I did all the work," Terry cried.

"You are both nothing but pathetic lackeys in his mind," Carly told her, realizing what game Luke was playing, turning them against one another.

And still, Harry Green held the remote.

But she continued, thinking Luke must have a solid plan to get the remote from Green.

"Especially you, Terry. A woman? Oh, come on. You must realize you are less than a third-rate assistant in Harry's mind."

"Do something," Terry ordered her husband. "You bastard!"

she said to Green. "Guess what? I don't want to die. I don't want to be part of your ridiculous—"

"Oh, Terry, Terry, Terry," Green said, and he turned to stare at Carly. "You should have seen her in action. She loved watching her husband with a woman, and then moving in to do a little slicing on her own. She is far better at torture and murder than any man I've come across."

That isn't really a surprise, Carly thought.

She felt a presence behind her.

Kenneth.

"It's all right, lass. Luke is in control."

She wasn't sure how Luke had come up from behind them, except...

Who knew exactly how these tunnels and vaults cut through the ancient mound?

"What fool ever said the female was the weaker of the sexes?" Luke said casually. "But who did exactly what doesn't really matter. Here we are! And it looks as if you're the man in control, Mr. Harry Green—or whoever you really are. H. H. Holmes reincarnated? No. He wouldn't have made so many mistakes—"

"Oh, yes, he did," Green muttered. "He made a deal with a fellow prisoner when he was being held on a lesser charge and then he didn't follow through and the idiot was furious and gave witness against him and that's... I didn't make any stupid deals. I just joined with stupid people!"

"How dare you!" Jim Allen raged again. He suddenly made as if he would lunge at Green in spite of his injured, bleeding hand. Carly couldn't let that happen. She easily tripped the man and he went down, screaming in fury.

That brought Terry Allen to a frenzy; she sounded like a snarling bobcat as she turned to jump on Carly in return.

And in that melee, Luke fired.

A single shot.

Harry Green screamed in agony. He had not received a mortal wound, but rather, his hand—that holding the control—appeared to have exploded in a burst of blood and tissue.

The remote went flying.

Luke caught it as Carly felled Terry Allen with a counterweight blow.

"We've got to get the hell out of here!" Luke said. "That's only one of the controls. He planted others—the Allen couple were not supposed to survive this, either."

"I have one!" Daniel Murray announced. "But it seems they were set to trigger in certain areas if anything happened to the others." He stood over the Allens, who remained on the floor. They both looked like rabid dogs, all but foaming at the mouth.

"By the way, he apparently meant to get out without either of you—you would have gone up with the house and be blamed and found guilty of every crime committed here," Daniel told the couple.

"Let's go!" Luke urged. "Carly—"

She stooped to try her best to gently pick up the poor woman they'd found on the torture table. She had not awakened; maybe it was best.

But Daniel was at her side, smiling at her. "May I? I would never be so foolish as to doubt your abilities. I'm just bigger."

Carly grinned, allowing him to lift the young woman.

"Up!" she ordered Jim and Terry Allen. "We're going to try to save your lives."

The ghost of Kenneth Menzies was at Carly's side. "Lead them this way, lass. Lead them this way... The tunnel here breaks out at the cliff down the western road."

"Shouldn't we go back through the house?" she wondered aloud.

As she spoke, they heard the sound of an explosion, coming from the area beneath the ground where the elevator shaft lay.

Still screaming, Harry Green, the would-be Holmes, began to laugh, and his agony and amusement became hysteria.

"This way!" she urged, jerking Terry Allen to her feet and allowing Jim to rise on his own. "And you *want* to live, so move!"

Luke caught hold of Harry Green with his left hand; with his right, he kept his Glock trained carefully on the group in case one of them resisted again.

Kenneth moved ahead. The light in the tunnels was dim, the going was over rough rock. Different vaults occasionally broke off.

They heard another explosion.

Closer this time.

"Move!" Carly shouted again.

Terry started running; Jim was right behind her, crying and cradling his injured hand, and Carly kept pace.

Many of the tunnels were lined with crypt shelving; bodies lay in disintegrating shrouds, some down to nothing more than bone.

"I'd not been here," Kenneth murmured. "But St. Ninian came in the year of our Lord 397, bringing the Christian religion, but it was some time before the old ways died out. Perhaps the early followers laid their dead here, protecting them from the vengeance of others."

"Centuries go by," Carly murmured softly. "At least…"

"At least these monsters did not murder all of them? They'll never know the full truth."

"Ah, they'll know," she returned. "They will face arrest. And they will tell the truth."

I hope that's true.

Neither the whining Jim nor his wife were giving her any heed, and if Daniel was listening, he would understand. And no one cared about speech or even sobs—they were well aware that the entire structure, the tunnels and even the ground above could blow to pieces.

They kept running. Harry Green, also emitting anguished

HEATHER GRAHAM

and furious sounds, was running behind her, and behind him, Luke brought up the rear.

Then she saw that Kenneth had stopped. "There! There ahead. Up the wall."

Up the wall?

But then she saw it—the opening that was little more than a crawl space about four feet up the wall. On the surface, the rich growth of shrubbery, leaves and branches created the disguise that there was nothing there on the hillock.

"Daniel, go—we'll balance this woman between us, Carly will cover us and we'll get her up. We can't send the Allen couple first, even if Jim is bleeding all over. We'll get them out—then Carly, Green and then me," Luke said.

"Makes sense," Daniel muttered, hiking himself up.

Carly kept her Glock on the group as Luke helped balance the young woman—who still clung to life with a faint pulse but never opened her eyes—out of the tunnels.

She had to wonder if there was any hope the young woman would survive in the end.

Then again, none of them might survive.

Jim Allen, cradling his bleeding hand, moved forward, pushing his wife aside. He wanted out first himself.

"No!" Terry shrieked.

But Jim Allen was halfway out despite his injury and Carly held Terry back, telling her, "Let him go. You're next."

She gave Terry a push and then managed to hike her own weight up. She burst through the tunnel into the dim glow of a starry night. And for a brief split second, she was just grateful for the sweet kiss of the cool night and the strange peaceful beauty of the rolling green earth.

"Green coming up!" Luke shouted, and while Daniel kept his gun trained on Jim and Terry, Carly hunkered down to grasp Green's good wrist and help drag the man out.

He lay on the ground, panting, crying, cradling his wrist

where his hand used to be. But when Luke's head emerged, Harry Green came to life, howling in fury and twisting to shove Luke back down.

A foolish move. Luke jerked himself up, a move that sent Harry Green crashing back into the hole.

And even as he did so, they saw a spill of light coming from the hole.

"Go!" Luke roared. He paused long enough himself to sweep up the unknown young woman.

"Right! Move!" Carly commanded Jim and Terry.

They began to run. Downward along the slope. Jim tripped and went rolling down, far down, and Carly ran after him with the spirit of Kenneth Menzies at her side. Daniel continued to prod Terry Allen, keeping the sobbing woman running.

Then the explosion occurred. It rocked the earth. Carly stumbled and fell; Terry Allen did so; and Daniel went down as well, almost on top of Terry.

The night was no longer gentle and dim; the ensuing fire lit up the night.

The sound of sirens followed. Carly stared at the sky before she could rise, but she dared smile at last. Officers from Police Scotland and the National Crime Agency were scurrying over the ground, taking Jim and Terry.

And Luke was there, smiling grimly, reaching down for her. "Terry, Jim—"

And as she stood, she saw Brendan Campbell was there, too.

"Amazing work, my American friends. Amazing work," he said.

"We had Daniel," Carly reminded him. "And without the four—" She broke off.

Without Kenneth Menzies, they seriously might not have made it. But she couldn't say that.

She smiled. "My head is still reeling, I'm afraid. Without Daniel, we couldn't have…"

"Blown up half a hill?" Daniel asked, joining them.

"Stopped killers who would have slaughtered many more," Campbell finished.

"The woman! The young woman—" Carly worried.

"Already on her way to the hospital," Campbell assured her. "Now, I am afraid that the house went up, too. We'll have to get you some clothes. And, of course, when the dust settles, a new place to sleep for the night." He smiled and shrugged. "Well, if there's any night left when we've finished here."

There wasn't to be. The once-quiet hillock was still alight with the remnants of the fire and the many officers moving about, when Carly, standing by Luke's side, saw Daniel Murray seated on a rock, looking toward a tree.

Curiously, she moved over to take a better look. The spirit of Kenneth Menzies was standing before him. He smiled when he saw Carly. "Lass, as ye saw in the tunnel, he sees me! The lad sees me, as fully as ye do yerself," he said excitedly.

"Yes, I know he felt you before. Kenneth, you're very special, you bring out the best of the gift in all of us. Daniel—"

"I heard him!" Daniel said. "I heard him! Oh, sir, we can't thank you enough. We can't—"

"Ah, laddie, nay, perhaps I perished on that long-ago day to be here now. My pleasure."

"I can't wait to see you again!" Daniel cried.

But Kenneth Menzies shook his head. "I've a feelin', and a good one. 'Tis, I think, my time to forgive my enemies and to join me fellows. Forgive me, but 'tis time!"

He nodded to Carly and Luke, who now stood behind her. "Fine warriors ye all be! And to fight with such true and loyal brethren, ah, that be the greatest reward!"

"Kenneth, thank you, thank you," Carly told him.

Luke echoed her words.

He lifted a hand and disappeared through the trees.

"Oh, my God," Daniel breathed, looking at them. "I saw

him. I talked to him. I... You were right, Carly. It—it developed in me late and it's not a curse to me at all but something wonderful. Well, mostly wonderful. I mean, no one else would believe this, right?"

Luke laughed softly. "There's always room for one more in the Blackbird unit of the Krewe of Hunters," he told him. "Did I say that aloud? Campbell would have my head!"

"Oh, we don't do that anymore in Scotland," Daniel said, laughing. "But...ah, who knows? Speaking of Campbell..."

There was the inevitable paperwork. The relief of knowing that they had, indeed, saved a young woman. The knowledge that Jim Allen was also being treated, but that he and his wife would remain incarcerated while awaiting trial.

A forensic crew *thought* they had found enough remnants of the body of "H. H. Holmes" to verify the fact that he was indeed dead; positive ID might be a ways off, with only dental records to work with.

They believed the man's birth name had been Richard Howard, but that would come later on down the line.

And finally...

Daylight.

And they were left at a hotel with a promise that clothing would be delivered.

Closing the door when they entered the room, Luke leaned against it and grinned.

"Good thing we don't need clothes tonight," he said with a shrug.

And Carly started to laugh. "Have you seen yourself?"

"Uh, I have not. Have *you* seen yourself?"

They were both covered in soot and dirt and grit, smudged with it from head to toe. But that didn't matter. She stepped forward, sliding into his arms, catching his hands and drawing them up with her own to press against the door, her body flat on his as she teased him with a long, long searing kiss, a burst of adrenaline, of the simple pleasure of being alive...

And of being with someone who seemed to fulfill her, a second half to create a whole and...

"What?" he whispered against her lips. And then he teased her with, "You were thinking that I'm a great partner, strong as an ox, but noble and thoughtful and—"

"Nope. Not at all. I was thinking that you do have a passable body and that there is a certain sensual charisma about you."

"I'll show you passable!" he countered, sweeping her up.

She burst into laughter, ruffling his filthy hair.

"Luke! We are total messes!"

"I can be *passable* in a shower!" he assured her.

And so...

The hours passed...sleeping...touching...fulfilled, urgent, resting, awaking...

And then, just before night fell again, there was a knock at their door.

Carly looked at Luke, grimacing. They had never managed to put their tattered clothing back on.

But she needn't have worried. She heard the sound of laughter—a laughter she knew.

"It's okay—don't open the door until you're ready. It's Daniel. I went to pick up the clothing that Campbell had Liz go out to get for you guys—we decided she'd be the best shopper, even for you, Luke, so, you know, whenever. But if you've had enough, um, sleep for a wee bit, we'll be having dinner down in the main restaurant in about an hour and a half. There's a surprise for you, should you make it. Oh, and by the way, I grew up in Glasgow. My home is still down there but I'm here at the hotel...until the paperwork is all tied up. That's why I was elected to knock on your door. See ya!"

He left them both laughing. Carly slipped into a robe and secured their clothing from the hallway. Liz had not managed just to fit them well, but purchased items they might have chosen for themselves.

"She's good," Carly said.

"They're all good," Luke agreed. "Duncan, Ian, Liz and Daniel."

"And now Daniel is happy, but…"

"You're afraid he'll be unhappy?" Luke asked her.

She nodded. "He… Oh, Luke, don't you remember trying to work before the Krewe? Having help that lets you know something, but having no way to make someone who doesn't see the dead understand?"

"The Krewe makes everything so much easier, yes," Luke told her. "But Blackbird…we'll work here often. Weird crimes—"

"Don't all happen in Scotland or even Britain," she reminded him.

"He'll find his way. He is a great asset, wherever he may work."

They did head down to dinner and were delighted by the "surprise."

Jackson Crow and Angela had flown in, and even better, Della Hamilton and Mason Carter were there as well, along with Brendan Campbell and Daniel Murray.

"Does this mean that…?"

"Yes!" Della said. "While you were bringing down the head of the Society, we cut down the two-man crew who had been working in France. Finally! That seemed to take forever. But seriously, we were going from place to place, stopping things after atrocities were uncovered, but now the website is down for good and the head is off the snake."

"I wish we could have brought him in," Carly said.

Della took a breath. "Listen, I hate it just as much when we can't mete out due justice—bring criminals in and let trials by juries and sentences given by judges decide on punishment. But you didn't even kill the man—he killed himself with his own mechanism of death. Oh, and you saved a life, and that couldn't have been easy."

Carly nodded. "I know all that. I just hope—"

"That there aren't still others active?"

"Exactly."

Mason spoke up, shaking his head. "At every location, the founder of the Society made a stop—it was his way of assuring that his instructions were followed. Others were often allowed in to carry out their own fantasies about revenge, but when that was done, they were usually dispatched as well. So… Jackson ordered champagne. This is a win!"

It was a great evening. Jackson and Angela were heading back in the morning; they had just come because of the American law enforcement angle on the case. It was great seeing them, and they made finishing the paperwork Brendan Campbell needed that much easier.

And they were getting to know Daniel Murray, who was both funny and entertaining as he regaled them all with the history of Stirling that night. The castle had been extremely important in medieval history; it was central, the gateway to the Highlands. And there, William Wallace had won his all-important victory at Stirling Bridge, and later, Robert the Bruce had cemented his kingship by taking the stronghold itself and winning the day.

The evening at long last came to an end and there were good-byes to be said. Brendan Campbell was heading down to London. Angela and Jackson were returning to the States.

"I'll still be here for a bit," Daniel told them. "Aren't you thrilled!"

Carly laughed and said that yes, she was.

She and Luke spent another night teasing, taking the time to play, to be urgent, to bask in one another's company.

To plan the vacation they had been promised.

"Campbell says he can get us a stay in any of the bed-and-breakfast castles," Luke told her.

"No, no, no. No castles! A beach somewhere."

"French Riviera, Spain—Italy has some beautiful beaches."

"So hard to choose. Let's look up some places in the morning, make a decision and head out," Carly said.

That was the plan.

It was doomed to change.

There was a knock on their door again in the morning.

"Ah, guys, it's Daniel. Sorry, this isn't social. Can you be downstairs in thirty minutes?"

Carly looked at Luke, frowning.

He pulled her to him. "Okay, let's remember. Seize every minute."

She nodded.

And they were downstairs in exactly half an hour.

Jackson and Angela were already on their plane back to the States, but this was a strange case that didn't relate back to the US.

"I need your help again," Campbell told them.

"What is it?" Luke asked him.

Campbell passed a printed sheet across the table to him and Carly.

He'd given them a photograph. It was of a dead man.

Missing the middle portion of his body.

Then he passed over another.

It was of a skeleton, one that might have been found in a medical museum.

"And then," Daniel said, "there's the media headline."

He passed over his phone, showing the major headline on a search engine.

"Burke and Hare—At It Again?"

Luke turned to Carly. "I guess we're not getting to a beach."

"No," Campbell said grimly. "We four will be heading back to Edinburgh."

★ ★ ★ ★ ★